Perfect Peace

Perfect Peace

DANIEL BLACK

St. Martin's Press ⢎ New York

This is a work of fiction. All of the characters, organizations, and events portrayed in this novel are either products of the author's imagination or are used fictitiously.

PERFECT PEACE. Copyright © 2010 by Daniel Black. All rights reserved. Printed in the United States of America. For information, address St. Martin's Press, 175 Fifth Avenue, New York, N.Y. 10010.

www.stmartins.com

Book design by Susan Yang

Library of Congress Cataloging-in-Publication Data

Black, Daniel.
    Perfect Peace / Daniel Black. — 1st ed.
        p. cm.
    ISBN 978-0-312-58267-8
    1. African American girls—Fiction.   2. Gender identity—Fiction.
3. Domestic fiction.   I. Title.
    PS3602.L267P47 2010
    813'.6—dc22

                                                                2009040237

First Edition: March 2010

10 9 8 7 6 5 4 3 2 1

For all of you who were mocked, scorned, and silenced because you were different, it's now your turn to speak. . . .

And for my newest niece, Punch (Olivia).

Acknowledgments

To every elder who prayed for me and believed in me, this novel is proof that your prayers have power.

To the Fialio: Your excellence and constant love helped me climb this steep mountain.

To the Nation of Ndugu-Nzinga: I'm sure I would've died if all of you hadn't been there to save me. I bow before you in reverence. Thanks for honoring the gift in me, and for allowing me to take this spiritual journey with you.

To all who read this novel before its publication and affirmed its worth, I shout your names to the ancestors! Keith Hamilton Cobb, Kariamu (Dr. Maisha Handy), Aminata (Lisa Noel), Rose Norment, Nazapa, Mawu, Ocheing, Tendaji, Chinasa, Makata, Molefi, Sedrick McDaniel, Ligongo, Muthoni, Darius, Ernest Dillon, Karyn Lacy, Reverend Timothy McDonald, Okafanus, Ra Min Anki Maa, and Anela: Might you have nothing but health and prosperity the remainder of your living days.

To Maurice Culpepper: Thank you, sir, for reading all four drafts of this novel and providing the wisdom and insight necessary to mold it into a solid literary work. I'll never thank you enough for your mental energy and invaluable criticism.

Perfect Peace

Chapter 1

Gus stood beside the living room window, waiting for the annual spring rains. They should have come by now, he noted, glancing at the battered Motley Funeral Home calendar hanging from a nail on the wall. It was May 17, 1940, and Gus's wilted crops made him wonder if, somehow, he had angered Mother Nature. Usually the rains came between March and April, freeing him to hunt or fish the latter part of spring while cabbage, collard, and tomato sprouts strengthened in the moistened earth. That year, the stubborn rains prolonged the daily sojourn Gus and the boys took to the river and back—locals called it the Jordan—carrying five-gallon buckets of water for both their own and the sprouts' survival.

Gus loved the rains. As a child, he lay in bed listening to the thunderous polyrhythms they drummed into the rusted tin rooftop. Something about the melody soothed his somber soul and allowed him to cry without fear of his father's reprisal. After all, he was a boy, Chester Peace Sr. loved to remind him—as though his genitalia didn't—and tears didn't speak well for one who would, one day, become a man. The indelible imprint of Chester Sr.'s inordinately large hand on Gus's tender face whenever he wept never bothered the boy who, in his heart, wanted nothing more desperately than to emulate his father. But as he grew, he never learned to control his tears. He learned instead to hide whenever he felt their approach.

The rains awakened something in him. Maybe it was their steady flow that eroded his makeshift stoicism and caused water to gush from his eyes as if from a geyser. Whatever the connection, Gus always wept along with the rains. He'd convinced himself that the sky, like him, was cursed with a heavy heart that required annual purging. So every spring since his tenth birthday, when the scent of moisture filled his nose he escaped to the Jordan River and stood amid the rain, wailing away pain like a woman in labor. Whether it lasted for hours or even a day, no one expected his return to normalcy until the showers subsided.

Gus was grateful others didn't ask why he cried, because he couldn't have explained it. Had he known words like "injustice" or "inequity" he might've been able to translate his feelings into words, but with a third-grade vocabulary, such articulation was out of the question. All he knew was that he cried when things weren't right. He wept as a child when other children mocked his holey shoes, and then he wept when God refused to grant him the courage and the will to fight. He wept for mother birds that couldn't find worms for their young. He wept for cows left freezing in the snow. He wept for Miss Mazie—the woman whose husband slashed her with a butcher's mallet for talking back—and wept even harder when he overheard that they put the man away. Most of all he wept because he thought people in the world didn't care.

His hardest days were between the rains. At the most inopportune moments, in the middle of the summer or the bitter cold of winter, he'd witness a wrong and water would ooze, unannounced, across his cheeks and he'd be forced to retreat into some private place where his tears wouldn't be cause for ridicule. Yet these momentary cleansings never resulted in Gus's complete healing. Only the annual spring rains set his heart aright again, so, after the third grade—the end of Gus's formal education—he began anticipating the rains' arrival. As soon as the first buds bloomed, he'd watch the heavens for signs of inclement weather, and when the dark clouds gathered, he'd run to the Jordan and welcome the downpour. After 1910, locals noted the beginning of spring when they heard Gus wailing in the distance and, whether out of fear or simple disinterest, no one bothered traveling to the riverbank to see exactly what Gustavus Peace was doing, much less why.

He needed the rains of 1940 worse than he'd ever needed them, for the impending birth of his seventh child—the only one he had never wanted—incited rage he feared he couldn't restrain. Yet the rains wouldn't come. Each morning he jumped from his sleeping pallet on the floor, sniffing the air like a Labrador retriever, hoping to smell the sweet scent of moisture, only to be disappointed when his nostrils inhaled particles of dry, pungent, red dust. Having never mentioned to his wife, Emma Jean, that he felt deceived by the pregnancy, Gus had waited since her ecstatic November announcement to unleash with the spring rains instead of strangling her. His greatest fear now was that an overflowing heart would cause him to crumble before his sons. Each day, his eyes glazed over and his hands began to tremble, and he cursed the rains for seemingly having abandoned him. So far, he had remained composed, but he knew he wouldn't last much longer.

When Emma Jean screamed, Gus released the curtain, turned from the window, and looked toward their bedroom. It was really *her* bedroom, he thought, for he had slept on the floor since learning of her pregnancy. He liked it that way. It kept him from touching her and creating another mouth to feed. He wouldn't have touched her this last time had Emma Jean not convinced him that she couldn't have any more children. Gus asked why, and Emma Jean said that she was going through *the change*. He didn't know exactly what that meant, but he took her at her word. The day she confessed her pregnancy, Gus nodded and promised in his heart never to touch her again. That would keep the children from coming, he reasoned, and that was exactly what he wanted.

"Push!" Henrietta coaxed with her hands cupped around the wet, slimy crown of the baby's head.

Beads of sweat danced across Emma Jean's shiny black forehead as she panted. With borrowed might, she clutched the sheets on which she lay and bellowed, "Ahhhhhhhhhhhhhhh!" tossing her head from one edge of the pillow to the other. "Oh my God! I thought havin' a girl"—breath—"would be easier than havin' them big, knucklehead boys."

Henrietta chuckled. She had delivered almost every child in Conway County, Arkansas, since the 1920s, and if nothing else, she had learned that a baby's gender could never be predicted. "This might be another boy, Emma," she warned softly. "Don't get yo' hopes up too high. Plenty women think they havin' one thing and have somethin' else. Now breathe and push again."

Emma Jean sighed, refusing to relinquish hope that she was finally birthing the daughter she'd always wanted. That hope lent her strength to push again. "AHHHHHHHHHHHHHH!" she growled, exposing the rich, deep alto for which folks at St. Matthew No. 3 Baptist Church were grateful. It was this voice that had caught Gus's attention years ago, teasing his soul one Easter Sunday morning with a rendition of "He Rose" that left him tingling inside.

He called the feeling *love* and asked Emma Jean to marry him. That was fifteen years ago. Back when he was a fool, he always said.

"It won't be long now!" Henrietta encouraged. "Just a few more pushes and we'll have ourselves another baby."

Emma Jean gripped the iron bars of the headpost and stared at the ceiling, delirious. She wanted to push again, but couldn't find the strength. In the meantime, she wondered if Gus had decided upon a name, since he hadn't liked any of her choices.

"What about Rose?" she'd posed one night, leaning over the edge of the bed.

Gus grunted something unintelligible and pulled the battered quilt over his head.

Emma Jean interpreted the response as a no. "Then what about Violet? Or maybe Priscilla?"

Too sleepy to care, Gus hoped his words would close the matter. "Them don't sound like no colored girls' names to me," he murmured. "And, anyway, it's probably gon' be a boy, the luck we been havin'."

Emma Jean scoffed. "Just 'cause a girl be colored don't mean she gotta have no ole, tired, country-soundin' name."

Gus peeked from beneath the quilt. "You got one."

"I know!" Emma Jean shouted. "But that don't mean my baby gotta have one."

"Well, it don't make no difference right now noway. The baby ain't even here yet. Good night."

Emma Jean stopped discussing names with Gus. Why, she wondered, had she consulted a fool in the first place? What would a man know about choosing a baby's name?

"I got de head in my hands," Henrietta said excitedly. "Just give me one more good push! Come on! You can do it!"

The dance of the sweat beads devolved into a slow waltz around Emma Jean's thick brows as she lay exhausted upon the feather pillow. Her good, baby blue sheets, which she had intended to remove from the bed in a few days, would now have to be discarded. Thinking she had at least another week before the baby's arrival, she had prioritized other more immediate chores, but when her water broke while she was preparing Sunday breakfast, she knew those sheets were history.

Gus and the boys sat in the small living room and waited. Knowing no other way to pass the time, Gus read passages from the Bible—the few he *could* read—in hopes that something from the Word might still his rumbling heart. He would love the baby, he resolved, but he would never forgive Emma Jean. Never. And if the rains didn't come, he wouldn't forgive them, either.

Still in their church clothes, which was a clean shirt beneath their work overalls, the boys anticipated the sister they didn't have. Of course another brother would be okay, they agreed silently, but a sister would add spice to an otherwise dull household. Mister, the youngest brother, didn't care either way. He simply wanted someone else to be the baby of the family.

"What if it's a boy?" Mister asked.

"Shut up, will ya?" Authorly insisted. "If it's a boy, then it's a boy. That's all. And if it's a girl, then it's a girl. Jes' be quiet 'til we know."

Mister grimaced and stuck out his tongue. He hated his brother's uncensored authority. *Why don't you shut up!* he almost said, but didn't. One day he would say it, he swore, but for now he held his peace.

Everyone assumed Authorly the eldest, but James Earl was fourteen months his senior. No one had ever heard James Earl speak more than a passive phrase or two a day, so they deemed him far too timid to lead a pack of six brothers. Authorly's muscular disposition and loquacious tongue, on the other hand, granted him the position of eldership among the boys, causing the others to wonder at times if he perceived himself their father instead of their brother. Having no resolve to challenge him, the others obeyed Authorly, calling him names behind his back whenever he infuriated them. Even James Earl acquiesced, yielding his obedience as an offering of gratitude for Authorly's willingness to lead. Locals called James Earl "slow"—some said "retarded," others said "off"—and wondered what woman would ever tolerate such a puny, no-count man.

"You sho dat boy all right?" Miss Mamie Cunningham sneered, watching six-year-old James Earl stumble down the church steps.

"He's perfectly fine," Emma Jean huffed. "He just in his own world."

"And he in it by hisself, too!"

Kiss my ass, Emma Jean wanted to say, then remembered that Miss Mamie was twice her age. Anyway, it was true that James Earl was a bit different, she had to admit. He weighed only four pounds at birth, and once Gus scribbled his name and birth date—

James Earl Peace, June 13, 1928

—in the huge white family Bible resting on the sofa end table, Henrietta guaranteed he wouldn't survive. But he did. He didn't eat much, but he kept on living. Emma Jean forced her nipple in his mouth every three or four hours, but, most days, James Earl lay in her arms like a corpse, seemingly unable to discern what to do. Usually once a day for ten minutes or so he'd suckle and whine like a sick puppy, and Emma Jean would cry as she prepared to wake any day and find him stiff as a board. But he just wouldn't die. He was three before he took a step and four before he said a word. At five, he began eating solid food, so Emma Jean gave thanks for his life and stopped worrying.

The day Authorly came, Gus half-read a flyer at Morrison's General Store announcing the release of a book some author had written. Mistaking "author" for the writer's name and unable to distinguish phonetically between "author" and "Arthur," Gus exited the store proud he could spell the first half of a name he liked. Walking home, he discovered he couldn't spell the other half. He knew it started with an *L*—he had learned his consonant sounds well— but *Le* didn't look right in his mind. Trying to recall other names with the *E* sound, he said several aloud until he stumbled upon the final sound in his mother's name. "Lucy," he mumbled. "The *Y* must be the *E* sound," he decided, sticking out his chest as he visualized the entirety of his second son's name. Afraid he might forget some of the letters, he scratched the name on the Sheetrocked wall of the Peace living room the moment he arrived. When Henrietta announced that Emma Jean had had another boy, this one damn near ten pounds, Gus said his name would be Authorly. He pointed to the childlike letters on the wall as he copied the name, one letter at a time, into the family Bible.

Authorly Peace, August 23, 1929

Henrietta smiled. Not having the heart to correct his spelling, she simply nodded as Gus's pride multiplied. Whenever Authorly felt the need, he referred his brothers to the inscription on the wall as evidence that his coming was obviously divine since none of their names was thus inscribed.

"This'll all be over in a minute, Emma Jean, if you can give me one more good push."

Emma Jean panted.

"Just relax and try to control your breathing. We're almost there now."

She nodded.

"Take a few deep breaths like this"—Henrietta inhaled and exhaled slowly—"and give me what you got."

A weary Emma Jean gasped. She had given birth before, but she didn't remember it being so exhausting. Maybe, after birthing six boys, she wasn't the woman she used to be.

"This one's got a head full o' hair, girl! I feel it!" Henrietta said, winking at Emma Jean while tugging the baby from her womb. "This might jes' be the little girl you been waitin' for!"

Emma Jean was hopeful, but refused to celebrate until she knew for sure. She hadn't even chosen a name yet, although recently she'd considered Octavia or maybe Scarlet. If it was a boy, she didn't know what she'd do, and she definitely didn't know what she'd call him.

Gus returned the oversized family Bible to the sofa end table. He'd give those damn rains a piece of his mind whenever they finally came, he thought. It wasn't fair, making him carry an overflowing heart for months now, and if, at any moment, he collapsed and unleashed in front of his boys, those rains would have to pay.

Woody, the third boy, slithered out like a slimy black garden snake, Henrietta said. She had never delivered a baby twenty-five inches long, so she told Gus to beware the devil in him. Gus said he would, then scribbled

Woody Peace, July 2, 1931

into the biblical registry. The child grew so quickly some folks said they saw him grow before their very eyes. Who had ever seen a five-year-old stand three feet tall? And as if that wasn't strange enough, he laughed incessantly as he grew. Gus tried beating him, in hopes of calming his unbridled mirth, but the spankings only made him laugh harder. Perplexed that the jeering seemed unstoppable, and obviously unable to drive the devil from him, Gus stopped whipping Woody and started laughing with him. By 1945, an inch shy of his six-foot-two father, fourteen-year-old Woody was charging people a dime an hour to listen to his outrageous tales. Most paid without complaint. It was Emma Jean's idea. "Don't let folks use you, boy! Make these niggas pay if you gon' entertain 'em. Colored folks always want somethin' for free!" Woody obeyed and cut a slit in the plastic top of an empty Folgers coffee can, which then became his personal coffer. Some Saturday evenings, he filled the can, at which point Authorly's huge, rounded palm collected the remaining admissions. The Laughins, as Gus called the gatherings, occurred on the front porch with folks scattered across the yard. Some walked for miles to hear Woody talk shit about things he couldn't possibly have known. Thin as a young sapling in winter, he had elongated arms that swung freely from his torso as he clowned, while his pencil-shaped legs wobbled beneath him. His erratic movements made others fear he'd fall over, but he never did. That was part of the fun, people said, watching this rail-thin Goliath drama- tize stories and jokes as his arms flared wide and his fourteen-inch feet danced awkwardly upon the wooden porch. Gus couldn't tell whether peo- ple laughed with Woody or at him, but after weeks of all those dimes, he stopped caring.

"A country man went to a fancy party one night," Woody began one sultry summer evening. At first, folks milled about the yard casually, but when Woody started, they shuffled toward the porch as though it were magnetized. His booming voice, echoing across the yard, complemented his dramatic pre- sentation and caused others to laugh long before he reached the punch line. "He was dressed in his best red suit, with red shoes and a matchin' red hat! The nigga was sharp!"

Emma Jean yelped. Whenever Woody performed, she screamed like one being stabbed to death.

"They had food everywhere, of all different types. Ribs, chicken, casse- role, all kinds of salads, and the man was eating like he ain't never ate befo'! Well, like I said, this was a fancy party, so the white folks had labels on each table to let folks know what they was eatin'. The man walked 'round to all the different tables, trying a little bit of this and a little bit of that, then he ap- proached a table with a label he couldn't pronounce. He stared at the little piece of paper a long time, trying his best to figure out what it spelled, but he hadn't never seen that word befo'. He wanted to try the food on the table, but since he couldn't pronounce the word on the label, he just stood there, star- ing. The white chef behind the table said, 'May I help you, sir?' " Woody laughed as he mocked the chef's voice. A few men turned away and hollered. "The Negro country man didn't wanna look stupid, so he threw his head back real grand"—Woody exaggerated the movement—"and started talkin' like the educated white chef. 'Um, yessir,' he said. 'I'd like to try some of your whores de overs, please?' " People shouted and scattered as if a bomb had exploded. Even Gus covered his bad teeth and laughed freely. Others tried to retell the story later, but no one could perform it like skinny Woody Peace.

Emma Jean hoped the boy would become famous one day. Maybe then, she wouldn't have to work anymore.

Gus and Emma Jean agreed their fourth child *had* to be a girl, so they never bothered thinking of another male name. Disgusted and disappointed when another boy arrived—this one the blackest of all—Gus suggested they call him King Solomon since, according to Reverend Lindsey, King Solomon had been a wise man. Emma Jean liked the idea so Gus scribbled

King Solomon Peace, May 20, 1933

into the family Bible.

No one paid Sol, as the boys called him, much attention until Christmas of 1939. Dressed in James Earl's old Easter suit, he rose, prepared to recite "Silent Night" as his Christmas speech, but suddenly decided to sing it instead. His rich vibrato mesmerized the audience initially, but when Sol belted "All is calm, all is bright," complete with runs and trills adult vocalists couldn't manage, people ignored his age and let the Holy Ghost have its way. Miss Mamie cried, "Yes, Lord!" as others stared in awe and wonder. The real phenomenon, Gus noted, was that the boy's voice was identical to his mother's. Gus felt the same tingling sensation whenever Emma Jean sang, and, to keep from crying, he rocked violently in every direction with Authorly whispering "Shhhh" into his right ear. No one could believe it. Sol switched to falsetto and ended sweetly with "Sleep in heavenly peace." A momentary hush befell the hypnotized congregation. Miss Mamie broke the silence with "Ouuuuuu we! That boy's gotta gift!" "Shonuff!" others confirmed. Sol didn't comprehend exactly what he'd done, but he loved the crowd's response to it. So he started singing to anything and anyone who would listen. His voice became the clarion call for others to rise each morning in the Peace household, so if he overslept, everyone did. He loved that his voice disturbed people, leaving them weepy and vulnerable. He loved that birds gathered and chirped along as he serenaded the universe. And he loved that, in the spring of 1940, Gus asked him to sing to the seedlings and maybe they'd grow. People laughed at the boy, moving from row to row like a ministering evangelist, grazing his tender fingertips across fragile sprouts and singing at the top of his tenor range, but when, weeks later, peas, corn, okra, snap beans, and cabbage jumped from the earth in green abundance, the naysayers fell silent. Gus was grateful, but warned Sol not to get a big head.

On Sol's first day of school, Miss Erma Briars was taken with his brilliance. He was precisely what a burnt-out country schoolteacher needed. Yet Gus saw things differently. He asked Emma Jean, "If the boy already smart, what's de point o' sendin' him to school?" She ignored him and smiled at the As plastered across Sol's worksheets. He tutored his older brothers in reading and math and loved that Authorly submitted to him, if only for a while.

"How you get smart like that?" Gus asked Sol one night before bed. "Me and yo' momma ain't smart."

He shrugged. "I don't know."

Gus shrugged, too.

And Sol honestly didn't know. Things just came easily to him, he said. And quickly. Sometimes he'd stare at other pupils, wondering why the simplest concepts appeared so difficult for them, but he never belittled anyone. Gus had told him that if you don't use a gift to help others, God'll take it away from you, so Sol assisted his classmates, whenever Miss Erma allowed, until most comprehended what he had understood days earlier. Little King Solomon Peace was the joy of the classroom until the day Emma Jean insisted he stop going.

Gus and Emma Jean's fifth child was born blind. Kicking in the womb as though frustrated with its confinement, the baby reminded Emma Jean every day that she would surely regret having conceived out of desperation. In her sixth month, she knew it was a boy because, as she told her sister Gracie, "Only a man would kick a woman this hard." Miss Mamie confirmed her fear. "High as you carryin' that load, girl, can't be nothin' but a ole' big-head boy." Thirteen minutes after her first contraction, her fifth son burst forth without uttering a sound. Emma Jean screamed.

"He all right," Henrietta said. "Just quiet, I guess. That's all."

Having run out of boy names two boys ago, Emma Jean simply called him Baby and said that somewhere, somehow his name would surface. Gus thanked God the child was alive and felt relieved that at least the boy didn't seem slow.

Baby was even punier than James Earl had been. At six weeks, he weighed seven pounds and always seemed to be staring into oblivion. Emma Jean fed him and told God that if He were going to take him, then go ahead and do it. When God didn't, she asked Henrietta to take another look at the child. "He all right," Henrietta reassured after further examination. "Just little. And blind as a bat." Emma Jean sighed, then remembered that Reverend Lindsey had preached about a blind man who, despite others' objections, cried out to Jesus on the Jericho road until Jesus restored his sight. Hoping for a similar miracle, Emma Jean prayed, and named her son Blind Bartimaeus. She dictated each letter slowly, repeatedly, until Gus had it engraved in the family Bible:

Blind Bartimaeus Peace, July 31, 1934.

Of all the boys, Bartimaeus was most like his father, and Gus hated it. He had prayed that his sons wouldn't inherit his oversized heart—that's how he thought of his emotional fragility—but as Bartimaeus cried throughout his formative years for reasons no one could discern, Gus knew his prayer had gone unanswered. What the boy couldn't see, he felt even more intensely, and only when Gus held him did he calm and drift to sleep. Grateful the child couldn't see him, Gus often walked the dirt roads of Swamp Creek with Bartimaeus cradled in his arms, smearing tears into both his own and the child's high cheekbones. Only then did Gus ever see the boy smile and cackle like a normal baby. When the rains of '37 came, he wasn't surprised that Bartimaeus's two-week crying spell ended abruptly. He simply knew he'd have to teach the boy to hold his heart until he found a safe, obscure purging place.

As Bartimaeus grew, his sensitivity multiplied. The rains of '39 marked his transition from a shy, quiet youngster into a talkative, perceptive one. Gus groomed contempt for this new self, especially once people started calling the boy "sweet." "He ain't sweet!" Gus insisted. But Bartimaeus *was* sweet, people declared, and his blindness made him sweeter. Who had ever seen a child feel his way from one person to the next, hugging everyone as though trying to feel the beat of people's hearts? And who had ever seen a boy raise his arms in frozen ecstasy as floral fragrances wafted by his nose? Yes, he was the sweetest boy in Swamp Creek. Probably in the whole state of Arkansas, Miss Mamie declared. Sweet, blind Bartimaeus. Nothing Gus said could redeem the boy's public reputation. Gus thought to beat him, like Chester Sr. had done him. Surely that would allay the boy's sensitivities and quiet people's tongues. The only problem was that whenever he raised his hand to strike Bartimaeus, the child sensed the impending violence and recoiled in utter fear. All Gus could do was cry and hold him.

Never attending school—how in the world, Gus argued, could a child learn to read if he couldn't see?—Bartimaeus let his imagination become his reality. In his mind's eye, he saw the world as a place of perfect love, where people exchange hearts simply to know what others' feel like. Uninhibited by frowns and stares, Bartimaeus touched everything within reach as he attempted to see what those with eyes often overlooked. He would have given anything to glimpse, if only for a moment, the honeysuckle bush that smelled so sweet or the mountain range that Mister said touched the sky. At night, he grazed his hands over his brothers' faces, creating a family portrait only he could see, but how would he ever know the accuracy of his imagining? Maybe there was a reason God had denied him sight, he thought, and each day he hoped to discover that reason.

The last child—or so Gus had thought—was also a boy, and Gus thanked a merciful God he'd never have to raise a girl. He'd wanted Bartimaeus to be the last, but Emma Jean's desperate hope for a girl compelled him to relent once again. She'd always foreseen a herd of children, but girls were her preference, so with each birth she prayed the curse of the boys would end. Believing the sixth child was a girl and too sick, after the seventh month, to endure another day, Emma Jean induced her own labor. Unable to find Henrietta, Gus told her that she'd have to birth the child alone, so she did. When she saw its penis, she looked heavenward and mumbled, "Damn you." Then she screeched, "Gus! Come get this!" He knew it was another boy. "You name him whatever you like. It don't make me no difference." Gus said, "Well, people gon' call him mister somethin' when he get grown, so we might as well start callin' him Mister now." Emma Jean would have hollered had she had the strength. After waking from a nap and hearing the other boys call him Mister, she decided to let the name stand. Gus wrote

Mister Peace, August 16, 1935

in the family Bible and closed it with finality. "When I have my little girl, I'll name her something pretty," Emma Jean promised herself.

"We almost got the shoulders out," Henrietta said. "If you can give me one more good push—"

Emma Jean raised herself, almost to a full sit-up position, and roared, "AH-HHHHHHHH!" then collapsed heavily. "Oh my God!" she gasped. "This has gotta be my little girl. It's just gotta be."

"Let's just get it here first," Henrietta cautioned. "Then we'll see what it is." She dabbed Emma Jean's forehead with a cool, moistened cloth.

Gus didn't have to worry about this ever again, Emma Jean thought. Boy or girl, she had had enough of childbearing for the rest of her life.

After one last, feeble push, Henrietta said, "Dear Jesus! Here it is." Slowly, she lifted the baby, showing Emma Jean her seventh son.

Emma Jean closed her eyes and trembled. What had she done to make God mock her so, she wondered. Hadn't she been an obedient daughter, even when her mother beat the shit out of her? Hadn't she fed and clothed her children to the best of her ability? Hadn't she married and loved—well, not loved, but at least respected—a husband whom she was sure no one else had wanted?

"He's jes' as cute as he can be, Emma Jean," Henrietta pacified, after severing the umbilical cord. "This one's kinda golden. Not as black as the others. Soft, curly hair. Yep! He's a beauty."

Emma Jean wouldn't look. All she could think about was the promise she had made as a child to love and pamper a daughter the way someone should've loved her. She'd dreamed of stroking a little girl's hair and binding it with golden ribbons, then sending her off to be admired by the world. But that couldn't happen now. How would she ever spite her mother without a daughter of her own?

"Don't be disappointed, honey. A healthy child's a blessin', don't care what it is. And this one's the cutest one yet. Plus, a house full o' boys is always a blessin'."

Henrietta sat the newborn in a small basin of lukewarm water and began to rinse the guck from him. "Yep, he's the prettiest! Just look at all this hair, girl!" Emma Jean's silence compelled Henrietta to add, "All dese hyeah boys sho nuff gon' take care o' you one day. You mark my word. Boys take care o' they momma!"

Emma Jean ignored Henrietta. She certainly loved her boys, especially Authorly, but she couldn't foresee a future without the daughter she'd imagined. *God must think this is funny,* she thought. *Why does He love to watch people suffer? What kind of God is He anyway? Aren't people supposed to get* something *they want before they die, especially if they've never had anything?*

Henrietta wrapped the infant in the pink towel Emma Jean had bought weeks ago at Morrison's, and handed the baby to its silent, stoic mother. Emma Jean received the bundle like one receiving an eviction notice. She shook her head as tears welled, but she refused to cry. What would've been the point? Why couldn't she ever have what she wanted? After six boys—six!—didn't she deserve a girl?

"I may as well go tell the menfolk now," Henrietta slurred. "At least Gus'll be happy."

A yellow-breasted chat appeared on a branch outside the bedroom window. Emma Jean studied its color and smirked. She loved that shade of yellow. She had foreseen it in dresses and matching hair barrettes adorning her little girl, and now she couldn't relinquish the image. Of course a boy *could* wear yellow, but most didn't. What father, including Gus, would allow it? And who would call him beautiful? That's why Emma Jean needed a girl. She needed someone others would deem beautiful, someone around the house who would care as much as she did about dainty, frivolous things.

"Emma Jean?"

Someone who wanted her and thought she was the greatest mother in the whole wide world. Someone who *needed* her like her sisters had needed their mother, Mae Helen, years ago. Someone who justified why she, Emma Jean, hadn't murdered Mae Helen back when she had the nerve. Yes, she needed a girl. She had to have one. And if God thought He was going to deny her, Emma Jean resolved, He had another thing coming.

"Yes! Yes! Of course!" She burst into triumphant laughter. Her dismay lifted like fog on a cold, cloudy morning.

"Emma Jean? Are you all right? What is it?"

Emma Jean unveiled the baby, caressing its limbs, hands, and feet. "Hi, honey," she whispered. "You finally made it, huh? You just as pretty as you can be."

"Emma Jean? What are you talkin' about?"

"I prayed for you a long time ago, and now you're here."

Henrietta's mouth twitched. "Emma Jean? You all right?"

The mother blinked tears of joy. "I'm just fine, Henrietta Worthy. Just fine!" She stroked the baby's head gently.

"Well, I'ma go on out and tell the menfolks—"

"You ain't gon' tell 'em nothin'," Emma Jean said. "Nothin' but what I tell you."

Henrietta turned, confused. "Excuse me?"

"You gon' tell 'em they got a new baby sister. That's what you gon' tell 'em. And she's just as cute as she can be!" Emma Jean smiled.

"What?" Henrietta said, approaching the bed. "What did you say?" Her eyes narrowed to small, oval slits.

"That's right! This is my baby girl! She's jes' as pretty as she can be! You said so yourself!"

"What chu talkin' 'bout, Emma Jean?"

"This here's my baby girl," Emma Jean repeated. "At least now she is."

"That ain't no girl! I know you wanted one and all, but—"

"And now I got one!"

Henrietta glanced frantically from Emma Jean, to the ceiling, to each of the four walls, and back to Emma Jean. "What?"

"You heard me. I said, this is my baby girl. And that's all there is to it."

"I don't understand what you sayin', Emma Jean Peace." Henrietta stood with arms akimbo.

"Oh, sure you do. It ain't deep."

"It must be deep 'cause I ain't gettin' it."

Emma Jean wrapped the child again and cleared her throat. "This is my *daughter*," she stressed, peering into Henrietta's bulged eyes. "And don't look at me like I'm crazy."

Henrietta blinked repeatedly. "You is crazy! You must be done lost yo' mind, Emma Jean. That baby ain't no girl!"

"I know what it is, but it's gon' be a girl. From now on."

Henrietta's mouth fell open.

"You ain't got nothin' to worry about. This is all my doin'. I just need you to keep yo' mouth shut. That's all."

"Keep my mouth shut?" Henrietta shouted. "Is you plumb crazy, Emma Jean Peace?"

"Shh! Like I said, you ain't got nothin' to explain to nobody. Just let my business be my business."

"You can't be serious! What kinda mother would do this to a child?"

Emma Jean looked away. "Just let me handle this my own way, okay? And anyway, a child gon' believe whatever you tell it. As long as she thinks she's a girl, that's what she'll be. So that's what she is now."

Henrietta clasped her mouth in horror. "Emma Jean, don't do this! You can't jes' make a person be what you want 'em to be! That's sick!" She backed away from the bed slowly. "You can't make a daughter outta no boy!"

"Sure you can. Just think about it. You don't know what most folks is. Not really. You ain't seen 'em naked, is you?"

Henrietta paused.

"Well, is you?"

"No, I ain't, but . . ."

"But what? Most folks *look* like a boy or girl, but you don't *know* for sure what they is, do you?"

"Come on, Emma Jean! Don't try to justify this mess! I don't care what you say. It ain't right!"

"Maybe it ain't, but it's what we gon' do."

"We?" Henrietta hollered.

"That's right. Me and you. We in this together."

"I ain't in nothin' with you, Emma Jean Peace! You ain't nothin' but a ole connivin', black heffa!"

"Maybe I am, but I'm a damn good one! And, like I said, I ain't got to explain nothin' to you or nobody else. All you gotta do is be quiet 'bout my business."

Henrietta shivered. "What's wrong with you, woman? You think ain't nobody got good sense but you? Who gon' believe this boy is a girl? You may as well admit you had a boy and be done with it. You can't just turn no boy into a girl."

"I can do whatever the hell I want to, Miss Lady, and you gon' keep yo' mouth shut about it!"

"Stop this, Emma Jean! Stop it right now!"

The menfolks wondered why Henrietta was stomping, but they dared not enter the birthing room.

"I know you been wantin' a girl, but it wasn't God's will. You gotta take what God gives you and try to see the blessin' in it."

"And sometimes you gotta make a blessin' out of it."

Henrietta shook her head and breathed deeply. "You can think whatever you want to, Emma Jean, but I ain't goin' 'long wit' no mess like this." She turned to exit.

"Oh, sure you will," Emma Jean sassed, "unless you want folks to know 'bout Louise's baby."

Like Lot's wife, Henrietta turned and froze. "Don't you dare! You don't know nothin' 'bout Louise's baby! She ain't got nothin' to do with this shit you doin'!" Henrietta's bottom lip trembled like a gospel soloist's.

"You right! That ain't none o' my business and this ain't none o' yours. Not really. So jes keep yo' mouth shut and we'll all be fine."

"But, Emma Jean, I ain't 'bout to tell folks you had no girl. I can't lie like that!"

"Oh yes you can. Sure you can. You did it for Louise, didn't you? Well, now you'll have to do it again."

"Louise's baby died, Emma Jean. Ain't nothin' else to know."

"Ha!" Emma Jean mocked. "That's what most folk think, ain't it?"

Henrietta saw the truth in Emma Jean's eyes and knew she couldn't deny it any longer. She studied the crevices in the hardwood floor, then said, "Don't do this to me, Emma Jean. Please."

"Do what?" Emma Jean squealed joyfully. "I ain't doin' nothing to you. Nothin' at all."

Henrietta sat at the foot of the bed, unable to believe that Emma Jean Peace, of all people, knew what no one else in the world was supposed to know.

"Any time you go sneakin' 'round, thinkin' you hidin', I guarantee you somebody watchin'. Guarantee!"

Henrietta sighed. Nothing to do now but set the record straight. "It ain't what you think."

"I don't think about it. And that's what you should do about this—just don't think about it."

Henrietta couldn't yield so easily. "I wouldn't neva blackmail nobody into doin' somethin' so evil. You shonuff got the devil in you, Emma Jean."

"Well, you musta had him in you, too, to take another woman's child."

"I ain't took nobody's child! It didn't happen like that."

"Well, however it happened, it happened. That's yo' business." She lifted the baby to her bosom. "And this is mine."

Henrietta rose. "You gon' answer to God for this."

"Ain't we all? Who ain't got somethin' to answer to God for?"

Henrietta said nothing.

"That's what I thought. Now. Let's make sure we're on the same page with our little . . . *arrangement*. What is this?" Emma Jean pointed to the infant.

Henrietta looked away. "It's whatever you say it is."

"That's right. And what do I say it is?"

Henrietta hesitated. "A girl. It's a girl."

"That's right! And she's beautiful. Couldn't be more perfect, could she?"

Emma Jean's wink drove Henrietta toward the doorway. "You'll never get away with this."

"Get away with what? Lovin' and celebratin' my perfect little girl?" Suddenly, Emma Jean shrieked, retarding Henrietta's exit. "Oh my God! That's it! That's her name—Perfect. Because that's what she is. Don't you think that's a pretty name?"

"It's yo' chile."

"Yes it is! And Perfect's her name. Oh, this is wonderful!" Emma Jean beamed.

Henrietta closed her eyes and said, "If it's the last thing I do, I'll get you for this one day. I promise you that."

"Don't make promises you can't keep," Emma Jean said.

"Oh I'll keep it. And when I do—"

"You can go now, Henrietta. Thanks for everything. And, on yo' way out, tell Gus and the boys 'bout the new woman in the family."

Chapter 2

When the rooster crowed, Emma Jean leapt across the two sisters with whom she shared a bed, declaring, "It's my birthday! It's my birthday!" Gracie and Pearlie grunted their annoyance and burrowed themselves deeper beneath the homemade quilts. Their indifference didn't stifle Emma Jean's joy. "It's my birthday! It's my birthday!" she sang as she slung her battered housecoat around her scrawny shoulders. The floorboards whined and squeaked as she shuffled, and Emma Jean hoped she hadn't awakened Mae Helen. If she had, her birthday would be ruined. Mae Helen had told her countless times to do her morning chores quietly so as not to disturb her sisters. They needed their beauty sleep. Whenever Emma Jean disobeyed, the sting of Mae Helen's back-hand lingered across her cheek for days. Yet Emma Jean purposed in her heart to celebrate her eighth birthday, if she had to do so alone.

"Cut out all dat damn noise!" Mae Helen shouted from the other end of the house.

"But it's my birthday, Momma!" she exclaimed, skipping softly down the narrow hallway.

"So what!" Mae Helen screamed. "Who is you? The goddamn queen o' Sheba? You think everybody's s'pose to jump up just 'cause it's yo' birthday? Shit. Everybody got a birthday."

They met in the kitchen.

"I just thought it might be fun maybe"—Emma Jean swallowed hard, trying not to cry—"to do something special today."

"Special?" Mae Helen sneered. "You better be glad I ain't slapped de shit outta you for wakin' me up wit' all dat hollerin'."

Emma Jean gathered kindling for the woodstove. Once the fire was brewing, she filled the coffeepot and placed it atop the warming surface. Mae Helen sat at the table, mumbling something about having to wash white folks' dirty drawers, and Emma Jean turned and risked, "I just thought that maybe, um, we could have a li'l party or somethin'? You know. Nothin' big or fancy. Just a fun little party."

Mae Helen glanced up. "A party? Shiiiiiit! Ain't nobody wastin' no time on no goddamn party. We got work to do 'round here, girl." She stood and stared at Emma Jean. "I mean, who you think you is for real? You ain't nobody special. That's what I shoulda named you—Nobody."

Emma Jean's solid hope began to liquefy. "I know I ain't nobody, Momma, but since I ain't neva had no birthday party in my whole entire life, I thought that, maybe, I could have one this time. I ain't talkin' 'bout nothin' big or nothin'. Just a li'l yellow cake, maybe, and a scoop o' ice cream or somethin'. I ain't even got to invite nobody."

"Ain't gon' be no goddamn birthday party 'round hyeah today, you black heffa!" Mae Helen screamed into Emma Jean's watery eyes. "You must think you some rich white girl or somethin'. Well, you ain't! You's a po', ugly, black-ass nigga. That's what you is!"

Emma Jean recoiled and trembled.

"You think de world s'pose to stop and dance"—she mocked a jig—"jes' 'cause it's yo' birthday?"

Tears burst free across Emma Jean's deep chocolate cheeks. Now she wished she had jumped into the Jordan like she had contemplated weeks earlier.

Mae Helen stared hatred into Emma Jean's eyes. "You's a selfish li'l bitch, you know that?"

Emma Jean couldn't figure out what to say or do.

"We already ain't got nothin' and you want us to spend what little we do have on you jes' 'cause it's *yo'* birthday? What about everybody else? Huh? I guess we ain't got no birthday, huh? Don't nobody have no birthday 'round here 'cept you? You de only one whose birthday really matter?" Her condescension made Emma Jean nauseous.

"I didn't mean it like that, Momma," the child whispered.

Mae Helen retrieved a cast-iron skillet from a nail on the wall. "That's exactly how you meant it. It's always about you, ain't it?" As though by reflex, she slammed the skillet against Emma Jean's forehead, then placed it on the stove. "Now get that broom and sweep this floor. I bet you done woke yo' sistas."

The room was swirling like a merry-go-round. Emma Jean couldn't maintain her balance. She leaned against the small rectangular kitchen table, trying to steady herself.

"Did you hear me, girl? I said git that broom and sweep dis floor! And I mean now!"

Mae Helen's voice echoed in Emma Jean's head as though her mother were shouting from a distant mountain. Emma Jean stepped forward uneasily, hoping to avoid another blow. Stumbling to her knees, she was grateful that, now, Mae Helen would know that at least she was trying to be obedient.

"Girl, if you don't git up off dat flo', I'ma beat yo' ass fo' real! I didn't even hit you dat hard." Mae Helen stepped around the child and sat at the table, peeling potatoes.

Emma Jean managed to utter "Yes, ma'am" and lift herself, climbing a badly splintered table chair. The high-pitched ring in her ears reminded her of the incessant chirping outside her screenless window every night, or maybe it resembled the chiming of the church bell on Sunday morning. That, along with the fact that everything she reached for seemed to back away from her, made Emma Jean wonder why God didn't just take her away. The beautiful colors of the trees and flowers outside had all turned gray in her head, and the dingy nightgown she wore seemed to float away from her flesh. If only she could uncross her eyes, she thought.

"If I have to tell you one more time to sweep this floor"—Mae Helen scowled without facing Emma Jean—"you gon' really be sorry."

Emma Jean hadn't the strength to wipe her tears. She wanted to move, wanted it more than her birthday party, but she feared her wobbly legs couldn't carry her. Her only recourse, she concluded, was to return to the floor and crawl to the corner. Having done so, she climbed up the broom handle, caressing it gently like one might a lover, hoping all the while it had the strength to bear her weight.

On her feet, she clutched the wooden handle to her flat chest and sighed heavily after the three miles, it seemed, she had crawled to reach it. "Thank you," Emma Jean whimpered. Then she shuffled slightly, dragging the broom along. It was a kind of two-step waltz, the movement she and the broom made, like a three-legged creature fumbling through a basic choreography. The three-quarter time structure provided a rhythm conducive to a tremulous little girl and a broomstick, especially since, after being knocked senseless, Emma Jean shared the broom's mental wherewithal. The swoosh of the first beat allowed Emma Jean to breathe on the second and third, giving her just enough strength to perform the movement again before the wrath of Mae Helen befell her. Sweat and trickles of blood covered her once-hopeful brow and made her regret the mention of her birthday. Breathing like someone in danger of drowning, Emma Jean dragged the broom across the floor in no particular direction, praying that whatever dirt her mother saw, the broom collected. She dared not ask whether her effort was satisfactory. It never was. She dreamed of the day Mae Helen said, "That looks great, honey!" or "Momma's so proud of you!" But after she was struck with the black cast-iron skillet—with which she shared a complexion—Emma Jean's dream shattered and scattered like dandelion seeds in the wind.

"You ain't doin' shit, gal!" Mae Helen said. "And you want a birthday party?" She rose and snatched the broom from Emma Jean, who, shivering like a newborn calf, almost tumbled to the floor. "Go git dem eggs outta de hen house, and don't let it take you all day."

Grateful to be out of harm's way, Emma Jean stumbled through the screen door and onto the front porch. Fumbling down the cinder-block steps as though inebriated, she hobbled through the dusty dirt yard until she reached the chicken coop. How she would gather eggs without breaking them she didn't know, since the violent tremors wouldn't subside, yet presenting Mae Helen with cracked shells was definitely not an option.

Leaning against the cedar-post gate, Emma Jean panted and allowed her right hand to find the latch. She then entered the chicken yard and fainted, facedown, in the midst of miniature white feathers and moist chicken shit. Several hens approached her limp form, jerking their heads curiously as though trying to ascertain why a little girl would choose their space in which to lounge. Seconds later, a bold one pecked at her arm and startled enough consciousness in her so that she could rise, drag herself inside the coop, and collapse intentionally.

Within moments, her senses returned. Unsure of how long she had been incapacitated, she gathered eggs quickly and rushed back inside.

"You musta gone to a chicken coop five miles away," Mae Helen reprimanded.

Emma Jean hung her head and lamented, "I'm sorry, Momma. It's just that my head keeps swimmin' 'round and—"

"Oh, shut up, chile!" Mae Helen spewed, snatching the basket of eggs. "Ain't nothin' wrong with you. I barely even touched you. But de next time you prance around dis house like you somethin' you ain't, I'ma really knock de shit out o' you. Then yo' head *will* be swimmin'." Mae Helen placed the basket on the table. "Now go ask yo' sistas what they want for breakfast."

Gracie and Pearlie, four and six years Emma Jean's senior, slept Saturday mornings until they rose naturally. "Pretty folks need plenty o' sleep," Mae Helen reminded Emma Jean constantly. It must be their golden hue, Emma Jean guessed, that granted them something her ashen blackness didn't. Or maybe it was their silky hair, which Mae Helen combed tirelessly. When Emma Jean sat before her, Mae Helen grabbed the thick bush and said, "This is yo' daddy's nappy hair. My hair is nappy, but not like this. You need a mule and a plow for this briar patch!" Such rumbling continued until, ten minutes later, she had worked Emma Jean's hair into four thick, ribbonless plaits. "That'll do," she always said, pushing the child away from her.

Sampson Hurt, one of Swamp Creek's two heartthrobs, had fathered Pearlie and Gracie, much to Mae Helen's boastful delight. Whether he was actually handsome or not was debatable, but his straight hair and golden skin tone were sufficient for black folks to think he was. Mae Helen offered herself to Sammy simply as a necessary sacrifice for a modicum of coexistent pleasure, and of course Sammy didn't refuse. He never said he loved her—or even that he liked her—and Mae Helen never asked. His presence alone, especially inside her, allowed her to believe that someone at least *could* love her. So when Sammy disappeared without ever saying good-bye, she celebrated the two daughters and the precious memories he left behind.

Claude Lovejoy, Emma Jean's daddy, was a shade yellower than Sammy. Mae Helen lay with him in hopes of being used, once again, by a man every other woman wanted. Yet when Emma Jean emerged with Mae Helen's navy blue complexion, Mae Helen swore she'd never sleep with the son of a bitch again. She told him to pack his shit and get out and that Emma Jean would never carry the Lovejoy name. She would be a Hurt, like her sisters, so others would at least associate her with beauty. When Claude chuckled and told Mae Helen, "She looks jes' like you!" Mae Helen said, "Fuck you, nigga. Get the hell outta my house."

Claude left. Emma Jean would wonder, years later, if he had offered to take her with him.

* * *

Pearlie sat on the edge of the bed, brushing Gracie's hair. Both sisters turned when Emma Jean entered.

"Ugh! Why you so dirty, girl?" Pearlie asked. Gracie pursed her lips sadly.

"Momma hit me, then I fell out in the chicken coop." Emma Jean began to disrobe.

"You sho smell like it!" Pearlie screeched, and resumed stroking Gracie's hair.

"Leave her alone," Gracie admonished sympathetically, staring into Emma Jean's transparent eyes.

"I wunnit pickin' on her! I was jes' sayin' that she smell like—"

"Shut up, Pearlie!" Gracie leapt up. "Just shut up. You don't know what happened so just shut your big, fat mouth."

"What's wrong with you?" Pearlie asked, unable to explain Gracie's new-found compassion.

"Ain't nothin' wrong with me. You just ain't gotta be so mean. That's all."

Pearlie frowned.

"It don't make no sense to laugh at Emma Jean. You know Momma don't like her."

Pearlie shrugged and walked out. Emma Jean stood naked in the middle of the room and wept with her face buried in her palms.

"Don't cry, Emma," Gracie soothed, patting her shoulder. "It's gonna be all right. I'll take care o' you. Just try to stay out o' Momma's way."

"But I ain't done nothin' wrong!" Emma Jean protested. "All I done was ask Momma for a birthday party and she hit me with the skillet."

Gracie blinked slowly. "Don't ask Momma for nothin'. Just do whatever she say."

Together, the sisters wiped Emma Jean's face, hands, and feet with moist washcloths. Gracie noticed the fresh wound, circling from Emma Jean's forehead around to her right temple. In years to come, Emma Jean would try to hide the C-shaped mark with strands of straightened hair, only to be disappointed that it never quite reached far enough. When people inquired as to the origin of the scar, she would say, "It's my birthmark." Most left it at that although they knew better. What child had ever been born with a rough, raised keloid blemish like that? Yet, not wishing to pry, they let Emma Jean construct whatever truth she needed.

Sliding a clean cotton sack dress over her little sister's head, Gracie said, "Don't say nothin' else 'bout yo' birthday. You can have a party when you get grown if you want to."

"But what's so wrong about havin' a party now? I ain't neva had no party befo'."

"I said forgit about it! You ain't gon' do nothin' but make Momma madder, and this time ain't no tellin' what she might do to you. Jes' be quiet."

"Okay," Emma Jean said as the image of the pretty lemon cake dissolved in her head.

Chapter 3

The Peaces lived in a rather large A-framed house in the backwoods of Swamp Creek. No one ever stumbled upon their dwelling because it would've been impossible to do so. From Highway 64, you'd turn right onto Fishlake Road and follow its winding trail, past shacks and shotgun houses, until the main road ended. That's as far as most ever went. Yet, those seeking the Peaces, Tysons, and Redfields made a ninety-degree turn onto a dirt path mules and wagons had carved out, and continued on, several hundred yards, passing first the Tysons', then the Redfields', until suddenly, far in the distance, the Peace home appeared.

Gus and Chester Jr. built it months before Gus proposed to Emma Jean. He'd marry somebody, he assumed, and they'd need a place to live. Hopefully, she'd like it, but if she didn't, she'd simply have to get used to it, he told Chester. Gus said that a man's job was to provide a dwelling place for his wife; whether she liked it or not was her problem. Yet Gus hoped she would, and in fact she did. The full-length porch, stretching the width of the house, attracted her most as she imagined children, hopefully girls, leaping from it and into the yard, screaming and playing tag on hot summer afternoons. She envisioned herself in a porch rocker, on rainy days, mending holey socks while humming church songs to the rhythm of the downpour. She'd always wanted a porch. A porch invited people's company, and that's what she longed for.

The rest of the house was fine with her. There were two bedrooms, a wash area, a sizeable kitchen, and a huge living room. When Emma Jean walked in, she gasped at the enormity of the living space and mentally began to decorate it. If she had a boy in the midst of her daughters, he'd sleep on the sofa. Boys didn't mind that kind of thing, she told Gus.

Emma Jean's only insistence was that the house remain immaculate. She hated clutter and filth even more than Mae Helen had. Or maybe *because* Mae Helen had. For fifteen years, her Saturday morning chores included cleaning up behind her mother and sisters, and she would kill a man—children, too!— if they thought she was going to do more of that. Of course she would clean, she told Gus, but she wasn't a maid and didn't intend to feel like one. He nodded, but offered no assurances.

Gus inherited the twenty-acre lot on which the house sat the day Chester Sr. died. He left Chester Jr. thirty acres north of the Jordan. Gus's land was deeper in the woods and he preferred it that way. Once the house was complete, a hundred yards off the wagon path, he combed the nearby forest for wild ferns, flowers, and other greenery, which he then uprooted and transplanted to his own front yard. The result was a lush, colorful oasis the likes of which Emma Jean had never seen. Each spring, when the rains came and Gus escaped to the Jordan, ferns burst forth and flowers of every color bloomed and peppered the lawn. Gus was meticulous in its maintenance, beating Authorly severely whenever he mowed across something he thought was a weed. People complimented Emma Jean on her horticultural skills, and she accepted the praise, for both her own and Gus's sakes.

Gus liked that his picturesque lawn contrasted with what he called the ugliness of the adjoining cotton field. As a child, he promised Chester Sr. that none of his children would ever pick cotton a day in their lives. If he had to work like a mule to provide for his family, that's exactly what he'd do. And it's exactly what he did. Kissing white folks' asses by picking their cotton was simply out of the question. So when he inherited the twenty acres and his boys started coming, he taught them how to work and, with their assistance, he kept his promise.

Wilson Peace, Gus's grandfather, had done the same thing. He refused to slave for white folks, and, even in the winter of 1907, when his family practically starved to death, he forbade any of them to bring white money into his house. That's the winter Chester Sr. resolved not to emulate his father. His hunger had been far greater than his pride, so the day he turned eighteen, Chester Sr. started chopping cotton for whites, and stopped a day shy of his seventy-eighth birthday only because his legs gave out. Gus reverenced his grandfather's pride and sought nothing more desperately than to replicate it. Chester Sr. warned that pride comes before a great fall, but Gus said he was willing to fall if it meant he didn't have to submit his labor to whites. Wilson smiled. It wasn't that Gus didn't admire his father; Gus loved Chester Sr. and respected the fact that they always ate. Gus simply hated that whites called his daddy "boy" and treated him like shit. So Gus explained his defiance as the only way he knew to keep white folks from destroying another generation of Peaces.

To keep his family together, Wilson's father took his master's surname when slavery ended. Baxter Pace owned some three hundred slaves in South Carolina and sold one of Wilson's uncles to a plantation somewhere in Louisiana. Hoping to find his brother one day, Wilson kept the Pace name at first in hopes that, wherever he was in the world, his brother might search him out. Yet once slavery ended and Wilson's father made his way to Arkansas—where folks said money was growing on trees—he dropped the hope of ever seeing his brother again and added an *E* to "Pace," thus naming himself what he desired most—Peace.

Henrietta emerged from the master bedroom, feigning a smile. "It's a girl."

"Yeah!" the brothers cheered. Their boisterous applause almost deafened Gus, who nodded and sighed with relief.

"What's her name?" Authorly asked.

"She ain't got no name yet," Gus said. "Hell, she just got here. Yo' momma gon' think of a name pretty soon."

Not meaning to contradict Gus yet afraid the least omission might cost her, Henrietta said, "Her name's Perfect. That's what yo' momma said."

"Perfect," the boys repeated in chorus.

What kinda name is that, Gus thought, and grimaced as he retrieved the family Bible. Sol leaned over his right shoulder, spelling the name seven or eight times before Gus had it correct:

Perfect Peace, May 17, 1940.

"Who she look like? Can we see her? Can we hold her?" Mister's questions came faster than Henrietta could answer.

"No!" she snapped. The boys' faces went blank. "I mean, not quite yet. It was a tough birth and yo' momma needs a little time to recover. Just give her a little while." Henrietta paused to collect herself. "Your mother's tired now and the baby's sleeping. He—I mean she's really pretty though. Perfect—just like your mother calls her." Henrietta hadn't planned to say that, but in the midst of forced deceit, she didn't know what else to say. She turned abruptly and reentered the bedroom.

"I can't do this, Emma Jean. I can't."

Emma Jean nodded. "Of course you can. And you will. It's already done. I have a beautiful baby girl and that's the end of it."

"This ain't gon' work. There's no way." Henrietta's strength dissolved like sugar in hot water. She sank onto the edge of the bed.

"Listen," Emma Jean murmured, grabbing Henrietta's arm. "Just call her a girl and be done with it! There's nothin' to think about, nothin' to rationalize, nothin' to justify, nothin' to pray about, and nothin' to do except love her the way she is."

"That's the whole problem! The way she is ain't right 'cause she ain't no she!"

"Of course she is. She's jes' a little different from most other little girls, but she'll never know that if don't nobody tell her."

Henrietta stared at Emma Jean, perplexed.

"I knew God wouldn't let me down. After raisin' all these boys, He owed me a girl."

Henrietta stood. "Don't bring God into this, Emma Jean!"

"What chu mean? God's the One Who made this possible. And I thank Him for it."

"You know what?" Henrietta tossed her hands into the air. "Do what you want. But when you go befo' God on Judgment Day—"

"I'll meet you there!"

Emma Jean was out of her mind, Henrietta decided, so once again, she turned to leave.

"If you ever tell anybody about this, you'll be sorry. I promise you that. You and that *daughter* of yours."

Henrietta seethed with anger.

"Oh, don't worry." Emma Jean shrugged. "Don't nobody know the truth but me. Well, me and the person who told me. But I ain't gon' tell. I understand why you did what you did. I really do. A woman does strange thangs sometimes."

"It ain't the same thing, Emma Jean, and you know it!"

"Oh, sure it is! Since you didn't have no children of yo' own, although you had done delivered everybody else's, you thought you'd just take one."

Henrietta swiveled and faced Emma Jean. "That ain't what happened."

"No? Sure it is. Louise died anyway, right? Or maybe I'm wrong. But I know enough to know you did somethin' you didn't have no business doin'."

Henrietta slid to the floor and relinquished the fight. "Who told you, Emma Jean?"

"That's some more o' my business. It don't make no difference noway. Just know that you ain't the only one who know."

"I was takin' care o' my sister. That's all," Henrietta said, dazed. "She never wanted no babies, but that preacher husband insisted. After she went into labor, it lasted four days, and she was so exhausted I thought she was gon' fall out dead. But then the water broke and the baby came. In the middle o' pushin' with what little strength she had left, Louise stopped breathin'. I thought she was jes' so tired she quit pushin', but after the baby came, I realized somethin' was wrong 'cause don't care how tired a mother is, she wanna see her baby when it come out.

"I washed the baby girl and wrapped her real tight in one o' Louise's little blankets. Then I stood over Louise and patted her cheeks and arms and everything, but she didn't respond. Her eyes was wide open like she had done seen a ghost, but her body didn't have no life. I started cryin' and askin' God to bring her back 'cause she didn't want no babies noway, but she just laid there and never did move. Preacher was in the kitchen, smokin' his pipe real proud, and when I seen him and thought about what he had done done to my sister, I knew what to do. It was what Louise woulda wanted. She had done told him she couldn't have no babies"—Henrietta clenched her teeth—"but, no, that wasn't good enough for him. He needed somebody to carry his name, and it was her duty to provide it. That's what a wife's s'pose to do, he told her. I heard him say it. And since Louise didn't want to be no bad wife, she at least had to try."

Henrietta stared through the window at the woods in the distance. "One Sunday morning, right as we wuz walkin' into church, Louise whispered and told me she was late. I asked her if she was pregnant, but she didn't say nothin'. 'Bout halfway through service, she tiptoed out back, lookin' real sick. I snuck out there and saw Louise throwin' up all over the ground. I knowed she was pregnant.

"So when Louise was strugglin' in childbirth, and Preacher Man was sittin' up there with his chest stuck out like he had done done somethin' grand, I knowed I had to fight for Louise 'cause she couldn't fight for herself."

"So you told Preacher Man the baby died?"

"I told him that both of them died. But I took the baby and raised it myself. What was he gon' do with a little girl all by hisself? What a man know 'bout raisin' a girl?"

Emma Jean nodded and mumbled, "Right, right. But what happened to your baby? You was pregnant, too. Y'all shoulda delivered 'round 'bout the same time, if I remember right."

Henrietta ignored the question. "He didn't deserve no baby, the way he had done treated my sister. And he didn't want no girl noway. Louise didn't mean nothin' to him 'til she got pregnant, and then all he was concerned about was the baby. He had done already named it 'fo she had it. I knowed in my heart he was gon' throw my sister and that child away if it was a girl, so when it came, I told him that Louise died and the baby girl died, too."

"And nobody knows that Trish is really Louise's daughter." Emma Jean snickered.

Henrietta rose. "Trish is my daughter. I raised her."

"You right about that! If a woman raise a girl, that's shonuff her daughter. But how did you get the baby outta the house without Preacher Man knowin'?"

Henrietta's head dropped as she remembered. "I bundled her up in a sheet and set her outside the window on the ground. She never mumbled a sound. When I left, I went 'round de house and put her in my medicine bag and took her home. I kept what part o' my sister I could keep."

"Oh! That's why you disappeared for a while. You needed folks to believe you had gone off and delivered yo' own child. I see! Wow. You good, girl, 'cause they believed it. I believed it, too. 'Til I learned better."

Emma Jean's assumptions weren't correct—she was so very wrong!—but Henrietta refused to tell her more than she already knew.

"Trish deserved somebody who wuz gon' love her."

"And that somebody wuz you, right?"

"Yes, it was."

"Of course it was. You knew what you could do and you knew what the child needed. A woman always knows."

"She was my baby sister, Emma Jean. She was all I had."

"I understand. That's why yo' secret is safe with me. Now, you gotta help me out, too."

"What you doin' ain't nothin' like what I did, and you know it!"

"What's the difference?"

Henrietta couldn't explain the difference, but she felt it in her heart. "It just ain't the same."

"So what you did was right?"

"I ain't sayin' it was right. I'm just sayin' I *thought* it was right."

"Okay. And I think this is right."

"No you don't! Ain't no way you think twistin up dat boy's mind is right!"

Emma Jean smiled. "What's right changes from one minute to the next. You ever noticed that?"

Henrietta wanted to disagree, but couldn't.

"So yo' job now is to keep yo' mouth shut about my business. Like I did for you."

Henrietta reached for the doorknob. "God gon' make you pay for this, Emma Jean. You mark my word. He gon' git you sooner or later."

"Then He gon' git all of us."

Stumbling through the screen door, Henrietta leaned against the nearest porch pillar and covered her mouth as if she might vomit. She couldn't crumble right there, she thought, not in the middle of Emma Jean's territory. She'd never give her the satisfaction. No, she needed to get home, to be surrounded by things familiar, to examine herself and see how she'd let Emma Jean do this to her. Emma Jean Peace . . . of all people. Black, ugly, insignificant Emma Jean Peace. Who would've thought? And who had told her? Who else could've known? Henrietta hadn't told anyone. And of course Emma Jean hadn't been there, had she? No, she couldn't've been. And since God wasn't in the habit of telling other people's business, Henrietta couldn't figure out how Emma Jean had somehow become Swamp Creek's omniscient one.

She cleared her throat and extracted from her bag a handkerchief with which she dabbed her sweating forehead. Yes, she needed to get home. Her feet felt like concrete cinder blocks, dragging beneath her as she staggered down the front steps and into the weeded lane. On an ordinary day, she was a relatively pretty woman, tall and slender as bamboo stalks. Her head seemed a bit large in proportion to her body, but her eyes, nose, and mouth sat in perfect proximity, causing people to nod subconsciously when they beheld her. Her shape was unimpressive though. Even when she tried to stick out her ass, it simply wouldn't protrude, so she accepted that it would be flat forever. Her once-perky breasts, which never filled a C cup, were now shrunken and limp like deflated, miniature balloons. Standing five foot ten, she towered over her girlfriends and stared awkwardly at men. Her short natural, which she wore long before it became fashionable, sat atop her head like a black crescent moon. Yet, even with these foibles, everyone agreed that she was definitely prettier than her other two sisters. On an ordinary day.

But this was no ordinary day. Henrietta wondered, in fact, if she'd even recognize her own reflection in a mirror. She felt her facial features shifting, as if Emma Jean's proposal sought to distort her very flesh. Tenderly and frightfully, she touched her cheeks, nose, forehead, mouth, just to make sure they were still there, and pressed her way home. Everything stable enough to bear her weight she grabbed along the way—saplings, fence posts, road signs—until she was sure Mother Nature marveled at the strangeness of her behavior. At one point, she wilted against a young maple tree and wailed as though giving birth again. Yet fearful that someone might come along and inquire as to her state, she quickly composed herself, lifted her dress tail, and fumbled the rest of the way home.

The worst part about it, she thought, flinging open her front door and tossing her bag onto the sofa, was that Emma Jean really didn't know the truth. Not the *full* truth. She certainly knew too much, but she didn't know everything, and for that Henrietta was grateful. Emma Jean knew that Henrietta and Louise were pregnant at the same time—everyone knew that—but no one knew that Henrietta's baby was stillborn. No one except her husband and Louise, who helped her deliver. Too devastated to face reality, she asked them not to say anything. Not right away. So they didn't. She lay in bed for two days, with the dead baby pressed against her bosom, sulking and asking God why, knowing in her heart that, at her age, she'd never conceive again. Then when Louise went into labor on the third day, she rose and helped her deliver a beautiful, healthy baby girl. But there were complications that Henrietta hadn't expected. When Louise died, Henrietta knew exactly what to do. She laid her own dead daughter next to her dead sister on the cooling board behind Preacher Man's house and told him that his wife and baby had both died. She had done all she could do. Preacher Man was sad, but he wasn't devastated, and that's what confirmed for Henrietta the rightness of her decision. Her strength returned and, overnight, she was back to her old self again. No one knew anything. Or so she thought. Henrietta saw the hand of God orchestrating things, and she gave thanks. There was a problem, however. Her husband wouldn't sanction the plan—not at first—so Henrietta convinced him to let her breast-feed the child for a while, just to make sure it survived, then promised to give it back without a fight. Feeling sorry for Henrietta's loss, her husband reluctantly agreed. Someone needed to care for the child, he thought, and Preacher Man certainly couldn't do it alone. He didn't even have a wife anymore! So maybe Henrietta was right. She should keep the baby for a spell, just to make sure the child survived. *I bet Emma Jean don't know that!* Henrietta smirked.

After two weeks, Tom told Henrietta that enough was enough. The child couldn't stay any longer. So Henrietta bundled the baby, and together they went to return the child to its rightful home. But Preacher Man wasn't there. Tom looked in the front window and noticed that everything was gone. Everything. They scoured the community for information as to his whereabouts, but no one knew anything. There were no relatives to approach or to hand the child to, since Preacher Man had migrated from somewhere out West, so Tom and Henrietta took the baby back home and decided to raise her as their own, at least until Preacher Man returned.

And he did return—with a bride—five years later. By then, Tom had died from a heart attack and Henrietta had become far too attached to Trish to let her go. She contemplated telling Preacher Man, having promised Tom she would, but after losing everyone she'd ever loved, she simply couldn't. Whenever she saw him and Georgia, who returned to Swamp Creek to take care of her mother, Henrietta smiled apologetically. Too much time had transpired to fix things. She simply couldn't undo what she'd done, so she left things as they were. Once she learned the woman was barren, she fell to her knees and begged God for forgiveness. That was the difference, as she saw it, between herself and Emma Jean. She'd wanted to fix what she'd done, had even gone to Preacher Man's house to do so, but he'd disappeared. Once he returned, it was too late. That wasn't her fault, right? She wasn't evil like Emma Jean. She had saved a life. Emma Jean was destroying one.

And even this wasn't the worst of it, Henrietta thought, collapsing into the rocker and rocking wildly. The worst of it was that Preacher Man's longing for children increased as he grew older, causing Henrietta immeasurable distress whenever she saw him. He stopped her one Sunday after church and revealed that, now, he'd give anything for a child. The gender didn't matter anymore. Henrietta smiled and said she'd pray for him and his wife to have the favor of Abraham and Sarah. It never happened. Henrietta saw the longing in his eyes whenever he beheld Trish, the spitting image of Louise, so she knew she couldn't tell him. Preacher Man would kill her if he found out the truth.

The rocker slowed as she heard her mother's voice say, *Lies never work out the way you think they will.* Henrietta chuckled sadly. What else could she do but yield to Emma Jean's scheme?

Well, there was one thing she could do, she thought. Lifting herself from the chair, she took her medicine bag out behind the house and set it ablaze. She didn't want to deliver babies anymore. Somehow, doing so had left her entwined in the intricacies of their lives, and this thing with Perfect—Henrietta shook her head repeatedly—was more than any human should ever be asked to bear. There were other ways she could make a living. She felt sure of it. But she didn't have the slightest idea what she'd say to Perfect if the child lived long enough to ask her, very simply, "Why?" The more Henrietta thought of it, the more she hated Emma Jean. Her only prayer now was that God would grant her the years to watch Him make Emma Jean pay.

Chapter 4

Once Henrietta left, Gus told the boys to be patient while he checked on Emma Jean and the baby.

"Can we see her?" Authorly shouted.

"Be quiet, boy, and wait a minute." Gus raised his hands like one under arrest. "Li'l girls gotta be handled real gentle. You can't be rough with 'em like y'all is with one another."

"We'll be gentle, Daddy," Mister promised. "I bet she look jes' like Momma."

Gus tried to imagine a toddler version of Emma Jean, complete with double-D breasts, a rotund behind, and a scar on the side of her face, but he couldn't conceive it. His greatest concern, though, was not whether the child looked like Emma Jean, but whether she'd act like her.

Gus tiptoed into the bedroom, searching for something nice to say. "Hey."

"Hey?" Emma Jean squealed. "Is that the best you can say to yo' wife and daughter?"

"Yeah," Gus mumbled. Had he said what he was thinking, he was sure Emma Jean's feelings would've been hurt. "The boys is waitin' to see they new sista."

Emma Jean paused. "All right. But don't unwrap her. Babies gotta stay warm."

Gus nodded and received the child cautiously.

"Make sure you bring her right back. She gon' be hongry in a minute."

"I'll bring her back."

"And make them boys wash they hands. 'Specially Mister. You know how nasty—"

"I know what to do, woman." Gus chewed dead skin from his parched lips, but didn't move.

Emma Jean waited.

"You finally got what you been wantin', didn't you?"

"Yes, I did."

"Well, good, 'cause ain't gon' be no mo' babies 'round here. We barely eatin' as it is."

"We'll make it. We always do."

"Like I said," Gus huffed, "ain't gon' be no mo' babies. I'ma love this one 'cause she mine, but you didn't have no right to lie."

"I ain't lied to you 'bout nothin', Gustavus Peace!" Emma Jean lifted her head. "I thought I couldn't have no mo' babies, but de Lawd saw otherwise."

"De Lawd ain't saw nothin', Emma Jean. I ain't neva been smart, but I ain't no fool, neither. You wanted a girl soooooo bad—"

"That I *made* you get me pregnant? Is that what you tryin' to say?"

It didn't make sense now that Emma Jean had said it. "I ain't sayin' that, woman. What I'm sayin' is that you tricked me."

Emma Jean gasped. "Tricked you? *I* tricked *you*? You gotta be kidding. How the hell did I trick you, man? You know how womenfolk get pregnant."

"Yeah, but you said you couldn't get pregnant no mo' and I believed you. If I hada knowed you could, I wouldn't a eva touched you."

Gus saw the hurt in Emma Jean's eyes. He hadn't imagined she cared one way or another about his desire for her.

"I didn't mean it like that. I just meant that I woulda been . . . you know . . . mo' careful. You knowed I didn't want no mo' chillen. I told you that."

Emma Jean feigned indifference. "Well, that's all behind us now. God done blessed us with a beautiful little girl, so let's jes' be thankful and do the best we can."

Gus turned as the scent of rain filled his nostrils. He began to shiver. "I'ma let the boys hold her and Authorly'll bring her back. I gotta go."

"Tell him to bring her *right* back!"

Gus dropped Perfect in Authorly's lap and sprinted through the front door. At almost six, Bartimaeus stood at the screen, longing to accompany his father to the Great Cleansing. That's what Authorly called it. Lurking in the overgrown wheatgrass the previous year, he had followed Gus when the rains came, hoping not to violate his father's privacy but to understand exactly what the rains did for him. After watching Gus remove his shirt and stand at the Jordan with outstretched arms like Moses must have stood at the Red Sea, Authorly's confusion only multiplied. The torrential downpour blurred his view, causing Gus to look gigantic one moment and miniature the next. When his father fell upon his knees and moaned like a sick bull, Authorly abandoned the search for clarity and, instead, wept on his father's behalf. Gus's soulful lamentation reminded the boy of churchwomen who hummed and cried simultaneously as they begged God to do the impossible. A man purging that way, however, overwhelmed Authorly. Having never witnessed his father's—or any man's—absolute vulnerability, he had no context in which to understand how Gus surrendered to the universe so completely. Had he not known better, he could've convinced himself that the figure in the distance was some monstrous creature—not his father at all—then, maybe, his conventional notions of men and masculinity wouldn't have been disrupted. As it was, Authorly was forced to admit, against his understanding, that men could be as emotional as women, and that one of those men was his own father.

Upon his return, he told his brothers that Gus paced the riverbank, thinking and praying.

"Was that all he did?" Bartimaeus inquired later.

Authorly sighed. "I can't really explain it."

"Can you try?"

"All right," Authorly began. "He was bent over cryin' like somethin' was painin' him so bad it was 'bout to kill him. It scared me at first. Then he stood up and raised his hands in the air and started screamin'."

Authorly paused, but Bartimaeus wanted more.

"Then he hugged hisself and started moanin' like he had a bellyache."

"Ummmmmmmmm. Yes." Bartimaeus smiled.

"Yes what?"

"He was cleanin' out his soul."

Authorly didn't understand and now he didn't want to. Whatever Gus was doing at the Jordan was his own business, Authorly decided, and he left it at that. The day Perfect came, he distracted his brothers away from their father's sudden escape by inviting each of them to hold the baby, giving Gus time and space to do whatever his soul needed.

"Don't you wanna hold her?" Authorly asked Bartimaeus.

"No. I wanna go to the river."

Authorly passed Perfect to Mister instead. "Be careful, boy. Don't drop her."

"I ain't gon' drop her. But why she so little?"

"All babies is little when they first born," Sol explained. "But they grow fast. This time next year, she'll be walkin'."

James Earl, Woody, and Sol huddled around Mister while Authorly motioned for Bartimaeus to follow him. Standing on the porch, talking above the hum of the rain, Authorly said, "I'ma walk you to the fence, then you'll have to follow it the rest of the way. It'll lead you straight to the river."

"I can get there."

"When you get close to the water, just listen for Daddy's voice and follow it."

Gus's screaming filled the surrounding woods with an unmistakable echo. As Bartimaeus walked, he, too, began to wail—an octave higher than his father. Feeling his way to the Jordan, he anticipated a purging that would leave him emotionally transformed. Authorly watched his blind brother shuffle alongside the fence until his form fused with the rain.

Back in the living room, Authorly said, "Perfect look kinda like Daddy, huh? All that hair!"

Mister handed Perfect to Woody, who then rubbed her forehead softly. "I think she look like me!"

Everyone laughed.

"Give her to James Earl," Authorly said.

"No!" he whimpered.

"Why not? You can't hurt her," Mister said.

"No," James Earl repeated.

"Oh stop, boy!" Authorly demanded. "It ain't nothin' but a baby."

"I don't want to!" he cried.

"Fine. Forget it. Give her here."

Just then, Emma Jean called for Authorly to return Perfect for feeding.

"How come her eyes ain't opened?" Mister asked.

" 'Cause she a baby and babies ain't got enough strength to hold they eyes open when they first born," Sol explained.

"Give her time," Woody said. "She'll get stronger in a little while, then you can look her in the eyes long as you want to."

"I'll be glad when she's old enough to play with us."

"She ain't gon' play with us, fool!" Authorly said as he reentered. "She's a girl, and girls is real delicate. They not tough like boys, so they have to play with other girls."

"But ain't none o' us girls, so who she gon' play wit?"

Woody roared.

"She'll find some other girls around," Sol assured him.

"Ah, man! I wanted to play with her myself."

"You might get to play with her a little bit, but not too much. You too rough. Girls don't like to play rough," Sol said.

"Well, how do girls like to play?"

"They play soft," Woody teased, rubbing Mister's head sensually. "They comb baby dolls' hair and play house and cookin' and stuff like that."

"I don't wanna play none o' that."

"That's 'cause you a boy," Authorly said. "Girls like girl stuff and boys like boy stuff."

"So what's the good o' havin' a sista?"

" 'Cause she'll help Momma with the house chores," Authorly explained, "and then she'll cook for us and stuff."

Mister's demeanor brightened. "I hope she can cook good!"

Woody chuckled.

Bartimaeus heard the roar of the Jordan. Walking cautiously, like one approaching the edge of a flat world, he tiptoed toward Gus's voice—mingled with his own—and sensed that he was precisely where he needed to be. Where the fence met the water, he turned left and kept his right foot in the river and his left on dry ground. He and Gus created an alto-bass duet, which, louder now, confirmed to Authorly that Bartimaeus had arrived. The father greeted his son with the right hand of fellowship, and instinctively the boy unbuckled his overalls, removed his shirt, and took his place on the banks of the Jordan.

When the rains intensified, the two joined hands and waded knee deep into the river. Bartimaeus shivered from the initial shock of the cool, rushing waters, but Gus's strong hand allowed his son to relax and feel safe in the midst of the Jordan's healing powers.

Time watched Gus and Bartimaeus cleanse their souls. Conversing in moans and hollers, both appreciated having someone with whom to share the experience. Gus further appreciated his son's blindness now, for it allowed him to usher Bartimaeus through the cleansing without fear that the boy was gawking at him. With no physical limitations, they spent the afternoon exposing their hearts to one another, unconcerned about what others thought and glad that at least one person in the world knew they weren't crazy.

Father and son returned to the riverbank hours later when the rains subsided. Still humming away vestiges of hurt each had found difficult to release, they sat on the banks of the Jordan until Gus believed he could tolerate Emma Jean again and Bartimaeus forgave God for denying him the gift of sight.

By dusk, they were renewed. The soft drizzle confirmed the conclusion of the ritual, and, like his father, Bartimaeus sighed heavily and said, "Thank you," both to the heavens and to a merciful, ever-flowing Jordan. Father and son then embraced, buckled their wet overalls, and walked home with their shirts slung across their shoulders.

And they were not ashamed.

Chapter 5

Gus said good night to the boys and entered Emma Jean's bedroom. After unrolling the sleeping pallet, he closed the door, reclined, and sighed heavily. He had never seen the rains come and go so quickly. It was as though they had come only for his sake, and now he felt confident that he could love his daughter as much as he loved his sons. Emma Jean was simply grateful the rains had come at all. Now, maybe, Gus would stop fussing about having another mouth to feed.

"Ain't you gon' kiss yo' daughter good night?" she said, peering over the edge of the bed.

"No, I ain't," Gus grumbled. "I'm tired. And, anyway, she don't know nothin' 'bout that yet. She don't even know she in the world."

"Ah, hell, man," Emma Jean said, returning her head to the prickly feather pillow. "Ain't no need in bein' mad now. The baby's here. You might as well be glad about it."

"I'm glad enough."

Emma Jean sucked her teeth. "You ain't got nothin' to worry about. I'll take care o' her myself."

"Good. You the one wanted her." After a brief pause, Gus added, "I'll do whatever I can, but I can't promise you nothin' else. I don't know nothin' 'bout raisin' no girls."

Perfect whimpered sweetly and Emma Jean unbuttoned her gown, allowing the child to suckle.

As badly as Gus wanted sleep, it wouldn't come. The cleansing had certainly drained him, but his anxiety about having another child kept him awake. "We might get a decent crop after all, now that de rains done come," he said, staring at the ceiling.

"Un-huh. Might."

"Yeah, look like we gon' be all right. You'll have a lot to can this year if de tomatoes, peas, and corn make de way they oughta. In a coupla years, that girl oughta be ready to give you a hand."

"Perfect. Her name's Perfect."

"All right. Perfect." Gus frowned. "And why did you name her that anyway? I ain't never heard o' nobody named Perfect."

"'Cause I like it," Emma Jean sassed, rubbing the baby's silky-smooth, featherlike hair, "and because the name tells people exactly what she is."

"Okay, but, like I said, I ain't never heard o' nobody named Perfect before."

"Of course you ain't. My baby's special."

Gus mouthed the name repeatedly, hoping the awkwardness might subside, but it didn't.

"Hand me that towel over there," Emma Jean asked.

Gus rose and passed her the towel resting on the back of a chair. When he saw her breast, he turned away quickly and returned to the floor. Emma Jean almost screamed, finding it ridiculous that an exposed breast disturbed a father of seven, but then she reminded herself that Gus hadn't often seen her naked. Months ago, when they used to touch, it always happened in the dark, she recalled, so maybe Gus didn't connect the sight of breasts with the joy he once got from them.

Perfect drifted back to sleep and Emma Jean rolled to the edge of the bed again.

"A girl needs thangs boys ain't gotta have, you know," she said as though introducing Gus to the concept of calculus.

"That's why I didn't want one."

"Well, we got one now, and raisin' a girl is different from raisin' dem knucklehead boys. She gotta have pretty ribbons for her hair"—Emma Jean smiled—"and dresses to match."

"You know we can't afford no expensive stuff like that. We barely eatin' as it is!"

". . . and cute li'l pocketbooks for Easter Sunday morning. Course it ain't got to be nothin' too fancy, but then again ain't nothin' too good fu my baby girl!"

"Stop it, Emma Jean. Just stop it. You know we can't buy none o' dat stuff. This is 'xactly why I didn't want no mo' chillen. Boy or girl."

"Well, fine, we won't have any more, but we can't act like Perfect ain't here 'cause she is, and li'l girls gotta have thangs li'l boys don't."

"We ain't got no money fu dat shit you talkin' 'bout, Emma Jean! We can't even keep dese boys' feets covered in de winter, and now you talkin' 'bout buyin' needless stuff like hair ribbons?" Gus slammed his right fist into his left palm. "I knowed this was gon' happen. I knowed it."

"Well, yes, it's done happened now," Emma Jean commented casually, "and you ain't gon' have my li'l girl runnin' 'round here lookin' like no black pickaninny!"

"She gon' look like whatever she look like," Gus said. "And she ain't gon' git no mo' than what these boys gits. I know a girl wear dresses and all, but she can't be walkin' 'round lookin' like a princess while de boys lookin' like slaves!"

"All I'm sayin' is that Perfect is a girl, and girls need thangs boys don't. And she gon' have whatever she need."

"She'll get whatever we can give her," Gus said matter-of-factly.

Emma Jean cackled. "That's fine. I'll have Authorly paint the bedroom yellow. Girls usually like yellow."

Gus was silent.

"It's gotta look like a girl's room."

"I don't care what color you paint it."

"Fine. Then yellow it is. She'll love it. You'll see."

In the living room, Mister whispered in the dark, "Can Perfect swim wit' us in de pond when she get bigger?"

"No, fool!" Authorly said. "Girls don't swim naked wit' boys."

"Why not?"

"'Cause they girls! Boys ain't s'pose to be seein' no naked girls 'til they get married."

"Why not?"

"'Cause Momma say it ain't right. She say it's a sin to see a naked girl before she become yo' wife."

"But Perfect ain't gon' neva be my wife! She my sister!"

"Don't make no difference. She still a girl, and if you see her naked, you goin' to hell. Remember what Momma said: we can't even change her diapers."

"Oh yeah," Mister moaned. "But she can sleep wit' me, right? I don't mind at all. Not even a little bit."

James Earl rubbed Mister's head lovingly but said nothing. Sol added, "She'll get her own bed, li'l brother. She'll probably get the other bedroom all by herself."

"Of course she'll get it," Authorly said. "We'll all just have to sleep out here 'cause girls and boys can't sleep in the same room. Dang, Mister, you don't know nothin' 'bout girls, huh?"

"I ain't never knowed none, 'cept de girls at church, and they ugly."

Authorly and Woody chuckled. Bartimaeus snored.

"All you gotta know is dat girls and boys is different, and the two don't get together 'til they get married."

"Momma play wit' us sometimes, and she's a girl!"

"No she ain't," Authorly corrected. "She a woman."

"Is Perfect gon' be a woman, too?"

Woody snickered. "All girls grow up to be women, boy."

"Well, I'll play with her then."

"No, you won't," Authorly said, "'cause women cook and sew and piece quilts and stuff like that. They don't play with li'l boys."

"Anyway," Woody added, "when Perfect becomes a woman, you'll already be a grown man, and you won't wanna play wit' her anyway."

"I bet chu I will! And we'll have a lot o' fun, too!"

"A sister ain't s'pose to be fun." Authorly sighed. "She s'pose to do woman stuff so she can be a momma one day."

"They don't have no fun when they little?"

Woody said, "They play with baby dolls and stuff."

"Yeah, but even when they play wit' baby dolls," Authorly said, "they practicin' how to take care o' they own kids. That's de whole point o' givin' them dolls in the first place."

"Oh," Mister said, and nodded. "But why don't boys play wit' baby dolls, too? Don't they need to learn how to be daddies?"

The brothers laughed.

"No, man!" Authorly screeched. "Bein' a daddy is easy. It don't take much. All you gotta do is work. That's why boys ain't got to practice. They jes' learn how to work, and when they get married and babies come, they jes' keep workin'. But bein' a momma is a whole different story. That's why girls gotta learn how to take care o' everybody—de husband and de kids—all at de same time."

"Why they gotta do everything?"

" 'Cause de Bible say so, stupid. Raisin' kids is a woman's job. Didn't you hear Reverend Lindsey last Sunday? Dat's why God make women carry de babies. De man is s'pose to work and de woman is s'pose to raise de kids and take care o' de husband and de house."

"That ain't fair," Mister said.

"It *is* fair," Authorly assured him. "And anyway, Reverend Lindsey say women like it. He say God make 'em dat way."

"Okay, but I'd rather be a boy."

"Sure you would. Everybody would. But everybody cain't, 'cause then who would carry de babies? I'm sure bein' a girl ain't so bad if that's all you ever been."

Mister relinquished the hope of ever playing with Perfect. He drifted to sleep praying she would learn all the things necessary to become a good wife one day.

The next afternoon, Gracie arrived slightly before dinner.

"Hi, Aunt Gracie!" Mister shouted from the porch.

"Give her time to get here," Authorly reprimanded. "You see she comin'. Ain't no need in hollerin'."

Gracie switched toward the house in a soft pink and lavender pastel summer dress. Her hefty breasts, bouncing vertically, distracted boys and attracted men. Most agreed that, physically, she was peerless, although Gus quickly reminded them that her looks didn't fix her snobby disposition.

"Good afternoon, boys."

"Momma had de baby!" Mister belted before anyone else could speak.

"Yes, I heard. Henrietta told me yesterday. You boys have a sister now, I understand."

"Yes, ma'am," they answered.

"Well, I'm sure you'll take good care of her. With six brothers, a young lady should be well-protected."

"Yes, ma'am," they repeated.

"I'm going in to check on your mother. You boys be good."

"Yes, ma'am."

When Gracie entered the house, she sashayed past Gus without ever acknowledging his presence.

"Um," he grunted.

She lifted her head a few centimeters higher and entered the bedroom.

"How you doin', girl?" Emma Jean saluted groggily after her eyes focused. "You got choself a niece now."

"So I hear."

"Ain't she pretty?" Emma Jean folded back the bedspread from Perfect's face.

Gracie sat her pocketbook on the floor and rubbed the baby's head gently. "She's beautiful. All that hair! Wow. Looks sorta like you—thank God."

"All right, girl. Don't start that."

"I'm just joking."

Gracie's face went sour.

"What's wrong?"

She sat on the bed lightly. "Momma's sick, Emma."

Emma Jean's lips puckered. "I know."

"I know? Is that's all you can say, *I know*? Why haven't you gone to see her?"

" 'Cause I didn't want to. The boys go by sometimes. They tell me how she's doin'."

"Why don't *you* go, Emma Jean?"

" 'Cause ain't no need to. She got plenty o' visitors without me. I'm the last person Momma ever needed."

"She wants to see you, Emma. She needs to see you. She asked for you."

"Well, she know where I live. She can come anytime."

"No, she can't. She's too sick to get out. You know that."

"Well, I'll pray for her."

Gracie shook her head. "She doesn't need your prayers, Emma Jean. She needs you. I know why you hate her. It makes sense. But it doesn't make sense to take it to your grave."

"What chu talkin' 'bout, girl?"

"Aw, come on, Emma Jean. I was there! Remember? We grew up in the same house! I saw how Momma treated you."

"Well, if you saw it, you sure didn't say much."

"We were kids! What was I supposed to do?"

"I don't know, but you coulda said somethin'."

Gracie stood. "I did!"

"When?" Emma Jean bellowed.

"That day you came back from the chicken coop all dirty! You remember that? I was the one who helped you get cleaned up!"

Emma Jean nodded. "That's true. Thanks."

"I don't need your thanks, Emma Jean. I want you to go see Momma before it's too late."

Emma Jean rolled her eyes. "Me and Momma ain't got nothin' to say to each other. I have perfect peace in my heart, so just leave it alone."

Gracie resumed her seat on the bed. "Emma Jean, look. Momma gon' have to pay for what she did to you, but you don't have to suffer for it. Not anymore."

"Me? Suffer?"

"Oh, come on, Emma Jean! Let's not play games. Denial makes people repeat what they aren't willing to acknowledge."

"What are you talkin' about?"

"I'm talking about how Momma treated you! That's what I'm talking about. I'm talkin' about that Easter Sunday morning when Momma handed Pearlie and me those brand-new yellow dresses but didn't give you one. I re-member that, Emma Jean. I remember the look of disappointment on your face. I remember telling myself that I was going to be nice to you from then on. I started saving pennies and nickels in that snuff can under the bed so I could buy you a yellow dress myself. I just never saved enough. I remember it like it was yesterday."

Emma Jean couldn't hold back the tears.

"Momma was wrong. She didn't have no business treating you that way. I remember you asking where your dress was and she told you to shut up and wear my old one. Of course it was too big and she never could get that huge chocolate ice cream stain off the front. Everybody told me and Pearlie how pretty we were, how pretty our hair was, how pretty our new shoes shined, and that was enough for Momma. We sat next to her on the front pew and she told you to sit behind us. She hadn't even done your hair."

"Okay, Gracie. Just leave it alone." Emma Jean sniffled. "It's all in the past now, so just let it go."

"That's the thing! It *is* in the past, but *you* can't let it go! That's why you haven't been to see Momma. 'Cause you can't let it go!"

"I don't even think about that stuff anymore."

"You're lying, Emma Jean."

"Don't call me a liar, girl!"

"I'll call you a liar until you start telling the truth!"

"Fine!" Emma Jean shouted. "Fine! I remember it! But that don't mean I gotta think about it every day!"

"Who could forget it? Of course you think about it every day. So do I. We just can't change it."

"No, we can't, so let's stop talkin' about it."

"Emma Jean, we gon' talk about this now, if we don't ever talk about it again! You might not have another chance."

"Another chance to do what?"

Gracie cleared her throat. "To forgive Momma. To stop hating her."

"I don't hate her."

"You think you do. Maybe you do. Who wouldn't? But that's not wrong. What I'm trying to say, though, is if something happens to Momma, you'll never get the chance to confront her and free your heart. That's why I'm begging you to go see her. Say whatever you want, but please go. Please."

Emma Jean wiped her cheeks.

"And, anyway, Momma's not the woman she used to be. She's really not."

"Oh really," Emma Jean sneered.

"Really. You'd be surprised. The last few years, especially once she got sick, she's turned into a woman I've never known."

"Probably thinks she's gon' die. Everybody gets righteous before they think they goin' to meet the King."

"Maybe," Gracie pondered, "but even before she got sick, she said something that made me believe she was sorry for how she had treated you."

Emma Jean refused to ask, so Gracie volunteered, "She said, 'Everything I ever wanted Emma Jean got.'"

"Ha! What I got?"

Gracie shrugged. "I don't know. Whatever it is, Momma wanted it. I mean, think about it. You got a husband who loves you, six boys and a beautiful little girl now, and you got your health."

"This ain't what *I* wanted!"

"Maybe not. But Momma would've been happy with it. That's what she said."

"Well, I can't do nothin' 'bout that. She'll have to take that up with the Good Lawd."

"Will you go see her, Emma Jean?"

Emma Jean sighed. "I doubt it. But I'll think about it if it'll make you happy."

"It's not for me, Emma Jean. It's for you."

"Well, if it's for me, then I ain't goin'. I'm through with her, Gracie. You can tell her you saw me and I was doin' fine."

"I'm not telling her anything. You go and tell her yourself." Gracie rose, retrieved her pocketbook from the floor, and said, "Please, Emma Jean. Go. Even if you don't say anything, let Momma clear her heart. Hearing her out might clear yours, too."

"Clear my heart? Clear my heart?" Emma Jean wept again. "Did you say clear my heart?"

"Yes. And Momma can clear hers, too."

"So I been keepin' Momma from clearin' her heart? All dese years, I been de one wit' de key to her heart and didn't even know it?"

Emma Jean's tone left a putrid taste in Gracie's mouth. She wished she'd simply glanced at Perfect and left.

"You can't change the past, sister. All you can do is forgive people for it."

"You gotta be kidding! Girl, listen. If I hadn't forgave Momma years ago, I probably woulda killed her by now, so please don't talk to me about no forgiveness."

"You didn't forgive Momma, Emma Jean. You jes' tried to forget."

"How you know what's in my heart?"

"Because the heart always tells on itself. Even when we think we hidin' it."

"Well, mine feels fine to me. If Momma got somethin' she need to say, she can come over here and say it. Otherwise, I'm through wit' de whole thing."

"Very well." Gracie gave up and clutched her purse beneath her arm. "I just wanted you to know that Momma's time is limited just in case you wanted to make things right between you two. Before it's too late."

"That ain't fu me to do. She de momma."

"All right. Just don't let the sun go down on your wrath. That's what the Bible says."

Emma Jean chuckled. "You reap what you sow. It says that, too."

Chapter 6

Gracie left, convinced that Mae Helen would die before Emma Jean saw her again. Still, she was glad she had tried. A child's hurt obviously evolves into an adult's resentment, she told herself, so after years of abuse, the possibility that Emma Jean might forgive and forget was a virtual impossibility. Maybe she should have fought more directly for Emma Jean when they were children, Gracie considered, but what could she do about that now? Even if she apologized, which she felt she'd done, Emma Jean's pain wouldn't decrease. All Gracie knew to do was promise to love any child she birthed—even if, like Emma Jean, it was ugly.

Yet children never came for Gracie. Pearlie neither. They were too uppity and saddity, Gus said, to be somebody's momma. Gracie wanted a college-educated man like herself, and Pearlie refused to look at anybody if he wasn't lighter than she was. Mae Helen told both of them, once they turned thirty, "Y'all ain't *that* damn gorgeous! You better get you somebody before it ain't nobody to have!" But the girls refused to settle. In their forties, Gracie and Pearlie married Stanley and Buster Wilson, the ugliest, most unrefined brothers in Swamp Creek. They did that only because Mae Helen told them she was tired of feeding their stuck-up asses.

Once Gracie left that day, Emma Jean tried frantically not to think about Mae Helen, but the more she tried, the more impossible it became. It was always Gracie who kept mess going, she thought. Always sticking her nose in somebody else's business. So what that she hadn't seen Mae Helen in months. Who says a daughter *must* visit her mother?

After their last encounter, Emma Jean swore she'd never set eyes on the woman again, even in a casket.

"What's that smell, girl?" Mae Helen had declared, walking into Emma Jean's kitchen years ago without knocking.

"Hey, Momma."

"That meat musta been spoiled, girl. I wouldn't eat it if I was you." She pinched her nose and frowned.

Emma Jean offered her a seat and continued washing dishes.

"Where de boys?"

"Out fishin' with Gus. They gon' be disappointed they missed you."

"I'll see them nappy-headed niggas soon enough."

Emma Jean sat a glass of iced tea before Mae Helen, who drank it in one gulp. "Needs more sugar."

"Momma, that tea's fine. It's almost syrupy as it is!"

"You drink it the way you want to. I'll make my own at home."

Emma Jean huffed. "It's never enough, is it?"

"Huh? What'd you say?"

"Never mind." She rinsed the empty glass and returned it to the cabinet. "I have some cake if you want some."

"Oh no. I don't care for sweets."

Emma Jean recalled Mae Helen's sweet tooth and chuckled lightly. "The boys is really growin,' you know."

"I guess they is, sittin' 'round here eatin' like hogs."

Emma Jean struggled to ignore her. "You're welcome to stay for dinner. I cooked more than enough."

"No, no. I jes' come by to see what that new baby o' yours look like." She grunted, "Ump. I shoulda guessed."

"He's pretty, Momma, but he ain't no baby no more. He's almost a year old!"

"Better late than never." She studied the kitchen in apparent disapproval. "What'd you name him?"

Emma Jean smiled. "Mister."

"Mister? Mister what?"

"Mister Peace."

"Hell, I know his last name. I'm askin' 'bout his first name."

"Mister *is* his first name," Emma Jean slurred, never having considered how ridiculous the name might sound to her mother.

"What? Are you serious? That's kinda stupid, ain't it? I bet Gus named him, didn't he?"

"He's a sweet boy, Momma. Grin all de time. Happy as he can be."

"Yep, Gus named him," Mae Helen murmured. "Ain't no way in the world I woulda let that fool name my baby no Mister. That's 'bout de dumbest thing I ever heard of, but if you like it . . ."

"His name's fine, Momma. Like I said, he's a good baby. Don't do nothin' but laugh all the time. The boys love him."

"I guess they do! They don't know no better."

Emma Jean grimaced. "What's that suppose to mean?"

"Oh, don't worry about it. I was jes' talking to myself."

That's when Emma Jean broke. "Get out, Momma!"

Mae Helen trembled. "What did you say, girl?"

"I said, get the hell out of my house!" Emma Jean went to the screen and held it open. "You ain't never said a kind word to me my whole life. Pearlie and Gracie were *your* precious daughters, and I was the garbage my daddy left behind. I thought that maybe you'd start bein' nice to me when I got grown, but obviously I thought wrong. You talk about Gus like a dog and treat my boys like they ain't nothin'!"

"What?" Mae Helen stood. "I speak to dem ugly children all the time!"

"Can you say something nice for once! Huh? Can you? Would it kill you to be kind just for a day?"

"It's nice enough of me just to come over here!" Mae Helen declared, sashaying past Emma Jean and into the yard.

Emma Jean followed. "Don't chu know what it do to a child to call 'em mean names? Don't chu know you cain't treat children that way and get away with it forever? Don't you know I dreamed about stabbing you every night I slept in that house?"

Mae Helen smacked her lips.

"You ain't got to care 'cause I ain't got to have you no more. And God have mercy on yo' soul if you ever need me!" Emma Jean panted.

"Why, you ungrateful heffa! How dare you talk to me like that after all I did for you."

"Oh, Momma, please! All you did for me was make me hate you."

Mae Helen shuddered. "Pearlie and Gracie would never talk to me like this."

"I'm sure they wouldn't! Perfect Pearlie and Gracie."

"You always was jealous of them."

Emma Jean hollered, "Oh kiss my ass, Momma!" and marched back into the kitchen.

Mae Helen pranced away, leaving Emma Jean overwhelmed. She loved her mother and that's what she hated most. Her childhood had been spent praying for a change of Mae Helen's heart, although it never happened. She thought she'd gotten over things by now, but Mae Helen's demeaning of her boys conjured memories of Emma Jean's dream of killing her. Now that she was a mother, she could live without her own, she determined, but what she couldn't tolerate was the possibility that her boys might grow up like she had, feeling ugly and rejected. She'd stab Mae Helen directly in the heart before she'd let her do that to another child.

The cussing felt good and relieved Emma Jean of years of repressed emotions. Fear had always made her contain her tongue, lest she disrespect her mother beyond repair, but now it didn't matter. Emma Jean wished she had beaten her. That's what she had felt like doing, and that would have cleansed her heart completely. Or so she thought. The truth was that the episode left her shaken for three days. The least noise caused her to glance over her shoulder, thinking Mae Helen had returned to whip her good. She hated how much she feared her mother, and she hated even more that she couldn't stop loving her.

Emma Jean laid Perfect in the bassinet and dreamed of all the things they'd do together. Like pick blackberries along the banks of the Jordan and talk about boys the way she and her sisters once did.

"Ain't Virgil Ponds 'bout the cutest thing you ever seen?" Pearlie said dreamily one hot July morning. She'd just turned twelve.

Gracie and Emma Jean giggled.

"He's tall, and lean, and got some soft curly hair. Oh my God! He's so gorgeous!"

"He's all right," Gracie said, "but he ain't cuter'n Phillip Hampton."

"Phillip Hampton?" Pearlie cried. "That boy ain't cute. His head is round as a plate!"

"Yeah, I know, but he's still cute to me. Momma said he got some Indian in him."

"He does have some good hair," Pearlie conceded, "but he ain't cuter'n Virgil."

Gracie noticed Emma Jean's silence. "Who you like?" she asked.

Emma Jean shrugged. "Nobody." She ate a handful of overripe blackberries.

"Don't you think Virgil's cute?" Pearlie asked.

"He's okay I guess. Look kinda mean most of the time. Don't never smile."

"You mean he don't smile *at you*?"

"He don't smile at nobody!" Gracie said.

"He smile at me. And anyway you can't ask a man to like *everybody*."

"Well, I'm just sayin' I wouldn't choose him," Emma Jean said, and continued berry picking.

"You *couldn't* choose him, even if you wanted to!" Pearlie sneered.

"Guess not."

Emma Jean filled her bucket, then began filling her sisters'. "Do y'all think I'm pretty?"

Pearlie hollered. "Of course not. But you nice, and that counts for somethin'."

Gracie agreed. "Everybody ain't gotta be pretty, Emma Jean."

"But I wanna be pretty."

They couldn't think of anything else to say.

"Momma's dark like me, and she's pretty, ain't she?"

Their silence surprised her.

"You not ugly," Gracie said. "And, like I said, you're real smart and sometimes that's worth more."

"But I wanna be pretty, too."

"Your looks come from your daddy," Pearlie explained, "and *your* daddy's people are real black jes' like you. He jes' happens to be yella."

"But cain't chu be dark *and* pretty?"

The sisters frowned and said in unison, "No."

Emma Jean's head fell as though guillotined.

"Don't worry about it," Gracie said. "Everybody's pretty in their own kinda way."

"You jes' look like yo' folks," Pearlie repeated. "You cain't help that."

"How you know how my folks look?"

" 'Cause I done seen 'em! They live down in de Bottoms. It's a lotta dem Lovejoys runnin' 'round. They breed like rats, Momma said."

Emma Jean was glad she didn't live among them.

"Yo' daddy jes' happen to be light, but de rest o' his folks is real black. That's where you get it from."

Gracie softened Pearlie's blow. "You can still make somethin' outta yo'self though. If you try real hard. Like you could be a hairdresser or somethin'. They make good money!"

Emma Jean wanted to be a dancer, but Mae Helen wouldn't hear of it. She'd said, "Is you ever heard of a black nigga dancer, girl? Huh? Is you?" Emma Jean shook her head slowly. "Well then! Do somethin' you can do." When Emma Jean mentioned nursing, Mae Helen clutched her hips and said, "Girl, find a man who'll have you and have as many babies as you can. Good as you sweep and clean up, you oughta be somebody's wife. If they'll have you."

Emma Jean told Gracie, "I don't wanna do hair!"

"Well, you oughta want to!" Pearlie interjected. "Then maybe you could do somethin' with that briar bush o' yours! And who knows? Maybe you could help all your people *down there*." She pointed toward the Bottoms.

Emma Jean swore she'd never step foot in the Bottoms long as she lived. The last thing she needed was to encounter, in the face of some ashy black woman, her own spitting image. Maybe her daddy was one of the bottom people, but she promised not to be caught dead down there.

"What if Claude Lovejoy ain't my daddy?" she mumbled.

"Then who is?" Pearlie asked.

Emma Jean didn't say. She certainly couldn't claim Sammy Hurt since she shared none of her sisters' features, and, anyway, Mae Helen reminded her constantly whose child she wasn't.

To Emma Jean's chagrin, Claude Lovejoy appeared one day out of nowhere. The girls turned and there he was. Emma Jean was almost nine.

"Howdy, y'all," he said kindly.

As though spooked, Pearlie and Gracie ran into the house, screaming, "Momma, Momma! That man's back! He's here!"

"Who's here?" Mae Helen asked, walking onto the porch. When she saw who it was, she sucked her teeth and said, "Aw, shit! That ain't nobody. I thought y'all was talkin' 'bout somebody important," and walked back into the house, allowing the screen to slam behind her.

Emma Jean lingered only because Claude was staring at her.

"You's real pretty, honey. Black and beautiful jes' like my momma. Your name's Emma Jean Lovejoy, ain't it?" He smiled and sat on the edge of the porch. "You my baby girl."

"My name's Emma Jean *Hurt*," she corrected nastily, "and if you is my daddy, you a sorry one 'cause I ain't never seen you in my whole life."

Claude's smile vanished. "I been workin' on de railroad, baby. I wanted to come see you, but seem like every time I got a day off, I was either dog tired or called back to work. I thinks about you all de time, sugar. Really I do. Don't chu neva think yo' daddy don't love you."

Emma Jean almost jumped into his arms, but restrained herself. "Okay," she said.

"I wanna take you to meet my folks so you know yo' people. They'll like you right off, pretty as you is."

"No, thank you."

"What chu mean, 'no thank you'? Don't chu wanna know yo' family?"

Emma Jean heard the disappointment in her father's flat voice, but her pride outweighed her empathy. "I already know my family," she sassed, "so you can jes' tell all dem bottom folks that I'm fine right where I am."

Claude shook his head. "What's wrong, baby? You actin' like you hate me or somethin'."

"Ain't nothin' wrong wit' me. I jes' don't wanna go with you down in dem Bottoms. I don't wanna go wit' chu nowhere, so you ain't gotta come back here no more if you don't want to." She turned to walk away.

Claude stood. "I don't know what you done heard 'bout me, but I's a good man and you got a whole heap o' folks jes' waitin' to love you 'cause you mine."

"No I don't!"

"It's fine though 'cause you can't run from yo'self. Don't care how hard you try, when you turn around, that self is starin' back at you. You's a Lovejoy, baby, and you gone stay one 'til de day you die. I jes' hope I'm still livin' when you come to yo' senses. Yo' momma and everybody else 'round hyeah done told you a bunch o' mess 'bout me and my folks, but one day you'll know de truth." He wiped his eyes and left.

For a second, the thought of being shown off like a prize excited Emma Jean, yet fearful of her sisters' ridicule, she decided to let Claude Lovejoy go.

Mae Helen returned to the porch. "Why didn't you go with him? You coulda gone if you wanted to."

"I jes' didn't," Emma Jean mumbled.

"Well, you shoulda. You need to know yo' people. You look jes' like 'em."

Emma Jean had hoped Mae Helen would say, *Oh, honey, I was so scared you was gon' leave me. Thank God I still got my baby*, or something like that. Instead, she told Gracie and Pearlie, "Ump, ump, ump. Y'all almost had a bed to y'allself."

For the rest of her life, her mother's words lived in her head. Even in her dreams, she heard, *Y'all almost had a bed to y'allself, y'all almost had a bed to y'allself, y'all almost had a bed to y'allself*, as though someone were trying to convince her of her own selfishness.

By sixteen, Emma Jean was praying for Claude's return. She promised herself that, if he came again, she'd accompany him to the Bottoms and wouldn't care what Gracie or Pearlie or anyone else said. She might not even come back. That way, Mae Helen could forget she'd ever lain with Claude Lovejoy.

Yet the next time Emma Jean encountered her father, he was lying in a coffin. Some pretty black woman killed him, people said, for cheating on her with a white woman. The white woman confronted the black one—went to the Bottoms all by herself, they said—but the black woman held her peace. The next night, though, she stabbed Claude in his heart while he slept.

"He was already dying though," Emma Jean overheard one woman tell another at the funeral. "Ain't been right since he fooled with dat Mae Helen what's-her-name."

"Oh yeah!" the other woman said. "Dat uppity-ass heffa wit' dem two yellow girls and that black one that's s'posed to be his."

"Yep. Dat's her. He said he went up there to see 'bout his daughter but she didn't want nothin' to do wit' him. Said she looked at him like he was crazy."

"Get outta here, girl!"

"That's what he told me. I was anxious to meet my niece, but he said she frowned at him like he was a dog or somethin'."

"Ain't no tellin' what dat woman told dat girl 'bout Claude."

"Well, whatever she told her, dat li'l girl missed out on the nicest man God ever made." They nodded vigorously. "He said she was so pretty"—the lady smiled—"but she turned her nose up at him."

"She didn't know no better."

"Guess not. But she gon' want him one day."

Emma Jean walked away. The only reason she had gone to the funeral was because, at twenty, she couldn't remember exactly what Claude looked like, and she knew this would be her last chance to see him. When the family processed, she stood with other tertiary attendees and marveled to see herself replicated, to varying degrees, in almost every mournful face. During the eulogy, when the preacher said, "Claude Lovejoy left this world with only a daughter to mourn his passing," Emma Jean covered her mouth in shame. He went on to speak of Claude as a man with an enormous heart, one any child would have been lucky to have as a father. Emma Jean resented that he kept looking at her.

At the end, after family members had recessed, she asked the officials if she might have one final glance at the body. They said, "I'm sorry, ma'am, but once we close the casket, only next of kin—"

"I'm his daughter," she whispered softly, and immediately they raised the lid. Death had darkened him, she noticed, and now she saw the irrefutable resemblance. Emma Jean nodded her thanks and asked the officials not to repeat what she had said.

Chapter 7

Gus told Bartimaeus never to divulge their activity at the Jordan. People wouldn't understand, he said, and no mother—Mae Helen had been a desperate exception—would ever let her daughter marry a man *like that*. As long as they kept their mouths closed, folks' gossip would always be just that—gossip. It was a private affair anyway, Gus said, and the first lesson of manhood Bartimaeus needed to learn was how to keep other folks out of his business. So the two set about their daily chores as though the previous day's cleansing had never occurred. Woody joined them, cleaning out the cruddy woodstove while James Earl and Authorly split logs under the bright morning sun. Sol and Mister attended the house, the best they could, and half-burned enough breakfast to go around.

Moments later, they took Emma Jean a plate of biscuits, molasses, eggs, and burnt salt pork.

"Y'all tryin' to burn my house down?" she teased.

"No ma'am. We jes' tryin' to help out."

Their long faces made Emma Jean feel ungrateful. "Oh, I'm sorry, boys. I know y'all mean well. I really do thank you." She took the plate. "I'll be back to my old self in a day or two."

"Oh, don't worry, Momma," Mister said. "We don't mind takin' care o' you."

Emma Jean forced herself to eat. She knew the day would come when Bartimaeus would accompany his father to the place of purging, but she didn't know it would come so soon. What would she tell the neighbors about that other voice? How had Bartimaeus gotten to the river anyway? And why couldn't he and Gus cry like normal people?

Perfect squirmed, and Emma Jean retrieved her from the bassinet. Rocking her gently, she offered her nipple and Perfect suckled gratefully. All Emma Jean wanted was to protect her and make her happy. She'd definitely have to sacrifice to provide the kind of life she envisioned for her only daughter, but she was determined to do it even if she had to do it alone. Of course she'd be the only one attending to Perfect's personal needs, but that was as it should be. Menfolks ain't got no business in womenfolks' affairs, she had told Gus and the boys months before the birth. They were all relieved. *Good*, Emma Jean now thought. *This is working just like I need it to.*

Truth be told, Gus had been more relieved than the boys by Emma Jean's edict. He knew about boys, but a woman's world was as foreign to him as China. Even when he and Emma Jean used to do *it*—as he called sex—it was always in the dark, and Gus liked it that way. He had seldom seen Emma Jean naked. He had certainly felt her many times, but he would have failed miserably had he been required to draw or describe the contours of her body. He knew how the vagina felt, wrapped like a warm, moist blanket around his throbbing penis, but exactly how it looked he didn't know. It never occurred to him to look at it—much less taste it, as Emma Jean once suggested. Yet he loved Emma Jean's fellatial performance. Penetration was the extent of Gus's sexual participation and once he climaxed, he simply rolled over and went to sleep. On one occasion, Emma Jean spoke his name as they did *it*, and Gus stopped altogether, asking, "Huh? What is it?" She reverted back to their silent exchange and Gus decided that women call men, even during sex, when they obviously don't want anything. Gus never knew that women climaxed, and once Emma Jean stopped dreaming of it, they marked his overflow as the aim and the end of *it*.

Authorly and James Earl stacked the wood neatly against the west side of the house.

"Daddy and Bartimaeus sounded funny yesterday," James Earl said out of nowhere.

At first, Authorly didn't respond. Then he slurred, "Don't worry about it."

"Okay. But they was real loud."

"I said don't worry about it!"

James Earl shuddered and began to cry.

"I'm sorry. I didn't mean to hurt yo' feelin's. It's just that what Daddy and Bartimaeus do ain't nobody's business. You know what I mean?"

James Earl wiped his eyes.

"Good. Let's just leave it alone."

They entered the house.

"Breakfast is ready!" Mister screamed.

Authorly and James Earl washed their hands in the kitchen basin and sat at the table.

"Come on, Woody," Authorly called. "You can finish cleaning that thing after we eat. Daddy! Bartimaeus! Y'all come on!"

The menfolk joined hands and Authorly prayed, "Dear Lawd, we thank You fu dis day and fu blessin' us wid a li'l baby sister. We thank You for de rain"—he peeked at Gus—"that waters the crops and helps . . . other thangs grow, and we thank You for Momma and ask that she get better real soon, and we thank You for dis food and for a roof over our heads. Amen."

"Amen," the others murmured.

Mimicking their mother, Mister and Sol set plates before Gus and their brothers, hopeful the food was satisfactory.

"I ain't neva seen no black biscuits before," Woody teased. "This must be a new recipe." His shoulders jerked.

"Everything's fine," Authorly said. "We 'preciate you boys' effort."

He sound just like Daddy, Mister thought.

Authorly glanced around the table, insisting that everyone clean his plate. Then Gus said, "Sol, you and Mister handle the dishes and Authorly, you and James Earl go see 'bout de crops. Me and Bartimaeus gon' see 'bout de cows and fix de fence. Woody, you finish the stove."

Everyone obeyed. It would be another day before Emma Jean resurrected, and Gus wanted things in order so she'd have nothing to fuss about.

Outside, Authorly told James Earl about his love for Eula Faye Cullins.

"She's real pretty. And black. Just like I like 'em. You know Eula Faye, right?"

James Earl shook his head.

"Yes you do. Mr. Buddy's oldest girl? The one with the real big booty?"

James Earl looked away.

"Well, anyway, you'll like her. She got a pretty smile, and she's sweet as pie. I'm gonna marry her one day, I think."

"Okay."

They surveyed the crops as Authorly droned on. James Earl appeared unmoved, but of course that never stopped Authorly. After an hour or so, he said, "I want you to be in the wedding, okay?"

James Earl smirked. "Okay."

Then they returned to the house. Yes, he'd like Eula Faye, Authorly decided—as much as he'd like anybody—and they'd be happy together. All three of them.

Inside, Sol sang "All of My Help Comes from the Lord" as he and Mister tidied the kitchen. Woody paused occasionally, letting his brother's high tenor voice ease his frustration with the cruddy woodstove.

"I like that song," Mister said. "Sing it again."

Sol began, "All of my heeeeelp," and Mister hummed along as best he could. The last of the dishes was dried subconsciously as both brothers found themselves entangled in spiritual jubilation. Each time Sol crooned, "Whenever I need Him! He's riiiiiiiight by my siiiiiide," Mister's head swayed, and he put plates where pots should have been. Then he wiped the table in a circular, rhythmic motion while Sol swept the floor. Neither knew that Woody shared their ecstasy, weeping inside the old woodstove. Covered with a thin layer of powdery black soot, his face looked warrior marked from the streaks his tears left behind. He wanted Sol to stop singing and he wanted him to go on forever. When Authorly and James Earl entered, followed by Gus and Bartimaeus, they all succumbed to the moment instantly, distracting themselves by straightening up the living area, which Sol and Mister had already straightened. All five boys moved like electronic objects, refusing to be totally overwhelmed by Sol's gift, while entrapped in its healing power. When his voice faded, they collapsed simultaneously as though having been suspended in midair.

Emma Jean had also been entranced. Perfect lay snuggled between her mother's breast and the bed when Sol began, so Emma Jean closed her eyes and welcomed the soothing melody. Having gotten the daughter she begged God for, she now forgave Him for taking His sweet time in the sending, and asked if they could even be friends. She never hated Him, she said. She just didn't understand His ways. But now, after having a daughter—or, rather, making one—she understood that, sometimes, God expects people to work with what they get. That's how she thought of it. She apologized to God for waiting on Him to give her everything she wanted instead of meeting Him halfway. Now she understood the adage, "If you take one step, He'll take two." She smiled at their reunion.

With Sol belting from the living room, supported by his brothers' humming, Emma Jean and Perfect relaxed amid the quartet performance. Carrying the lead, Sol improvised slightly before and after the beat, Billie Holiday style, doing half-step runs only Daryl Coley would ever emulate. Bartimaeus and Gus, with their off-key humming, gave the melody a gospel pathos both hypnotic and healing. Emma Jean's only sorrow was that she would probably never hear the melody again—not in its exact replica. With the boys getting older, she thought, who knew what tomorrow would bring? Sol sang constantly, but usually he sang alone. Emma Jean tried to record the melody in her memory, yet, once it ended, she couldn't remember how it went.

At the end of the day, Gus and the boys sat in the living room, listening to the *Amos 'n' Andy* radio show.

"What does she look like?" Bartimaeus asked Authorly.

"She jes' look like a baby, I guess. Kinda brown like Daddy." He wanted Bartimaeus to be quiet until the show ended.

"What does brown mean?"

Authorly tried to contain his frustration. "Look, she got black, curly hair and brown eyes. I don't know nothin' else to say. She jes' look like a li'l baby girl," he huffed.

Bartimaeus got the hint. He stared into nothingness and tried to imagine what "brown" looked like. Then he eased into Emma Jean's bedroom.

"Momma?" he whispered, holding on to the door.

Emma Jean looked up. "Hi, baby. You all right? I heard you went with yo' daddy yesterday."

"Yes, ma'am."

"Well, that's good, that's good."

"Momma?"

"What is it, baby?"

Bartimaeus felt for the bed. "Can I hold her? I won't drop her. I promise."

"Well, she's sleepin' right now. Maybe a little later."

"Can I hold her now, Momma?" he asked sincerely. "I won't wake her up."

Emma Jean relented. "All right." She lifted Perfect from her left side.

Bartimaeus extended his arms with great expectation. The weight of the child made him giggle. Gently, he moved his forefinger across her forehead, eyelids, nose, mouth, and chin. "She's beautiful," he said, counting her toes and fingers. "I can tell. A baby sister. Wow."

"That's right!" Emma Jean affirmed.

"She's got my nose," Bartimaeus said.

Only then did Emma Jean realize that Perfect, Bartimaeus, and Gus shared identical wide, flat noses. Perfect's was tiny, but its shape was unmistakable. "I guess she does."

As Bartimaeus rocked her, he imagined that, one day, boys would seek Perfect to accompany them to a picture show or on a picnic, and she would deny most of them the privilege. But a really handsome fellow might come along whom Perfect would not deny, and hopefully he'd love her even with her difference.

"You'd better let me have her now. She's startin' to squirm."

Bartimaeus passed her back and stood. "I know she's pretty, Momma. Jes' like you."

"Ha!" Emma Jean retorted. "Ain't nobody ever told me that!"

"Daddy don't tell you you pretty?"

Emma Jean almost said, *Hell no*, but instead said, "You'd better get you some rest, son. You and yo' brothers oughta be real tired from all that work today. Go 'head now."

Bartimaeus shuffled back to the living room. Something about Perfect felt eerie, but he couldn't discern what it was. He would find out soon enough.

Chapter 8

Six weeks later, Emma Jean introduced Perfect to the St. Matthew No. 3 Baptist Church congregation. Yellow ribbons adorned the child's greasy black hair, and only Gus and the boys knew that Perfect's exquisite white lace dress had been fashioned from the one good tablecloth the family owned.

When Emma Jean entered, the crowd gasped. Some covered their mouths, others stared in stark incredulity. It wasn't the floral peach dress that sent them over the edge, or even the rhythmed two-step with which she walked, but rather the bouquet of flowers sitting atop her hat. She had picked them herself, she later bragged, and stuffed the stems into the hat wherever they'd fit. Most people stifled their screams and waited to see if Emma Jean could prance down the aisle without the flowers tumbling in every direction. The assortment contained at least ten different species, with a rose hanging low enough to shield the crescent-like scar. She tried to brush it aside, so as not to miss the faces of her neighbors as they gawked, but the rose kept brushing the scar irritably until she yanked it from her head and tossed it aside. One woman laughed until she collapsed. Another raised her index finger and exited, screaming, "I can't take this! I just can't take Emma Jean Peace!" With sky blue eye shadow, maroon lipstick, and enough foundation to lighten her complexion four shades, Emma Jean smiled at her neighbors, who then snickered and shook their heads at the most ostentatious presentation they had ever seen. Authorly whispered, "Go 'head, Momma!" then laughed with the rest of the crowd. Emma Jean's strut resembled a first Sunday Black Baptist gospel choir march, complete with the step-hesitation, step-hesitation rhythm. As she approached each row of pews, people marveled in absolute disbelief. "How y'all doin'?" she mouthed along the way. No one responded. They knew her question was rhetorical, and, in fact, understood the greeting simply as Emma Jean's way of securing attention. Gus's inability to watch her strut intensified the joy of the audience, causing many to whisper, "How in the world does he live with that woman?" Emma Jean strolled gracelessly until she reached the front pew, which was already packed. "Excuse me," she said repeatedly to the entire row until someone felt compelled to relinquish their space. "Thank you," she then murmured, and reclined. Others were too shocked to scold her and a few clapped vigorously for an award-winning performance. What Emma Jean didn't know was that a bee circled above the flowers, outlining a perfect halo, and various members dared one another to swat it. After she sat, the congregation fanned as though on fire, and Gus coiled in his seat in the back of the church. He had endured all the drama he could handle in a day.

Before the sermon, Reverend Lindsey said, "I wanna take this time to celebrate the newest member of the Peace family. A girl this time—thank God!"

The congregation laughed heartily.

"And I wanna ask the proud parents if they would bring that pretty little girl on up here and let's dedicate her to the Lord."

Gus's head began to swim. The only thing he despised worse than crowds was being the center of them.

Authorly whispered, "You can do it, Daddy. Go 'head."

Gus nodded and rose like one approaching the Judgment Seat of God. Emma Jean, on the other hand, leapt instantly. Her bouquet-hat wobbled as if it might fall, and most hoped it would. She pranced toward the pulpit, shaking her head as though the cheap hat were priceless. With Perfect bundled in her right arm, she waved her left hand like a beauty pageant contestant. Congregants yelped without shame.

Mamie Cunningham leaned forward and asked another woman, "Do she think that peach dress go with that tired, ugly hat?"

The woman shrugged and shook her head.

"And what mother in her right mind would *ever* put that many bright yellow ribbons on a black baby?"

The woman screeched.

"After all dem boys," the preacher teased, "this girl must be an answer to prayer."

He reached for Perfect, but Emma Jean murmured, "I better hold her, Reverend. She can get cranky with strangers."

Reverend Lindsey frowned. "Well, all right," he said, and stood between Gus and Emma Jean as though he didn't belong there. "What's her name?"

Gus squeezed his eyes shut.

"Perfect!" Emma Jean shouted.

"Excuse me? I'm sure she's perfect, but what's her name?"

"Why, I just said it, Reverend. Perfect. Her name's Perfect!"

The crowd muttered its confusion. Miss Mamie cackled and whispered into her comrade's ear, "Didn't I tell you that bitch was crazy?"

Reverend Lindsey looked at Gus, who looked more disturbed than the audience. "I didn't have nothin' to do with it," he said.

Emma Jean became incensed. "Is something wrong, Pastor?" She studied his frown, then examined the faces of her neighbors.

"Um . . . no, I guess not," Reverend Lindsey stammered. "It's just that I've never heard of anyone named Perfect, so it seems a little strange, I must admit. I mean, nobody's truly perfect but the Good Lawd, so—"

"Well, somebody is now. My baby girl. And that's her name." Emma Jean's eyes pierced Reverend Lindsey's.

"I see," he said, and paused. "Perfect. Perfect . . . Peace."

"That's right!" Emma Jean declared.

"I didn't have nothin' to do with it," Gus repeated, embarrassed. "By the time I seed her, Emma Jean had done already named her."

"It's fine, honey," Emma Jean said. "Her name is exactly what it oughta be. Now go ahead, Reverend, and bless her real good."

He wanted to explain to Emma Jean that calling a child "Perfect" was definitely blasphemous. What had possessed her to do such a thing? Instead, he sighed and said, "Let us bow," then prayed, "Blessed is this child, given to Gus and Emma Jean, for the perfecting"—he paused awkwardly—"of the kingdom of God. May she grow to show the world what it means to walk as a godly woman. Might her friends call her loyal, her parents call her obedient, her teachers call her brilliant, her elders call her wise, and her suitors call her lovely. In everything she does, might you, oh Lord, be glorified. If she chooses to marry one day, might she be the crowning glory of her husband. Let her children call her honorable, holy, and righteous."

Some mumbled "Amen," assuming the dedication complete, but Reverend Lindsey continued: "None of us is perfect, oh Lord. No, not one."

Emma Jean turned her bowed head and peeked from one eye.

"Give us the humility, precious Savior, to know that all have sinned and fallen short of your glory. No one," he shouted, "can be called perfect in your sight, oh Lord. No one!"

The crowd affirmed his vehemence with a hearty "Amen!"

"Don't let us forget, Lord, that when we exalt ourselves, you bring us low to remind us of our place. Our job, Great Master, is to keep our heads bowed that you might exalt us in due season. Give this child the ability to accept her own *im*perfections"—Reverend Lindsey peeked back at Emma Jean—"so that she won't think more highly of herself than she ought. I pray this precious little girl good health, prosperity, and godspeed. Let the church say amen."

"Amen."

Emma Jean rolled her eyes at Reverend Lindsey. *"My* little girl *is* Perfect!" she hollered, stomping back to her seat. How dare he, she thought, imply that Perfect had been misnamed. The gall of some people! "If you wuz so spiritual, Mr. Preacher Man," she burbled from the pew, "you'd know that God gave me that name anyway! You ain't been called to preach! All you want is money! And, anyway, it ain't yo' business—"

"Shhhhhhhh!" her neighbors hissed.

"Shush yourself!" Emma Jean grumbled, and fell silent. *Everybody ain't gon' understand the ways of God 'cause everybody don't walk with God*, she told herself. *That includes some preachers.*

"That baby ain't right!" Sugar Baby screamed. "That baby ain't right!"

Emma Jean turned. She would have cussed him out had they not been in the sanctuary.

Everyone usually ignored Sugar Baby's outbursts. He hadn't been himself since he was a child. Homeless and alone, he had snapped, folks said, the day his mother died. Then, when his father passed, Miss Mamie said he went completely off the deep end. If he agreed to act right, families would shelter him for a day or two, then Sugar Baby would disappear for weeks without a word. No one ever knew where he went. How he survived without money or food was the unsolved mystery of Swamp Creek, and children were often told that he was somebody's spirit returned from the dead. Reeking of smoke, liquor, and piss, Sugar Baby was usually avoided, and once he reached adulthood, people disregarded him altogether, especially whenever he opened his mouth. When he was a baby, his mother named him Walter Lee Fletcher Jr. but called him Sugar Baby because he was so sweet. Others adopted the nickname the moment they beheld his smile, and most forgot his birth name by his first birthday. He never cried, his mother boasted. If he was hungry or wet, he simply whimpered, and even his whimpering was soothing. She killed herself, folks said, because her husband questioned Sugar Baby's paternity. She couldn't prove it one way or the other, and she was too afraid to know the truth. At the funeral, Walter Sr. bellowed, "I woulda loved ya anyway, honey. I sware 'fo God I woulda," but it was too late. No one ever said who the real father was. They simply said, "Sugar Baby and W. C.'s oldest boy sho do look alike, don't they?"

Too emotionally distraught to care about the needs of a child, Walter Sr. left the boy to heal his own ten-year-old heart. Rumor had it that Sugar Baby found his father's moonshine and began drinking his cares away. By thirteen, he was a bona fide alcoholic. He and his father ate most days only because sympathetic churchwomen brought them food. The deacons repaired their dilapidated house once, free of charge, but refused to do it again. On August 17, 1903, Walter Sr. died, and Sugar Baby drank so heavily thereafter that folks thought he'd drink himself to death. But he didn't. The old house caved in, so Sugar Baby moved out. Or, rather, he left and wandered the woods, stealing food until folks started giving it to him. Occasionally he'd talk to Gus—the only person he trusted—but Gus never shared the content of their conversation. "What you and Sugar Baby be talkin' 'bout?" Emma Jean asked once, but Gus only said, "Li'l bit o' this, li'l bit o' that." Emma Jean shook her head and murmured, "Two peas in a pod."

"That baby ain't right!" he slurred again, more loudly. "That baby *ain't right*!"

"Shut up, Sugar Baby!" Emma Jean shouted. "You ain't nothin' but a ole drunk heathen!"

The crowd snickered.

Sugar Baby exited as congregants pinched their noses. Emma Jean was glad. Her worry was that most of what he said was true—or later came true—and left people embarrassed and uncomfortable. Miss Mamie said he had the gift of Insight. Others mocked her observation until the summer Sugar Baby shouted to the congregation, "A flood is a-comin'! A flood is a-comin'! It's gon' raaaain!" Nobody believed him. It hadn't rained in weeks and there were no clouds in sight. Yet, in the middle of the night, droplets began falling, and by morning the Jordan had swelled past its banks and swallowed many of those who had ignored Sugar Baby's prophecy. More than thirty people drowned. Even after that, folks didn't heed Sugar Baby's words, but Emma Jean didn't dismiss him quite so easily.

That's why she couldn't stand him. She hated his untempered declarations, and she hated even more that her cursings didn't stop him. Whenever she told him off, he laughed as though she were making a joke. Her inability to control him left her nervous that one day he'd say something for which she'd have to hurt him. Maybe this was the day, she thought.

After the benediction, she found Sugar Baby slumped against the outside wall of the church, chugging Jack Daniel's and puffing homemade cigarettes.

"Hey you!" she called, marching toward him.

He turned slightly, clearly inebriated.

"You stay out o' my business, you hear me! You don't know nothin' 'bout my baby. Heal yo'self befo' you start talkin' 'bout somebody else!"

Sugar Baby chuckled with indifference.

"My baby's just fine. She's exactly what she's supposed to be. Now mind yo' own damn business!"

Emma Jean almost reached the front of the church before Sugar Baby reiterated, "That baby ain't right!"

Others heard him and awaited Emma Jean's response. "Stupid fool!" she hollered.

Mamie intercepted her. "Emma Jean! Oh, Emma Jean!" she called in her scratchy, screechy soprano.

Yes, hussy? Emma Jean wanted to say, but smiled instead.

"You know I couldn't let you git away without seein' that pretty li'l girl o' yours. Come here, baby!" she babbled, reaching for Perfect.

Emma Jean resisted, but Mamie pulled Perfect from her grasp.

"Ouououwee!" Mamie sang. "Jes' look at her! Lookin' jes' like . . . like, um . . ."

Emma Jean's fist tightened in case Mamie said the wrong thing.

". . . like her daddy. I see Gus all 'bout de eyes and de nose. Yep! He couldn't deny this one. At least not this one!" She laughed, then turned to her deaconess comrade. "You ever seen a girl look so much like her daddy? Almost look like a li'l boy, don't she?"

Emma Jean snatched Perfect from Mamie's arms. "I . . . uh . . . gotta get home and get supper ready. Dem boys gon' be real fussy if they ain't got nothin' to eat after church."

But before she could escape, Mamie asked, "And you said her name's Perfect?"

"That's right. Per-fect." Emma Jean over-articulated each syllable.

"Oh dear," one lady said.

"My, my, my," another offered.

Only Mamie was bold enough to ask, "What kinda name is that? That don't sound like no name I ever heard of."

"Well, that's her name," Emma Jean sassed. "I named her what she is."

"I see," Mamie said, and grimaced.

"Good," Emma Jean returned, rolling her eyes and walking away. Over her shoulder, she added, "Then that settles that!"

Mamie chuckled and whispered to her comrades, "If yo' name is what you is, then Mae Helen shoulda named her Stupid-ass!"

The women roared.

Gus's aim had been to exit the church from the rear and disappear before the deacons caught him, but it didn't work out that way. They were huddled in a circle as though awaiting his arrival.

"Whatcha say there, Mr. Gus!" W. C. hollered playfully. Woodrow Wilson Cunningham was his formal name. Folks said he was going to heaven not because he had accepted Jesus as his personal Lord and Savior, but because he had tolerated Mamie fifty years, and even Jesus couldn't have done that.

"Doin' fine," Gus returned, trying not to stop.

"Where you rushin' off to?" another deacon asked.

"Nowhere, I guess." Gus hated himself for giving in so easily.

"You got chu a daughter now, huh?" W. C. said.

Gus didn't know how to respond. Of course he had a daughter, but W. C. already knew that.

"You and Emma Jean 'bout to overpopulate de whole county, ain't cha?" he teased.

The other deacons laughed. Gus didn't.

"I thank God for all my kids," he said.

"Oh yessir! Chillen is a blessin' from God shonuff! I got eight o' my own, twenty grands, and four great-grands! But I thought de last time we talked, you said you wuz through."

"Well, I wuz," Gus said, then decided not to attempt an explanation. "De Lawd do thangs mighty strange sometime."

"De Lawd? De Lawd did that?"

The deacons screamed while Gus grinned sheepishly. Never able to think quickly on his feet, he always left the male gatherings feeling belittled. "Naw, I guess I did it, didn't I."

W. C. screeched, "I guess you did! 'Less Emma Jean done become de Virgin Mary!"

Since he couldn't outwit them, Gus decided to laugh along. Maybe that would quell the emotion rising in his chest.

"Now how in de world did y'all come up wit' de name Perfect?" W. C. finally asked.

"I didn't have nothin' to do wit' it. Dat was all Emma Jean. By de time I seed de baby, she had done already named her."

"You didn't say nothin' 'bout it?"

"Nope. What could I say? Emma Jean de momma."

W. C. nodded. "You right about that. Mamie did de same thang wit' my oldest boy."

"You mean E. J.? I thought his name was just E. J."

W. C. shook his head. "That's what we call him, but his real name is Ecclesiastes Job."

The deacons screamed and scattered in every possible direction.

"Shiiiit! Stop lyin', W. C.!" one man said, bent over with laughter.

"I ain't lyin'!" W. C. hollered.

"Did you say 'Ecclesiastes Job'?" another man asked. "Dat boy's name is actually Ecclesiastes Job?"

"Dat wuz some o' Mamie's bullshit!" W. C. said. "I thought his name was just E. J., too. Hell, I didn't find out 'til de boy was damn near grown!"

"Aw, get outta here, W. C.," Gus said. "You didn't even know yo' own son's name?"

"No!" W. C. frowned and lifted his right hand. "This de God's honest truth! Mamie said she had a dream de night befo' she went into labor, and in dis dream she was readin' 'bout Job in de book o' Ecclesiastes."

"Job ain't in no Ecclesiastes!" one of the deacons said.

"I know dat! Shit!" W. C. defended. "Dat's why she said somethin' wuz special 'bout it, and I guess she thought that wuz s'pose to be de baby's name. Hell. You know how womenfolk think."

Gus was glad another man had a wife he didn't understand. He was relieved, too, that someone else was the butt of the joke for a change.

"Well, wit' all dem brothers, dat li'l girl o' yours sho ain't gon' have no trouble. Dat's fu sho," W. C. said.

Gus smiled, but couldn't think of anything to say.

"Dat's why de Lawd told men not to let women run nothin'," W. C. commented, " 'cause they get a idea and go crazy wit' it."

"I know dat's right!" the others agreed.

"You gotta keep a woman in check, boys. Don't chu neva thank you don't. Else she'll start thinkin' she runnin' thangs, and then you'll look up and have a big ole mess on yo' hands."

"That's right!" one deacon said.

"But I'ma tell you what," W. C. said, pointing to each of them. "A woman don't respect no man who won't put her in her place. She lookin' for a man strong enough to tell her when to shut up."

Gus's head dropped. He tried to imagine controlling Emma Jean but couldn't.

"B'lieve what I'm tellin' you! They ack like they don't like it, but really they love it. God made 'em dat way, and He made de man to stand up and take charge. How you thank I done stayed wit' Mamie fifty years? 'Cause she do what I tell her, that's how!"

"Aw, come on, W. C.," the deacons bantered. "Don't nobody run Mamie Cunningham! Includin' you! If she tell you to jump, you go ta hoppin' 'round like a black-ass jackrabbit!"

W. C. hollered, "Sheeeeit! I know y'all crazy! I runs my house de way a man s'pose to!"

The jeering evolved from one topic to the next, and once the laughter subsided, Gus gathered the courage to say, "Well, I guess I'd betta be gettin' on to de house. My folks waitin' on me to eat."

"All right, all right," the others said.

"Take care o' yo'self, Gus," W. C. said. "The way you and Emma Jean goin', this time next year you liable to have yo'self number eight."

"Oh no," Gus said, and waved. "I'll see y'all later."

"Tell them two oldest boy o' yours to come by de house dis week and cut my grass if they wanna make fifty cents," W. C. called to Gus's back.

"Sho will," Gus returned over his shoulder. "I thank ya fu helpin' my boys out."

A hundred yards down the road he collapsed against a huge white oak. Sweat meandered across his forehead, and his heart beat as though trying to escape his chest. He hated that his mind always proved inadequate when around other men. Instead of joking with them freely, he found himself reticent and afraid, as though they were men and he a boy. Sometimes, while plowing, he would rehearse things to say at the next gathering, but, inevitably, the men would talk about some topic he hadn't thought about. Others' spontaneous wit left him envious and desirous of a mind that moved so quickly. He was simply slow, his father had told him. He would never be smart and that was okay. Everybody couldn't be smart anyway, Chester Peace Sr. had said. That was the same day Gus left school for good—not because, like other black sharecropping children, he was needed in the fields, but because his presence in the classroom was, in his father's words, "a humongous waste of time and space." Education was too precious, the sympathetic father argued, to waste it on a mind which, on a good day, comprehended an hour's worth of basic information. "Let somebody wit' a sharp mind have that seat," he told Gus. "Some folks is cut out for school and some is cut out for work." It took Gus a week to realize he was in the latter group, and instead of feeling dejected, he was amazed at his father's incredible discernment. By fourteen, Gus could read most four-letter words—five-letter words gave him a headache—so Chester Sr. concluded that, as long as the boy worked, he'd make it in the world.

Occasionally Gus had dreamed of being smart, but usually he never thought about it. Anyway, he didn't understand how smart people make money and feed their families. "Who get paid to sit around thinkin'?" he asked himself on his last day of school. "Everybody I know git money after they done done some work." He knew he'd always eat because he'd always work. He had neither seen nor heard of a male schoolteacher—the only occupation he knew of for smart people—so the mystery took its place among others in Gus's mind and accompanied him to his grave.

When Emma Jean first paid Gus any mind, he was picking cotton for Thomas Washington. Nothing about Gus was the least bit attractive to her until dusk when his cotton sack weighed in at three hundred pounds. She had never heard of anyone picking that much cotton in a day, so she knew Gus had to be a work mule, and more than anything, she liked working men. However, his sharp African features disgusted her. With lips three times the size of her own, and big open nostrils that flared with each breath he took, Gus was rejected by most women, and Emma Jean most of all. Who would ever marry such an ugly, purple-black brute, she wondered. His smile and frown were barely distinguishable, and the first time Emma Jean saw his crusty, flat, fourteen-inch feet, she actually vomited.

"You betta try to git dat man, girl!" Mae Helen admonished after witness-ing Emma Jean's repulsion. "What other choices you got?"

Emma Jean was eighteen then and swore she'd never lay with Gustavus Peace. A year later, after having been ignored by every other man in Swamp Creek, she cried her way to the altar and married the man she loathed. They never talked about love. Their union didn't require it. What Emma Jean needed, she told Gus, was the promise that he'd never quit working. Gus raised his right hand like a courtroom witness and said, "I promise." The only thing he wanted was a son and Emma Jean said she'd try. They married on a Saturday afternoon, in Mae Helen's front yard.

Later that night, in the house Gus and Chester Jr. had built, Emma Jean asked, "Do you think I'm pretty?"

Gus stared at her sleepily and said, "I ain't never really thought about it."

Emma Jean almost slapped him, but decided that, as long as he worked, she wouldn't trouble him about such frivolous matters.

Chapter 9

Gus pushed away from the tree and shuffled home. Trying to avoid another embarrassing encounter, he hid, like an escaped convict, behind nearby trees and high grass whenever he thought he heard someone coming. Had a psychiatrist observed him, he would've been bound and transported to the Arkansas State Mental Facility. As it was, he simply took two hours to walk what should've taken him thirty minutes.

He thought to pick Emma Jean a bouquet of wildflowers along the way, but reconsidered when he remembered that vased flowers always die. Why did they always die? Why didn't at least some of them survive? *Can't something stay pretty forever? Something?* Then he figured out the answer and exhumed a handful of black-eyed Susans—dirty roots and all—and presented them to a stunned Emma Jean.

"I got you some flowers," he announced proudly, walking through the back door. The clock chimed four. "Now they'll live forever."

Emma Jean snarled, "Sit down, man, and eat yo' supper." She tossed the plants out the back door.

"They gon' grow like that? You sho you ain't gotta plant 'em first?"

Emma Jean shook her head and watched the boys play with Perfect on the bare hardwood floor.

"Is she ever gon' talk?" Mister complained.

"She ain't old enough yet, fool! I told you that already," Authorly said. "She jes' six weeks. Most babies don't talk 'til they at least two years old."

"Two years old!" Mister screamed.

Sol chuckled. "It won't be long, little brother. Just be patient. One day you'll look up and Perfect'll be walkin' and talkin' like everybody else."

"But I want her to talk now!"

"You cain't rush God, boy," Authorly said. "Thangs happen whenever God say they happen, and not before."

"I'ma ask God to make Perfect talk tomorrow. I bet He'll do it!"

"Bet He won't," Sol teased.

Authorly buried his face in Perfect's stomach and blew forcefully. After she giggled, he scowled. "Whea! She done boo-booed, Momma."

"Why don't chu change her then since you know everything," Mister said.

"No!" Emma Jean yelled.

The boys flinched.

"Y'all remember what I told you: boys ain't got no business lookin' at they sister naked. Never!" She retrieved Perfect from their midst. "It ain't right. A girl gotta be tended to by her mother. Men ain't got no business doin' nothin' like that."

The boys nodded agreeably as Gus continued eating. Emma Jean retreated to the bedroom, then returned Perfect to her brothers.

"Is you gon' have another baby, Momma?" Mister asked.

"Hell, naw," Gus mumbled before Emma Jean could speak. "She betta not."

"I doubt it, sweetie. I got boys and a girl now, so I don't need no mo' chillen."

"You got dat right! I love de chillen I got, but I shonuff got enough."

Knock, knock, knock, someone banged on the front door.

"Come on in," Gus yelled as though he were miles away.

"How y'all doin' today?" a boisterous voice returned.

"Uncle Chester!" the boys screamed, and leapt upon him as he entered the house.

"Goddamn!" Chester hollered in jest, hugging each nephew. "You niggas bigger'n me now! Last time I seed y'all, you wunnit nothin' but li'l ole stumps. Shit, now I gotta look up to ya!" His wife and four children followed.

"Hi, Aunt Margaret," Mister slurred, begrudging the sloppy, wet kiss she always left on his cheek.

"There's my baby!" she moaned, and slobbered as he had predicted. "You almost too big to kiss now, boy."

His brothers muffled their laughter. They'd tease him about it later until Mister would feel compelled to fight one of them.

"You chillen go play!" Chester instructed. "I ain't neva seen chillen love to sit up in de house and look grown folks in de mouth. Y'all go 'head on now."

After their stampede, Margaret cackled, "Girl, you and Gus gon' have a army afta while, ain't cha? Let me see dis precious li'l girl." She reached and Perfect yielded.

"I guess she like you, Margie. She don't go to most folks."

Margaret smiled and whispered, "All chillen like me. It's des titties, girl. They like to put they head on 'em and jes' relax."

"I like to do that, too!" Chester taunted.

Gus looked away and Emma Jean hollered. The men stood, as though on cue, and walked out the front door.

"Let's see what all dese damn chillen doin'," Chester grumbled lovingly.

He and Gus scuffled to the porch and fell heavily into old, high-back wooden chairs. Gus studied the children in the yard, glad his childhood days were long gone.

Chester was more nostalgic. "We gon' look 'round and dem chillen be grown, Gus."

"Yep. That'll be good."

"Funny how fast chillen grow up, ain't it?"

"Yeah, it is."

"Me and Marg thought we'd betta come and see dat new li'l girl o' yours."

"She's in de house."

Chester bit his bottom lip. "I know she's in de house, man! I was jes' sayin' . . . oh shit. Forget it."

Chester's frustration always left Gus nervous. He would've introduced a new subject had he been able to think of one. Instead, he closed his mouth and waited for his big brother to continue.

Reminding himself that Gus couldn't help it, Chester smiled and said, "My niece is jes' as cute as she can be. Looks jes' like you, boy."

Gus lifted his head. "Folks been sayin' that."

"Well, it's de truf. She look kinda like a li'l boy, now that I think about it."

Gus frowned.

"Oh, don't get me wrong. She's a cutie. I'm jes' sayin' she look so much like you dat she coulda passed for a li'l boy. That's all."

"De boys is crazy 'bout her. I'm glad about that."

"Oh yeah! Boys always love dey sister. Dat's why it's good to have the boys first, so they can look after her. They'll take care o' her de rest o' they lives. You mark my word."

"Hope so," Gus moaned. "Hope so."

"But, now that I think about it, I thought you said you didn't want no mo' kids after Mister? I told you Emma Jean was gon' come up pregnant again, didn't I? Dis ain't de last one, neither!" His hearty laughter vibrated across the front porch.

"De hell it ain't! I didn't want this one, but I didn't have nothin' to do wit' it."

"What chu mean, you didn't have nothin' to do wit' it? If you didn't, you need to be out kickin' some nigga's black ass right now!"

Gus's stoic expression never softened. "You know what I mean."

"Well, long as y'all keep doin' de do, Emma Jean gon' keep on poppin' out babies. She ain't gettin' 'em by huself."

"I know." Chester's words reinforced Gus's decision to sleep on the floor. "This one snuck up on me though. We ain't havin' no mo'—not if I can help it. Emma Jean don't want no mo' noway."

"Is that right? Well, y'all betta stop fuckin' if you want this li'l girl to be de last! What's her name, by the way?"

"Perfect," Gus sighed. "Dat's what Emma Jean named her."

"Perfect? What kinda crazy-ass name is dat?"

"You tell me."

"You didn't have no say-so in de matter?"

"Naw, I didn't."

"Well, I'll say! Perfect Peace. That's a name for ya!"

"Yes it is."

Chester howled. "It's plenty folks with crazy names though. You 'member dat girl we used to call Sticks? De one who lived in dat old shack behind de church?"

Gus couldn't remember.

"De one with fourteen brothers and sisters?"

"Oh yeah. I remember her. What about her?"

"Well, did you eva know her real name?"

Gus searched his brain. "I guess I didn't."

Chester hollered before he ever spoke it. "Man, that girl's name is Buster-lina!" His entire body shivered.

Gus laughed wide enough to expose his rotten wisdom teeth. "What?"

"Her daddy's name was probably Buster and I guess they named her after him."

"Why didn't they jes' name one o' de boys after him?"

" 'Cause when Sticks come 'long, it wunnit no boys yet. It wuz eight girls and I guess it looked like wunnit no boys comin'. Then, after Sticks, six come straight in a row."

"Busterlina," Gus repeated in disbelief.

"Ain't that some shit?"

"Yeah. But I guess it wasn't so crazy to her momma."

Inside, Emma Jean and Margaret cut old clothes into quilt blocks. Perfect lay in the bassinet between them.

"Well, you got yo'self a li'l girl now, Emma Jean. I guess you through havin' babies."

"You better believe it, chile! After all these boys, I got me a daughter, so I don't never intend to be pregnant again!"

They cackled like adolescent girls in a schoolyard.

"I know what chu mean, honey. I *know* I ain't havin' no mo'. I'd shoot myself befo' I start *that* over again."

They nodded.

"What's her name?"

Emma Jean didn't hesitate. "Perfect. I named her what she is."

"What? Did you say 'Perfect'?" Margaret burbled in shock.

"Yeah."

"Wow. I ain't neva heard o' nobody named Perfect before."

"Well, I think it's pretty."

"Well, it sure is *something*. That's for sure!"

Emma Jean chewed the inside of her bottom lip. She dared not sass Margaret as she had done Mamie, for Margaret was known for being a bigger fool than Emma Jean.

"Gus like dat name?" Margaret risked.

"I don't know. I didn't ask him."

She treaded further out on the limb. "Well, I know some real pretty girl names. Like Angel or Crystal or Stella . . ."

"Stella? Dat sound like a ole woman's name. That ain't no pretty name for a li'l baby girl."

"Well, it depends on how you hold yo' mouth when you say it. If you say"—she protruded her lips like one preparing for a kiss—"'Stella,' it do sound like you callin' a old woman, but if you say"—she glanced heavenward, dreamily—"'Stella,' it got a nice ring to it." Margaret nodded, agreeing with herself.

"Oh well, it don't matter anyway." Emma Jean shrugged. "She got de name she s'pose to have and dat's what folks gon' call her."

"Fine wit' me! All I know is, she sho look like Gustavus Peace. Lawd have mercy, she look jes' like dat man!"

Emma Jean contemplated telling Margaret everything. A co-bearer of the truth would be nice, she thought, and that way, if anything ever happened to her, someone else could complete what she had begun. Margaret was about the best friend she had, if she had any, and surely she would understand. If she didn't, she would keep the secret anyway, Emma Jean assumed, for anyone with a past like Margaret's was morally obliged to keep her mouth closed.

But Emma Jean couldn't tell it. Every time she tried, her lips clung together like magnets. In her mind, the confession began something like *Margaret, you a woman jes' like me and I know you understand stuff a woman gotta do. And since I didn't have no daughters, I had to make one . . .* but that was far too abrupt. She needed a smoother segue if the thing were going to make sense, and having never been a person of tact, she feared she'd confuse Margaret before she made an ally of her. Now she was glad Mae Helen had taught her to keep her business to herself.

"You can have Izella's old clothes if you want 'em. Perfect'll grow into 'em in no time."

Emma Jean frowned. "No thank you."

"Oh, they ain't no rags! Don't get me wrong! No, no. I bought good clothes for my baby girl. Some of 'em I made, but most of 'em I bought straight out de sto'!"

Still, Emma Jean said, "I thank ya right de same, but my Perfect gon' have her own brand-new thangs."

"Suit yo'self," Margaret said, and changed the subject before she told

Emma Jean off. The women giggled until the old clock chimed eight times. Chester hollered, "Let's go, woman."

"You boys wash yo' hands and feet and get ready for bed," Gus instructed as the boys charged into the living room.

Chester and Margaret said good night, loaded their children onto the wagon, and made their way to the other side of the Jordan.

Emma Jean placed her sewing things in a brown paper bag and returned it to the corner, next to the upright radio Gracie had given them as a wedding gift. Emma Jean then lifted Perfect from the trough-shaped crib and met Gus in the bedroom.

"Maybe we could call her somethin' else," Gus said, unable to shake Chester's ridiculing of Perfect's name. "You know . . . a nickname or somethin'." He disrobed with his back to Emma Jean.

"She already got a name!" Emma Jean screamed. "And it's the name I like."

"Okay, okay. But folks say it's mighty strange." He unrolled the pallet. "They laughin' at it."

"So what! Most folks ain't got no sense noway."

Gus reclined. "Maybe we could call her something else," he repeated quickly, and rolled over.

"We ain't gon' call her nothin' but what I named her. Other folks can kiss my behind if they don't like it. That includes you."

Gus rose, blew out the coal oil lamp, and resettled onto the floor. "I guess it don't make no difference."

Perfect lay peacefully where Gus once had. He resolved to drop the matter and shoulder the ridicule, while Emma Jean decided to slap anyone who mentioned the name issue again.

Slightly beyond midnight, Perfect whimpered irritably and Emma Jean shifted to feed her. Gnawing ravenously, Perfect suckled as though this meal were her last. Gus, who usually slept like a hibernating bear—and snored like one, too!—was awakened by the sound of Perfect's lips smacking on Emma Jean's nipple, and, for a brief moment, he wished the lips were his own. However, as he recalled the connection between sucking Emma Jean's breasts and her subsequent pregnancies, his erection subsided and he returned to sleep. Emma Jean, on the other hand, battled insomnia most nights as she stared into the dark, imagining what her life might have been like under different circumstances. But that night, with Perfect nestled against her bosom, she couldn't have been happier. "Hush li'l baby, don't say a word," she sang softly, stroking Perfect's hair, "Momma's gonna buy you a mocking bird. If that mocking bird don't sing, Momma's gonna buy you a diamond ring." Each time Perfect paused to breathe, Emma Jean kissed the crown of her head. Remembering only a few lines of the standard lullaby, Emma Jean composed verses of her own: "Sweet little Perfect, you're real fine, Emma Jean's baby, yes, you're mine. And if these folks don't love you right, I'm gonna love you with all my might," and so on until Perfect stopped sucking and drifted back to sleep.

Chapter 10

Christmas of 1944 was bitter cold. A raging fire warmed the boys in the living room while, in the master bedroom, Emma Jean shivered under a sheet and three heavy quilts. Gus was equally bound, lying on the frigid hardwood floor, but he felt content, especially since his actions guaranteed the end of little Peaces. Perfect lay in the other room, similarly burdened with layers of covering, longing to join her brothers and partake in the living room's limited, precious heat, but the last thing she wanted on Christmas morning was another of Emma Jean's spankings. She had been told, countless times, not to leave her room in the mornings until she heard her mother's voice. The boys might not be decent, Emma Jean had explained, and a girl ain't got no business seein' a boy's business. The first time Perfect disobeyed, Emma Jean whipped her with a thin sapling from the old peach tree in the front yard, and the last time, she left welts crisscrossing down Perfect's thick legs. Perfect finally understood that what Emma Jean Peace said, she meant. And, anyway, it was Christmas morning and Perfect didn't want anything to come between her and her presents.

Overnight, a storm had dumped two inches of snow in Swamp Creek, and residents declared the first blizzard of the season. Perfect rolled from beneath the quilts and tiptoed to the window. She loved snow. She loved watching it fall from the sky slowly, softly, gracefully, blanketing everything in pure white. She loved its silence, too, how it descended without making a sound and covered things gently. She loved its unmarred beauty, and its tendency to hide things normally unattractive. Like the old, rusted wagon. Emma Jean had begged Gus to get rid of the thing, especially after they got another one, but Gus insisted he could fix it and make a profit. He never did. Now, covered in snow, it looked like a miniature mountain. Birds stood atop the mound, jerking their heads in every direction as though excited about their view of the world. Perfect wanted to grab her coat and join them, but she hadn't yet heard Emma Jean's voice. It was probably too cold outside anyway, she thought. And she hated being cold.

"Y'all gon' sleep the day away?" Emma Jean bellowed, stepping into the living room at 5:45. "It's Christmas morning! Children s'pose to get up and be glad about it!"

Perfect bolted from her room with two plaits sticking up like devil's horns. She was stout now, like Emma Jean had been as a child, and her behind was beginning to take shape. By all standards, she was a pretty girl, with mildly slanted eyes and a smooth, cocoa brown complexion. Emma Jean had seen to it that nothing tarnished Perfect's face. No scratches, no mosquito bites, no natural blemishes. Only her beaming smile jumped out at others, forcing them to smile in return. Even when her hair was a mess, as Emma Jean complained incessantly, it never hid her pretty brown eyes. She had Gus's wide, flat nose, which normally wouldn't have been attractive on a child, but her extra-long eyelashes and high cheekbones gave the nose context and made Swamp Creek women call her a "pretty li'l thang." Her brothers knew she'd be a knockout one day, and that made them proud. "Good mornin', Momma, good mornin' everybody!" she called.

"Hi, honey. Merry Christmas."

"Merry Christmas, Daddy," Perfect said as Gus scraped crust from the corners of his eyes.

"Merry Christmas, baby. Merry Christmas, boys."

"Merry Christmas, Daddy," they said in chorus. Authorly asked about breakfast.

"We gon' eat in a minute," Emma Jean said. "You must be the greediest child the Good Lawd ever made!"

Emma Jean sat the coffeepot on the stove and started a fire underneath. The children awaited her permission to open their gifts.

"Y'all go 'head," she murmured after teasing them with her silence.

"Yay!!!!" they screamed, and scrambled for packages scattered beneath the tall Christmas tree that Gus had dragged in two weeks earlier.

"Everybody got they own present," he said, "so ain't no need in fussin'. It ain't nothin' much, but it's the best me and yo' momma could do. Children 'cross the water don't have nothin', so y'all betta be grateful."

Authorly distributed the gifts, wrapped in newspaper, as though he were Santa Claus. Emma Jean had written each child's name in large print across the packages, and now the children ripped them open with unbridled anticipation.

James Earl, Authorly, and Woody said thanks for new overalls. Bartimaeus, Sol, and Mister would now inherit their brothers' old ones, so they smiled their appreciation for the new shirts they discovered beneath the newspaper wrappings. They were grateful. Of course, months earlier, they had mentioned things like choo-choo trains and baseball bats and gloves, but even then they knew Gus couldn't afford such things. They were content with knowing that he *would've* bought them if he could've.

"What'd you get?" Mister asked Perfect, who seemed unable to open her gift. He volunteered to help.

"No! I can do it myself!"

"Leave her alone, boy," Gus said. "She's a big girl now."

Mister recoiled and sat on the end of the sofa. He knew she'd get something different, something special. She always did.

"Ohhhhhhhh," she cried as shreds of newspaper fell to the floor. "Oh, Momma! Look! My very own baby doll!"

"That's right, honey, your very own baby doll. Now make sure you take care o' her. Me and yo' daddy spent good money for that."

I didn't spend nothin', Gus thought.

"Oh, I'll take care of her, Momma! I promise! She's so pretty!" Perfect studied the doll's yellow hair and aqua blue eyes, cast against an off-white face. She wore a frilly pink dress that flared at the waist, and snow-white shoes. The doll's legs were thick like table legs.

"How come she get a baby doll and we don't get nothin' but—"

"Close yo' mouth, boy," Gus warned. "You ain't no girl. Dolls is for girls."

"I know, but she got somethin' to play with and I didn't get nothin' but a old—"

Slap!

"I said, shut up! Be grateful for what you got! Lotta boys would be happy to have a brand-new shirt."

Mister touched his stinging face. He wanted to say more, to explain that he didn't want a baby doll; he wanted a boy's toy, something like a train or a baseball glove, but he dared not go on. Instead, he sucked his teeth and sulked.

"Keep on, boy, and you gon' get a good whippin' on Christmas mornin'."

Perfect's joy wasn't diminished by the commotion. She clutched the doll to her chest and showed it to Authorly.

"Ain't she pretty?"

"Yep," he said casually. If Gus hadn't known better, he would've thought Authorly was jealous, too.

Perfect scampered to Emma Jean in the kitchen. "Thank you, Momma. I like her a lot!"

"I'm glad you do, baby. She's brand-new."

"Wow."

"And she's yours all by yourself."

"Really, Momma?"

"Really. And remember what I said: take good care of her. Most little Negro girls in Swamp Creek ain't never had no baby doll, and they sho ain't had no new one."

"I love you, Momma!" Perfect embraced Emma Jean's waist tightly. "You the best momma in the whole wide world!"

Emma Jean kissed Perfect's head. "You welcome, sweetie. Ain't nothin' too good for my baby girl. Now run on and play and let me get breakfast ready."

The boys were putting on coats in preparation for morning chores.

"Put somethin' on y'all heads!" Emma Jean hollered. "I don't want nobody barkin' 'round here tonight."

Perfect went to her room to get dressed. She sat the doll upon her bed and smiled.

"Since you my baby now, I guess I'll have to give you a name."

The doll held a constant grin, as though frozen in merriment. Perfect contemplated names as she removed her housecoat and slipped into one of her good Sunday dresses. "Let's see," she murmured, mocking her mother's verbal drama. "I don't know a lotta names, but there's gotta be one . . ." She lay in the middle of the bed, facing the doll. "How 'bout . . . um . . . Josey?" Perfect quickly frowned. The doll didn't like it. "Okay. Well, what about . . . Ella?" The doll didn't like that one, either. Perfect laid her down, then rolled onto her back, thinking aloud. "Corine's pretty, but it's for old ladies, huh? Yeah, I know. Margaret's okay, too, but I don't really like it. Not really." Then it hit her. "Olivia! That's what I'll call you." The doll seemed to like it. "That's the woman's name on the radio show. She sounds really pretty. And white. Just like you."

Perfect ran to Gus, who was filling his pipe. "Guess what, Daddy?"

"What is it, honey?"

"Guess what her name is?" Perfect extended the doll to Gus.

He chuckled. "I don't know, sweetheart. I ain't neva named no girl before."

"It's Olivia!" She bounced on her toes. "She likes that name, and so do I!"

"All right, then Olivia it is." Gus handed the doll back.

"But I wanna ask you somethin', Daddy."

"Okay."

"Do you think Olivia's a pretty name?"

"Well, I guess so. Sounds all right to me."

Perfect scowled. "But do you think it's pretty?"

Gus scooped Perfect and sat her on his lap. "It's a mighty pretty name, honey." He tickled her until she screamed for mercy.

"Then I have another question, Daddy."

Gus's patience was thinning. "Yes?"

"Can we put her name in the Bible?"

"I don't think so, baby. De Bible is for real. It ain't nothin' to play with."

"But Olivia *is* real. I mean, I know she ain't livin' and stuff, but she's a real baby doll, and now she got a real name."

Gus hesitated. "Tell you what. Let's put her name on your wall. Then, she can see it every day."

"Okay!"

The two entered Perfect's room and Gus retrieved his pocketknife. "Where you wanna put it?"

"Um . . ." Perfect surveyed each wall, then pointed to an area just above the bedpost. "Let's put it there, Daddy. That way, she'll see it every morning when she wakes up!"

"All right."

Gus moved the bed and would've commenced carving except that he couldn't spell "Olivia." "Emma Jean!"

"What is it?"

"Come give me a hand."

Emma Jean suggested that she do the carving since she was the speller, but Gus wouldn't hear of it. "Perfect asked *me,* so I'm gon' do it. Just tell me the letters. I cain't spell too good, but I ain't no dummy, neither."

Choosing not to embarrass him in front of Perfect, she relented. "Ooooooo, lllllllll, iiiiiiiiii, vvvvvvvvvvv, iiiiiiiiiiiii, aaaaaaaaaaa," holding each letter's sound long enough for Gus to remember its shape, until, finally, he had it carved into the wall.

"There," Gus said. "Now she'll never forget."

"Thank you, Daddy. Thank you, Momma." Emma Jean smiled and returned to the kitchen. Gus went to check on the boys.

Perfect leapt upon the bed with Olivia in her arms. "There's your name right there." She stood on the pillows—defying another of Emma Jean's rules—and rubbed her small fingers across Gus's carving. "Olivia," she sighed as though the name were divine. "You're my best friend now, so we have to tell each other everything, okay?" She lowered herself to the edge of the bed. "And I guess I need to do somethin' with that head o' yours." The words didn't make sense, since Olivia's hair was straight, but Emma Jean's example of motherhood was all Perfect knew. She got a brush from the top drawer of the small, two-drawer dresser and sat Olivia between her chunky thighs. As she stroked Olivia's golden hair, she said, "I cain't have you walkin' 'round here lookin' like you crazy. Folks gon' think I ain't raisin' you right." Olivia's head jerked with each stroke of the brush. "Be still, girl! This is for yo' own good. Don't you wanna be pretty?" Olivia appeared to comply. "Then sit still so I can finish."

Perfect rubbed the doll's hair with envy. She wished her hair was like that: soft, silky, easy to brush. Maybe then Emma Jean wouldn't make her cry when she did her hair. It was always an ordeal, as Emma Jean pulled and tugged Perfect's hair like one shucking summer corn, then drove the comb into her scalp with the same force as Gus driving the plow. Eventually, Perfect's hair was divided into four quadrants of bushy, chocolate brown Negro hair, as Emma Jean called it. She resisted words like "kinky" and "nappy," having promised herself as a child never to speak such negativity to her own daughter, but now she understood that the words carried some truth. Perfect's hair was so thick that, as soon as she untangled one portion, it retangled as Emma Jean untangled another. Usually, she simply plaited it as a tangled mass, grateful that it coiled enough to look neat. Perfect hated the nightly ritual. As soon as the sun descended, Emma Jean would call, "Perfect! Come on here!" and the child's head would began to ache and she'd weep in anticipation of the pain. But it had to be done. Perfect understood that. She liked how, at the end of the ritual, Gus and the boys smiled at her. Sometimes they took turns touching her heavily greased hair like one might touch the fur of a rare beast. Emma Jean warned them not to mess it up, but she didn't discourage the admiration. That was proof that her little girl was beautiful and that's what Emma Jean had always wanted.

"Now!" Perfect said, turning Olivia to face her. "You just as pretty as you can be." She kissed the doll's rosy cheeks. "Let's see if breakfast is ready."

Perfect bounced off the bed and skipped to the kitchen with Olivia dangling by one arm. She smelled a combination of biscuits and bacon, so she knew they'd eat soon.

"Look at how you carryin' her, Perfect!" Emma Jean scolded. "I told you to take care of her!"

"I am takin' care of her!" Perfect pouted. "What'd I do?"

"You swingin' her by the arm. That ain't no way to care for no baby. Babies is delicate and gotta be handled real gentle. You'll pull her arm off that way."

"Oh," Perfect said, lifting Olivia to her bosom.

"I woulda done anything for a doll like that when I was a little girl," Emma Jean said, retrieving biscuits from the oven.

"Grandma didn't never buy you one?" Perfect asked, and took a seat at the table.

"Chile, no! Momma wunnit spendin' no money on no baby doll. Not for me."

"Why not?"

"Well, let's just say we didn't get along too good."

"Why not?"

Emma Jean placed bacon and homemade jelly on the table. " 'Cause I wunnit as pretty as you." She tried to smile.

"But I bet you was pretty though."

Emma Jean thought of all the Christmases she and Pearlie and Gracie had dashed to the tree, only to find small paper bags of apples, oranges, and peppermint. One year, a large box rested beneath the tree and the girls spent days trying to guess what it was. There was no name on it, so they couldn't figure out whom it belonged to. Christmas morning, Mae Helen told them, "It's for all o' y'all. Open it together." Emma Jean waited as her sisters ripped open the wrapping.

"Momma!" Pearlie shouted. "A baby doll!" She rocked it like it was real.

"Share it with your sister," Mae Helen said. "And let Emma Jean see it, too."

Pearlie passed the tall stiff doll to Gracie, then, seconds later, asked for it back. "It ain't yours!" Gracie said. "Momma told us to share!"

"That's right! And that's what I mean. I'll take it back if y'all don't know how to act."

Gracie returned the doll to Pearlie. "You gotta give it back in a minute. Momma said so." They drifted into the bedroom.

"You can play with it, too," Mae Helen told Emma Jean. "Just don't hog it from your sisters."

"It's okay, Momma. They can have it."

"What chu mean, 'they can have it'?" She mocked Emma Jean's pitiable voice. "You don't like it? You think you too good for a baby doll?"

"Oh, no ma'am. I like it. I like it a lot. It's just that I don't wanna fight over it."

"You ain't gotta fight over nothin'. I bought the damn thing and I'll take it back if y'all don't know how to share."

Emma Jean knew Mae Helen had really bought the doll for Gracie and Pearlie. They had asked for it. Emma Jean hadn't asked for anything, trying desperately to save herself the disappointment. They'd never share with her anyway, she knew, and Mae Helen would absolutely never deny them for Emma Jean's sake. "Suit yo'self," Mae Helen said, and went to join Gracie and Pearlie in the bedroom. Sitting alone, Emma Jean ate the apple from her fruit bag, then ate Gracie's and Pearlie's, too.

"Do you think Olivia's a pretty name, Momma?" Perfect asked, trying to lighten the mood.

"I sure do."

"Wanna know where I got it from?"

"Yep."

Perfect squirmed with excitement. "I heard it on the radio." She bounced Olivia on her lap. "Remember that show that comes on on Saturday nights? The one that Daddy likes?"

Emma Jean couldn't recall.

"You know, Momma! The one with the man and woman who always be fussin'."

"Oh yeah!"

"Well, Olivia's the woman's name."

"Shonuff?"

"Yes, ma'am. And I kinda picture her with hair like this. I really like the name. It sounds so pretty."

"Your name's pretty, too. Why didn't you name her Perfect?"

Perfect shrugged. " 'Cause then there'd be two perfect little girls and that wouldn't be good."

"Why not?"

" 'Cause it's better if it's only one. Then nobody's confused about who's *really* Perfect."

Emma Jean howled. "Girl, you a mess! I don't know what I'm gon' do with you." She called the boys in for breakfast.

When Mister saw the doll again, his envy resurfaced. "She's ugly anyway," he whispered nastily into Perfect's ear.

"You shut up!" Perfect muttered.

"Ugly, ugly, ugly," Mister mouthed.

"Momma! Mister said Olivia's ugly."

"All right now," Gus said. "Be quiet 'til Authorly says the blessing."

Authorly sat at the foot of the table, opposite Gus, as though he were the other provider. "Lord, we thank You for this food and for lettin' us see another Christmas mornin'. Help us to be grateful for what we have and not to wish for what other people have. Amen."

"Amen," others said, and began to eat.

"Who's Olivia anyway?" Authorly asked, piling biscuits on his plate.

"This is Olivia," Perfect said, holding up the doll. "And she's pretty!"

Mister shook his head.

"Yes, she is!" Perfect cried. "Ain't she, Momma?"

"Of course she's pretty, honey. Don't pay Mister no mind." Emma Jean gave Mister a stern glance.

He wanted to yank the doll from Perfect's lap and rip it apart, one limb at a time. Of course Gus would've killed him. That's the only reason he didn't do it. He hated the stiff, stationary smile she wore and the thin, yellow hair that looked like corn silk. The more he thought of Olivia, the more enraged he became. Why did Perfect always get everything? None of her clothes were hand-me-downs like his were. Obviously Emma Jean loved Perfect more than she loved the boys, Mister concluded. That was the only explanation he could conceive. But why was she special just because she was a girl? What was so special about girls? Weren't boys special, too? At least some of them?

"Eat yo' breakfast befo' you git in trouble," Authorly murmured. He had watched Mister stare at Olivia. "Don't worry about that ole doll. We'll play outside in the snow after we eat."

Mister obeyed, grateful that at least someone understood. He still hated Olivia though, and he began constructing ways to destroy her.

Chapter 11

"How come I cain't play with Mister and the other boys?" Perfect whined from the yard.

" 'Cause you a lady," Emma Jean said, stomping each word into the front porch. "And ladies ain't got no business rollin' 'round in de dirt wit' no boys. A lady is s'pose to stay clean and pretty."

"But I don't wanna be clean and pretty, Momma. I wanna play wit' de boys!"

"Well, you ain't! You's a girl and you gon' act like one!"

Tears welled and burst across Perfect's cocoa brown cheeks. She knew her resistance was useless. By six, she had learned that Emma Jean's word was law, especially concerning her upbringing. So knowing nothing else to do, she plopped down on the edge of the porch, sat Olivia beside her, and rested her chin in the palms of her hands. The pink dress and matching hair ribbons, for which Emma Jean had emptied the family coffer, meant nothing to Perfect, who wanted only to partake in the fun her brothers experienced daily. Of course Emma Jean wouldn't hear of it, so Perfect had no choice but to sit on the porch with Olivia and watch as her brothers climbed trees and raced down the dirt road. She still liked Olivia, but at six, Perfect preferred a friend who talked.

"Why don't chu go find Caroline and Eva Mae, and play with them?" Emma Jean suggested. "It's a beautiful Saturday afternoon, and I'm sure those girls would love to play with you."

Perfect frowned, but boredom persuaded her. "Okay," she huffed. "But what if—"

"There they go now!" Emma Jean pointed toward the road. "De Lawd always show up on time. Why don't chu jes' go over there"—she pressed Perfect's shoulders gently—"and ask them to come play with you? They real sweet girls. And pretty. Jes' like you."

Perfect complied although, had she had her way, she would have been entangled in the limbs of the oak tree with Mister and Sol.

"Hey y'all!" she hollered lazily, sauntering toward the dirt lane with Olivia swinging from her right hand. "Y'all wanna play somethin'?"

"Sure," Eva Mae said. "What chu wanna play?" She wiped sweat from her glistening brow and ran fingers across what her mother said was the nappiest hair she had ever seen. Never bothering to comb or brush it, Mrs. Free usually washed it on Saturday mornings and let it dry on its own. Most days, Eva Mae's long, kinky hair coiled like a snail and stood on her head, pointing in every conceivable direction. It never warranted ribbons or bows. The left strap of her baby blue sundress hung off her shoulder, semi-exposing a tender young eight-year-old breast, anxious, but unready to bloom. She was barefoot, as was Caroline, whose sandy red plaits made Perfect jealous.

"I don't know," Perfect returned. "Whatever y'all wanna play, I guess."

"Then let's play house," Eva Mae suggested, and led the girls back to the porch. Caroline and Perfect followed like naïve ducklings.

"I'm the momma!" Perfect said as they reached the front steps. She slung Olivia onto the porch.

Eva Mae nodded. "Okay. Then I'll be de daddy and Caroline, you be de daughter."

"Why you always gotta be de daddy?" Caroline complained.

" 'Cause I'm bigger'n you," Eva Mae said matter-of-factly.

"So!" Caroline hollered.

"And I'm older'n you. I'm eight and you're only six. And me and Perfect both bigger'n you, so you have to be the daughter. And since I can beat both o' y'all up, I gotta be de daddy 'cause daddies beat people. At least they gotta be able to. That's what makes them daddies."

Caroline wanted to be the daddy, for once, but unable to usurp Eva Mae's authority, she sighed and assumed her secondary role.

"Perfect, you start cookin' supper over there"—Eva Mae pointed to an imaginary kitchen at the end of the porch—"and I'll start gatherin' kindling for de woodstove." She began to move, then added as an afterthought, "And, oh yeah, Caroline, you . . . um . . . play with your friends in the front yard."

Caroline sat on the green lawn and immediately began conversing with invisible companions. For an instant, Eva Mae and Perfect stared, troubled that Caroline required no transition from reality to fantasy, but since her actions contributed to the fun of the game, they didn't disturb her.

Perfect scurried back and forth in front of the porch, huffing complaints about sweating over a hot stove for niggas who didn't appreciate it. With pursed lips and limp wrists swinging freely, she moved from pot to imaginary pot, stirring nothingness and daring anyone to touch it before it was done. Ocassionally, she switched her narrow hips like Emma Jean, unsure of why women did it at all until Eva Mae slapped her buttocks.

"Whatcha do that for?" Perfect asked.

"'Cause dat's what my daddy do when my momma walk in front o' him like that."

"Oh," Perfect said, wondering why Gus had never responded to Emma Jean that way. Simulating her mother's coarse alto, she turned to Caroline and said, "Girl, git in here and sweep dis floor!"

When Caroline didn't answer, Perfect huffed, "These kids! I swear they git on my nerves!"

Across the yard, Eva Mae swung her arms as though the make-believe ax were real. Every few minutes, she stopped and panted, "Whew! Shit! Lawd have mercy!" just as her father did, then she resumed the chore with renewed vigor. Her sweat confirmed her paternal authority, she believed, and now she knew why her father ate so ravenously at the dinner table.

"Y'all come on!" Perfect hollered sweetly, and wiped her hands on an invisible apron.

Caroline jumped and said, "I gotta wash my hands, Momma." She went to the well on the side of the house and drew a bucket of lukewarm water with which she rinsed her hands and face.

"You got some dinner ready, woman?" Eva Mae growled. "I done worked hard all day, and you betta have somethin' ready fu me to eat."

"It's ready, it's ready," Perfect mocked. "Just sit down, man, and I'll put everything on de table. Caroline, git in here!"

Caroline ran from the side of the house. "Good evenin', Daddy," she said with a smile.

"What's good about it?" Eva Mae grimaced.

"Um . . . I don't know," Caroline whimpered.

"Then don't say it no mo'. Jes' sit yo' ass down and wait fu yo' momma to put de food on de table."

Eva Mae's cursing was off-putting for Caroline and Perfect, but since she was the daddy they didn't object.

Perfect set the fictitious table, complete with pots, pans, and cutlery, and said, "Go 'head and eat, man, befo' de food git cold."

Eva Mae lifted a lid and said, "What is this shit anyway?"

Perfect wanted to ask her not to say bad words in case Emma Jean was near, but instead she answered, "Meat loaf, mashed potatoes and gravy, string beans, and homemade lemonade."

"I hate meat loaf," Eva Mae said.

Perfect was dumbfounded. She couldn't imagine Gus saying something like that to Emma Jean, who certainly wouldn't have cared anyway.

Caroline intervened. "It'll be good, Daddy. Momma made it extra good jes' for you." She smiled and the tension eased.

The girls spooned imaginary food into their mouths, but chewed as though it were real. Never uttering a sound, Perfect and Caroline watched Eva Mae to make sure Daddy was satisfied.

After several silent seconds, Perfect rose and said, "Let me clear these dishes up." She gathered plates, forks, and glasses from before Eva Mae and Caroline, saying, "Y'all don't do nothin' but dirty up a bunch o' dishes that somebody else gotta wash. I tell ya, I'm sick o' y'all."

"Shut up, woman!" Eva Mae shouted. "Just do what you s'pose to do. Don't nobody wanna hear yo' mouth."

"I speak when I want to, man," Perfect returned. "You don't own me."

Eva Mae's slap startled Perfect. "Stay in yo' place, woman!"

Too shocked to cry, Perfect wailed, "That's not part of the game!"

"Sure it is," Eva Mae said. "I'm the daddy and the husband, remember? Don't yo' daddy slap yo' momma when she get smart at the mouth?"

"No. At least I ain't neva seen him do it."

"Well, he *is* the man of the house, ain't he?"

"I guess so."

"Then he can do whatever he want to. That's what bein' the man of the house means. And if anybody make him mad, he can hit 'em."

Perfect didn't care for the notion, but since Eva Mae's explanation was logical, she acquiesced. "Okay, but don't hit so hard."

"All right." Eva Mae smiled. "Now finish cleanin' dis kitchen and git dese kids a bath."

Caroline stared at Eva Mae like she did her own father whenever he hit her mother. She would have shot him by now, but she couldn't reach the shotgun hanging on the living room wall. One day, she stood in a chair and retrieved it, only to discover that it was too heavy to hoist. All she could do was stare her hatred at him in hopes that the memory of the contempt in her eyes would one day convict his heart.

She never looked at her mother immediately after the abuse. Instead, Caroline would escape outdoors and reenter later as though nothing had happened. The black eyes and bruises made the charade difficult to execute, but Caroline thought this delusion the least she could do to help her mother retain at least a modicum of dignity.

So when Eva Mae slapped Perfect, Caroline ran across the yard and hid behind a rosebush, only to return seconds later, skipping and calling, "Hey, Momma. What cha doin'?"

Perfect was wiping off the imaginary table. Neither of them looked at the other.

"Get in here, girl, and get yo'self a bath," Perfect fussed playfully.

"Yes, ma'am," Caroline said, and went to the far end of the porch where the invisible washtub rested. Sliding the spaghetti straps off her shoulders, she let the loose, thin dress crumple to the ground. Then she rubbed her body as though bathing, scrubbing vigorously under her arms and between her skinny legs. "All clean, Momma!" she announced in nothing but her panties.

"Good, baby," Perfect said without turning. "Now put on your nightgown and git ready for bed."

"Your bed is up here," Eva Mae said to Caroline, pointing to the porch. "Our bed is down there." She nodded toward the area beneath the house.

Caroline stretched across the edge of the porch and said, "Good night, Momma, good night, Daddy."

Perfect grabbed Olivia, and Eva Mae ushered them into the abyss beneath the house. It was dark and damp down there, for although the sun shone brightly, the three enclosed sides blocked most of its light. As the husband, Eva Mae led the way, assuring her wife that everything was all right. Perfect had played under the house before, but, for some reason—maybe submission to a man—she now felt helpless and lost.

The young couple tripped over miscellaneous items—empty buckets, garden shovels, fishing cane poles, gas containers—and came to rest in the far back corner. For the cooler temperature, Perfect was thankful, but for Eva Mae's boldness, which certainly exceeded her own, she was envious.

"We can lay down right here," Eva Mae said spryly, noting a vacant spot on the moist earth. "This'll be fine."

Perfect wanted to protest, simply for the sake of challenging Eva Mae, but in truth she had no objection.

The two reclined easily as though careful not to make a squeaky bed squeak. Perfect's back fit snugly into the concave of Eva Mae's arms and chest, and, acting like she thought a good husband should, Eva Mae grabbed Perfect and said, "Come here, woman." She took Olivia and cast her aside.

"Don't be so rough with her. It ain't nice."

"All right, all right," Eva Mae said, and began to caress Perfect's left arm sensually. Her touch sent chill bumps racing across Perfect's body.

"Just relax," Eva Mae coached. "I won't hurt you."

Perfect sighed.

"Good, good."

Everything's okay, Perfect told herself. *Ain't no need in bein' scared. We just playin' house and this is part of the game.* She couldn't understand why she wanted to cry.

Eva Mae released Perfect's body and gently rolled her onto her back. Perfect resisted slightly, sensing something wrong, but Eva Mae insisted. "You ain't playin' right! I'm de husband and you de wife, so you s'pose to do whatever I tell you!"

"No, I ain't! My momma don't do that."

"Well, she oughta! Dat's what de Bible say and dat's what Reverend Lindsey say, too. De man is s'pose to rule over de woman and she's s'pose to help him do whatever he dream of doin'. Don't yo' daddy work every day and yo' momma stay home and cook and stuff?"

"Yeah, but that's work, too!"

"Of course it is. But dat don't mean de man ain't s'pose to tell her what to do. She can work all day and night, but de Bible say she still s'pose to mind the man."

Perfect recalled Reverend Lindsey saying those things. She'd wanted to ask him exactly what a "help meet" was, but she never did. Now, she couldn't challenge Eva Mae's explanation, so she huffed and gave in.

On her back, Perfect looked up into Eva Mae's fierce eyes. "Ain't you s'pose to say you love me or somethin'?"

"Hell no!" Eva Mae said. "Colored men ain't gotta say that to their wives. You musta heard some white folks on de radio or somethin'."

She had.

"Just lay back and relax."

Eva Mae unbuttoned Perfect's blouse and began rubbing her flat chest as though smoothing out a rough surface. Perfect glanced at Olivia, whose smile eased her discomfort. Then Eva Mae bent and softly kissed the place she had anointed, and Perfect hated that Eva Mae's lips felt so good. Without asking permission, Eva Mae grazed Perfect's tender nipple with her tongue, leaving a trace of murky saliva, which Eva Mae subtly wiped away with her one free hand. All Perfect knew to do was stare at Olivia as her play husband introduced her body to sensations she would later wish she had never known.

Perfect could have sworn that, for an instant, Olivia's smile softened. The sharp, upturned corners of the doll's mouth seemed to descend slightly, and the glow in her eyes appeared to dull momentarily.

"This is fun," Eva Mae said, raising her head. "My daddy do this to my momma all the time. I watch 'em sometimes." She buried her face, once again, in Perfect's belly button and licked around it like one licks the head of a lollipop.

Stop! Perfect heard a voice cry deep within. Yet her pleasure muffled that voice and begged Eva Mae to go on. Go on where, she didn't know, but Perfect sensed there was a climax to these feelings, and she wanted to reach the mountaintop. So when Eva Mae reached under Perfect's skirt and rubbed her inner thighs, Perfect parted them willingly, welcoming whatever Eva Mae intended.

"That tickles," Perfect chuckled.

Eva Mae glanced up and smiled. Suddenly she lifted herself and planted a wet, soft kiss on Perfect's virgin lips. "You like that?"

Perfect nodded excitedly, so Eva Mae kissed her again and again.

"Perfect! Girls!" Emma Jean called. "Y'all come and get somethin' to eat."

The husband and wife jumped up, brushed off the backs of their clothes, and, after retrieving Olivia, Perfect said, "Come on! We gotta get outta here."

Eva Mae followed this time, asking, "Can we play again tomorrow?"

* * *

The next day, Eva Mae coaxed Perfect under the house again and told her they were best friends. Olivia watched in silence.

"Really?" Perfect beamed. "I ain't neva had no best friend before. Not a real, live one."

Eva Mae smiled. "Well, you got one now. But we cain't tell nobody. It's our secret, okay?"

"Okay."

"Everything we do is our secret. Everything." She winked.

"Okay," Perfect said more slowly.

"I wanna show you something," Eva Mae said excitedly, and grabbed Perfect's hand, leading her to their imaginary bedroom.

"It's our anniversary today, so we have to do something special."

"What's a anniversary?"

"It's when two people celebrate the time they done been together. You ain't neva heard of it?" Eva Mae took Olivia and sat her aside.

"No," Perfect felt ashamed to admit.

"Well, don't worry about it. I'll show you what to do."

Perfect was fine with things as they had been the day before—Eva Mae's tongue on her nipples, then her stomach, then her hand playing between Perfect's legs—but she was also eager to see what Eva Mae had in store.

"Just lay back and close yo' eyes," Eva Mae instructed.

Perfect obeyed and lifted her blouse voluntarily. Eva Mae's gentle kisses around her nipples made Perfect smile and shiver. She didn't want to see Olivia's face this time.

Eva Mae smiled, too. "It's our one-day anniversary, and this is what people do on their anniversary."

Perfect's breathing increased. Eva Mae raised her head and leaned forward until the couple's lips met. Though awkward at first, Perfect relented and moved her lips slightly as Eva Mae pecked them repeatedly.

"I love you," Eva Mae moaned.

"I love you, too," Perfect felt compelled to say.

When Eva Mae stopped, Perfect thought the anniversary had ended. She leaned up on her elbows.

"Wait a minute," Eva Mae whispered. "I ain't gave you yo' present yet."

"What is it?"

Eva Mae kissed Perfect again and thrust her tongue into Perfect's mouth.

"Ugh!" Perfect moaned, jerking away.

"What's wrong? You didn't like it?"

She frowned. "It felt funny. And nasty."

"Yeah, but didn't it feel good, too?"

Perfect pondered. She didn't want to disappoint her husband. "I guess so."

"You just gotta keep doin' it, that's all. The more you do it, the more you'll like it. It's fun. I like it a lot. Especially with you."

Perfect blushed. She wanted to like it, too.

"Can we do it again?"

Perfect didn't object, so Eva Mae engulfed Perfect's lips with her own, but this time inserted her tongue much more slowly, moving it around as though tasting something unfamiliar. Perfect began to like it.

"See? Told ya it was fun. And we can only do it with each other, bein' best friends and all."

Perfect agreed. She had no one else to do it with anyway, she thought. They held hands and returned to the front porch, anxiously awaiting their next anniversary.

Chapter 12

"Hey, boys!" Gus screamed. "Come give me a hand!"

It was a gusty October day in 1947. Yellow, brown, and burnt orange leaves swirled in the yard like miniature tornadoes as Gus hopped excitedly from one side of the wagon to the other.

"Boys! Hurry up!"

Authorly led the pack, wondering why Gus was so anxious. Bartimaeus stopped at the edge of the porch. He, too, had never heard such enthusiasm in his father's voice. "What is it?" he asked.

Gus flung back the tarp like one revealing a wagonload of cash. "Isn't she a beauty?" he said.

Authorly motioned for his brothers to hold their peace. "Daddy, what are we suppose to do with that thing?"

Gus looked disappointed. "Thing? Are you kidding? This is our new coffee table!"

The boys gawked.

"Well, it wasn't *suppose* to be a coffee table, but it *can* be. Help me get it in the house."

The boys didn't move until Authorly nodded. Each tried to recall when Gus's mind had begun to slip, only to conclude that it was probably long before their time. The new coffee table was heavy, so the older brothers lifted it from the wagon like pallbearers and ushered it into the Peace living room.

Bartimaeus touched the top as it passed and knew this wasn't a good omen.

"Sit it in front of the couch!" Gus instructed gleefully.

The boys obeyed.

"Yes, right there! That's perfect. Now go get yo' momma. She gon' be so happy!"

Authorly screamed out the back door for Emma Jean. When she entered, she stumbled in shock.

"What the hell?"

"Don't chu love it!" Gus said. "And it's brand-new, too. Didn't cost a dime." His chest protruded with pride. "It's a coffee table. At least now it is."

Emma Jean studied Gus's face as though he were a stranger.

"Okay! It's a wooden coffin, but if we drape a cloth over it, nobody'll ever know the difference! Undertaker gave it to me free. Somebody was s'pose to die who didn't, so he told me I could have it. You been talkin' 'bout wantin' a coffee table, so now you got one!" He smiled.

Emma Jean trembled. Had Gus gone completely crazy?

"You don't have to thank me. A good man provides for his family."

Gus exited while the others stood frozen in horror. It would be several minutes before Emma Jean thawed and said, "Just throw a sheet over the damn thing. Hurry up."

Still traumatized, Authorly laid the sheet gently, as though the coffin were too fragile to hold its weight, and the family never spoke of the matter again. A month later, Emma Jean converted the coffin into the family chest, filling it with memorabilia, especially Perfect's childhood things, then using it as the coffee table Gus had suggested in the first place. He knew she'd come around.

A month after that, Authorly shifted the memorabilia to the foot of the coffin, and Bartimaeus began sleeping in it. Padded with one of Emma Jean's old quilts, it would definitely be more comfortable than the floor, Authorly explained, and since Bartimaeus wasn't troubled by it the way others would have been, he lay in it without reservation and slept there until he moved out of the house. He loved Authorly for deferring unto him a place of such comfort.

When company pointed and whispered, "Is that a . . . um . . . coffin under there?" Gus shouted, "Yeah! Ain't that a great idea?" while the rest of the family coiled in shame.

* * *

Bartimaeus was the only brother Emma Jean trusted to be alone with Perfect. His handicap convinced Emma Jean that he was a safe companion, so she relaxed her guard and let the two do as they pleased. Sometimes they'd play hide-and-seek in the front yard—Perfect was always the seeker—but most times they'd walk the back roads of Swamp Creek with Bartimaeus holding Perfect's narrow elbow and talking about whatever he happened to be wondering that day.

"Do fish sleep?" he posed one lazy Sunday afternoon. He had recently turned thirteen. Perfect was seven.

"I don't know. I ain't neva thought about it."

"I bet they do. All living things sleep, don't they?"

"I guess so."

"Maybe they only need a few minutes since they don't work or nothin'."

"How you know they don't work?" Perfect asked, eager to prove Bartimaeus wrong whenever she could.

"Because they don't need money. You only work if you need money, right?"

"I guess so," Perfect said, defeated.

"God takes care of all their needs."

"Then why don't God do it for people, too?"

"I don't know. Maybe He don't like people as much as He like everything else."

"But Reverend Lindsey say God made people in His own image, so it wouldn't make sense for Him not to like 'em."

"You got me on that one." Bartimaeus smiled. Perfect did, too.

They walked farther, and Perfect saw a bull mating with a cow.

"Why's that cow sticking her thing inside that other cow?"

Bartimaeus laughed. "That's how they make baby cows, Daddy said. But the one with the thing is the boy. The other one's the girl."

"No it's not," Perfect contested. "The girl's the one with the thing. Just like I got."

Bartimaeus hollered. "What? You ain't got no thing, girl!"

"Yes I do!" Perfect insisted.

"No you don't."

"Yes I do!" she screamed louder.

"Okay. If you say so, then I guess you do."

"I do," Perfect repeated. "Girls have little things down there"—she pointed to her genitalia—"but I don't know what boys have."

"You'll know soon enough."

Perfect shrugged. They walked farther.

"Something smells sweet," Bartimaeus said, sniffing the air.

"Oh, that's the honeysuckle bush right in front o' you."

"What does it look like?"

"Um . . . it's big with little green leaves and yellow flowers. It's real pretty."

"I wish I could see a honeysuckle bush." His eyes moistened as he reached forward.

"Maybe you will one day."

"I doubt it. I won't ever see a honeysuckle bush or anything else."

"How you know? God might make you see one day."

"God ain't gon' make me see 'cause once God do somethin' He don't neva change. That's what Daddy said. He said He de same yesterday, today, and tomorrow, so I ain't gon' neva see nothin'.'"

Perfect took her brother's hand and said, "Don't worry about it. Momma say miracles still happen. Sometimes."

"If I could just see for a day," he whimpered, "that would be good enough for me."

Perfect didn't know what to say.

"I just wanna know if I imagine things right. That's all."

"Well, I'd give you my eyes if I could. At least I'd give you one of 'em."

Bartimaeus blushed. "Thanks, Perfect, but I guess God didn't mean for me to have 'em."

"I'll describe the whole world to ya!" Perfect shouted. "That way, you'll see everything everybody else see. At least sorta."

"It don't matter. I bet I imagine it better than it is anyway. I'd probably be disappointed if I saw the truth."

Perfect looked around. "I don't know. The world is beautiful. Everything's green or purple or yellow or brown and everything changes colors from one part of the year to the next." Perfect paused.

"Tell me more."

"Well, the sky is real blue and birds fly all around—"

"What does blue look like?"

Perfect was dumbfounded. "I don't know. I can't describe it, but it's pretty. It makes you feel warm inside."

Bartimaeus nodded.

"And the trees are real big with leaves hanging from them. The leaves are green. They make you feel . . . well . . . excited, I guess."

"Un-huh."

"And the grass is green, too, but it's a lighter green than the leaves. It feels soft and fuzzy like black people's hair." She pressed Bartimaeus's hand to the earth and he smiled. "And the flowers are all different colors and they make you wanna cry 'cause they so pretty." She picked a honeysuckle blossom and handed it to him. "Just feel it and you can tell what it looks like."

Bartimaeus obeyed.

"And the wind blows, but can't nobody see it."

"Why not? It don't have no color?"

"I guess not."

"I'm glad can't nobody see it, so everybody know what it feels like to be blind. At least sometime."

"But I ain't blind."

"If you can't see de wind, you a little blind. I guess everybody is though."

Perfect blew into her palm, straining to see what she obviously felt.

"Wow. I ain't never thought about it like that."

"I guess everybody's blind to a certain extent. Some people jes' more blind than others, but if nobody can't see de wind, then, yeah, everybody's a little blind."

Perfect felt enlightened.

"There's a bee over there." Bartimaeus pointed to his right.

Perfect didn't see it. "Where?"

"Right over there." His index finger outlined a small circumference.

When the bee rose and flew away, Perfect murmured, "Wow. How'd you know there was a bee over there if you can't see?"

" 'Cause I can hear real good. I guess if God don't give you one thing, He give you a whole lot more of somethin' else."

"What else can you hear?"

"Close yo' eyes," Bartimaeus said. "And keep 'em closed 'til you start hearin' stuff."

Perfect tried, but didn't hear anything more than usual.

"I can hear the Jordan."

"The river?" Perfect screeched. "We ain't nowhere near de river!"

"But I can still hear it."

She closed her eyes again, but heard nothing.

"And I can hear a animal walking in de woods."

Perfect surveyed the trees, but saw nothing.

"And I can hear those birds' wings flapping way up in the sky."

"Way up there?"

"Yep. It's not loud, but I can hear it. And sometimes, if I get real quiet, I can hear my own heartbeat."

"Really?"

"Un-huh. Like I said, I guess when God takes one thing away He gives you twice as much of something else."

The two sat at the edge of the road, one seeing, the other hearing and feeling God's creation.

"I wanna try something," Perfect said suddenly.

"Okay."

She lifted Bartimaeus's hands and pressed them against her cheeks. "Can you tell what I look like?"

He smiled. "Of course."

"Really?"

"Sure."

He grazed her tender face slowly, nodding as the familiar image coalesced in his mind. "You real pretty," he said. "Ain't nothin' too big or little. You jes' right." He felt her smile.

"But what about my legs? Everybody say my legs is real thick."

"Yo' legs is just fine, girl."

Perfect guided his hands down to her kneecaps. "You feel 'em and see if they feel fine to you."

"Aw, these is great legs," he teased. "They gon' hold you up for a long time."

"I'm glad you like 'em!" she said, relieved. Then, she pressed his hand against her private.

Bartimaeus jerked away. "What was that?" He tumbled backward.

"I told you girls have things down there, dummy!" she chuckled.

"What was that!" Bartimaeus cried again.

From his tone, she knew something was wrong. "What did I do?"

"Oh God! What was that? What was it!" he kept asking.

"It was my—"

"You ain't s'pose to have that!"

"Why not?"

"Oh God, oh God, oh God, oh God!"

"What is it?"

Her innocence calmed him.

"L-l-l-listen, Perfect. Somethin' ain't right. I don't know if it's you or me, but somethin' ain't right."

"What chu talkin' 'bout, Bartimaeus?"

He tried to still his trembling hands. "Listen to me real good, Perfect. I know you a little girl and all, I know you are, but . . . um . . ."

"But what?" She was practically in tears.

"Somethin's wrong."

"What chu mean?"

"I mean, you ain't s'pose to have that! You a girl!"

Perfect was confused. "I know I'm a girl."

"And girls is s'pose to have somethin' else!"

"Huh?"

He rubbed his head. "Perfect, somethin' ain't right."

"Why you keep sayin' that?" She was becoming annoyed.

"Because it's true. I . . . um . . . don't know what it is, but somethin's real wrong."

"Then what is it?"

Bartimaeus knew he wasn't making sense. "Something's wrong," he said again.

"What chu mean 'wrong'?"

Bartimaeus shook his head. "This ain't right."

"Huh?"

"I don't know how to tell you this"—Bartimaeus rubbed his head in confusion—"but you ain't no normal little girl."

Perfect didn't understand. Bartimaeus didn't, either.

"Listen to me, Perfect." He reached for her hands. "Don't never, *ever* let anybody touch you down there again! Do you hear me?"

She thought of how Eva Mae tickled her thighs, although she had never touched her private parts.

"I said, do you hear me!"

"Okay! But why not?"

"Because you cain't! Never! Don't ever let anybody touch *that* again. No-body!" Bartimaeus shivered as though naked in the snow.

"I didn't do nothin' wrong, Bartimaeus," she pleaded.

He reached for her hand. "I know you didn't. I'm sorry for hollering, Per-fect. You right—you didn't do nothin' wrong. I just want you to be careful so others don't hurt you."

"Why would somebody hurt me?" She still didn't understand.

"Please, Perfect. Just do what I said. Please."

"Okay."

He rubbed her head soothingly, trying to ascertain what to do. Should he mention this to Gus or Emma Jean? Surely they already knew. After all, she was their daughter. Emma Jean definitely had to know. She had changed Per-fect's diapers, so of course she knew. But why hadn't she told anyone? Didn't the brothers deserve to know that their sister had a penis? It would be their job to protect her if others found out, but they couldn't do that if they didn't know. And that was a penis, wasn't it? Of course it was. Bartimaeus knew what a penis felt like, having felt his own countless times, but he couldn't understand why his sister had one.

"Promise me one thing," he repeated as he released her hand.

She sniffled. "Okay. What?"

"Don't ever tell anybody else what you got down there."

"Why not? Every girl's got—"

"Don't *ever* say it again. Ever! They won't understand and they might try to hurt you."

Perfect couldn't understand why he was saying this again. "Who are you talkin' about?"

"Just don't say it no more, Perfect! Ever! To nobody! Promise me!"

"All right. I won't."

Perfect knew Bartimaeus loved her. She didn't see the big deal in others knowing she had what she thought every other girl had, but Bartimaeus's re-action convinced her never to speak about it again.

Sauntering home, Perfect asked a million other questions, none of which Bartimaeus heard. He tried to blot out what he knew, even to wipe the feeling from his hand, but he couldn't. Maybe he was mistaken, he considered again. Maybe what he had felt wasn't a penis but a . . . a . . . what? Nothing he re-called felt remotely similar, so he found himself unable to formulate the lie he needed so desperately.

Perfect didn't share his trauma. She couldn't figure out why, every few steps, he stumbled like old, drunk Sugar Baby. She thought that maybe he was hungry or fumbling over stones unseen. Yet, unable to take refuge in the material world, Bartimaeus walked in darkness, rushing to the comfort of his coffin, where he hoped God might clarify his confusion.

God didn't. In fact, God didn't say anything. Bartimaeus lay in total silence, waiting for God to send a vision of what he should do, but instead Bartimaeus drifted off to a vacuous sleep, only to be awakened by Mister knocking on the coffin.

"I can't sleep," he complained.

"Leave me alone!" Bartimaeus muttered. His voice sounded hollow and distant.

"But everybody else is 'sleep. I don't got nobody to talk to!"

Bartimaeus opened the top slowly as though rising from the dead. "What do you want?"

"I can't sleep."

"What do you want me to do about it?"

Mister shrugged. "I don't know. I thought that maybe you couldn't sleep, neither. Daddy said you don't know night from day."

Bartimaeus climbed from the coffin and whispered, "Come on, boy."

He took Mister's hand and felt his way to the front porch. The balmy night welcomed the brothers, offering a breeze a few degrees cooler than the ninety-degree air circulating in the living room.

"What chu wanna be when you grow up?" Mister asked.

Bartimaeus was in no mood for small talk. All he could think about was Perfect and his inability to help her. "I don't know. I ain't thought about it much."

"I wanna be a preacher," Mister volunteered. "You wanna know why?"

Bartimaeus nodded.

" 'Cause preachers get all the food they want! And they get the best of it, too. If Momma burn some o' de fried chicken, she don't neva give them pieces to Reverend Lindsey. She give 'em to us and give him the pretty pieces."

Bartimaeus said, "You s'pose to love God in order to preach."

"I do love God!" Mister said. "Plus, I like to talk. Aunt Gracie said I have the gift of gab."

It was true. Mister could speak for hours without pausing, and most people simply walked away when they tired of listening. Whether he'd preach or not was yet to be seen, but what was certain was that, whatever the occupation, he'd have to talk. He'd die otherwise.

"We gotta go back to bed now, boy," Bartimaeus said, interrupting Mister's disjointed discourse. Together, they reentered the house and returned to their respective sleeping places.

"Good night," Mister said kindly.

"Good night, boy," Bartimaeus returned, and began praying for Perfect's safety. He forgot, for the first time in his life, to ask God to restore his sight.

Chapter 13

At Perfect's eighth birthday party, Eva Mae told Caroline, "I know a secret you don't know." They and several other children sat around the Peaces' rectangular kitchen table, anticipating the homemade ice cream and cake Emma Jean had promised.

"Tell me!" Caroline murmured, tight-lipped.

Eva Mae smiled devilishly and raised her head like one marching in a parade. She never intended to tell Caroline the secret. Her joy was in taunting others with it. The power and authority she felt each time she broached the subject made her giggle and understand how insecure people are. She had determined, years ago, never to tell that she and Perfect were kissing buddies, because someone might find it objectionable and bring an end to their private joy.

Their intimacy always occurred in the same place—under the house, far away in the back corner. Because they had anointed the space with their sweat and innocence, it felt clean, honest, and sacred every time they entered. In school or church, Eva Mae would whisper, "See ya at *home*," speaking the final word sensually, and Perfect would smile, anticipating the moment. "You real pretty, Perfect Peace," Eva Mae always told her, and although Perfect didn't believe it, she loved hearing it. Emma Jean said it all the time, but she was her mother and she was supposed to say it, Perfect thought. When Eva Mae said it, Perfect heard something else in the words, something more convincing. It was as though Eva Mae's words were more sincere or more trustworthy, and Perfect began to believe Emma Jean precisely because of Eva Mae. Whenever the husband whispered the affirmation, Perfect giggled, freeing Eva Mae to kiss her repeatedly until Perfect lost count of how many times.

On one occasion, Perfect reached to tickle Eva Mae between her legs, but the husband refused. "You just relax," she said, pushing Perfect's trembling hand away. "I'm de husband, and I'm s'pose to make you feel good." Such altruism was strange to Perfect, who had certainly never witnessed Gus cater to any of Emma Jean's pleasures, but Perfect didn't mind. If Eva Mae preferred giving to receiving, then Perfect was fine with that. Where others might have been bored with such monotony, the girls enjoyed their respective roles and thanked Emma Jean silently for forcing them to play together that day in the sun.

Three days before the party, Emma Jean had strutted throughout the community with her hands cupped around her mouth, heralding Perfect's eighth birthday party like Gabriel proclaiming the birth of Christ. Folks rushed to their doors, wondering what in the world Emma Jean was screaming about. "Party! Party! Party!" her raspy voice belted. "Birthday party! Saturday afternoon! All children welcome! Bring gifts!!" Everyone knew it had to be Perfect's birthday since Emma Jean never made a fuss about any of the boys. Mothers smiled politely while simultaneously murmuring, "That bitch is crazy. She think that li'l heffa is better than otha kids 'round here." Children began to ask permission to attend.

Gus found the notion ridiculous. "Everybody got a birthday every year," he said, perceiving himself profound, "so what's so special 'bout Perfect's?"

"This is yo' daughter, man!" Emma Jean said, trying any angle she could to justify the expenses.

"I know who she is," Gus said. "I'm jes' wonderin' why we gotta make such a big hoopla 'bout her birthday."

" 'Cause she's a girl," Emma Jean said pitifully. "And girls need stuff like this."

"Why?"

"Because I said so!"

Gus shrugged.

The day before, Emma Jean had taken a shiny new quarter from Gus's overalls and given it to Perfect, who then bought enough yellow ribbon to decorate the entire living room and kitchen. Perfect rose early Saturday morning, too excited to sleep. After Emma Jean forced the menfolk up and out, Perfect cut the ribbon into foot-long strips, tied them in bows, and taped them everywhere she found a bare spot. She put three on Bartimaeus's coffin. Then, like God on the seventh day, she looked around the living room and said, "I like it."

As she swept the floor, she hummed a tune Eva Mae had taught inadvertently during their moments beneath the house. With the broom handle as partner, she danced—Fred Astaire style—sweeping many places repeatedly before scooping the dirt onto a piece of used cardboard and casting it out the back door. Perfect then shifted furniture, three inches to the right or two inches to the left, until she convinced herself that the room had been rearranged. "There," she said, and clapped excitedly.

She named aloud the guests she was sure about: "Eva Mae, Caroline, Christina, Joyce Ann, Bonita, Martha Jean, Angie Faye, Trutisha, Jackie, Sandy, Ethel Faye . . ." and she wondered what each girl would wear. Emma Jean told her not to worry—none of the other girls would be prettier than her—so Perfect focused on making the house something both she and Emma Jean would be proud of.

"What the hell?" Gus mumbled when he reentered the front room, rubbing his eyes as though having awakened in a foreign land. "Who did this?"

"Don't chu worry 'bout it, Mr. Gustavus Peace!" Emma Jean intervened before Perfect attempted to explain. "It looks real nice, baby. Real nice." She surveyed the room like a museum observer.

"This is gonna be the best party ever!" Perfect declared, skipping to the kitchen. "Can I help make the birthday cake, Momma?"

Emma Jean smiled warmly and toyed with Perfect's short plaits. "Of course you can, honey. But then we gotta do somethin' with that head o' yours."

"Okay," Perfect said, and retrieved the mixing bowl from the cupboard. She placed it on the table and waited. Olivia sat in the chair beside her.

"What about breakfast?" Gus asked, primarily for his and Authorly's sake.

Emma Jean's narrowed eyes made him wish he hadn't said anything. "You greedy niggas cain't go without breakfast fu one day? Don't y'all see all the work me and dis girl gotta do to git ready fu this party? Menfolk can be so selfish sometimes." Emma Jean shook her head.

"That mean we ain't gon' eat?"

She stared at Gus until he went away.

"Get four cups o' flour, baby," she told Perfect, "and pour it into the mixin' bowl. Then sift it."

"Why you gotta do that, Momma?" Perfect said as she obeyed.

"So yo' mixture won't be so lumpy. You want the cake to come out right, don't chu?"

"Yes, ma'am!" Perfect hollered. She sifted the flour carefully like one panning for gold. "I'm done!"

Emma Jean ran her fingers though the flour. "Good. Now put in two cups o' sugar, a tablespoon o' baking powder, and a teaspoon o' salt."

"Salt? You put salt in a cake?"

"Dat's right, girl. You didn't know dat?"

"No, ma'am. I thought a cake was s'pose to be sweet."

"It is, but you still gotta add a touch o' salt. I think it does somethin' with the baking powder."

"Oh." Perfect sighed and added the ingredients.

"Now mix it all up real good. And when you get through with that, add six eggs." Emma Jean smiled as her eyes moistened.

"What is it, Momma?"

"Nothin', chile. I jes' cain't believe my baby girl is growin' up." She clasped her hands over her mouth.

Perfect chuckled. "I'll always be yo' baby, Momma. That's what you always say."

"Yeah, but you ain't no baby no mo'. Seem like jes' yesterday you wuz layin' next to my tittie, suckin', and now you a big girl!"

Perfect stirred a bit too forcefully, splattering small portions of cake batter with each whip of her wrist.

"Take yo' time, honey," Emma Jean admonished tenderly. "Try not to spill nothin' or the cake won't be but so big."

"Yes, ma'am."

"And when you crack the eggs, crack 'em clean. We don't want no shells in the batter if we can help it." Emma Jean began putting dishes away.

"Momma, can I ask you somethin'?" Perfect murmured as she added the eggs. She slid from her knees to her bottom in the kitchen chair.

"Sure, baby. What is it?"

"Caroline told me I was gon' start bleedin' one day soon down between my legs. Is that true?"

Emma Jean tried to hide her trembling hands, but couldn't. She turned her back to Perfect, talking slowly in hopes that a sensible lie might materialize.

"Some women do," she began, "and some women don't. Everybody's different." She braced herself for the next question.

"Then why do some women bleed?" Perfect continued stirring the batter freely.

"Um . . . some women . . . bleed to keep . . . um . . . pure." Emma Jean cleared her throat. She glanced at the white-faced image of Jesus hanging over the living room sofa. "Some women have to be reminded of the sacrifice Christ made for them. Other women never forget."

Emma Jean knew her explanation made no sense, but she couldn't think of anything else to say. People always shut up after preachers mention the cross and the blood, and Emma Jean hoped Perfect would do the same.

"Do some men bleed, too?"

"No."

"Why not? Don't some of them fugit, too?"

Emma Jean's confidence was disintegrating. "I don't know what happens to men who fugit 'cause I ain't no man. You jes' be sure to love the Lord and remember, and you'll be fine." She turned abruptly. "And anyway, a lady don't talk about her personal business to otha folks. Tell Caroline that!"

Perfect didn't understand Emma Jean's sudden wrath, but she was determined never to bleed if she could help it.

Emma Jean added, "Every woman got her own particular life, honey, and no two womens is de same. Jes' stick with de Lawd and you'll be fine. That's why I named you Perfect."

She smiled and said, "Yes, ma'am."

Emma Jean sighed.

Once the cake rested in the stove, Perfect went to the picture of Christ hanging above the living room sofa. "I love you," she whispered to it. "Thank you for bleeding so I don't have to." She then ran her finger across the picture, wondering how anybody could stand to have nails driven through their palms and ankles without dying from pain. She guessed that's why he was so special—'cause he could endure what others couldn't. And he wasn't even crying! Yes, she loved his fortitude and his soft countenance, especially in the midst of tragedy. And to think, as preachers demanded, that he died for her? Especially for *her*? Perfect smiled at the picture and promised never to let the sun set without acknowledging him. If Caroline broached the subject again, she'd tell her all about Christ and that he could keep her from bleeding, too.

Perfect's party guests represented the who's who of Swamp Creek's black elite. Mamie Cunningham's granddaughter Christina was there, taking notes to report back to her grandmother. "If the food don't look right, don't eat it, honey," Mamie had instructed. "Emma Jean can sing, but she sho can't cook!" Christina gave Perfect a brand-new olive green scarf from Morrison's, the kind only white girls usually wore, and Emma Jean would have been elated except that it came from Mamie. "Always tryin' to outdo otha folks," Emma Jean muttered. Then she said more loudly, "Tell your grandmother thank you. We sho do 'preciate it." Christina was a pretty, milk chocolate–colored child with long, thick Indian-like hair, and she liked Perfect. That's why Emma Jean liked her. The girls would have been friends if Emma Jean and Miss Mamie got along, but since they didn't, Perfect and Christina waved vigorously as their parents pulled them in opposite directions.

The Chambers twins came, much to Emma Jean's surprise. They were nice boys, but usually they never played with any of the local kids. Authorly said that, for nine-year-old boys, they were mighty soft, and, in fact, only came to the party because they could dress up and sit around looking cute. They were the only black boys in Swamp Creek who went to school absolutely every single day and whose hands were not scarred by physical labor. Whenever you saw one, you saw the other. Authorly wanted some ten-year-old boy to whip their asses and toughen them up a bit, but they probably wouldn't fight back, he thought. And the only thing worse than a crying sissy country boy was two of them. Didn't they see they were the only boys at the party?

"What's the secret?" Caroline leaned over and asked Eva Mae. Other children seemed not to notice.

Eva Mae stuck out her tongue. "Ain't tellin'."

"Come on! Tell me!"

Perfect noticed the private exchange and said, "Why don't we play something everybody can play?"

"That sounds fun!" Eva Mae said, glad to be rescued from Caroline's begging.

"Then y'all go outside for a while," Emma Jean said, "but don't get dirty. The party's jes' beginning."

Gus and the brothers wanted to know when it would end. They were starving and, even if there was extra cake and ice cream, they wanted real food. Authorly and James Earl tried to ignore their hunger as they repaired the barbed-wire fence and Sol and Mister laughed at Woody's jokes while weeding the vegetable garden. Gus walked with Bartimaeus, teaching him how to feel his way around the world without fear.

"You hear the chillen playin'?"

"Yessir," Bartimaeus said.

"Where they at?"

He turned to his left and pointed.

"Good. Good. Now where is that bird?"

Bartimaeus pointed to a treetop far to the right.

"Good. You doin' good. Now. You gotta be able to walk around in all o' this without bein' scared you gon' bump into everything. All you gotta do is listen. I been teachin' you this kinda stuff since you was little, so you gotta start doin' it on yo' own now. I know you blind, but you still gotta be a man."

Bartimaeus nodded.

"Go get that bucket from under the old cypress tree in the backyard and bring it back to me. Picture everything in yo' head. You know where the house is and you know everything 'round it."

Bartimaeus walked with outstretched arms. The children suspended their play and watched as though beholding a performance. When he disappeared behind the house, they waited, unsure of what he was doing, but somehow aware that the show wasn't over. His return with the bucket made them jittery, and when he placed it before Gus, only inches from where his father stood, Gus shouted, "Yes!" and the children cheered. Gus told them to return to their play.

"How 'bout hide-and-seek?" Caroline suggested. "We can play that without gettin' dirty."

Eva Mae hated hide-and-seek, but consented for everyone else's sake. Her desire was to take her "wife" home and say happy birthday in her own private way. Of course she couldn't do that, at least not in the moment, so she hid in obvious places, allowing other kids to find her and deem themselves clever.

"Cake's ready, children!" Emma Jean called from the porch. "Come and get it!"

"Yeah!" they screamed, and herded past her into the house. Just as she turned to reenter, Sugar Baby declared from the road, "A change is a-comin'! A change is a-comin'!"

"Go home, fool!" Emma Jean shouted before remembering he didn't have one. "This party ain't for grown folks and it sho ain't for drunk folks!"

"He's all right," Gus yelled. "He can't hurt nothin'."

"Yes he can! He might scare the children away."

"Oh, stop it, woman. You know better'n that. Ain't nobody scared o' Sugar Baby. Go 'head and have the party. I'll take care o' him."

Emma Jean let the screen door slam. Then she brightened and said, "Okay, children. Everyone have a seat."

The children chatted excitedly as they sat around the table. Emma Jean placed a three-layer lemon cake before them, complete with chocolate icing and eight candles bunched in the center. Their "oohs" and "ohs" were precisely what she had hoped to elicit.

"Okay, children." Emma Jean clapped. "Now's the moment we been waitin' for."

They bounced in their chairs with exhilaration.

"But first we have to sing 'Happy Birthday.' So here we go."

The children's shrill voices gave Gus and the boys hope that the party was coming to an end.

"Now, Perfect, you have to make a wish and blow out the candles. If you don't blow them out all at once, the wish won't come true, so take a deep breath and blow hard as you can."

Having nothing she longed for, Perfect snuggled Olivia in her lap, closed her eyes, and asked God to restore Bartimaeus's sight. Then she blew out all the candles.

"Yeah!" the children shouted.

"Don't tell nobody what you wished for," Emma Jean warned, "or else it won't come true."

She served each child a hearty slice of cake, hoping it tasted as good as it looked. Mamie would certainly let her know. Then she scooped homemade vanilla ice cream from the churn and lumped it atop each slice. The eager children ate and asked for more.

Emma Jean stepped back, folded her arms, and smiled with pride. This was the party she had envisioned forty years earlier. The yellow ribbons, chocolate-frosted cake, neighborhood friends, homemade ice cream . . . she had dreamed it all. Why couldn't Mae Helen have done this? It wouldn't have cost much and, unlike Perfect, Emma Jean had promised to clean up afterward. Was it too much to ask for a simple birthday party, where a girl could feel special and loved for a change? Emma Jean's anger rose until she resolved to simply let it go. What mattered most was that Perfect had been given the party, which Emma Jean had been denied, and now, Emma Jean chuckled, Mae Helen could *really* go to hell.

"Momma!" Mister screamed from outside. "Here come Aunt Gracie and Aunt Pearlie!"

"Pearlie?" Emma Jean burbled. "What Pearlie doin' here?" The last time her oldest sister had been to the Peace house was a week after Emma Jean ran their mother away.

The sisters knocked like traveling missionaries, afraid their presence might be unwelcome.

"Hey in there," Gracie called.

Emma Jean met them on the porch without taking her eyes off of Pearlie. The weight she had gained was unbelievable, but Emma Jean decided not to mention it. "Well. Ain't this a surprise."

Pearlie appeared not to have heard her.

"The party's almost over now," Emma Jean said. "The least y'all coulda done was try to make it on time for your niece's eighth . . ." Emma Jean noticed that something was wrong. "What is it?"

Pearlie and Gracie joined hands. "Momma died this morning, Emma Jean. She's gone."

Emma Jean fought the tears she had thought wouldn't come. "Oh wow." She sat in a nearby chair.

"She had been in pain so long. Almost ten years. But she's resting now." Gracie rubbed Emma Jean's back.

Emma Jean wiped her eyes. "This is good!"

"Excuse me?" Pearlie said in disbelief.

"Now, she's gone to meet her maker—whoever that is!" Emma Jean smirked.

"Emma Jean, don't do this," Gracie said. "It's okay to hurt. I know you and Momma didn't get along, but don't do this now."

"Don't do what?" Emma Jean asked indignantly. "Don't be happy that I'm finally free?"

"Momma wasn't your enemy, Emma Jean."

"The hell she wasn't! You don't remember how she treated me? Huh?"

Pearlie said, "Nobody's perfect, Emma Jean, but Momma tried her best."

Emma Jean stepped toward Pearlie, but Gracie halted her approach. "Is you serious, Pearlie?" Emma Jean said. "You gon' stand on my porch and tell me that Momma did her best by me?" Emma Jean's anger radiated.

"Well, she's dead now anyway, so ain't no need in bein' mad," Pearlie sneered.

"You right about that! I ain't mad about nothin'! In fact, I'm 'bout glad as I can be!" She danced a two-step across the porch.

"I don't have to stand here and watch this . . . this . . ."

"This what! Huh? This what?"

"This performance!" Pearlie joined the shouting match. "Fine! You didn't like her, and, yes, we all know you wasn't her favorite, either, but you don't even respect the dead?"

"Aw shit!" Emma Jean said, smacking her lips. "It's the livin' who need respect. What the dead gon' do with it?"

"Oh, forget about it!" Pearlie said, and hobbled away.

Gracie sniffled. "You're still our sister, Emma Jean, and we thought you'd want to know. That's why we came." She descended the front steps.

"Well, now I know."

"Would you do me one favor, sister?" Gracie turned and asked. "Please?"

Emma Jean stared and waited.

"Come to the funeral. I know you don't owe it to her and I know you've probably promised yourself you wouldn't, but please come. Please."

"You gotta be kiddin'! You got the nerve to ask me to stand over that woman's dead body with everything she did to me? You askin' me to respect her after she treated me like shit? Gracie Mae Hurt, you got some nerve!" Emma Jean was hysterical. "I can't believe you askin' me this! I just can't believe it. You know what she did to me! You know!" Emma Jean's finger trembled at the tip of Gracie's nose. "And still you gon' ask me to come watch folk lie about how great she was? What I went through all dem years wasn't enough?"

"Momma?" Perfect whimpered, standing with the other children at the screen door. "What about my party?"

Emma Jean didn't hear her. "Well, my answer is hell naw! I'll be goddamn if I put on good clothes to watch de rest o' y'all turn that woman into the saint she ain't! She was mean, Gracie! And hateful! At least to me. And ain't no way on God's blessed earth I'm carryin' my ass to no funeral for her. Shit! I didn't go see her when she was livin', so I sho ain't goin' now!"

"But this will be your last chance, Emma Jean, and I just didn't want—"

"She beat me, Gracie! Don't you remember that?" Emma Jean was screaming. "She slammed a cast-iron skillet upside my head! And, now, I'm s'pose to feel sorry that she's dead? Huh? I'm s'pose to make everybody 'round here believe she was a good mother to me? Well, she wunnit! And I'ma tell you this: I ain't neva cussed nobody out, at least not all the way out, in my whole life but I sware 'fo God I'll cuss yo' ass out today if you ask me that again!"

Some of the children were crying.

"I'll be goddamned if you see me at that woman's funeral! Goddamned!" Emma Jean stormed past the children into her bedroom and collapsed across the bed. She hated that tears always came when she was angry. And why hadn't she smacked Pearlie across the face? And why did Mae Helen have to die right before Perfect's birthday?

Emma Jean collected herself and returned to the living room. Gracie was comforting the children as Perfect pouted that her birthday party had been ruined.

"Everything's fine, honey," Emma Jean said, fluffing her matted hair. "Momma just . . . um . . . had a moment, but she's fine now. Anyone for more ice cream and cake?"

The children's confusion wasn't so assuaged. They stood statuesque as though afraid to speak or move.

"Oh come on, children," Emma Jean said. "Relax. Everything's fine. Come back and finish your cake."

In slow motion, the children returned to the table and sat quietly. A few tried to nibble on soggy cake, but most simply wanted to go home.

"Miss Emma Jean?" Christina whispered. "I think I better be gettin' on now. I gotta do my chores before dark."

The others rode her courage, offering similar excuses.

"No!" Emma Jean cried. "You can't leave yet! We haven't even opened all the presents! And what about the games you're supposed to play?"

No one said anything. Perfect folded her arms in disgust.

"Momma told me not to stay too long. The sun'll be goin' down pretty soon." Christina tried to smile, but didn't quite manage.

Eva Mae said, "We'll come back and play another time. We promise. I think we all better be gettin' on home."

The children thanked Emma Jean for the party and promised to tell their parents how much fun they had had. Perfect went to her room and cried.

"All right," Gracie said, once the children were gone, "you ain't gotta come. But I'm afraid you'll regret it later. Funerals have a way of bringing closure to things."

"Gracie, I'm through talkin' about this. My baby's birthday party done been ruined and now I gotta get her back together. Whatever you and Pearlie wanna do is fine with me, 'cause I don't want nothin' to do with no funeral. Y'all can throw her in the ground for all I care."

Gracie left. She vowed never to press Emma Jean again about her feelings for Mae Helen. If Emma Jean wanted to carry hatred in her heart, Gracie resolved to let her.

Chapter 14

*Am I gonna start bleeding down there? Am I gonna start bleeding down there?
Am I gonna start bleeding down there?*

Emma Jean couldn't get the echo out of her mind. She knew what it meant:
her scheme was coming to an end. What did big-mouth Caroline know about
a woman's period anyway? Nasty heffa. She was just like her nosy momma,
Emma Jean thought, always talking about things she didn't have any business
talking about. Now Perfect was asking questions that should've come years
later.

"Oh well," Emma Jean murmured, and shrugged. All of this was inevitable.
It was only a matter of time before the secret began to unravel, and Emma
Jean didn't want to find herself in a whirlwind of lies from which she couldn't
escape. But what could she do now? Who would be sympathetic after all
these years? Gus would probably run to the Jordan and scream his head off,
she considered, but what about the brothers? What would Authorly say?

Emma Jean had to do something. She couldn't just watch her life disinte-
grate. After all, she was Emma Jean Hurt—well, Peace now—and if she were
going to give up on life, she would have done that a long time ago.

Yes, she had to take control of things, especially with that damn Eva Mae
around. Caroline was bad enough, Emma Jean thought, but Eva Mae was
downright dangerous. Emma Jean hadn't said anything, but she knew about
Eva Mae and Perfect's disappearances. She didn't know where they went or
what they did, and at first it didn't trouble her. They were both little girls, she
told herself, so what harm could they do? But then, one day, she called for
them, and saw the look of deception on Eva Mae's face. Clearly the child was

hiding something, but Emma Jean couldn't discern what it was. She almost asked Eva Mae, *What you and Perfect be doin' down there?* but changed her mind, not wanting to disturb their obvious affinity. Only Perfect's oblivious expressions calmed Emma Jean's suspicions and convinced her that there was nothing to worry about.

That was then. The day of Perfect's party, Emma Jean's mistrust of Eva Mae resurfaced. What was she whispering to Caroline about? It had something to do with Perfect, Emma Jean guessed, since Eva Mae stared at Perfect throughout the party as though she owned her. *Yes, that girl is dangerous*, Emma Jean reminded herself. What if she knew already? What if she was taunting Caroline with the secret only Emma Jean—and Henrietta—was supposed to know? What if Eva Mae, with her fast self, had convinced Perfect to undress, and now was surreptitiously planning to make a public spectacle of her? Emma Jean shuddered at the thought. She couldn't let anyone hurt her baby. There was only one way to protect Perfect, and Emma Jean had to do it before someone else did.

"What's the matter with Momma?" Mister asked Authorly the day after Perfect's party. They were gathered for the Sunday meal. "Why ain't she eatin'?"

"I don't know," Authorly said with a drumstick in each hand. He'd noted her strangeness in church, the way she looked out the window as though in another time and place, and decided he'd ask her about it later. But now he sensed she wanted to be left alone.

Sitting on the couch with her forehead buried into both palms, Emma Jean knew there was no turning back. She wasn't afraid for herself. Her entire life had been a struggle. It was Perfect she was worried about. Was she as strong as she'd need to be? Could she withstand the frowns and verbal abuse sure to come? She was only a little girl, Emma Jean told herself. But she had to do it. It was the only way to give Perfect a life, some hope that would sustain her, regardless of what happened to Emma Jean. It was what she knew had to be done.

She'd seen Eva Mae wink at Perfect during church and that's when she decided she couldn't wait any longer. There was something that girl knew and Emma Jean feared she'd tell it. Maybe Eva Mae didn't know everything—she couldn't have known *everything*—but she knew something. And if it was what Emma Jean feared, and if Eva Mae told, her whole family would be ruined and nobody would ever trust her again. No, she had to act today. It couldn't wait.

Dreading the moment like Sisyphus must have dreaded another rolling of the stone, Emma Jean rose and said, "Perfect, honey, come with me." She slung a bag over her shoulder and walked out the front door without ever turning back.

The boys gathered at the screen and watched Perfect walk behind Emma Jean until both vanished down the road. Emma Jean turned and led Perfect into the forest. She hadn't had the time to grab Olivia, and she would soon regret having left her behind. Perfect thought that maybe they were headed to the Jordan for some reason.

"Sit on that stump there," Emma Jean said, and pointed.

"Okay, Momma."

Emma Jean couldn't face her. All she could think about was what she was prepared to do and whether Perfect could handle it. She paced several seconds with her eyes closed, then said, "Listen, sweetie. Momma's got somethin' to tell you, and I need you to hear me. This ain't gon' be easy, but it's gon' be okay. At least afterwhile."

Perfect smiled. "Is this about my birthday party yesterday? I know it was ruined, but it's okay. We can always have another one if you want to."

"No, honey, this ain't got nothin' to do with that." Emma Jean chewed her thumbnail and continued, "This got to do with you. Just you."

"What about me, Momma?"

Emma Jean looked heavenward and asked for strength. "You just gotta hear what I'm 'bout to say and believe I wouldn't never do nothin' to hurt you. I swear I wouldn't."

"I know." Perfect nodded.

"And I'm doin' this for your own good. You understand that, don't you?"

"Yes, ma'am." Perfect had no idea what Emma Jean was talking about.

"This ain't gon' be easy, sweetie," she repeated, "but it's the only way."

"Okay."

Emma Jean knelt. "Years ago, I did . . . um . . . something I shouldn't have done."

Perfect frowned. "What?"

"And I need to fix it now. So no one hurts you in the future."

Perfect's blank stare made Emma Jean's purging difficult. "See, honey . . . um . . . when you was born I wanted a little girl so bad I woulda done anything to get one."

"Then you got one!"

"Um . . . yes . . . well . . . sorta."

"Whatcha mean?"

Emma Jean huffed and shook her head. "I mean that . . . um . . . I wanted a girl so bad that I . . . um . . ."

"What, Momma? You can tell me anything."

". . . that I . . . um . . . made you into one." She glanced into Perfect's eyes and saw nothing but confusion. Then she reached for her small, soft hands and clutched them harder than she had intended.

"I know this don't make no sense, baby, but you gotta know. Before somebody else tell you."

Perfect's brow furrowed. "Tell me what?"

Emma Jean blurted, "That you ain't no girl!"

"What do you mean, Momma? Of course I'm a girl. I got long hair and everything."

Emma Jean stood. "Listen, Perfect. You been thinkin' you a girl yo' whole life. I understand that, because that's how I raised you, but you wunnit born that way."

"Huh?" Perfect began to tear up. "I don't understand, Momma."

Emma Jean struggled to remain composed. "I know you don't, baby, but just listen to what I'm telling you."

"I ain't no girl?" Perfect whimpered.

"No. Not really. I mean, no. When you was born I decided to raise you as a girl 'cause I wanted one so bad, but—"

"Then what am I?" Perfect cried.

"You're a boy. That's what you are." Emma Jean covered her mouth at the horror of it all.

"No I'm not! I'm a girl. Just like you."

"Honey, listen," Emma Jean tried to explain. "I know you're confused and don't none of this make much sense to you right now, but you gotta believe me. You was meant to be a boy."

"But I don't wanna be no boy!"

"It don't make no difference what you want!" Emma Jean screeched. "You was born a boy. I *made* you a girl, but that ain't what you was suppose to be."

"How you know, Momma? Huh? How you know?"

Emma Jean began unbuttoning her dress.

"I like bein' a girl and havin' pretty things and stuff. You even said yourself that I was a girl and that I was gon' grow up and marry a handsome man and—"

"I know what I said, Perfect," Emma Jean said as she lifted her dress over her head. "But I was wrong. I shouldn't o' said those things to you. You ain't no girl."

"Yes I am, Momma!" Perfect was inconsolable.

"No, you ain't!"

Perfect nodded and sobbed.

Emma Jean pointed to her panties and said, "This is what girls have!"

Perfect gawked. Where was the lump?

"Only boys have what you have. I'm sorry, honey. I'm really, really sorry."

She hadn't meant to be crude, but she couldn't think of another way to convince Perfect of the truth.

"Now. I know this ain't easy, but we can survive it," Emma Jean said, pulling her dress back over her head. "If I hadn't told you, somebody else would've, and then you'd been real upset with me, and you probably wouldn't ever trust me again. This way, you heard the truth from me. I know I was wrong, but this is the best I can do now. Trust me. I'm lovin' you more right now than I ever have before."

Perfect hadn't said a word since beholding Emma Jean's nakedness. Where was her *thing*? She thought desperately. It couldn't be true, could it? Was she really supposed to be a *boy*?

"So from now on, you gon' be a boy. A handsome little black boy. It'll be strange at first, but you'll get used to it, and this'll all be over afterwhile."

"But, Momma, I—"

"Shut up! I done told you the truth and ain't no more to say about it. I'm sorry for what I did, and this is the only way I know to fix it." Her tone softened. "I know this hurts, Perfect, but if somebody else told you, you wouldn't ever forgive me. You might be mad at me now, but you'll thank me one day for telling you the truth."

"But I cain't be no boy!"

"Yes, you can. And you will. We gon' start with this." She extracted a battered pair of overalls from the bag. "Here. Put 'em on."

Perfect sat transfixed.

"I said, put 'em on!"

She received the overalls with tremulous hands. Emma Jean lifted Perfect's dress and manipulated it over her head. "Put these on first."

Perfect wept as she removed her panties and slid on a brand-new pair of boy's underwear. They felt thick and heavy, and Perfect didn't like them, but

she was too perplexed to argue. She needed Olivia now. Someone who understood her. Someone who could verify that, in fact, she was a girl and had always been.

"Now. Step into these." Emma Jean held open the overalls as Perfect
obeyed. "Good. You're gonna be fine." Emma Jean buckled the straps.

Perfect stared at her mother as though she had never seen her. Was this
some sort of joke? Why was Emma Jean doing this? Perfect couldn't be a boy
for real. Not really. Could she?

"Now. One more thing."

Emma Jean motioned for Perfect to sit, and, like a robotic zombie, she
complied. Her tears continued to flow, but the sobbing had ceased. She gazed
straight ahead as though out of touch with reality. The straps of the overalls
drooped over her thin shoulders, and she still wasn't sure why Emma Jean
was doing this to her.

After rummaging through the bag, Emma Jean removed a pair of scissors
and stood behind the paralyzed child. "This hurts me more than it does you.
Believe me. I wish there was another way, but there ain't. If I didn't do this
now, you'd hate me later, and I couldn't live with that. This way, we'll go
through everything together." She removed the ribbons from Perfect's hair
and began to clip it away in clusters. Stray pieces fell slowly, quietly across her
shoulders and onto her lap, and all Perfect could do was weep. She couldn't
imagine what she'd look like without hair, but she had a feeling others
wouldn't call her pretty anymore. "You gon' always be my baby," Emma Jean
assured her. "Don't make no difference if you a girl or boy." She cut the hair
as short as she could manage with a pair of scissors, then tried her best to
shape it. "There. That'll do for now." She stepped from behind Perfect and
inspected her work. "You real handsome." She collected the clumps of hair
and put them in the bag. Perfect never moved.

Emma Jean then pulled her to her feet. "All right. This is a new beginning.
You a boy now. It ain't got to be hard 'less you make it hard. It'll feel a little
awkward at first, but, like I said, you'll get used to it. Now wipe your face and
let's go."

Emma Jean was speaking jibberish for all Perfect knew. She felt like un-
wanted lint, picked and, tossed to the wind without a care. What would her
brothers say? Wouldn't they ask where their sister had gone?

Every few steps, Perfect stumbled or bumped into trees as Emma Jean
dragged her home. Years later, she would try to recall exactly how the transi-

tion had occurred, only to find a blank space in her memory where details should have been. All she remembered was crying and begging her mother to stop—had she actually said it or did she just think it?—but Emma Jean was determined to accomplish the mission at hand. She had decided that Perfect's life as a girl was over, so, without warning or preamble, she ended it—just like that. That's what she remembered. And her life was never the same again.

Emma Jean had practiced what she would say to Gus and the boys, but when she stepped through the door, her mind went blank. Authorly was the first to notice, and his "Oh shit!" captured everyone's attention.

Gus turned, prepared to slap Authorly in the mouth, but froze when he saw his distorted daughter.

"Everyone," Emma Jean announced slowly, "ain't no easy way to say this, so I'm just gon' say it." She positioned Perfect in front of her and rested her hands on Perfect's shoulders.

Mister's mouth fell open. His brothers stared and waited. Gus glanced from Perfect to Emma Jean, unable to imagine why someone had done this to his baby girl. He stood slowly.

Gus's facial contortions ruined Emma Jean's resolve. She had planned to tell the truth, and then to ask the men for forgiveness. Simple as that. It would be awkward, she knew, but she could endure it. She hadn't planned for Gus to rise and gape at her like one prepared to destroy her if her explanation wasn't sufficient.

"When Perfect was born," Emma Jean muttered, "I wanted a girl. Gus, you remember. I always wanted girls, but I didn't have none. You boys was fine, but I needed a girl. Someone I could dress up and make feel pretty. You know what I mean?" She tried to smile, but no one smiled in return. "So I did . . . something I shouldn't've done." Her voice broke. Perfect had been crying the entire time. "I lied. I told y'all the child was a girl, but it wasn't." She dropped her head. "It was a boy."

Now Bartimaeus understood.

Gus inched forward in slow motion, studying Emma Jean's face.

"I needed a girl!" she proclaimed. "Cain't you understand that? Every mother wants a girl. It's a woman's dream."

"What?" Gus whispered in fury. "You did what?" He was approaching like a starving lioness before the kill.

"Gus, listen. Please. I know this don't make much sense to you right now, but you gotta try to understand where I was then."

"I ain't understandin' nothin' you sayin,' woman!" he screamed. Authorly stood beside him.

"I'm sorry," Emma Jean whined. "I didn't mean for it to happen like this. It just got out of hand."

Gus lifted Perfect's bowed head and, for the first time, saw his own reflection, although he still didn't believe what Emma Jean was saying.

"You lyin', Emma Jean. My baby girl ain't no boy."

Authorly touched his father's shoulder, but Gus jerked away violently.

"Do you think I'd lie about something like this, man?"

Gus looked at Perfect and said, "You my little girl. You gon' always be my little girl, and ain't nothin' gon' change that."

"Stop, Gus! Listen to what I'm sayin'! I lied to you, I lied to everybody when this child was born 'cause I needed a girl. I knew it couldn't last forever, but I—"

Gus slapped Emma Jean so hard the boys gasped and held their breaths. Authorly stepped toward him, but the look in Gus's eyes made the boy halt.

"I don't know what you done done," he whispered vehemently, "but this ain't no boy." His pointed finger trembled.

Emma Jean sobbed and nodded. "Yes, it is, Gus. Yes it is. I'm sorry. I didn't know it would do this to you. I never knew you even wanted a girl."

"I wanted a girl when I got one!" he shouted. "Now I don't know why you cut her hair off and I don't know why she got on them clothes—"

" 'Cause he's a boy, Gus," Emma Jean sniffled. "He's a boy."

Gus's eyes watered and his mouth quivered. "If what you sayin' is true, you prove it to me right now."

"I'm tellin' you—"

"Don't *tell* me nothin'! I said prove it!"

"But the only way you gon' know for sure—"

Suddenly he turned to Perfect. "Take them clothes off."

"Oh no, honey. Don't do this. Not now. Don't embarrass him in front o' his brothers. He ain't ready for nothin' like that."

"I said, take them damn clothes off!"

Emma Jean reached to assist, but Gus wouldn't allow it.

"Not you!" He pushed her hands away. "You," he said to Perfect. "You do it yo'self."

Perfect submitted, dropping his overalls to the floor. Only his underwear remained. Gus thought he saw a bulge, but was still unsatisfied.

"Take 'em off," he demanded.

"Please, Gus, don't do this! Not in front of the boys! Take him in the room or outside, but don't—"

"Shut the hell up, Emma Jean!"

Perfect's sobbing returned as he lowered his underwear to his ankles.

When Gus saw the miniature penis, he screamed, "No! Oh God, no!" and crumpled to his knees. Authorly embraced him.

The brothers looked on in disbelief.

"I'm sorry! I'm so, so sorry!" Emma Jean repeated. "If I could do it all over again, I'd do it different." She knelt beside Gus. "Baby, I know you upset, but please try to understand."

Gus lunged at her before Authorly could restrain him. He smacked Emma Jean's face three or four times, then pinned her neck to the floor with his thick, rough hands. "What did you do this for! You ain't got no right to do nobody like this! What the hell is wrong with you!" Emma Jean couldn't breathe. "You didn't have to do this!" He might have strangled her to death had Authorly not jumped on Gus's back and, with Woody's assistance, wrestled Gus's hands away from her throat.

Emma Jean squirmed upon the floor in breathless agony. Perfect had closed his eyes once he removed his underwear, and never knew that it was Mister who had replaced them.

Gus sat panting in the middle of the living room floor. Emma Jean's heavy gasping meant nothing to him. A boy? Perfect was a boy? All these years he had been kissing a boy? He thought of Perfect in his lap and shook his head. Gus had absolutely no way to comprehend what, now, he couldn't deny—he had seen the penis himself. How had Emma Jean done it? How had she lied to him—and everyone else—without detection? Why didn't he suspect something? He had never been clever, he admitted, but shouldn't a father know instinctively about his own kids? Shouldn't he at least have *sensed* that something was different?

Mister escorted Perfect to the sofa and wiped his face with a ball of tissue. His quivering elicited Mister's sympathy and caused him to whisper, "Just be still. It's gonna be okay. Don't say nothin' right now. Just be quiet."

Perfect nodded. His uneven, partially straight, stubby hair made him look as though he had been in a brawl and lost badly. Wedged between Mister and Sol, who kept looking at him sympathetically, Perfect watched Emma Jean crawl into the bedroom and kick the door closed behind her. As the rains of

'48 began, Gus exited clumsily, tripping over the upturned edge of the bat-tered living room rug, but never made it to the Jordan. Too angry and con-fused to purge, he simply escaped to the barn and shouted every curse word he knew instead of murdering the mother of his children. With no one to guide him, Bartimaeus skipped the cleansing, too, and wept openly, right in the middle of the living room, about all the ways he could have protected his family. Especially Gus. He didn't deserve this. He was a good daddy, Barti-maeus thought, who worked hard and treated people kindly. And now Gus was devastated, all because Bartimaeus was too afraid to act.

An hour later, Authorly gathered the brothers together in the living room. He sat in the chair opposite the sofa and, with the coffin/coffee table between them, said, "Woody, Sol, Mister, James Earl, Bartimaeus . . . we got ourselves another brother. I ain't sho how this happened, but we all know it's true. Can't nobody deny that. We done seen it for ourselves. Ain't nothin' nobody can do about it now but accept it and keep on livin'."

Perfect never lifted his head. He knew he wasn't beautiful anymore. His brothers' energies convinced him that, now, he was ordinary, simple, common just like them. It was strange to Perfect how his world was shifting without his consent. He didn't feel safe like he once did in his brothers' presence. Sitting on the sofa shivering, with his head practically touching his knees, he felt his previous life ooze away as his brothers ushered him into a more harsh, less sympathetic reality. And they did this without uttering a word. Perfect sensed that if he cried now, Authorly's normally protective gaze would be replaced with something more corrective, so Perfect trembled and covered his mouth. What he really wanted was to run and hide in Emma Jean's bosom, but some-how he knew that wasn't an option. Who would touch and hold him now? Usually when he cried, someone embraced him and reassured his heart, but now all hands avoided him. That's how he knew he was different. Or no longer different. His pain was insignificant to his brothers and, for the first time in his life, he was responsible for his own healing.

Sol dragged his heavy heart to the edge of the porch and sang sweetly, "Sometimes I feel like a motherless chiiiiild, sometimes I feel like a mother-less chiiiiiild, sometimes I feel like a motherless child, a looooong way from hooooome, a loooooong way from home," while Perfect sat transfixed in a sea of sorrow.

Chapter 15

Moments later, Authorly knocked on Emma Jean's bedroom door. "Momma?" he whispered, then entered uninvited.

Emma Jean was curled in a fetal position upon the floor. She had tried to lift herself to the bed, but simply didn't have the strength. Gus had caught her off guard. She didn't know he had it in him to fight, but now she knew. He would've killed her, she was certain, had Authorly and Woody not intervened. Now she couldn't help but wonder what Gus might do when the rains ended.

"You all right, Momma?"

Her groan revealed that at least she was alive. Authorly lifted her as though carrying a new bride across a threshold and laid her gently upon the bed. He saw where Gus's fingernails had scratched her neck, and he knew that, for a while, she'd be terrified of him. *Good*, Authorly thought. *She deserves everything she gets.*

Emma Jean cleared her throat and massaged her neck. "Thank you, son. I'm all right."

Authorly walked to the window and noticed Mister talking to Perfect in the yard. "What's wrong with you, Momma? Why would you do something like this?"

Emma Jean sighed. "I don't know, son. It made sense then, I guess. I'm not sayin' it was right, but it made so much more sense then than it does now."

"You lied to everybody, Momma." Authorly turned from the window. "And you made Perfect think he was somethin' he ain't."

"I know what I did, and I'm gon' have to live with it the rest o' my life. But I meant well."

"How? How could you do somethin' like that and mean well?"

" 'Cause I wanted a daughter. That's all. I know you can't understand that, but that's what I needed then. I didn't mean to mess up the child's life, and I certainly didn't mean to cause confusion in this family."

"Well, you did. And I'll never see you the same way again."

Emma Jean's eyes begged for forgiveness, but Authorly refused.

"I don't know how he'll ever survive this, Momma. And it's all your fault."

"He gon' survive it," Emma Jean assured him. "We jes' gotta help him. He'll grow up and everything'll be okay."

"Be okay? He ain't never gon' be okay."

"Sure he will. If people let him be."

"But they ain't! You know that!"

"You probably right, but still Perfect got to live. And if he's willin' to fight, he can live good. Anybody can live good—soon as they decide the world can kiss they ass. We jes' gotta help him be clear about it. Me, you, yo' brothers, Gus."

Authorly's frustration overwhelmed him. "Momma, I can't believe you did this." His head shook continuously. "I'll never forgive you for it."

"You'll understand one day."

"The only thing I'll ever understand is that you ain't the mother I thought you was."

Emma Jean's eyes moistened, but she didn't cry.

"And now you got the nerve to ask the rest of us to help him? After what you done did? You a piece o' work, Momma. That's for sure."

"Who you talkin' to, boy? You ain't grown!"

"I ain't tryin' to be grown. I'm just sayin' you don't have no right to ask nobody for nothin'."

"You can't tell me what rights I got! You ain't nothin' but a chile! Don't forget who the momma is here!"

Authorly turned away.

"I'm sayin' we gotta help the boy 'cause he gotta live, and right now he don't know how to live. You de strong one 'round here, Authorly, so you could do a lot for him if you would."

Authorly chuckled. "I don't believe this! You tellin' me it's my job to fix what you messed up?"

"No, it ain't yo' *job*," Emma Jean emphasized, "but I hope you do what you can. All the boys look up to you, so maybe you could teach Perfect a thing or two 'bout bein' a man."

"Wow. You don't have no shame at all, Momma, do you?"

"You just don't understand, son. That's all."

"I ain't tryin' to!" He stomped angrily toward the door, then turned. "You ain't sorry for none o' this? You don't feel bad 'bout nothin' you did?"

Emma Jean rolled over and said, "Don't come in here judgin' me, boy. You don't know what I done been through and you ain't got no right to talk to me like that. I know you confused and all, but—"

"Confused? I ain't confused! I'm *real* clear 'bout what you done done. *Real* clear! And, like you always say, God don't like ugly, so get ready."

"Don't you threaten me, boy! I done spent my whole life sufferin', so don't you never talk to me like that again!" Emma Jean declared. "I done lost my only daughter and here you come—"

"You didn't have no daughter, Momma! He was a boy from the beginnin'!"

"I know what he was!" Emma Jean screamed. "But he was still my daughter as long as he thought he was. I ain't callin' it right, boy, but it's what I needed. Maybe everybody in dis house gon' be mad at me for the rest of my life, but, goddamnit, don't tell me I didn't deserve it! You don't know enough about my life to tell me nothin'! Shit!"

Authorly left. Emma Jean was apparently referencing things he had no idea about, and, really, he didn't care. All he knew was that his little brother's life would be hell now, and it was all because of Emma Jean Peace.

Authorly joined Sol on the porch. His soothing tenor calmed Authorly's nerves. From a distance, he studied his two little brothers and wondered how in the world they'd ever get the girl out of Perfect. The haircut and over-alls didn't amend the sway of his narrow hips or harden his soft demeanor, and as Authorly recoiled with repulsion, he promised—for the sake of the family, not Emma Jean—to make a boy out of Perfect if it was the last thing he did.

In the barn, Gus shouted, "Goddamnit! Shit! I shoulda knowed!" as he paced across scattered hay and mounds of dried mule dung, trying unsuccessfully to determine how all of this had happened right under his nose. Really, he was cursing himself for having been naïve. What a poor excuse for a father he was, he told himself. How would Authorly or the others respect him now? And what the hell was wrong with Emma Jean! What human being could think of such a thing? He had let her live, he rationalized, only because the boys needed their mother. Otherwise, he would have sent her to her grave, right behind Mae Helen.

It was the image of Perfect's penis that Gus couldn't shake from his mind. There it was, right in front of Perfect, hanging limp like it did on every other boy, and the more Gus thought of it, the more enraged he became. "How dare Emma Jean do something like this!" he screamed. "And think I wunnit gon' be mad!" *What father wouldn't be?* he thought. She had to know the truth would come out eventually, didn't she? In his head, he heard Chester Sr. say, "You can't lie a lifetime, son. Either you gon' tell the truth, or the truth's gon' tell on you."

Maybe Emma Jean didn't understand the bond between a father and his son, Gus considered. Apparently she didn't know that a father's joy is shaping his son into himself, then watching his son do the same with his son. But how could he do that with Perfect? In Gus's heart, Perfect was still a girl, but of course he was really a boy. Could he ever be like other boys? Totally? Would he chop wood and guide the plow one day like his brothers? Would he actually grow into a man? *Perfect? A man?*

For now, all Gus could do was stomp and screech in frustration. Bartimaeus found his way to the barn, hoping to comfort his father by holding his hand or touching his shoulder, but each time he approached, Gus recoiled until Bartimaeus knew his father didn't want to be comforted. He wanted God to tell him how to father a boy who used to be a girl. He wanted God to show him how not to hate Emma Jean—forgiveness was out of the question— so his family wouldn't fall apart, and he wanted to believe that, one day, his baby boy would be normal. But he didn't believe it, and God didn't confirm it. So he swung his arms wildly and cursed the entire world for making him see that perfect people only existed in his mind. He loved each of his boys for their own uniqueness, but he had no room in his heart for a son who, only yesterday, had been his daughter.

Bartimaeus was grateful that, in the midst of the chaos, no one had asked him anything. He felt guilty now for having held his tongue when he should have spoken up. He could have saved Emma Jean from Gus's deadly wrath, he thought, and, maybe, if he had explained things better, Gus could've digested the truth a little easier. Now, what would become of Perfect? Even he would know soon enough that Bartimaeus had lied or at least concealed the truth from him, and how would he justify that? *I was trying to protect you* wouldn't make sense to one who got hurt worse when the truth was revealed.

And what would the brothers say if they knew he already knew? He would be called a liar, a deceiver—along with his mother—and no one would ever trust him again.

So Bartimaeus wept, alongside a befuddled father, for having proven himself an accomplice to his family's trauma. "I should've told Authorly," he murmured regretfully, sure that, if he had, he could have ushered the family through the details of Perfect's transition without anyone being strangled. Yet since he didn't, he'd have to live with the fact that whatever pain his baby brother endured was, at least partially, his fault.

Eventually, Gus calmed and joined Bartimaeus in the wailing. Unlike in past years, their voices, echoing throughout the barn, carried a bluesy tone. It was a low, raspy moan, like an Ella Fitzgerald and Louis Armstrong duet, with the patter of the rain keeping time. Sol stood on the porch, listening to the muffled performance, swaying and humming like a nightclub attendee, until remembering that the sound wasn't supposed to entertain. It was supposed to soothe the soul, he guessed, and prepare one to endure another year of human frailty and transgressions. So, as though returning from a daydream, he shook his head rapidly and watched the rain nurture the earth as the voices faded among the thunder. He noted that, unlike in previous years, Gus's and Bartimaeus's voices weren't erratic and out of sync, but rather complementary and accommodating to the hum of the rain and the occasional claps of thunder. Together, the combined voices of God and man created a natural, harmonic orchestra, which Sol found at once eerie and intriguing. He told himself that if Gus and Bartimaeus sounded like that each year, maybe he'd start going to the Jordan.

Swamp Creek residents became alarmed when, listening throughout the night, they failed to hear father and son crying in the wilderness. Most wondered what had happened. Like Sol, a few stood on the edges of their porches, staring through the downpour, wondering if somehow spring had decided not to come that year. As much as they had criticized him, they needed ole Gus Peace now to confirm that the world wasn't coming to an end. It was all a bad omen, they agreed privately. Few remembered any spring's arrival without Gus's lament at the river, and Miss Mamie told W. C. that something bad was going to happen. She could feel it, she said.

Only Sugar Baby understood. But since no one consulted him about anything, his foresight was his alone to enjoy. If any of the Peaces, especially Sol, had bothered to look just twenty feet beyond the cocoon of their trauma, they would have noticed Sugar Baby's blurry form, standing at the edge of the road, studying the Peace home like one trying to memorize its exact measurements. As Gus had done in previous years at the Jordan, Sugar Baby stood amid the watery torrent with arms outstretched, bellowing words that were immediately usurped by the wind and the rain. Gus heard snippets of the familiar voice, but convinced himself that it was all in his mind. Bartimaeus also thought he heard someone say, "Beware the blaze!" but, like his father, he dismissed it as mental rubbish since talk of a fire made no sense in the midst of a storm.

By nightfall, after the rains had drizzled to a mist, Bartimaeus and Gus exited the barn for the house. Gus was still furious with Emma Jean—and intended to tell her so—but that wasn't what troubled him. What troubled him was that he still didn't know how to treat Perfect. Should he embrace the child or leave him alone altogether? Wouldn't he be a sissy, at least at first? And how in the world, Gus thought, was he supposed to fix that? The rains had dulled his fury enough for him to return inside without killing Emma Jean—although he wanted to—but God had not told him how to treat a son who acted like a girl. Those had been the only times Chester Sr. had beaten him—when he cried like a girl—and he promised his father, after the last lashing, that he wouldn't be a sissy. Now he promised himself he wouldn't raise one, either.

Gus entered the house without looking at Perfect. Of course this wasn't the boy's fault, he knew, but the whole ordeal made him sick all over again.

"I want everybody in this house to come here right now!" Gus demanded, standing in the center of the living room.

The boys gathered quickly, but Emma Jean remained in the bedroom.

"I said, *everybody*!"

Only then did she emerge, massaging her neck slowly, unable to elicit the sympathy she needed so badly. Leaning against the wall, she waited for Gus to go on.

"It's gon' be some changes 'round here from now on." Gus looked at each Peace. "What yo' momma did is a shame befo' God and man, and she gon' have to pay for it one way or the other." He shot Emma Jean a nasty look. "God gon' handle that. But I'm gon' handle this." Gus pointed to the four walls of the living room and the floor. "This is *my* house, and I'm the man in it! And ain't nobody, and I mean *nobody*, gon' destroy my family."

While the younger boys trembled, Authorly and Woody nodded their approval of Gus's newfound strength. Authorly almost said, *That's right, Daddy!* but feared Gus might reprimand him for interrupting.

"This boy ain't no girl no mo'." He pointed at Perfect, but didn't look at him. "He never was."

Emma Jean bowed her head.

"But he's still a Peace. And he's yo' brother and my . . . son, and we gon' have to make this work. It ain't gon' be easy, so ain't no need in thinkin' it is, but we can make it." Gus paused as he tried to maintain the resolve he had gathered in the barn, but it was slipping fast. "We ain't lyin' no mo' and we ain't hidin' from nobody. Folks can say what they want to, and we might as well get ready for that. But we been a family and we gon' stay a family."

No one knew if Gus was finished, so everyone remained still. Emma Jean dared not move.

"Now, boy, you got a hard row to hoe," he said to Perfect, looking at him for the first time since the transformation, "but whether you make it or not is up to you. We yo' family and we gon' help you, but we can't save you from other folks talkin'. You gon' have to be strong enough to take it and go 'head on 'bout yo' business. It's gon' be hard at first. Real hard. But you can do it. Ain't that right, Authorly?"

"Oh, yessir!"

"You a Peace man just like the rest of us now. And Peace mens is strong. My daddy used to say that all the time. It's yo' job to believe it."

Perfect didn't know if he should speak, so he didn't.

"Authorly, you and James Earl can sleep in the other room now 'til y'all move out. Then Woody, you and Sol'll get it and so on until everybody have it awhile. You"—he nodded toward Perfect—"gon' sleep out here from now on."

Mister rubbed Perfect's shoulders.

"Now everybody go to bed. We got a lot to deal with in the mornin'. Good night."

Gus moved toward the master bedroom, then turned abruptly. "And, by the way, we ain't callin' no son o' mine *Perfect*. I don't never wanna hear that name again."

Authorly asked, "Then what we gon' call him, Daddy?"

Gus shuffled to the sofa end table and retrieved the dusty family Bible. He opened it and drew a line through Perfect's given name—PERFECT—then, after a slight pause, said, "We gon' call him Paul—'cause he done been changed." Sol spelled it slowly and Gus wrote PAUL beneath the initial entry in the registry.

"All right," Gus said, closing the Bible. "That's that." He exited the living room as the boys mouthed their brother's new name. Paul never looked up.

In the bedroom, Gus rolled out the pallet without saying a word. "This is for you now."

Emma Jean reclined onto the floor without argument.

Gus sat on the bed and removed his shoes. "This ain't gon' neva make no sense to me, woman. Neva. I cain't believe no mother would do this to her own child. I jes' cain't believe it."

Emma Jean held her peace. Her neck was still sore from earlier, and the last thing she needed was another dose of Gus's wrath.

"Don't you neva call him Perfect again. And I mean *never!*"

Emma Jean twitched as Gus shouted.

"His name's Paul from now on. You remember that."

She nodded.

"I oughta beat you for real, woman," he said, staring at her, "but that wouldn't fix nothin', so I ain't gon' waste my strength." He set his boots beneath the bed. "I ain't neva met nobody like you, Emma Jean. Yo' name is Emma Jean, ain't it?"

She closed her eyes and hoped Gus wouldn't hit her.

"Ain't no tellin' how many lies you done told. If you'd lie about yo' own child, you'd definitely lie about anything else." Gus blew out the coal oil lamp. "You gotta lotta nerve. I mean, a whole *lotta* nerve. Most men woulda kilt you over somethin' like this."

Emma Jean heard Gus wrap himself in the quilt she had made last year. She was grateful he had spared her.

"And, now, I'm s'pose to make a boy out o' him? Huh?" He leaned over the bed in the dark. "I'm s'pose to make a man oughta that . . . that . . . child?"

What could Emma Jean say?

"You don't know what you done done, woman. You don't know what you done done."

Within minutes, Gus was snoring. Emma Jean had never imagined how uncomfortable and drafty the floor was, and now she knew her husband possessed endurance she simply didn't have. It was a reasonable price to pay though, she admitted, for what she had put Gus through. The boys, too. If she slept on that hard, uncomfortable floor the rest of her life, she knew it would never compensate for the pain she had caused. Yet, even with that, Emma Jean prayed for Gus's forgiveness as she continued rubbing her neck throughout the night.

Paul lay on Authorly's old cot, whimpering. How could Gus just take his name away? He'd been Perfect his whole life, and now he was Paul? *Paul?* He hated the name. The *L* made his tongue graze his upper lip every time he said it. But he'd have to say it. He had no other choice. Having stricken "Perfect" from the Bible, Gus obviously wanted to obliterate all histories of a daughter— starting with her name—and Paul feared what might happen to him if he relapsed into his former identity. He'd simply have to get used to the name, he told himself.

Now he understood why Bartimaeus had acted so strangely that day among the honeysuckle blooms. But why hadn't he explained things? Paul could've digested the news a little better, he convinced himself, had Bartimaeus explained the problem and told him what to do. He certainly wouldn't have suffered the way he was suffering now. Paul wished Bartimaeus had said, *You're a boy, Perfect*—or something like that—to prepare him for this impending transformation. As it was, Paul felt like someone who'd been pushed off a steep ledge into a mighty, rushing river.

Maybe Bartimaeus hadn't understood. Of course he knew what he'd felt, but, without sight, how could he have explained anything with absolute certainty? No, Paul couldn't blame him for anything. Bartimaeus's silence had been his way of protecting his sister, and for that silence Paul was grateful. It might not have been helpful, but it was loving, and love was something Paul needed more desperately than anything else now.

He clutched his arms around his shoulders and glanced at the shadows in the dark. Everyone agreed that he was a boy now, and there was nothing he could do about it. In the past, Emma Jean had made the lump irrelevant, but now it seemed to be the center of things, hanging freely and shifting slightly whenever he moved. It obviously meant more than Emma Jean had said. Gus and the brothers' reaction to it, lying at the base of Paul's flat stomach, suggested that, in fact, it meant everything. They had stood and gazed, waiting to see if Paul had what other men have, and when they discovered he did, they immediately began constructing for him a new, masculine Self. It was as if the penis were the male identifier, the main thing, the *only* thing that made a boy *a boy*, and Paul now knew why Emma Jean had gone to great lengths to trivialize it.

He reached beneath his underwear and felt it. There was nothing particularly striking about it—of course he had no standard of comparison—except that it was there. And it was supposed to be. Shifting it with his forefinger, he was surprised at its malleability. He had never really felt it, not *really*, since Emma Jean had taught him to pee sitting down and to wipe the tip instead of shaking the shaft. What else did men use it for, he wondered. And why had God chosen to place it *there*, in the center of a man's being?

Paul removed his hands and closed his eyes. With his hair gone, his head felt naked against the feather pillow. What would life be like when the sun rose again? Would he recognize himself? Would Eva Mae still want to be his friend? The only thing he knew for sure was that he wouldn't be special anymore. Those days were gone. Never again would he comb Emma Jean's hair or sit at the kitchen table, stirring cake batter. He would start going to the field with his brothers, he presumed, and doing only God knows what. And what would people say when they saw him? How would he explain that he *used* to be a girl? Who would believe him? Paul prayed no one asked him to disrobe as his father had. That had been the worst part of the ordeal—exposing himself to judgmental eyes. Gus's gasp had made him believe that something was terribly wrong with him. That maybe he was the carrier of a deadly, contagious disease that promised to eliminate all the Peaces. Now, lying among his brothers, he knew the problem wasn't biological. That had been proven. The trouble was something beyond his comprehension, something grown-ups knew more about than children. All he knew was that he represented an abnormality, a maladjustment, an aberration that folks in Swamp Creek knew nothing about. They'd have to make room for this absurdity, however, now that Emma Jean had revealed the truth, and all Paul knew to do was pray he could withstand it. If he could, then maybe he could live again, but that was yet to be seen.

Chapter 16

The following Saturday evening, Emma Jean found her way to the church cemetery. No one could've convinced her, days ago, that she'd be there and, truthfully, she didn't know why she had come. All she knew was that, more than ever, she longed for the mother she never had.

Graveyards made her uneasy as a child and scared the shit out of her as an adult. She swore she heard voices whenever she saw a tombstone. Logically she knew that dead people couldn't talk or feel anything, so there was no need to fear decaying flesh. That's what Mae Helen had said. Yet none of this allayed her fears as she approached the gate of the Rose of Sharon Cemetery.

With the slightest push, the gate yielded and groaned like one stricken with arthritis. Emma Jean hated that she'd waited all day to come. Now, at dusk, every sound made her jump.

She walked slowly, trying not to offend the invisible ones. Having boycotted Mae Helen's funeral and interment, she didn't know exactly where her mother lay. Reading name after unfamiliar name, she concluded that Swamp Creek must have been a thriving community once upon a time. W. C. had told her that, years ago, folks from plantations all over the South had come to Arkansas looking for cheap land and a place free of the Klan. They found the land. Then they intermarried and had scores of children, who then married and had more children, so that by the '30s, Swamp Creek had its own doctors and railway station. Lynchings and urban industry took most of them away, W. C. explained, but at its height, Swamp Creek's population numbered into the thousands.

After reading over names she didn't know, she saw Mae Helen's headstone.

"Oh my."

Her throat went dry and chills raced down her back. She read the inscription aloud.

MAE HELEN HURT

1880–1948

"OUR DEAR MOTHER"

Emma Jean couldn't restrain her weeping. "Momma!" She collapsed to the earth. "Why didn't you love me?" Her sobbing seemed louder here. "That's all I ever wanted. Somebody to tuck me in at night and read me bedtime stories. Like white folks do with their kids." Emma Jean sighed. "But you never did. I tried to clean up so good that you'd *have* to love me, but I guess I never did it good enough. And you know what's funny? I woulda done anything, I mean *anything,* to get your attention. The day my daddy came, I wanted to go with him 'cause I could tell he wanted me, but I wanted *you* to want me, so I stayed." She shook her head pitifully. "Now, I done ruined my child's life, just like you ruined mine. You wouldn't believe what I've done. I meant well, Momma. I just wanted a daughter so I could show you how horrible you had been to me. But it didn't happen like I planned. I guess it never does."

A setting sun cast purple and blue streaks across the skies. In her head, Emma Jean heard Mae Helen repeat, "I shoulda named you Nobody."

"I ain't mad at you the way I used to be. I didn't know bein' a mother was so hard. Maybe you didn't mean to treat me the way you did. I didn't mean to do my Perfect the way I did her, either. I really loved her. Still do. But ain't no way I can fix what I did. And ain't no way you can fix what you did. I guess we in the same boat, huh?" She smirked. "I don't know what's gon' happen, but I pray my child don't never hate me—as much as I hated you."

For the next several days, the Peaces conducted their lives in abject silence. Moving about the house like actors in a silent film, they struggled to make sense of a reality none of them had anticipated. Emma Jean cleared Perfect's bedroom of dresses, combs, hair ribbons, purses, and other miscellaneous girly things and burned them in the barrel behind the house. She wanted to keep a few mementos, like the floral bedspread, just to remind her that she had once had a daughter, but then she decided to let everything go. All except a strip of the yellow decorative ribbon from the party. She shoved it into her bra quickly, glancing around to make sure no one saw her. Even the patent leather shoes, which had cost more than she had ever divulged to Gus, went up in flames as Emma Jean shook her head. She would've burned Olivia if she could've found her. This was going to work, she told herself. It had to.

The most strenuous job was repainting the room. Authorly had painted it yellow the day after Perfect's birth, but Emma Jean couldn't ask him to paint it again—not after what she'd done. She couldn't ask anybody for anything, she knew, so she assumed the task herself. The paint was a shade of blue she liked, so she hoped the boys would like it, too.

She stepped back and examined her botched work. Spots of blue paint lay scattered across the floor and windows, and, try as she might, she couldn't paint over Olivia's name heavy enough to obliterate it from the wall. Oh well. The room was blue and that was the point.

Authorly broke the silence on the third day. He told Paul to sit in the chair while he shaped his hair into a neatly cropped Afro.

"Ain't no need in us tryin' to avoid this. You a boy now, so you gotta look like one." He waited for Paul to say something, but he never did. "And you gotta stop soundin' like a girl and start soundin' like a boy, too."

"How?" Paul whispered.

"Just talk deeper"—Authorly lowered his voice—"like this."

Paul tried, but lowered his chin more than his voice.

"No! That's not it!"

Woody, Sol, and Mister watched, praying that Paul met Authorly's expectation before his patience waned.

"You still sound like a girl."

"Of course he does," Woody said. "What else *could* he sound like? That's all he knows."

"That ain't no excuse. He's a boy now and he gotta sound like one. Right now. Today. What's gon' happen if other folks hear him and he sound like that?"

Woody didn't argue.

"So, from now on, you gotta sound like this."

Paul tried to mimic Authorly's rich baritone, but succeeded only in offering a raspy soprano.

"Stop that! You gotta do it right! You can't go 'round this community soundin' like no sissy!"

Woody shouted, "He'll get it, man! Give him time!"

"Why don't you shut up! I don't see you tryin' to teach him nothin'!"

"He'll learn everything he's supposed to know soon enough."

"What? Is you crazy? He's gotta know this now. Other folks gon' see him and know he's a boy, so he's gotta act like one."

"I know, Authorly, but just take it easy. He ain't gon' learn everything overnight."

"I know that! But he's gotta start." Authorly returned his attention to Paul. "Wipe your eyes and stop cryin'."

Paul obeyed. Under normal circumstances, he would've expected Gus to save him from Authorly, but, now, he knew he was on his own.

"Now try it again. Say your name."

"Paul," he whimpered.

Before thinking, Authorly shoved him to the floor. "Say it like a boy!"

"Stop it!" Woody said.

"I'll stop it as soon as he sounds like a boy!"

Paul trembled.

"You'll stop it right now! I might not can beat you up, but I swear 'fo God I'll try!"

Mister helped Paul from the floor.

"He ain't never gon' be no man," Authorly shouted, "long as y'all keep babyin' him! I don't want no sissy for a brother!"

"We don't, either," Woody said, "but you cain't change him in a day. It takes time. Just give him time!"

"Forget about it!" Authorly said, dropping the scissors and storming out. "I don't even care!" The screen slammed behind him.

Paul wanted to disappear. He hadn't meant to defy Authorly; in fact, he wanted nothing more desperately than to please him, but he simply couldn't. What was a sissy anyway? He had never heard the term, but he was sure he didn't want to be one. He certainly didn't want to embarrass his brothers, so he decided to practice his deep voice at night until it came. Maybe then Authorly would be proud of him.

"Let's go, boys," Gus called the next morning. "We got work to do." He put on his hat and walked through the door without looking back.

Paul's pleading eyes met Emma Jean's.

"I'm sorry," she mouthed.

Mister pulled Paul along before Emma Jean could cry out on Paul's behalf.

Unfamiliar with physical labor, Paul feared that, once again, he'd be proven inadequate. Outside, Gus told Mister, "Y'all pull dem weeds from 'round the sprouts, then take the cows some hay. I'll meet y'all back at the barn when you get through." By "y'all," Paul assumed Gus meant him and Mister, so he followed his youngest brother to the field and awaited instruction.

They bent to their knees and Mister said, "You take that row and I'll take this one. All you gotta do is pull these little grass sprouts up and throw 'em away. Just don't pull up the plants. Daddy'll be madder'n a wet hen if you do."

Paul followed directions. He hated dirt and grime beneath his fingernails, but somehow he knew not to mention this. The work was slow and uninteresting, and Paul's lower back ached before they reached the middle of the first row.

"How did it feel bein' a girl?" Mister asked, breaking two hours of uninterrupted silence.

Paul shrugged.

"You and Momma seemed real close. Like y'all was friends."

He whispered, "I guess we was."

"What did y'all talk about? You know, when y'all used to sit at the table and giggle?"

He shrugged again.

"Did y'all talk about boys?"

"Sometimes."

Mister wiped his brow with the back of his right hand. "I used to watch y'all. I'd be jealous, too. It seemed like y'all was havin' so much fun."

"It was okay."

"I knew you wanted to play with us though. I heard you ask Momma, but she said girls ain't s'pose to be runnin' 'round wit' no boys. I wanted to play with you, but I couldn't. Even when you was a baby, I remember askin' if I could play with you and everybody said no."

"It don't matter now."

"Guess not," Mister said, and continued pulling weeds. When they reached the end of the row, he said, "Authorly don't hate you. He just want you to act like a boy. So other folks won't make fun o' you."

Paul nodded.

"You ain't gotta be scared o' him. I mean, he's tough and all, but he's our brother and he'll take care o' us."

"I can't sound like him."

"It's okay. You'll start soundin' like a boy pretty soon, and then he'll leave you alone."

They squatted and began pulling weeds from the next two rows. Paul couldn't imagine how he'd make it another hour without fainting from exhaustion.

"Don't worry about it. Authorly'll be okay. I know it's hard, but you gotta do it. People'll laugh at you if you don't. They'll call you a sissy and stuff."

"What's that?"

"A boy who acts like a girl. People hate 'em, especially other boys. They beat 'em up sometimes."

"Oh."

"Men treat 'em real bad, too. Women just shake their heads. Nobody likes 'em."

"I don't wanna be no sissy."

"I know. Nobody does. That's why Authorly's so hard on you. He don't want you to be one, neither."

Paul nodded.

"So, like he said, just do what we do. Like you doin' now."

The two pressed on until they completed the field. It was lunchtime.

"Come on," Mister said, standing slowly. "Let's get somethin' to eat."

They met Gus and the other boys behind the barn.

"Y'all finish the field?" Gus asked, looking only at Mister.

"Yessir."

"Good. Get you some o' these biscuits and molasses and salt meat. It'll hold you over 'til suppertime."

Everyone ate in silence. Mister and Paul sat in the grass while the big boys stood.

Suddenly Paul screamed, "Ahhhhhh! A snake!" He jumped and began to run. Woody chuckled.

"Get back here, boy!" Authorly demanded. "And stop screamin' like that! You ain't no girl no more!"

Mister grabbed a hoe and chopped the snake's head off. "It's okay. I killed it." He resumed eating.

Authorly lifted the headless creature and presented it to Paul. "Hold this."

Paul froze.

"I said hold this! Ain't no country boy scared o' no snake. Here! Take it!"

Even Gus thought Authorly was a bit too much, but he didn't stop him.

Paul stared at the snake dangling from Authorly's monstrous hand.

"I'ma slap you if you don't take this snake, boy!"

Woody and Sol expected Gus to say something. When he didn't, they stepped toward Authorly simultaneously.

Paul wanted to obey, but fear paralyzed him.

Authorly's left hand came so fast that Paul never saw it, but he felt the sting. "I said hold this, boy!"

Before Woody and Sol could grab him, Gus said, "Y'all let Authorly be. That boy gotta learn somehow."

"But Daddy," Woody protested, "he's only eight! Authorly ain't gotta treat him like—"

"You wunnit scared o' no snake when you was eight, was you?" Gus asked.

"No, I wunnit, but I been a boy my whole life."

"Well, he been one, too! He just didn't know it. Now he gotta start actin' like one."

"He's doin' de best he can, Daddy!"

"You mind yo' own damn business, boy! I'm de daddy 'round here and I say how things go."

Authorly's eyes never left Paul's. "Here," he said, hoisting the snake in the air. "Take it."

"It won't hurt you," Mister said. "It's already dead."

Paul's arm felt heavy, like a solid steel rod, but he didn't intend to get slapped again. He reached forward, prepared to receive the snake with his thumb and index finger, like one might pinch his nose.

"Not like that!" Authorly pushed his hand away. "Like this." He clutched the snake with his entire palm.

If Paul dropped it, he knew he'd really be in trouble, so he closed his eyes and seized the snake as though angry with it.

"Good. Now. That's how you do it."

Woody winked at him. "See? It won't hurt you. You'll learn."

Paul looked at Gus, who looked away. Yes, Paul had held the snake, but, in Gus's heart, he still didn't seem like a boy.

"Finish yo' lunch," Gus said to everyone. "We still got work to do."

Sol extracted a book from beneath the bib of his overalls. Knowledge fed his soul *and* his body, he told Gus, although this made no sense to a father who had never read anything. Authorly taught Sol his ABCs at three and by five Sol read better than everyone in the house except Emma Jean. Sometimes he made up words for fun, asking his brothers if they knew what the words meant. Their puzzled expressions evoked his laughter and served as the origin of countless fights between him and Authorly. He would go to college one day, he told the family, although he didn't know where or how. Only Emma Jean believed him, and if she hadn't spent the family's meager savings on Perfect's birthday party, she would have contributed it to Sol's college fund. Now that Perfect was Paul, she wished she had.

Paul's noonday appetite dissipated the moment he touched the snake, and even Mister couldn't convince him that he'd soon regret an empty stomach. He felt proud of himself, having faced a fear that once seemed insurmountable. He almost thanked Authorly, but decided against it. Encouraging his traumatic—though liberating—approach was definitely not something he wanted to do.

Paul rose and disappeared behind the barn. He unbuckled the straps of his overalls, lowered his underwear, and squatted.

"You don't pee like that no more," Authorly said.

Paul hadn't noticed him following. He jumped, scattering urine across his clothes, unable to cover himself before Authorly beheld his nakedness.

"A man pees standin' up."

Paul tried to rebuckle the overall straps, but his trembling hands wouldn't allow it. "Like this." Authorly unzipped the fly of his overalls, motioning for Paul to do likewise. Then he extracted his penis.

Paul tried not to gawk at Authorly's gigantic extension. Would his grow into *that*, he wondered.

"You hold it like this. With one hand."

Paul looked, from the corners of his eyes, trying not to look at all. Authorly peed and Paul followed suit. "Then you shake it like this. So you don't leak into yo' drawers."

Paul shook his shaft, wondering if Authorly was laughing internally at his miniature penis.

"Then you tuck it back in like this"—Authorly demonstrated the move—"and you go on 'bout yo' business. Don't no boys pee sittin' down."

Paul zipped his fly and followed Authorly back to the others. For years to come, he would wait for his penis to evolve into what Authorly had, but it never did. He wondered if something might be wrong with his, if maybe its growth had been stunted during his girlhood days. Every day he looked to see if, finally, his penis size matched his brother's and every day he was disappointed that it didn't. Maybe if he could *act* more like a man it would grow, he thought. Yet after age sixteen, and very little success with masculinity, he stopped trying—although he never stopped hoping.

Chapter 17

Come Sunday morning, Sol's singing awakened the household as the sun peeked over the distant horizon. The boys rose, wondering if the family would attend church. Would Paul go, Mister asked himself. What would people say when they saw him?

"I don't think we better take the boy to church, Gus," Emma Jean said, leaning up and rolling her stiff neck. "It's just too soon. He ain't ready for that."

"We goin'," Gus said. "And he's goin', too. Ain't no need o' hidin' him, and it ain't gon' get no easier. The sooner the better."

"I know. You're right. But maybe if we waited just one more week, he'd be a little . . . um . . . you know . . . stronger so if people laughed at him he could take it a little better."

"We goin' today. All of us." He slid into his good overalls and entered the living room. "What y'all waitin' for? Y'all know we goes to church on Sunday mornins. Get y'all's behinds up and get ready for service."

They obeyed, each wondering how they'd survive the day. Authorly might fight, Mister considered, if someone said the wrong thing. Then Woody would have no choice but to assist. Sol hated violence, but Mister felt certain that Sol would fight if he had to. Of course James Earl couldn't be counted on for anything. The guarantee was that he'd watch and cry, squeezing his head until the commotion subsided.

Other boys would definitely have something smart to say. That was to be expected. Mister just hoped they wouldn't say it during church.

Eva Mae saw Paul first and wondered why she was dressed in boy's clothes. And why had someone cut her hair like that?

"Hey, Perfect," she called.

When Paul turned, he was relieved that Eva Mae wasn't horrified.

"What happened to your hair? And why you got on them boys' clothes?"

Before he could answer, Gus said, "Mind yo' business, li'l girl. This ain't got nothin' to do with you."

Eva Mae bit her bottom lip and stared at her best friend. "We ain't gon' sit together like we always do?"

Authorly pushed Paul away from Eva Mae as though she were the problem. What had she done, she wondered. Paul wanted to tell her that they were still best friends, if she wanted to be, but everyone made it clear that he was not to speak for himself. Not that day.

Within minutes, a crowd gathered around the Peace clan as though Paul were a celebrity. Or a freak. The frowns and whispers were more than Emma Jean could bear.

"What happened to that child?" W. C. asked Gus. "Who did that to her?"

Sugar Baby laughed and shouted, "He all right now! He all right now!"

The crowd awaited a response, but Gus said nothing. He tried to lead the family into the church, but the crowd blocked his way.

"Emma Jean?" Miss Mamie called. "What happened to that girl?"

"He ain't no girl," Emma Jean slurred. "He's a boy. Now."

"What! What chu mean 'he's a boy now'?"

Gus intervened. "Let it go, Emma Jean. They ain't gon' understand. You can't make this make sense to nobody."

The family pressed through the crowd and into the church.

"I told y'all that heffa was crazy!" Miss Mamie said. "Didn't I tell you? Lawd have mercy! Ain't no tellin' what that woman done done to dat chile. How you make a li'l girl into a boy? Huh? Somebody tell me dat!"

Folks shook their heads sadly. W. C. urged everyone into the church, saying, "Mind yo' own business. I guess we'll know soon enough."

Sandwiched between Emma Jean and Authorly, Paul slumped in shame. He heard every whisper, joke, and cackle as though people's voices had been amplified. Didn't they know their words hurt? Didn't they care?

Reverend Lindsey emerged from the pastor's study, wondering about the source of the commotion. He glanced across the congregation without noticing what everyone else had already seen. "Somebody give us an opening song," he said.

Miss Mamie stood and sang, "I woke up this morning with my mind!"

The congregation filled in the chorus: "Stayed on Jesus!"

"Yes, I woke up this morning with my mind!"

"Stayed on Jesus."

"Hallelujah, I woke up this morning with my mind!"

"Stayed on Jesus."

Together, everyone sang, "Hallelu, Hallelu, Hallelu . . . jah!"

Miss Mamie waved her arms, stared at Emma Jean, and sang, "It ain't no harm to keep yo' mind!"

Emma Jean stared back and mumbled with the crowd, "Stayed on Jesus!"

After the song, W. C. bent to one knee before a rusted fold-up chair and prayed, "It's once more and again we come befo' Yo' throne, Lawd, like empty vessels befo' a full fountain. You didn't have to wake us dis mornin', but You did, Lawd, and we can't neva thank You enough. Sometime we don't understand Yo' ways, Lawd, but we know dat You sits high and looks low, and everythang You do is holy and righteous. Send us Yo' power, Lawd, so we know how to walk right and talk right and treat our neighbor right. We cain't do nothin' 'til You come, Lawd, so we ask that You come on down and be in dis heah service, Lawd, and let de Holy Ghost have its way. Sometimes thangs happen we jes' don't understand, Lawd, but I ask You right now to give us understandin'."

"Yes!" The crowd shouted. Reverend Lindsey frowned.

". . . 'Cause You told us in Yo' word that with all thy gettin', get understandin', so I'm prayin' for understandin' right now, Lawd!" W. C. paused, clapping his hands vigorously, then added, "Visit de Peace household, Lawd, and give 'em comfort in dis time o' distress."

When Reverend Lindsey looked up, his eyes fell on Paul. W. C. had completed the morning prayer, and now the congregation sat in silence.

Authorly wanted to rise and scream, *What is you lookin' at, Reverend!* but he already knew, and, unfortunately, he had no explanation.

Reverend Lindsey couldn't speak. He blinked two or three times, but never closed his mouth. W. C. dismissed the congregation to Sunday school.

"Am I seeing things?" he asked W. C. once the sanctuary emptied.

"Nawsir, you ain't seein' thangs. I don't know what happened. Gus wouldn't say nothin'."

"It is a little girl, right?"

"I don't know. Emma Jean said it's a boy now."

"What!"

"Dat's what she said. Then they walked on in the church like they do every Sunday."

"Oh God."

"Yeah. It's crazy. I mean, it's really crazy."

Paul attended Sunday school with a bowed head. The teacher tried to ignore him, but couldn't help staring. Mister reminded her several times of the topic and eventually she dismissed Paul from her mind with the wave of a hand. He appreciated the gesture. Eva Mae decided she'd get to the bottom of this after church. Perfect was her best friend, and she felt she deserved to know.

Before Reverend Lindsey preached, he said, "I don't do this often, but I'm gon' ask Emma Jean if she wouldn't mind singing 'Amazing Grace.' I feel like I need to hear that this morning."

Emma Jean tried to deny the request, but the crowd insisted. Yes, she was crazy, and, yes, ain't no tellin' what she had done to that chile, but everyone in Swamp Creek forgave her shortcomings whenever she opened her mouth to sing. The opportunity to hear Emma Jean croon was simply a blessing no one was willing to forego. She rose, like a timid child awaiting reprimand, and shuffled to the front of the church. Gus stared out of the window, anxious for church to be over yet grateful it hadn't been as bad as he had imagined. At least not yet.

Paul lifted his head for the first time when Emma Jean began, sweetly, "Amazing Grace, shall always be my song of praise." She closed her eyes as tears poured. "For it was grace that bought my liberty. I do not know, just why He came to love me so. . . . He looked beyond my faults and saw my needs."

"You better sang, Emma Jean Peace!" people shouted. Hands were raised all over the sanctuary. Any minute now, they knew, Miss Mamie would faint under the power of the Holy Ghost.

"I shall foreeeeever lift mine eyes to Calvary!" Emma Jean belted. "To view the cross, where Jeeeesus died for me, how marvelous!"

Miss Mamie collapsed. Usher Board Number One fanned her violently as W. C. carried her out.

". . . was the grace that caught my falling soul." Tears dangled from Emma Jean's chin. "He looked beyond my faults and saaaaaaw my needs."

She returned to her seat as the congregation dried their weepy eyes. She needed the song, too, she thought, and now she felt a little better. Of course Paul's situation was all her doing, but if God and Gus could look beyond her faults, she didn't give a damn what other folks said.

After service, the congregation reconvened outdoors in front of the church. Gus had hoped to load the family onto the wagon and escape without incident, but that didn't happen.

"What's wrong wid that girl?" Snukey Cunningham, W. C. and Mamie's oldest grandson, asked. He and Authorly were only a month apart, but Authorly was twice his size.

"Ain't nothin' wrong wid him," Authorly said.

"*Him?*"

"That's what I said."

"How she get to be a him? She was wearin' dresses last week!" Other boys chuckled.

"It ain't none o' yo' business, Snukey, so just leave it alone."

"Oh, he must got a split *and* a ding-a-ling! So he can switch back and forth whenever he want to!"

Authorly pushed Snukey to the ground and pounced upon him. Children began screaming, afraid Authorly might hurt him.

W. C. came running. Snukey's blood was dripping from his nose onto his good white Sunday shirt. "Cut that out, boys! I said, cut that out!" Gus hadn't said anything. "You boys know better'n dat. Y'all on church ground!"

"He ain't got no business talkin' 'bout my li'l brother," Authorly panted.

"That ain't no boy! And if it is, he gon' be a faggot the rest o' his life!"

Authorly swung past W. C. and slammed his clenched fist against Snukey's left ear. The ringing lingered for days.

"I said stop it! That's enough! I don't wanna hear nothin' else 'bout it." He handed Snukey a handkerchief. "You go on home, and I mean now. I'll deal with you later. Authorly, you get wit' yo' folks and try to control yo'self."

Authorly brushed the front of his overalls. The crowd murmured about the strangeness of things as Gus motioned for Authorly to get in the wagon.

Suddenly, Emma Jean said, "Y'all wanna know what happened?"

"Momma, no," Authorly said. Gus didn't try to stop her.

"Well, I'll tell you!" she sassed, leaning on the wooden rail of the wagon. "I dressed him up as a girl 'cause I wanted one," she shouted. "And that's my business. All you need to know is that he"—she pointed to Paul—"is a boy now. I know how he used to look 'cause I made him look that way, and you can talk about me like a dog if you want to, but keep yo' mouth closed 'bout my child. He didn't have nothin' to do with it. He always been a boy and he gon' always be one. If you gon' chastise somebody, then chastise me, but keep yo' filthy mouth off my chile!"

Most women didn't try to conceal their horror. Miss Mamie said, "You did what?"

"You heard me! Now mind yo' own business and act like the Christians y'all claim to be!"

Gus loaded the family into the wagon before anyone could question them further. He then nodded to W. C. and directed the mules down the narrow path toward home.

"Mister, y'all get the cows feed," he said when they arrived. Everyone else went inside. When the task was complete, Mister and Paul saw Eva Mae approaching. Mister left them on the edge of the porch.

"Hi," she said.

"Hi."

Eva Mae sat beside Paul as though comforting him for his loss.

"What happened?"

Paul didn't know where to begin. "Momma cut my hair off."

"Yeah, I know. But why?"

He couldn't say it, so he shrugged.

"Folks is sayin' you ain't no girl no more."

Paul began to cry.

"Is that true?"

He nodded.

"Oh wow. That's sorta weird." She paused. "Who told you?"

"Momma."

"Oh." After another pause, Eva Mae asked, "Do you have a boy's thing down there?"

"Un-huh."

"For real?"

"Yeah."

Eva Mae smiled. "It's okay. I don't care anyway."

"You don't?"

"Naw. You still my best friend. Right?"

"Okay."

"And we can still play house. You'll just have to be the husband now."

"Okay."

"And I can be the wife. It'll still be fun."

"Okay."

Eva Mae hesitated. "People was talkin' 'bout you after y'all left today. I told them to shut up. They said you wunnit never gon' be right. Miss Mamie said you'd be a punk the rest o' yo' life. She said wunnit no way nobody like you was ever gon' be a *real* boy."

In his mind's eye, Paul saw the look of disgust on Miss Mamie's face.

"I don't like those people anyway. They don't know what they're talkin' about, huh?"

Paul shook his head, then added, "My daddy changed my name."

"For real? Yo' name ain't Perfect no more?"

"Naw."

"Then what is it now?"

"Paul."

"*Paul?*" Eva Mae said, frowning. "I guess it's okay. I liked Perfect though."

"I did, too, but you can't say it no more. I'll get in trouble."

"Okay. Come on." Eva Mae grabbed his hand.

He knew where they were going.

"It's okay. You de husband now, so it's all right."

They disappeared beneath the house.

"Just sit down and relax," Eva Mae said once they reached the corner. "The man ain't s'pose to do nothin' at home 'cept enjoy his wife."

Paul sat and followed Eva Mae's instructions.

"I kinda like you as a boy. You can take care o' me now. That's what men do. At least they s'pose to. My momma said so."

"Authorly said men s'pose to work. He didn't say they s'pose to do nothin' else."

"Well, they is. That's why women marry 'em, so they can take care o' 'em. Then the woman s'pose to do what he say."

"My momma don't do what my daddy say."

"She s'pose to."

"Well she don't."

Now Eva Mae shrugged. Then she brightened and said, "I peek and see my brother's thing sometimes. It's real big."

Paul thought of Authorly.

"Can I see yours?"

"Huh?"

"Your thing. Can I see it?"

"Um, I don't know. . . ."

"Why not?"

"I don't think you s'pose to."

"I seen my brother's and didn't nothin' happen."

"Yeah, but that's different."

"No it ain't. Not really."

They listened to the footsteps above them. Eva Mae moved closer to Paul and kissed him.

"It's okay. You my husband now."

Paul loved the taste of Eva Mae's saliva. It reminded him of the nectar from the honeysuckle bloom. He leaned forward to kiss her again, and they kissed countless times before Eva Mae said, "Lean back and get comfortable."

Paul complied, and before he realized what was happening, Eva Mae had unzipped the fly of his overalls.

He raised his torso.

"Just relax. My momma do this to my daddy all the time. I watch 'em sometimes."

Paul felt Eva Mae's mouth descend upon his penis. He yelped at first, then sighed as her lips massaged his private sensually. He loved the feeling, he discovered, and when she stopped, he wanted her to go on.

"Do you like that?" she asked, looking up.

Paul nodded, so Eva Mae repeated the act until his grunts and moans became audible.

"Shhhhhh," she hissed. "We'll get in trouble."

Paul covered his mouth, muting his uncontrollable response. He never wanted her to stop.

She lifted her head and kissed him again. "I gotta go now."

"Why?"

" 'Cause Momma gon' be lookin' for me soon. And if your folks catch us, they ain't gon' let us play together no more."

"I know."

"Hey! I know what!"

"What?"

"Why don't we meet someplace else, like the field of clovers? Nobody ever goes there and it's real pretty. Lots of wildflowers and stuff."

"Okay, but where's it at?"

"It's right next to the river. I'll show you. Just let me know whenever you can go."

"Okay, but I gotta work with my brothers from now on."

"That's okay. I'll show you one day soon. Just let me know."

In his heart, Paul declared his everlasting love for Eva Mae as she skipped away. She hadn't treated him differently and that's what he wanted. He hadn't said much since the transformation, but Eva Mae's unconditional love re-ignited life in his dying soul.

He wondered why Emma Jean hadn't simply let him live out the lie. He would have found out somehow, someday, but maybe by then it wouldn't have hurt so bad. Maybe it wouldn't have mattered. Maybe he would've been grown, or close to it, and then he could have dismissed what others said. But at the tender age of eight, his heart had no defense. Each frown, grunt, stare, and avoidance further wounded his already bleeding heart and made him resent Emma Jean's announcement all the more.

Even his brothers treated him like a leper. Sometimes they walked by him as though he weren't there, and other times they offered fake grins like church women who really don't want to speak. They talked around him—and about him—but rarely *to* him. They hadn't meant to be mean, Paul assumed. They simply didn't know what to say. What kind of conversation does one have with a brother who's been a girl all his life? What would they have in common? The boys feared that Paul would be the undoing of the Peace family since, now, folks demeaned all of them as though his abnormality were inherited.

"I'm sorry," Bartimaeus said.

Paul turned.

"I shoulda told you." He took Eva Mae's place on the edge of the porch. "I just didn't understand then. I wouldn't've guessed in a million years nothin' like this."

"It's okay."

"I feel like I shoulda knowed. I mean, what else could it be?"

Paul sighed.

"I failed you. I'm yo' big brother and I didn't protect you."

"It's okay."

"No, it's not. I shoulda told you something. Or asked Momma about it. She might not have told me the truth, but she might have told you." He hesitated. "Then again, maybe not. I don't know."

Paul wanted Bartimaeus to go away.

"I'ma do what I can. I don't know how much that is, but you my brother and I love you like I always did." He reached for Paul's hand. "You gon' make it. I'ma help you. I owe—"

"Ah! Somebody help me!" Emma Jean screamed from the kitchen.

She had been alone, preparing the Sunday meal, since no one could bear her presence. Paul dashed into the house, with Bartimaeus feeling his way behind him. The back of Emma Jean's dress was ablaze and smoke billowed out of the small kitchen window.

"Momma!" Paul screeched as he watched the fire crawl up her dress. Bartimaeus fumbled back to the front door and yelled, "Daddy! Authorly! Momma's on fire!"

Authorly ran from the barn and rushed into the house. "Get the water bucket!" he shouted to Paul. Paul obeyed and dipped several scoops into the bucket, spilling as much water as he saved.

"Oh my God!" Bartimaeus screamed and quivered. "What's happening?" He held on to the doorknob.

Authorly snatched the homemade quilt from the sofa and slung it across a hysterical Emma Jean just after Paul dashed cold water across her. Emma Jean fell to the floor, shivering like an epileptic.

"Go get Daddy!" Authorly shouted. "Hurry up!"

Paul ran into the front yard, screaming, until Gus appeared from behind the house.

"What is it, boy?"

Paul panted, "Momma's been burned. Real bad. Her dress caught on fire."

Gus sprinted through the front door and joined Authorly on the floor. "Aw no! Emma Jean! You all right? What happened!"

"I don't know!" Authorly said. "I just heard Paul scream for help and when I got in the house Momma's dress was on fire."

By this point, Woody, Sol, and James Earl were hovering over their mother in confusion.

Authorly added, "She's shakin' somethin' terrible and I think her back's been burned."

"Good Lawd! Woody, you and Sol go get Doc Harris. Run fast as you can! Bartimaeus, pass me that pillow on the sofa."

Paul stood still, staring at Emma Jean's quivering form, wondering how in the world all of this had happened so quickly.

Gus embraced Emma Jean from behind and said, "You gon' be all right, woman. Just hold on." He rocked her, but shed no tears.

"What chu want me to do, Daddy?" Authorly asked.

"Get a cool washcloth and bring it to me."

Authorly complied. "Here!"

Gus folded it and placed it on Emma Jean's forehead. She appeared unconscious.

"Is she all right?" Bartimaeus asked.

"We don't know yet, son. We gon' have to wait and see what the doctor says."

Emma Jean's trembling subsided a bit. Gus was afraid to move her. He didn't want to say it, but he had feared something like this would happen. It was only a matter of time. He didn't wish harm upon Emma Jean, but he knew God was going to have His say.

Mister took Bartimaeus's hand and led him to where Emma Jean lay huddled in Gus's arms.

"Don't touch her," Gus warned. "It might hurt."

Bartimaeus bit his bottom lip and clutched the sides of his head.

Moments later, Woody and Sol returned, bursting through the screen door with enough force to tear it from its hinges. Sixty-year-old Doc Harris panted behind them.

"She's over there," Woody said, pointing to the area behind the sofa.

"You boys get back," Doc said. "Let me see how bad it is."

The boys withdrew and Gus transferred Emma Jean's head gently from his lap to the pillow.

"She's alive, but probably in shock. You boys help yo' daddy get her to the bedroom."

Gus decided not to mention that Emma Jean's bed was on the floor. "How bad is it?" Gus asked.

"I don't know. I'm gon' have to examine her first."

Doc told Gus to remove her garments slowly and carefully, then he ordered Gus from the room. "I'll come tell you somethin' soon's I know."

Under an aura of gloom, the men waited. Bartimaeus envisioned what Emma Jean must have looked like, twirling and shouting while cloaked in a ball of fire. It was times like these that he hated his blindness most. It always limited his response to things. He seemed inept, he thought, for people never depended on him when it really mattered. Unlike his brothers, he was always assigned menial tasks so that if he failed, no one's life would be affected. But of course this wasn't the time to complain about being insignificant.

The heat had crawled up Emma Jean's legs from behind. On any other day, she would have been more cognizant of things, but her mind was consumed with the shocked faces of her neighbors at church. Their expressions highlighted the irreparable mistake she'd made. She knew it wasn't correct, but never did she consider that she had destroyed her own child's life. When people's eyes bulged so big that they almost fell from their heads, she was forced to admit that she hadn't told herself the truth. Not the full truth. And if she told herself now, she would feel like a bad mother and she knew she hadn't been a bad mother. Or had she? If, indeed, she *had* been a bad mother, maybe she was becoming more like Mae Helen each day, and the thought alone depressed her. She'd never live with herself, believing that she'd made Perfect—or, rather, Paul—hate her. Her aim had been the exact opposite, and now, somehow, everyone was scolding her for having loved a child so much she wanted to give her—him—the world?

It was these thoughts, fighting for prominence in Emma Jean's consciousness, that had distracted her and kept her from noticing that a spark from the old woodstove had set the hem of her dress on fire. By the time she noticed, it was too late to simply brush the fire away. As she screamed for help, she heard a voice in her head say, *You gotta tell the truth, Emma Jean. The whole truth.* But she didn't know what truth the voice was speaking of. She had told all the truths she knew. At least she thought she had. The truth that Mae Helen used to beat her for no reason at all. The truth that she was too black to be beautiful. The truth that she had lied to her family and the community about Paul's identity. She had told these already. What more was there to tell?

When she felt the skin on the back of her thighs begin to sizzle, she considered that her dying day had arrived. She'd never imagined it would come like this though. When her consciousness returned and she saw that God had not called her number, she lay in Gus's bed trying to remember what truth she hadn't told.

Doc emerged, closing the door gently. "It could've been worse, I'm glad to say. Much worse." He sat his satchel on the back of the sofa and snapped it shut. "She's gonna live."

Bartimaeus heaved a sigh of relief. Gus simply asked, "How bad is it?"

"Well, she has third-degree burns from the lower back down across her rear end and thighs. But, like I said, she'll live. It'll take a while for the sores to heal. Gus, you'll have to rub this salve"—he handed Gus a bottle—"on the wounds every day until you've used it all. It'll be painful for her, but it's the only way the burns are gonna heal. She'll have difficulty sitting, or lying on her back for a while, but after the burns scab over and peel away and a fresh layer of skin grows, she should be okay. She'll never be like she was, but she'll recover. Let her rest for a while before you go in."

"Is she woke?" Gus asked.

"Yes, but she's a bit disoriented."

"Huh?" Gus frowned.

"She shouldn't be disturbed right away. Give her time to get herself back together."

Gus thanked Doc Harris for everything and told Authorly to get him a basket of canned fruits and vegetables and a healthy side of bacon from the smokehouse. Doc received the payment gratefully and told Authorly not to let others worry Emma Jean during her recovery. He promised he wouldn't.

After Doc left, everyone fell silent until Authorly said, "Let's go to the table and eat."

"Ain't nothin' to eat!" Mister said. "The food's all burnt up."

"Just do what I said, boy. I'll find us somethin'."

Gus hadn't said a word. His heart vacillated between thanks for Emma Jean's life and frustration that he'd now have to usher her back to health.

Authorly scavenged the kitchen for enough leftovers to feed his brothers while Gus told him he wasn't hungry.

At dusk, Gus went into the bedroom and mumbled, "You need anything?" He hadn't meant to sound cold, but he knew he did.

Emma Jean was lying on her stomach with her face toward the wall. She whispered, "Water. Can I have some water?"

Gus held the dipper as she sipped slowly. "I don't wish you no harm, Emma Jean, but I knowed somethin' like this was gon' happen. I knowed it."

Emma Jean gulped, and breathed heavily.

"Don't think this makes me forget what you did 'cause it don't. I'll give you a few weeks, then you back on the floor. This is only the beginning." He turned to leave.

"Can you send Paul in? Please. I need to speak to him."

Paul tiptoed through the door. Emma Jean turned her head to face him.

"You all right, Momma?"

"I'ma make it, baby, I guess. You all right?"

"Yes, ma'am."

"I know this ain't been easy." She swallowed hard. "I just wanna say I'm sorry again. Just in case I don't make it, I need you to know how sorry I am."

Paul looked away.

"I hope you can forgive me. One day. All I meant was good. I didn't neva mean for you to suffer like this."

Her trembling hand reached for his and Paul surrendered. She pulled him to her side on the bed.

"When I look back, I know I coulda done somethin' else, but all I was tryin' to do was love you the best way I knew how. You can understand that, can't you?"

Paul wanted to say no, but under the circumstances he didn't say anything.

"If the Good Lord lets me live to see it, I'll make this up to you one day. I promise you that. I don't know how, but I will."

Paul eased his hand away from Emma Jean's and stood.

"Try not to be mad at me, honey. I love you so much."

He wanted to ask Emma Jean if she could send him somewhere to live by himself, free from the words and stares of everyone he knew. Then he wouldn't be angry anymore. But of course, in her current state, Emma Jean couldn't do anything, so Paul prepared to endure.

What he really wanted was the life he had before. The joy of waking in the morning to a family who loved him. Obviously things were different now. No one *said* they hated him, but he felt it, like people feel tension or excitement among a crowd. Their silence confirmed it. Even at church earlier, when others scowled at him, his own folks had said very little. They didn't say that he was still the joy of the family and that he was just as precious as he'd ever been. Shouldn't they have said that? Authorly had fought Snukey, but only because he felt embarrassed, right? Sure it was, Paul thought. Authorly used to tell him all the time how pretty he was, but, since his transformation, Authorly didn't tell him anything except how to work and be a boy. He didn't mind being a boy if the admiration continued, but clearly it did not.

"I gotta go now, Momma. Authorly told me not to stay long."

"Okay, baby. But just one more thing."

Paul hung his head and waited.

"You still *my* baby. Don't chu never forget that. I don't care what you do or what happens to you, you gon' always be my baby. I wouldn't take nothin' for you. Nothin'. And you still perfect."

Paul wiped his eyes as he exited. *You gon' always be my baby* echoed from one side of his skull to the other. That's what he needed to hear—that something about his former life was still intact. Maybe Emma Jean wasn't as bad as people were making her out to be, he told himself.

In the following days, women brought food to the Peace house and inquired about Emma Jean's health. "You can check on her yo'self," Gus told them, nodding toward the bedroom. Most followed propriety, whispering sympathetic words as they entered, although thinking that Emma Jean deserved everything she got.

"Yoo-hoo! Emma Jean!" Miss Mamie called early one morning. She had on her good wig and first Sunday hat. "I hope I ain't waking you. I heard what happened, so I just *had* to come see 'bout you."

Emma Jean convinced herself that she was having a nightmare. "How you doin', Miss Mamie?" she asked, trying painfully to sit up.

"Oh no! Don't get up, chile! You lay right there and get yo' rest. I'm just here to visit the sick—like Jesus would do."

Emma Jean swallowed her pride. "Well, I thank you for comin'. I'm doin' much better, thank the Lord."

"That's good. I'm glad to hear it. Those boys definitely need a momma." Miss Mamie paused. "How's that youngest one?"

Emma Jean knew it was coming. "He's fine. Just like the rest of 'em."

Miss Mamie cackled, "Naw, he ain't like the rest of 'em! Least I hope he ain't!"

"The boy's fine, ma'am, and I'd appreciate if you left him alone."

"Oh I ain't gon' bother *him*, 'cause *he* ain't done nothin', but I just cain't believe what *you* did. I just cain't believe it, Emma Jean."

"It ain't for you to believe, so don't worry about it." She hated that she didn't have her strength. That's the only reason Mamie Cunningham was trying her.

"Oh, I ain't judgin' you or nothin'. I mean, we all make mistakes. Even me! But come on, Emma Jean! This one takes the cake! How did you think you was gon' get away with somethin' like this?"

Before she cursed, Emma Jean closed her eyes and said slowly, "You'll never understand, so ain't no need in me tryin' to explain it to you. It ain't none o' yo' business nohow."

"You right, you right! You shonuff right about it. But I was layin' in bed the other night, tryin' to figure out how a mother can decide to change the baby she had. It just don't make no sense to me, Emma Jean."

"It don't need to! Leave it alone, Mamie, and mind yo' own business. We workin' it out the best way we can."

"Oh, I don't mean no harm, Emma Jean. I didn't mean to upset you, especially not in yo' condition. You done got enough punishment from God without me sayin' a word!" Mamie smacked her lips. "And He might not be through with you yet."

Emma Jean wanted to tell Mamie to go to hell, but of course that would've been rude.

"I'ma get on out of the way, girl. I just come by to see how you doin'. You be sho to let me know if I can do anything for you, you hear?"

Emma Jean nodded.

"I baked a sweet potato pie for the boys. *All* of 'em. I didn't want you to worry 'bout no cookin'."

Emma Jean was glad she couldn't move. She would've slapped Mamie Cunningham, elder or not.

"Let's just pray nothin' else happens. Sometimes, when God whips us, He gets out o' control. You know what I mean?"

Emma Jean refused to respond.

"Well, toodeloo!" she sang, sashaying through the door, glad that God's wrath had visited itself upon her neighbor.

Why had Gus let her in the room, Emma Jean wondered. He knew they despised each other. He had done it for spite, she concluded, but, angry as she was, she couldn't confront him. His anger might boil again and result in another thrashing. So she tolerated others as they came and went, and prayed that Mamie Cunningham would keep her nosy ass away from her house.

Then, one day, the most unexpected visitor arrived.

"Well, well," Henrietta joked.

Emma Jean opened her eyes. "What do you want?"

"I came by to see how you doin', honey!" She slapped Emma Jean's back.

"Ahhhhhhhhhhhh! Shit!" Emma Jean screeched. "That ain't funny! It still hurts!"

"Hurt? You wanna talk about hurt?"

"Oh, don't start that! I done told what I did, so why can't you let it go! Everybody knows now."

"Yeah, but everybody don't know what you did to *me*!"

"It don't make no difference. It's over. Everybody thinks I'm a bad person, and that's what you wanted, right? For everybody to think I'm a bad person?"

"It's always about you, Emma Jean, ain't it? You get burned and still you can't see the full truth."

There's that truth thing again, Emma Jean thought. "What is you talkin' about, Henrietta? What truth? I done told what I did."

Henrietta walked to the window and looked out. "If you can't figure it out, you don't wanna know. And I ain't gon' tell you. But God is. And when He does—"

"Oh, just get out, Henrietta! I'm tired of everybody comin' in here, actin' like they concerned. I ain't no fool."

Henrietta turned. "Fine. I'll go. But I get a feeling that, when we meet again, you gon' be *way* more sorry than you is now. We might be dead, but we gon' meet again. You believe that!"

"Oh, whatever!" Emma Jean mumbled as Henrietta left. "I ain't scared o' you!" And she really wasn't. Not yet.

Chapter 18

Three weeks later, Emma Jean was as close to her old self as she ever would be. She could only sit for a few minutes at a time, and lying on her back was out of the question. Gus relegated her to the floor again, and, like before, she reclined on her stomach without complaint. She never slept more than two or three hours a night, catnapping as often as she could during the day. That's what she hated most—the fact that she wasn't as functional as she'd once been. She felt old now. Her normally elegant, graceful stride had deteriorated to a slow, self-conscious gait, and she absolutely hated that, for comfort, she had to walk with a slight slump of frame. *But oh well*, she rationalized. *At least I'm alive.*

During Emma Jean's recovery, Paul began slopping hogs, chopping wood, and digging holes for fence posts. His once-soft hands became calloused and bruised, but he didn't dare whine. He told Mister that he despised physical labor, and Mister advised him to keep his opinion to himself. Sweat drenched his brow daily and his back ached constantly, but he never said anything to Gus. What would have been the point? This was a man's life, Gus had made him believe, so Paul had no choice but to live it.

He sneaked away one evening and met Eva Mae, who led him to a grassy expanse near the Jordan.

"Ain't this pretty?" she said.

"Un-huh."

"I come here a lot. By myself."

"Your momma don't care?"

"Naw, she don't care. She don't even know."

Paul surveyed the endless sea of clovers. They looked like tiny green trees, he thought.

"I sit on that stump over there." She pointed and led the way. The two shared the seat.

"I can hear the Jordan," Paul said.

"I know. It sounds angry, huh? Like God crying or something."

Paul watched a robin build a nest, one straw at a time, and wished he could help. It would take the bird a year to finish, wouldn't it?

"I want a real husband one day," Eva Mae said out of nowhere.

Paul continued studying the bird.

"A real handsome man who loves me. My momma talks about it all the time. She said if she could do it over again, she'd wait for one."

"Don't she think yo' daddy's handsome?"

"I don't know. I guess so. A little bit. But I think she means *real* handsome, you know. Like the men in the Sears and Roebuck catalog."

"Oh."

"Like you gon' be. When you grow up. I can tell. You gon' be real handsome."

"How you know?"

"'Cause you pretty now. I mean, I know you a boy and all, but you still pretty. At least to me." Eva Mae smiled.

"You think so?"

"Un-huh."

"Well, you pretty, too."

Eva Mae shook her head. "No I ain't."

"Whatcha mean? Sure you are."

"No I ain't. And it's okay."

"I think you are."

"No you don't," Eva Mae said. "You ain't neva said it before."

Paul couldn't argue.

"And, anyway, my momma don't say it, so I know it ain't so. If you pretty, yo' momma's the first one to tell you. Didn't Miss Emma Jean say you was pretty back when you was a girl?"

"Yep."

"Well that's how I know."

Paul didn't try to convince her otherwise.

"We can meet here whenever you want. Nobody ever comes here."

"Okay. I like it." Paul strolled and appraised the couple's new home. When he returned to the stump, Eva Mae said, "I want a nice husband, too. A man who'll bring me flowers and stuff."

Paul reflected on Authorly's teachings. "I don't know about that. As long as he works, he oughta be fine. I wouldn't worry about that otha stuff if I was you."

"Why can't he work *and* bring me flowers?"

" 'Cause ain't no colored man got no time fo' dat. He gotta work. Besides, you can't have everything."

Eva Mae suddenly felt selfish.

"Do yo' daddy bring yo' momma flowers?"

"No."

"Mine, neither. So why you think yo' husband gon' bring you flowers?"

"I don't know. I jes' thought it would be nice."

Paul kissed Eva Mae gently on the cheek. "Don't worry. When you get old enough to marry, a real nice man might come along and bring you all kinds of flowers and stuff. You never know. But if he don't, you can still live with him. Just like our mommas do. And they don't complain."

Paul's comments disturbed Eva Mae's vision. Her mother had told her never to settle—she shuddered at women like herself who had—for anything other than a beautiful, kind man. And by beautiful, she explained carefully, she didn't mean simply his face. "You want a romantic man," Mrs. Free had said, "one who understands the importance of love and giving a woman pretty things. Stay away from dumb, country niggas." The problem was that all the men Eva Mae knew were country and, in her estimation, only a few weren't dumb.

She began to hum a melody Paul didn't know. It always started this way, with Eva Mae offering a lyrical libation before the sensuality commenced. Paul didn't know if she borrowed the melodies from the radio or composed them herself, but he loved her rough contralto, the way notes tumbled around in her throat as though struggling through some deep, dark cave before release. Instinctually, he closed his eyes and followed Eva Mae's voice, imagining each note as a soap bubble he could never quite contain. Yet Paul's joy was chasing them nonetheless, and as Eva Mae's hum crescendoed, he felt better than he'd felt in months.

"I'm not so sure about this," he said as Eva Mae took his hand and pulled him onto the soft bed of clovers.

She nodded, but continued humming.

"What if somebody catches us?"

"Nobody ever comes here. Remember? I told you that already." She resumed the song precisely where she'd left off.

Paul looked around as Eva Mae hummed softly into his ear. The melody shifted, from alto to falsetto soprano, and Paul marveled at Eva Mae's vocal range. When she parted his legs with her own, he shivered a bit. Although they had done this umpteen times, Paul never participated without apprehension, and Eva Mae always knew what to moan to ease him across the fragile divide. Unable to face her, while grateful for her desire to please him, Paul usually closed his eyes and thanked God for having a best friend.

Eva Mae kissed his lips, then kissed her way south until, unzipping his fly slowly, she retrieved the miniature phallus. When her mouth embraced it, Paul took over as songster, trying his best to hum the melody exactly as Eva Mae had done. Eva Mae's sporadic "Ummmms" harmonized with Paul's voice, leaving him assured that his notes were correct and that his body was sweet and pleasurable. Occasionally Eva Mae looked up and asked, "You okay?" and Paul's vigorous nodding encouraged her to go on. His grunting validated her performance and made her glad that he was now a boy.

Eva Mae stopped. "We better go."

Paul covered himself and said, "Yeah."

They stood. "Come on." She brushed off the back of his pants. "Yo' folks gon' be callin' for you in a minute."

Together they ran until, from a distance, Paul saw Gus staring from the porch. "I think I'm in trouble," he told Eva Mae.

She squeezed his hand quickly and ran home. Paul couldn't think of a lie to explain his whereabouts, so he hung his head as he approached and waited for Gus to speak.

"Where you been, boy?" Gus said, looking above Paul's head.

"I . . . um . . . was out playin' with Eva Mae." He hoped the truth might save him.

Gus's left hand struck Paul's neck so hard he crumpled to the ground. "You don't play wit' no girls, boy! Boys play wit' boys!"

Bartimaeus heard Paul's scream and came running. "What is it?"

"This don't concern you, son."

"What happened, Paul?"

"I said, this don't conern you!"

Paul's wailing made Bartimaeus call, "Authorly! Momma!"

"I ain't gon' have no goddamn sissy in my house!" Gus kicked Paul repeatedly. "You gon' be a man if you gon' live here!"

The blows sounded to Bartimaeus like an ax falling on a block of wood. "Authorly! Hurry!"

Blood oozed from Paul's nose by the time the family appeared. Woody grabbed one of Gus's arms and Authorly took the other. "Stop it, Gus! Stop it!" Emma Jean shouted.

"What'd he do, Daddy?" Authorly asked.

Gus continued kicking him. "You gon' be a boy! You gon' be a boy! You gon' be a boy!" His voice faded as they pulled him away. James Earl knelt next to Paul and wept with him.

Sol lifted Paul from the earth and took him to the barn. Bartimaeus and Mister followed.

Paul's moan was deep and full of pain.

"What happened?" Bartimaeus asked.

"I don't know," Sol said. He sat Paul on a pile of hay. "Get some alcohol and a bandage," he told Mister while he leaned Paul's head back and held a handkerchief to his nose.

"Paul?" Bartimaeus said. "You okay?" All he heard was sniffing and huffing. Bartimaeus covered his mouth to keep from crying.

Sol returned with Woody.

"You're gonna be all right," Woody said, tending Paul's wounds and bruises. "Daddy didn't mean to do that. You know he didn't. He's not like that." Paul's wailing became audible again.

"Then he didn't have no business doin' it!" Sol said. "You don't treat yo' own child that way!"

"Why don't you just shut up!" Woody said. "This whole thing's been really hard on him."

"On him? What about on Paul?"

"He's a kid! Kids adjust easier than grown folks!"

"Oh my God!" Sol said, tossing his arms. "You don't know what it's been like for this boy! It's harder on him than any of us!"

"Well, what would you do if somethin' like this happened to your son? Huh? You gon' be all happy and smilin' 'bout havin a boy switchin' around like a damn girl?"

"It ain't his fault, Woody!"

"I know that! But so what? It's still the truth! How a man s'pose to be at peace with a son like *that*?" He pointed at Paul.

Sol shook his head and rolled his eyes.

Bartimaeus said, "Let's just take care o' Paul for right now, okay?"

Woody pressed a bandage against the cut on Paul's forearm. "There. You'll be all right."

Sol sighed. "What happened?"

Paul peered into Sol's eyes and explained, "I-I w-was playin' w-with"—he sniffled several times—"Eva Mae d-d-down by the river and w-w-w-when I come home, Daddy started b-b-beatin' me."

Bartimaeus felt his way to Paul's right side. Sol sat on the left.

"Why is you still playin' with girls!" Woody asked with disgust.

"'Cause won't no boys play with him!" Sol answered. "You seen any 'round here lookin' for Paul?"

"I guess not!" Woody said, and stormed away.

"Listen," Sol said, "I know this ain't been easy for you, but you gotta hang in there." He wiped tears from his little brother's face. "This ain't yo' fault. Daddy just don't know how to handle it."

Paul whimpered.

"Just stay away from Eva Mae. I know she's your friend and she means well and all, but for right now, just leave her alone."

Sol and Mister accompanied Paul to the living room where Gus sat stupefied. Bartimaeus lingered on the porch.

"What's wrong with you?" Authorly asked.

Bartimaeus hesitated.

"What is it?"

"I knew," he said, shaking his head.

"You knew what?"

"Oh no," Woody murmured.

"About Paul. I knew before Momma said anything." Authorly's hot breath brushed his face.

"Then why didn't you say somethin'!"

"'Cause I didn't understand it. It didn't make sense to me then."

"How'd you know?" Woody asked.

Bartimaeus chuckled uncomfortably. "Paul made me feel it one day, and I hollered 'cause I couldn't believe it. I promised myself I wouldn't say nothin'."

"Then this is yo' fault, too!" Authorly said.

"I know, but I didn't know what to do."

"You could've at least told us," Woody said. "Then we woulda knowed and maybe we coulda made this situation better."

"You're a liar!" Authorly shouted. He would've hit Bartimaeus had he not been blind.

"It just didn't make sense, so I didn't say nothin'."

"That's why you're a liar!"

"Come on, man," Woody said. "Ain't no need in blamin' him. He didn't do it."

"But he knew! And when Momma told us, he acted like he didn't. At least he didn't say nothin'. I'm sick o' this shit!"

"I'm sorry, Authorly. You right. I didn't mean to lie though. I just thought it was Momma or Daddy's place to tell it. If anybody said anything at all."

"You might be blind, but you ain't stupid! That's yo' little brother, too!"

"I know, I know! But what was I s'pose to do?"

"You was s'pose to tell me! I coulda done somethin' to make this a little easier."

"Like what?"

"Hell, I don't know, but I woulda thought o' somethin'."

"It's too late now," Woody said.

"Yeah, it is, all because *somebody* didn't think enough of the rest of this family to tell the truth."

"I'm sorry, y'all. I'm real sorry. I never thought it would come to this."

"Maybe it wouldn't've if you had been man enough to tell the truth!" Authorly stormed into the house.

"You know how he is," Woody said. "He'll be all right."

Bartimaeus nodded. Authorly wasn't the brother he was worried about.

Gus said nothing the remainder of the evening. On his way to bed, he paused in the center of the living room, and, without looking at Paul, said, "Sorry," and proceeded into the bedroom, closing the door softly.

Emma Jean was already on the floor. Gus slung his overalls across the footpost and reclined.

"Gus, you didn't have to do the boy like that. He's doin' the best he can."

Gus grunted.

"I know this is all my fault."

"It sho is."

"But don't take it out on the boy. He's just as sweet as he can be."

"Yeah," Gus murmured. "That's the problem."

Emma Jean waited. "You had every right to beat me. I cain't argue with that. But you didn't have no right to beat him. He gon' change with time. It ain't gon' happen overnight."

"I know that."

"Then what chu beatin' him for?"

Gus couldn't explain it. "I ain't been right since all this happened. I shoulda gone to the river."

"Well, I ain't in that, but ain't no need in you makin' that boy pay for what I done. Just give him time."

"He was playin' with that little Free girl, and I done told him about that."

"Gus, he been knowin' her all his life. She ain't gon' disappear just 'cause he's a boy now."

"I don't need her to disappear. I need him to find some boys to play wit'."

"Ain't none! His own brothers don't wanna fool with him, so what make you think some other boys gon' play with him?"

"I don't know."

Gus reclined heavily and studied the ceiling. He couldn't figure out what was happening to him. He hated violence—always had—and now he was its perpetrator?

"And why would you kick the boy like he some stray dog or somethin'? Kick me if you want to, but yo' own son?"

Emma Jean heard the sheets rustle, but Gus never responded.

"It's been a couple of months now, and you and Authorly don't do nothin' but torture the child. I know he gotta grow up to be a man, but that don't mean y'all gotta treat him like he ain't worth nothin'." She thought of herself at his age, facedown in the chicken coop. "Don't no child deserve that, Gus."

He asked God to forgive him.

"You ain't said two words to the boy since all this happened. I know it's hard, baby, and I ain't neva been mo' sorry about nothin' in my life, but it's done now. You might not be smart, but you ain't neva been mean, and ain't no need in startin' now. He cain't help who he is. Or what he is. He gon' always be different, but he's still our child."

Gus rose, slid into his overalls, and went to the living room. In the dark, he stood over Paul, lying on the cot between Mister and Sol, and almost reached to touch him. However, fearing the overflow of his heart, he stood there, like a ghost, unable to love the son he had adored as a daughter. Paul had heard his footsteps and now lay still, afraid that the slightest movement might rekindle Gus's fury and provoke him to beat him again. His father's presence was heavier than the quilt, and all Paul could do was pray the old man would go away.

Gus turned and ran into the front yard. Most of his tears were restrained, but a few broke free, running hard and fast down his scaly, razor-bumped cheeks. He wanted to love the boy, but his heart wouldn't allow it. Whenever he thought of Paul, he thought of the daughter he used to kiss on the lips, and the memory made him nauseous.

Peeking from behind the living room curtain, Paul watched Gus flail his arms wildly in the moonlight as though fighting someone he couldn't see. Paul couldn't discern what Gus was saying, but he heard snippets of "but why me?" and "how am I supposed to . . ." as Gus struck the air angrily. *He must be fighting God,* Paul thought. Who else could it be? God was the only one Who could've stopped this, and since He didn't, Gus was probably angry with Him, Paul concluded. He looked like he was giving God a piece of his mind and God was trying not to hear it.

With each swing, Gus stumbled, failing to make contact. Most of his expletives, which Paul heard as grunts and shrieks, were unintelligible, but Paul knew the battle was about him. At times he found himself rooting for Gus, wanting to believe that human flesh could actually overpower the spirit, and other times he hoped God would win and show Gus, finally, how to love him again. Either way, Paul knew for sure that a man couldn't fight God and come out unscathed.

"I ain't gon' let go 'til You explain this to me!" Paul heard Gus shout to the heavens. He could hardly make out his father's form in the dark. "You gon' tell me somethin' right now!"

The sight frightened Paul, so he retracted from the window and resumed his place between his brothers. He didn't know exactly what Gus had asked for, but he believed his life would be easier if God granted it, so he mumbled, "Fix Daddy's heart, God. Please."

A half hour later, Gus returned, panting, dragging a disjointed hip, and hobbled to the master bedroom. He would never walk fully upright again. The hip was frozen, refusing to shift or swivel, causing Gus to lean slightly in compensation for its stubbornness. Whenever people asked what happened, he said, "Me and God had it out." Only Sugar Baby knew the full story.

Emma Jean stirred when Gus reentered. "I didn't mean to make you upset."

"I ain't upset," Gus said, sliding out of his overalls again. "You can come back to bed if you want to."

Emma Jean didn't hesitate. She rose, folded the battered quilt, laid it at the foot of the bed, and thanked God her days on that cold floor were over. She believed erroneously that Gus had searched his heart and found the strength to forgive her. Actually he felt guilty that he couldn't love an innocent—and effeminate—son, so much so that he would kick the shit out of him. So how could he punish Emma Jean? He couldn't even promise that, given a similar circumstance, he wouldn't beat the boy again, so he had no choice, he felt, but to welcome Emma Jean back to her original resting place. Of course the devil in hell couldn't make him touch her—sometimes erections came when he thought of other women, but when Emma Jean crossed his mind, he immediately went limp—so Gus resolved to try to be kind, at least until the rains came again.

"I think he oughta go to school," Emma Jean said softly. "He ain't no good at field work. You said so yourself. Education's 'bout the only chance he gon' have to make somethin' outta hisself."

Gus frowned in the dark, rubbing his sore hip. "I can't send but one to school. I need all the help I can get in the field. We gotta eat."

Authorly's and Woody's education had ended after the eighth grade. They didn't complain. In fact, Authorly was glad. He never understood its utility anyway, especially since he knew he'd live out the entirety of his days farming in Swamp Creek. Woody simply hated homework, so he offered no resistance. James Earl's going would have been a colossal waste of time, his parents agreed, so he never missed what he never had. Mister wasn't moved by knowledge one way or the other, although Miss Erma said he was smart, so Emma Jean didn't mind him going to the field. It was King Solomon who'd have a fit when they told him he had to quit.

"What you gon' tell that boy?" Gus asked. "Seem like he oughta go to school if anybody go. He de smart one."

"Paul's smart, too. And, anyway, Sol know how to work. He'll be more help in the field than Paul ever will be."

Gus paused. "All right. But you gon' tell him. He gon' be mad, too."

"I know." Emma Jean sighed. "Ump, ump, ump. But it's for the best. He'll understand. One day."

Chapter 19

Gus rose before dawn the next morning and said, "Mister, you and Paul go down to Morrison's and get a bag o' feed for the cows. Don't let it take you boys all day."

This was what Paul had dreaded—the insensitive eyes of his neighbors, scrutinizing him, whispering, and asking him things he couldn't possibly know. But to disobey Gus would've been worse, so he grabbed his hat and followed Mister down the road. Along the way, Paul convinced himself that it was no big deal anymore, since everyone knew, but he had horribly underestimated the fears and curiosity of those who didn't understand.

From a distance, a group of old men, sitting on a worn church pew in front of the store, looked up as the boys approached.

"That's him right there," Stump murmured. Though he was born James Edwards Jr., folks called him Stump because at five foot three he stopped growing vertically and started growing horizontally. In his younger years, people called him stout. Now, after seventy-odd years, they called him big as a house. An unlit pipe protruded from the right corner of his mouth. "He don't look like no boy to me. You ever seen a boy twist like that?"

Charles Simmons, chairman of the trustee board at St. Matthew, shook his head sadly. He'd had a son *like that*, he remembered. Thirty years ago. Before he sent him away forever. "That chile ain't gon' never be right. You mark my word."

The other men agreed.

When Mister and Paul were within earshot, the men quieted. Paul felt their eyes on him like one feels a cold draft in the dark. They nodded cordially as the boys passed, and Paul tried to smile, hoping the gesture might soften their critique. The moment they thought he'd disappeared, they continued:

"That boy is sweet as sugar! Shit! I don't know what Gus gon' do with him," Stump said.

Paul was standing just inside the screen door, listening.

"I don't know, either, but I'm glad it ain't me. I couldn't have nothin' like that in my house." Charles spit tobacco into the road. "Gus need to send that child off somewhere."

"What good would that do?"

"A whole lot! Least folk 'round here wouldn't have to look at him every day."

"Well, maybe Gus is tougher than we thought. But I'm like you—I couldn't take it." His face grimaced as if he'd suddenly smelled something dead. "I can take a whole lot o' things, but I can't stand no punk. And that boy gon' be a punk the rest o' his life. That's for sure. Ain't nothin' else he *can* be."

"Well, not necessarily," Charles teased. "He might get some pussy one day. That'll straighten him out!"

The men hollered.

"Sheeeeeeit! You must be crazy, man. Pussy is good shonuff, but it ain't magical."

"The hell it ain't! First time I got a piece, it left me cross-eyed for a week."

The men howled as they slapped each other's palms.

"Yeah, I guess you right." Stump chuckled. "Been so long since I had some, I guess I done forgot what it's like."

"No siree!" Charles said. "If you done forgot what it's like, then you ain't neva had none! Pussy's kinda like God—it's too good to forget!"

"But what woman you know gon' open her legs for a ole sissified boy like *that*?"

"You never know! Some women is desperate."

"They ain't that damn desperate! If a woman give that boy some pussy, it's 'cause she like pussy herself!"

Charles collapsed across the other men as they screamed with laughter. Then he lifted a limp wrist and said, in a high falsetto, "But, Stump, I think you's mighty cute."

"Don't start no shit wit' me, Charles Simmons! You know I don't play like that! Hell, I believes in God."

The men cackled gleefully as Paul tried not to cry.

"I think it's a damn shame what that woman did," Stump said. "If it was me, I woulda beat that bitch 'til they had to call the law on me! Then I woulda set her crazy ass on fire, too!"

"You think Gus set her on fire?"

"I don't know, but I sho woulda! When I got through with her, she woulda been runnin' up and down the road hollerin' like she was in hell."

Paul covered his mouth as the men snickered.

"I sho hope don't no man mess with that boy," Charles said. "You know you can't put nothin' past Negroes these days."

Paul walked away. He'd heard enough. The men's laughter lingered like smoke. He kept looking back over his shoulder, wondering how in the world they could be so mean. He wanted to cry, but he wanted more not to, so he browsed the shelves and tried to forget what he'd heard. He knew the men and they knew him. That's what really hurt. Some of them were church officials, and others had visited the Peace home on several occasions. It just didn't make sense to Paul that those who had once smiled at him, who had taught him Sunday school and prayed until they wept, were now making fun of him. And they had absolutely no shame about it.

"Hi, baby," Miss Mamie said, interrupting Paul's thoughts. When he turned, she saw the tears in his eyes. "Aw, come here!" She pressed Paul's head into the center of her bosom.

Paul liked the sweetness of her perfume and the warm, comforting feeling of her flesh. It reminded him of how he used to lie on Emma Jean as she read to him. Back when he was somebody else.

"You gon' be all right, baby," she said, pushing Paul away from her. "You just stick with the Lord. He gon' bring you through. He do it every time!"

Paul wanted to ask how soon the Lord was going to do it, but he didn't.

"You still jes' as cute as you can be." She pinched his cheeks. "It's jes' kinda hard for folks, you know, to think of you as a boy. It'll probably take a little time, but afterwhile everything'll be okay. At least I guess it will. I certainly hope so." She smiled. "How's yo' momma?"

"Fine."

"Well, that's good. You be sho to tell her hello for me."

"Yes, ma'am."

"And don't you worry none 'bout what folks say. You jes' go 'head on and walk with the Lord. He'll bring you through." She swung the screen door open and walked away with an armload of groceries.

Paul wasn't exactly clear what she was talking about. Was God on His way to save him from something?

"Let's go," Mister called behind him.

Paul followed and entered the lion's den once more.

"You boys take care," Stump said.

Mister mumbled, "Yessir," while pulling Paul along.

"By the way," Charles Simmons asked, "is you a boy now *for real?*"

Paul's tears returned.

"Don't say that to that boy!" Stump admonished. "That ain't none o' yo' business. You'll mess around and hurt his feelings."

"Just come on," Mister said. "Don't pay them no mind."

Paul wished Gus would send him away like Charles Simmons had suggested. He didn't know where he'd go or whom he'd live with, but there had to be a place, somewhere in the world, where people loved him. Or at least liked him. He would've gone without Gus's permission if he'd had the money. He didn't need but a little. Now that he knew how to work, he convinced himself that someone would pay him for his labor. Someone in a faraway place. Not anyone near Swamp Creek. They knew too much about him. He wanted a place where all he'd ever been was a boy so no one could tease him about having been anything else. They'd look at his soft demeanor and sensitive ways, Paul thought, and think that was the way he'd always been, and no one would think twice about it. In Swamp Creek, his only friend was Eva Mae and since she was a girl, he wasn't supposed to play with her anymore. But since no boys wanted to play with him, he started hoping that what Miss Mamie said would come true. Soon.

Chapter 20

On Authorly's twentieth birthday—August 23, 1949—he announced at supper, "I'm gettin' married Sat'dey. Y'all comin', ain't cha?"

Gus was relieved. He didn't care that the boy had no other life aspirations; he was simply glad he wouldn't have to feed him anymore. Whenever Emma Jean fried chicken, she fried one for him and one for everyone else. He did his fair share of work, Gus admitted, but any child who consumed half of a man's entire fall harvest needed his own place.

"But you ain't got no girlfriend!" Mister said. "Ain't you s'pose to have a girlfriend before you marry somebody?"

"You don't know what I got! And, anyway, I do got a girlfriend and that's why I need to get out on my own."

Gus agreed. He didn't want to hurt the boy's feelings with expressions of jubilation, so he said, "You do what you thank you oughta do, son. You'll be fine. I done taught you how to work, so you ain't neva gon' starve. Not you!"

The others laughed.

"What about me?" James Earl asked softly.

Authorly said, "You comin' wid me."

Everyone frowned except Emma Jean. "That's a good idea," she said. "That way he'll have somethin' to do."

"You can live with me," he explained. "It'll be like us sharing a wife. Well, you can't *have* her, if you know what I mean, but she'll love both of us. She won't mind. I done already asked her."

Emma Jean touched Authorly's shoulder in gratitude. Of course she loved her firstborn, but what was she to do with him? All he wanted in life was

Authorly's approval, so it made sense to Emma Jean for him to stay with Authorly forever.

"I won't get in the way," James Earl promised. "And I'll do whatever you say."

"You're fine, little brother. Don't worry. We gon' be just fine."

Emma Jean hated to see Authorly go. He had been her measure of manhood around the house—the one she prayed the younger ones would emulate—and she made him promise to stop by often and talk to his younger brothers. Unlike Gus, she would miss his enormous appetite and his protective presence. In her mind, Authorly had been her man and, in some ways, she felt as if she were losing a spouse. But she couldn't stop him. She didn't even try.

Paul had mixed feelings. On the one hand, he was glad Authorly was leaving because another summer of his tyrannical teachings was more than Paul's sensitive spirit could bear. He especially hated maneuvering the worms onto the fishing hook. Each time he screamed, Authorly punched his arm, until he learned to keep his fears to himself. Then, he was beaten again when it took him too long to take the flapping fish off the hook. He would've shot Authorly, on several occasions, had he known how to use the gun, and he convinced himself that he wouldn't have regretted it for a moment. On the other hand, the cow milking, wood gathering, and general farm labor weren't so bad. Actually, he was beginning to get used to it, and he had no one to thank but Authorly. Paul was forced to admit that, although he had hated Authorly at first, the transition into boyhood would've been impossible without him. Now Woody and Sol would have to finish the job since Gus was obviously uninvested in anything concerning Paul.

"You and Eula Faye gon' be so happy!" Emma Jean said, smacking on a square piece of corn bread.

Authorly smiled. "Yeah, I know. Her daddy is grinnin' from ear to ear."

Authorly had stopped Eula Faye at Morrison's a year earlier. He had been watching her rotund behind since he was fifteen, but had never gathered the nerve to speak. Not until she switched past him, and his left hand accidentally brushed her bottom. He knew then she'd be his wife.

"I'm mighty sorry, ma'am," Authorly said, shoving his hands in his pockets. "I didn't mean to touch you that way."

Eula Faye beamed. "Well, you did, and I guess I forgive you, Mr. Authorly Peace." Reaching for a five-pound bag of sugar, she added, "And you can come keep company with me if you want to."

Authorly hollered. "Yippee! I do want to. I do!"

He carried her groceries home, and by the time they arrived, she was his girlfriend. She loved a thick black man, she said, especially one with battered overalls, 'cause that meant he loved to work.

"I got that from my daddy. I ain't neva seen him sleep past five, and even if he sick, he do somethin' 'round de house." Eula Faye laughed. Her father had told her that, if she prayed, God would send her a good black man one day. She didn't know it would be within a week. "I likes you, Mr. Authorly Peace."

"I likes you, too, Miss Eula Faye Cullins."

They stood in front of her folks' house and talked—well, Authorly talked—for the next three hours, and when he left, Eula Faye told her mother, "I'ma marry that man 'fo de month's out."

Authorly decided not to tell anyone about Eula Faye, afraid that if she changed her mind, he would be too embarrassed to recover. But the Friday he asked her to marry him and she said yes, he was the most confident young man in all of Conway County.

"When you wants to marry me, Mr. Authorly Peace?" she teased.

"Um . . . how 'bout a year from Saturday? That'll give me time to make some money," he said casually, and smiled.

Eula Faye leapt into his arms, kissed his forehead, and said, "Fine with me. I'll be waitin'."

Authorly hesitated.

"What is it?"

"It's about my brother. James Earl."

"What about him?"

"Well, I been takin' care o' him all his life. He kinda slow and I was wonderin' if you wouldn't mind him comin' to stay with us. He works real hard and he ain't no bother."

"Okay," Eula Faye said. Authorly's desperation suggested that if she was going to have the Peace she wanted, she'd have to take the Peace she didn't. "I guess I can live with that. Two men 'round the house oughta be better'n one anyway."

Mr. Buddy Cullins sobered up for the only wedding he'd ever attend, and he told Authorly that he and Eula Faye should have as many children as the Good Lord would allow. They obeyed, halting their reproduction only during the year of the tragedy. Twenty years later, Eula Faye awakened one morning in a battle with menopause she couldn't hope to win. "Oh well," she sighed.

"The Lord said be fruitful and multiply, and I done done that. Ten children oughta satisfy Him."

During the wedding ceremony, Eula Faye almost ran away when she looked up and saw both Authorly and James Earl marching toward her in matching suits. Folks turned their heads and covered their mouths. James Earl marched alongside Authorly as though he were the bride, and Eula Faye prayed she wasn't making the mistake of her life. Her fears were relieved once the three moved in together, and she discovered that James Earl was a better companion than Authorly. James Earl loved to listen to her rant and rave about arbitrary people or things, and his favorite pastime was rubbing her tired, aching feet. Authorly, on the other hand, loved to be listened to, and after twenty minutes of his self-absorbed babbling, she simply tuned him out and focused her attention on her second husband. He—not Authorly—made her feel special and important. James Earl was the daytime man, the one who accompanied her to the store or listened to the radio shows with her, and Authorly took the night shift, exciting her flesh and talking until the sound of his voice lulled her to sleep.

At the wedding, Paul wondered if he would ever marry. He didn't have a girlfriend and didn't want one, but he liked the idea of having a family. Emma Jean used to tell him, in his former life, "I can't wait 'til your weddin' day, honey. It's gon' be so wonderful. You gon' marry the man of your dreams and you gon' be the most beautiful bride anyone's ever seen! Oh, it's gonna be so great!"

Back then, Emma Jean's joyful anticipation made Paul laugh. Now, she never mentioned marriage anymore, and Paul understood clearly that, if he did marry, he wouldn't be the beautiful one, and that was the only reason he had wanted a wedding in the first place. Eula Faye looked pretty in her rose red dress, Paul noted, but Authorly looked like he did every day. If that was all the man was supposed to get out of the deal, then Paul decided it wasn't worth the trouble.

Gus patted Authorly's back and wished him well. Ten months later, the children started coming. They called both Authorly and James Earl Daddy. They weren't confused. Eula Faye explained that since two men took care of them, both men deserved equal honor, so the children acted accordingly. Whenever folks asked Nicodemus, the oldest boy, "Who's yo' daddy?" he would say, "Authorly and James Earl Peace." "But which one is *yo'* daddy?" "Both of them!" he'd say, nodding. The fact that some resembled James Earl made others believe that he had fathered a few, but had they mentioned this to him, he would have stumbled away in tears.

Normal Jean was the second child. Doc Baker told Eula Faye that something was wrong during her pregnancy and that more than likely the child would be abnormal in some way. Refusing to believe him, Eula Faye started calling the baby Normal in hopes of countering Doc's prophecy. It didn't work. Her Down syndrome, however, didn't make Eula Faye change the child's name. It just made people use it more enthusiastically.

The third baby was a boy James Earl named James Earl. Eula Faye handed the child to her second husband like one presenting a child to Christ, and he never left James Earl's side. He'd wave to Authorly as though saluting a stranger while clinging to his other daddy's pant leg. And since his mind, like James Earl's, was basically dysfunctional, Authorly and Eula Faye released the child unto one with whom they felt he could identify. After breast-feeding, Eula Faye would pass him back to James Earl, in whose bosom the child slept most easily. In his precious spare time, James Earl built a miniature bed and placed it next to his own, and that's where the boy slept until his fifth birthday. The day after, James Earl dismantled both beds and built a bigger one, and the two slept there, spoon fashion, until the rainy day, twenty years later, when James Earl Sr.'s heart stopped beating and he passed away.

Throughout the wedding, Paul noticed that all the men, including Gus, were most interested in—and amazed by—Eula Faye's voluptuous behind. Her form-fitting dress, which elicited both praise and profanity, outlined the contours of her buttocks as though someone had pasted the garment onto her skin. Men of all ages gawked in shameless awe and wonder.

"Goddamn!" one man hollered to the other menfolk. "Now dat's what you call a ass, boys! That ain't no butt. Nosiree. Shit, everybody got a butt. That's a ass!"

The men laughed freely. Paul now knew what men talked about when women weren't around. Was this the kind of man he was expected to become?

Chapter 21

What should've been an exciting first day of school for Paul began with immeasurable anxiety. He'd hoped that, like his brothers, he could avoid the drudgery of academic work, but when Gus told him he was going to school, Paul realized his personal desires meant nothing. Too afraid to protest, he simply nodded and hoped he'd do well. His prayer had been that his parents would continue to let Sol go since he was the one who loved knowledge, but Emma Jean had another plan.

"Get your satchel, Paul," she called cheerfully after clearing the morning dishes. "And don't forget your lunch."

Sol came in from feeding the hogs just as Paul was lacing his good shoes. To avoid the pain in his brother's eyes, Paul hurried through the door and dashed down the road. Sol was left staring his contempt at Emma Jean.

"I'm sorry, honey, but he needs it worse than you. You can read all you want. I'll even buy you a book the next time I'm at Morrison's."

Emma Jean's words didn't diminish Sol's fury. He would never forgive her for what she'd done. Never. And, unfortunately for her, the day would come when she'd need his forgiveness worse than anything she could imagine.

Eva Mae sat at the desk to Paul's right, surveying their classmates as though daring anyone to bother him. Most of the students were kids he knew, mainly from church, and most of them couldn't stop staring. The Chambers twins at least smiled when they looked—that smile that lets you know something's wrong with you—and Christina, Miss Mamie's granddaughter, waved softly. She was prettier now, Paul thought, than she had been at his birthday party, and maybe, outside of Emma Jean's and Miss Mamie's purview, they could be friends.

Then there was Johnny Ray Youngblood. Eva Mae said he was the cutest boy in Swamp Creek. She had spoken of him incessantly throughout the summer, and Paul remembered Emma Jean teasing him about marrying a Youngblood one day. That was back when he was Perfect. Now he was a boy and he knew that boys weren't supposed to call other boys cute. Or even think of them that way. Yet throughout the day he found himself looking at Johnny Ray, like most of the other kids, hoping he'd look back. He planned to tell Eva Mae on the way home that she had been right—he *was* the cutest boy in Swamp Creek. Maybe even the whole world. Paul hoped he and Johnny Ray could be best friends, too, like he and Eva Mae were. She wouldn't mind. Maybe the three of them could play together sometimes, he thought, after they finished their chores. Paul didn't really care what they did. He just wanted Johnny Ray's company. Maybe then kids would like him, too.

Miss Erma, the teacher, was a short, stout woman with an unusually small waistline. Women envied her figure while men dreamed of touching it. She was known for her stern disposition, and to be out of line at school guaranteed any child a firm ass whipping. Parents loved it. Whatever Miss Erma said happened is precisely what happened, as far as they were concerned, and a second beating was guaranteed if a first had been necessary. Paul feared her worse than he feared Gus.

"Good morning, class," she began at seven thirty sharp.

"Good morning, Miss Erma," the students responded.

"We have several new students with us this term, and I want you to welcome all of them."

Paul's nerves began to fray. He hoped Miss Erma wouldn't call his name aloud.

"I'm going to introduce each new pupil and the rest of you will greet them accordingly."

Oh no!

The Redfield boys, Swamp Creek's resident rascals, looked at Paul and began to snicker.

"I'll have none of that!" Miss Erma declared. She stared at all three of them, and they immediately fell silent. Paul wished he could run away. He knew what those boys were saying about him. He hadn't heard them, but he knew, and he couldn't imagine how he'd survive the ridicule without Authorly or somebody there to protect him. Caroline flashed a big, warm smile, and Eva Mae leaned and touched his shoulder lovingly. "You'll be okay," she whispered.

Miss Erma called name after name until finally she said, "And we have with us this year another Peace boy. His name is Paul, class, and I want you to welcome him."

Everyone hung their heads, but said nothing.

"I said *welcome* him!" Miss Erma admonished, and the class returned a pitiable "Hello." She studied each face angrily. "I don't know what you've heard or what you think about this young man, but in this classroom, he will be respected. Am I understood?"

A few murmured, "Yes, ma'am."

"Am I understood!"

"Yes, ma'am!" the children returned, louder.

"We are here to learn, young people. Education is the most precious gift a person can receive, and you must take it seriously. It's the key to Negro progress and freedom. We do *not* have time for vain foolishness."

Paul began to like Miss Erma. She had stood up for him and that made him want to please her.

"Furthermore, if Paul is anything like his brother Sol, we have ourselves a genius in the making." Miss Erma winked at him. Paul knew he was nothing like Sol, but he was determined to try.

For the next several weeks, Paul practiced his ABCs and learned how to spell his name. School wasn't so bad after all, he decided, although he still would've preferred manual labor. Miss Erma had whacked him across his fingers a time or two for sloppy penmanship and all he'd wanted to do was go home. But once his letters began to take shape and he could write his name legibly, Miss Erma praised his efforts and he forgave her strict demeanor.

One day in early November, eleven-year-old Lee Anthony, the second oldest of the Redfield boys, whispered to Paul, "Ain't you s'pose to be a girl?"

"No, I'm not. I'm a boy," Paul whined, and began to shiver.

"Leave him alone!" Eva Mae screeched.

"I ain't talkin' to you. I'm talkin' to *her*."

"He ain't no *her*! He's my friend and you better be quiet before I sock you in your big fat mouth!"

Paul wanted to speak for himself, but didn't have the courage.

"What's going on up there, Eva Mae?" Miss Erma called from the back of the room.

"Nothin', ma'am."

"Then why are you talking?"

Eva Mae lowered her head and whispered to Paul, "Don't pay him no mind. He's dumb and stupid like all of his brothers." But ignoring the Redfield boys was impossible, especially when, later, Lee Anthony said, "Hey you."

Instinctively, Paul looked up, and Lee Anthony winked at him. His brothers howled.

"If I have to tell you boys one more time to be quiet and do your work, I'm going to set your butts on fire! Do you understand me?"

"Yes, ma'am," they snickered, and hushed.

Eva Mae tried to kick Lee Anthony under the desk, but her leg wouldn't reach. She gave him the evil eye.

After the commotion subsided, Lee Anthony slid a note onto Paul's desk. He opened it reluctantly. Though he was unable to read the words, he certainly understood the image.

PAUL PEACE IS A FAGGOT!
AND A FREAK!

The picture was a stick-figured young girl with long, straightened hair that curled upward at the ends. She wore a mid-length dress and a smile that suggested contentment. What broke Paul's heart was his discovery of the penis behind the frills of the dress. He hadn't noticed it at first, but when he looked closer, he saw the thing dangling in midair. His hands began to tremble. The more he studied the image, the more uncomfortable he became. The penis looked awkward and out of place, like a tumor growing straight out of the child's stomach. A bad taste formed in his mouth. Then, as though taking on a life of its own, it seemed to grow the more he stared at it. He closed his eyes momentarily, then looked again. This time it was huge and undeniable. Now he hated the little girl in the picture. She didn't seem human anymore. She seemed like a monster or a beast—something that needed to be destroyed. So he crumpled the paper angrily and bit his bottom lip to keep from crying. His breathing grew more rapid. Had he once looked like that . . . that . . . thing? He leapt from his desk and dashed out the back door with Caroline chasing after him.

"What is it? What happened?" Miss Erma called.

Eva Mae snatched the note from Paul's desk, looked at it, and covered her mouth in shame. "Look at what Lee Anthony did, Miss Erma!" She extended the note and smirked to Lee Anthony. "You gon' get it now!"

Miss Erma unfolded the paper and beheld the image. She blinked several times saying, "Get out of my classroom, you vile, nasty heathens! All three of you! Get out right now!"

Lee Anthony and his brothers exited shamelessly.

The other children waited. They had never heard Miss Erma use such words or seen her mouth quiver that way. She followed the Redfield boys out the back door and found Paul weeping on Caroline's shoulder.

"Listen, son," she said, kneeling before him. "I'm not going to baby you through this. That wouldn't make you strong, and you need to be strong. You can't let those boys get to you. They need a good beating and I hope they get it tonight when I speak to their folks. But even then, there's no promise others won't tease you again in the future. I'm not going to let anyone harm you in my classroom, but you can't live there forever. You must learn to ignore ignorance, Paul. No one can save you from it. But you can't run out of the room every time another child teases you. Okay?"

Paul nodded and wiped snot onto his sleeves.

"Good. Now let's get back to the business of education. We have a lot to learn today, don't we?"

"Yes, ma'am," Caroline said.

Paul sat motionless the remainder of the day. Miss Erma's voice seemed far away, as though echoing from a distant mountain. Christina tried to cheer him by drawing a smiley face on his paper, but Paul's hurt was unreachable. He couldn't erase the image from his mind. The picture looked like a woman and a man—all in one—and he knew that wasn't normal. Now he knew why others were laughing at him, not just the old men in front of the store, but everyone in Swamp Creek. Folks must have discussed him at their dinner tables and in their private prayers. Children were probably told to leave him alone by parents who understood no more than they did. How would he ever survive this? All he knew to do was hope for Johnny Ray's company as Eva Mae plotted revenge on the Redfield boys.

Chapter 22

Sol was the first to see Miss Erma approaching. He hoped she was coming to plead with Emma Jean on his behalf. If Emma Jean let him return to school, he'd speak to her again, but if she didn't, he swore he'd ignore her the rest of his life.

His absence from school deteriorated Miss Erma's desire to teach. He had been her hope, her shining star, the only real reason she hadn't quit. Now, she questioned the worth of her sacrifice, wondering whether lesson plans, for instance, weren't simply a waste of time for poor Negro kids, few of whom attended school regularly. Having dreamed of an idyllic life as a Negro teacher in the South, she wished someone had informed her that colored children in Swamp Creek picked cotton better than they read, and only one or two had ever written anything. That way, she wouldn't have taken their poor final grades so personally. But she learned better. No use teaching about the wonders of the Eiffel Tower or the Taj Mahal, she told herself, when most of her pupils would never leave the county, much less the country. So, after Sol's abrupt disappearance, she abandoned her initial dream and taught mostly basic arithmetic and reading—the life skills country kids might actually use—sharing extraneous knowledge on occasion with Eva Mae Free and Napoleon Travis, the only two who shared even a fraction of Sol's remarkable genius.

He was reading Dickens's *A Tale of Two Cities* when Miss Erma and Paul entered.

"Good afternoon, everyone," Miss Erma said, following Paul into the living room.

"Oh my Lord!" Emma Jean screeched. "Come on in, ma'am! I didn't know you was comin'. This house is a mess!"

"Oh no, it's fine. Really. I wish you'd come clean mine."

Emma Jean smiled.

"I don't know how you do it with seven children, especially after the fire. And boys at that!"

"Do what? You know this house ain't clean! I do's—I mean, does—the best I can though." She offered Miss Erma a seat. "Can I get you some coffee?"

"No, thank you, Emma Jean. I'm fine."

"Dinner'll be ready in a half hour or so. I wish you'd stay and join us."

"Thank you. I just might do that."

"Well, jes' make yo'self at home," Emma Jean shouted, having nothing more to say. "I'll let you and Paul do . . . um . . . whatever y'all need to do." She returned to the kitchen.

Miss Erma followed. "I came by, Emma Jean, to tell you what happened at school today."

"Oh? Is everything all right?"

"Well, yes it is, but there was a little incident I think you should know about."

Paul turned away.

"What happened?"

Miss Erma swallowed hard. "Well, one of the Redfield boys drew a picture and gave it to Paul. It really hurt his feelings. I think he's okay though. I wouldn't worry. I just thought you and Gus should know about it."

"What kinda picture, ma'am?" Emma Jean's imagination ran wild.

Miss Erma gave her the note.

Emma Jean struggled to remain calm. "I see. Somebody needs to teach those boys some manners, don't you think?"

"Oh, absolutely! I'm going to see their folks when I leave here. Hopefully, nothing like this will ever happen again."

Emma Jean returned the wrinkled paper. "He'll be fine, ma'am."

"I'm sure he will, but maybe you should speak with him about it. You and Gus."

"Everything's gonna be fine."

Miss Erma cleared her throat. "You will speak with Gus about it, won't you?"

"I said, everything's fine—*ma'am*. I would appreciate it if you didn't mention this again. I'll handle it."

"I know this hasn't been easy for any of you. I can only imagine the difficulty—"

"Ma'am! I said I'll handle it."

Miss Erma clutched her chest in surprise.

"Now have a seat and make yourself comfortable. Dinner'll be ready in a little while if you'd like to stay."

Miss Erma dropped the matter and returned to the living room. She sighed and asked Sol, "What are you reading?"

He held up the book.

"Oh, that's a good one. I like Dickens."

"Yeah. Me, too."

"How have you been?"

"Fine." He blushed.

"I've missed you at school."

Sol nodded.

"You've still been reading consistently, I see."

"Yes, ma'am."

"I hope you're still writing, too."

Sol nodded vigorously.

"I wish you could come back to school, son. Of course you've missed a lot, but you'd catch up in a week. Maybe even a day."

"I've probably missed too much, Miss Erma."

"Certainly not. I'd be more than willing to meet you after school, if need be, to get you back on track. It wouldn't take long at all. I'm sure of it."

"The boy's gotta help his father," Emma Jean intruded, "so Paul can get a education. Sol's been real sweet about it."

"I understand, but couldn't he come back for a little while? I mean, he's so gifted!"

"I think it's better if Paul goes, 'cause the others can work with they hands. They're good at it and they like it."

Sol's eyes widened.

"Forgive me if I'm prying, Emma Jean, but I wish you and Gus would reconsider. I've never had a student like Sol. I mean, who reads Dickens just for the fun of it? He's something special and he *needs* to be in school."

"Paul is special, too," Emma Jean said with a smirk, "and the family thinks it would be better if he got a education since he's the baby."

Sol closed the book and stared at the floor. He didn't remember any such familial agreement, but he knew better than to contradict Emma Jean in front of Miss Erma.

"What is nine times eight?" she turned and asked Sol suddenly.

"Seventy-two," he blurted loudly, much to Emma Jean's chagrin.

"Seven times seven."

"Forty-nine."

"Eleven times eleven."

"One hundred twenty-one."

Emma Jean acted as if she wasn't listening.

"Who were the first five presidents of the United States?"

"George Washington, John Adams, Thomas Jefferson, James Madison, James Monroe, John Quincy Adams, Andrew Jackson . . ."

"My God," Miss Erma murmured. "And have you ever heard of any colored writers?"

Sol's brows danced. "Yes, ma'am! I have Frederick Douglass's book right here." He reached behind the sofa and retrieved *Narrative of the Life of Frederick Douglass, an American Slave.* "You ever read this one?"

Miss Erma smiled. "It's one of my favorites."

They chatted briefly about its contents, then Miss Erma tried one last time. "You must let this child come back to school, Emma Jean. You simply must!"

"I wanna go," Sol said, "but—"

"That's enough, boy," Emma Jean snapped. "You stay in a child's place. Ain't I done told you 'bout showin' out in front o' grown folks?"

"Please," Miss Erma pleaded, "let him come back. He's behind, but he'll catch up in no time. I've never met a more astute child in all my life."

"I don't need you tellin' me 'bout my children, ma'am," Emma Jean said, smiling nastily. "I know all of 'em. I raised 'em." *What the hell does "astute" mean?* she wondered.

"Then you must know what education would do for this young man!"

Emma Jean spoke louder. "We can't send but one, and it's gon' be my baby. Ma'am."

Miss Erma looked at Paul, who hoped desperately that she would win the argument.

"Momma, Sol can go! I don't mind at all! I really don't. He'd do way better'n me anyway 'cause—"

"Shut up, boy! You don't know what you talkin' 'bout! You need you some education. You different from yo' brothers. Sol can always work. He's good in the field."

"Emma Jean, we can't let a youngster with his erudition—"

"Ma'am! We ain't gon' talk 'bout this no mo'. Yo' big words ain't gon' convince me of nothin' I ain't already thought about. I done made up my mind, and I'd be mighty 'bliged if you'd respect my decision."

Obviously offended, Miss Erma sighed. "I see. Very well."

"Paul, get yo' homework done befo' supper. Sol, you go milk de cow." Emma Jean resumed cooking. "And Miss Erma, you still welcome to stay fu dinner if you'd like."

"I thank you all the same, Emma Jean, but I think I'd better be going. I have to get to the Redfields' before dark. Plus, I have papers to mark."

"I understand." Emma Jean nodded without facing her. "I thank you for all you doin' for my baby."

Miss Erma left, unable to understand why any mother wouldn't send such a naturally gifted child to school. She wanted to plead further, to ask if maybe she could tutor King Solomon in the evenings free of charge, yet, afraid of Emma Jean's wrath, she simply shook her head in dismay.

The day Emma Jean broke the news to Sol, he had wailed like Gus at the Jordan and remained inconsolable for weeks. Then, one day at supper, he wiped his last tear and said, "I'm goin' to school one day. Somewhere, somehow, I'm goin'." Paul asked Emma Jean to please let King Solomon go, but she wouldn't hear of it. The hatred in Sol's eyes was what scared Paul the most, and his subsequent guilt made him dislike school even more than he already did. Whenever he could, he rose early and escaped through the back door in order to avoid the longing in Sol's eyes.

At the beginning of his second year, Paul whispered to Sol, "I'll sneak you some books home if I can."

Sol smiled derisively. Everyone knew, although no one ever announced, that he—not Paul—read Paul's schoolbooks. Even the unassigned chapters. Whether fact or fiction, Emerson or Hughes, Sol fell asleep most nights with Paul's books upon his chest. He completed the homework assignments, too, eager to maintain his tradition of academic excellence. Paul wasn't the least bit ashamed to submit Sol's work as his own, believing, in fact, that to do so was his way of supporting Sol's vicarious education. Emma Jean loved it. Sol's meticulous penmanship and extraordinary analytical abilities kept Paul's As rolling in.

Sol resented it. His only life's passion, the thing he craved most, was knowledge, and having to fight to attain it seemed unfair. Actually, it infuriated him. Others didn't even want it, he rationalized, so why couldn't he have it? At twelve, he had been caught extracting a worn copy of *Uncle Tom's Cabin* from the garbage dump behind Morrison's General Store. Old Man Morrison drawled, "Ain't nothin' free, boy. You want that book, you gotta sweep de floor for it." Sol swept so well that Morrison hired him part time. He was there every day anyway, collecting pamphlets, discarded books, flyers, and whatever else he could gather to read, so Old Man Morrison said playfully, "Might as well hire you, huh?"

Sol was thrilled. "How much you gon' pay me, sir?"

"Pay you?" Morrison screamed. "You niggers expect white folks to give y'all de whole world? Dem books you take is yo' pay, boy, and I think that's mighty generous of me."

"I only take the ones in the trash, sir!"

"Well I'll be damned! Who you think own de trash?"

Occasionally, Sol would take new books off the shelf and mar them in some way to justify taking them home. Nobody in Swamp Creek bought brand-new books anyway, he noted. Most sat on the shelf in Morrison's the entire forty-three years it existed, having never been touched by black or white hands, so Sol felt justified in taking a few here and there, especially since he didn't get a paycheck. On the days he was required in the field, he took a few "old friends" with him, never able to simply read one at a time. When Gus let them break for lunch, he'd read as his brothers ate, telling them that reading was a kind of nourishment for the soul. Authorly always asked, "Then can I have yo' lunch?" Sol's extra-lean form worried Gus until, at thirteen, the boy lifted a railroad crosstie and carried it fifty yards. Gus stopped worrying after that.

Each year when school commenced, Sol's anger was assuaged only by the new books Paul brought home. Like an impatient fisherman awaiting the first bite of the day, he'd sit after supper and wait for Paul to pass along his satchel, anxious to encounter an unknown author or scientific concept. Paul would feign interest first, thumbing pages and nodding for Emma Jean's sake, then he'd extend the satchel to Sol, saying simply, "Here," and until bedtime, Sol would sit statuesque on the sofa, devouring worksheets, spelling books, and math lessons until he had learned far more than Paul ever would. Once he began excavating texts from Morrison's garbage, he eventually amassed his own makeshift library of discarded books, brochures, and newspapers and told Paul one evening, "You're on your own now. I don't need your books anymore." He hadn't meant to seem smug, although Paul took it that way, mumbling, "You think you're so smart." Paul's real frustration was that, now, he'd have to do his own homework and he knew his efforts would never equal his brother's. But, then again, having ridden the wings of King Solomon all those years, how could Paul complain?

A few wealthy whites, shopping at Morrison's, noticed Sol's insatiable thirst for knowledge and began giving him used books from their own personal libraries. Sol thanked them so enthusiastically that some dumped entire bags of books—like one slinging garbage into a Dumpster—onto Gus's immaculate lawn. Occasionally the Peaces would return home to find books (mostly old paperback romance novels) scattered across the yard or even dangling from the limbs of the peach tree. Emma Jean would marvel, "Look, y'all! Manna from heaven! Paul, you and Sol gon' be real smart after y'all read all dem books!" Everyone knew who read those books. *Why did Momma need to say that?* Sol wondered.

The boys would gather the books and wait for Sol's instructions. The one three-tier bookshelf Gus built for Sol's fourteenth birthday was filled to capacity in three months, and building another didn't make sense to a father who failed to understand why anyone needed to read more than two or three books in a lifetime. Sol asked Emma Jean if he could store books in the kitchen cabinets, and she teased, "Sure. Why not. Much as you Negroes eat, I cain't keep no food in 'em!" When the three cabinets filled, he began stacking books against the living room walls. Gus complained initially, then discovered, one frigid February morning, that books burn quickly and easily. When Sol caught Gus ripping pages from his only copy of *Native Son*, the boy fell to his knees and wept like the women at Jesus' tomb. He asked Gus why in the world he was burning his books, and Gus's innocuous response—"I was only burnin' de ones I thought you had done already read"—made Sol chuckle in disbelief. He began delineating the books he loved from the ones he could do without, and, that way, he avoided murdering the Peace family patriarch.

* * *

After dinner, the family migrated to the living room and listened to the radio. Emma Jean never mentioned the Redfield boys or the note and, for that, Paul was grateful. Within minutes, he tuned out the family's reverie as his mind wandered back to the days of pigtails and pocketbooks. He missed feeling beautiful, feeling special, as though his very existence was a divine gift to the world. Now, he felt ugly and unimportant. Lost in a sea of sameness among his brothers, his significance dwindled, he thought, once he became a boy, and all the manhood training in the world couldn't erase his memory of having once been the center of everyone's attention. He longed for those days. Why couldn't he be a boy *and* be beautiful? Some boys were beautiful, weren't they? Like Johnny Ray Youngblood. He was beautiful. Everyone thought so. Girls gawked whenever he approached, and boys looked away quickly as though afraid to admit what they beheld. Emma Jean had mentioned his name so many times that, now, Paul couldn't get Johnny Ray out of his mind. As much as Gus and his brothers teased him about liking girls—and he did like girls—he didn't like them the way they meant. His love for women was strictly platonic. That's why he couldn't understand when Gus beat him for playing with Eva Mae. What had he done wrong? Paul soon learned that men didn't mean for him to *enjoy* the company of women; they meant for him to *use* them for his personal pleasure. He had never thought of women that way. Emma Jean had planted in his consciousness dreams of marriage and intimacy with men while women were understood as confidantes and gossip buddies. Now he felt confused. Eva Mae was still his best friend—he sneaked and played with her in the field of clovers whenever he could—but he couldn't imagine marrying her. Certainly he loved her, but that tingling sensation Emma Jean said would come when he fell in love hadn't come. Not for her. He felt it, though, whenever Johnny Ray was around. The first time it happened, he leapt excitedly, declaring, "There's Johnny Ray, Mister! There's Johnny Ray!" Mister grabbed his arm and spun him around forcefully. "You don't do that, man! Is you crazy? Johnny Ray's a boy!" *Of course he is*, Paul thought. He didn't know then that boys couldn't celebrate other boys. Or love them. Or welcome that tingling sensation in their presence. Had it been Gus, Paul assumed, he might've been beaten yet again, and this time even more severely. So Paul learned, finally, why men keep their mouths shut about everything they think and feel. That way, they never have to explain themselves.

His feelings for Johnny Ray didn't matter anyway, Paul thought. Johnny Ray barely waved at him, so what difference did it make? Nobody would ever marry someone like him. Every day Woody or Gus reminded him to "Unfold yo' arms, boy! You ain't no girl." Or "Stop all dat damn drama! Men don't do that." Or "Put yo' hands down! Men don't swing their hands in the air like that!" There was simply too much about him that needed altering, he was made to believe, and Paul couldn't foresee a refined, polished, masculine product. He'd probably be alone the rest of his life, he told himself, but at least he'd have Eva Mae.

Chapter 23

Paul's girlhood faded into memory as the years passed. People still looked at him funny—and talked about him like a dog—but he'd learned to ignore them, for the most part. The day after his twelfth birthday, he met Eva Mae in the field of clovers.

"I can't stay long," Paul said. "Daddy'd kill me if he knew I was here."

"You mean if he knew you was here *with me*."

Paul didn't lie. "Yeah."

"Then I guess you better go," Eva Mae said.

"I don't wanna go. I like being here with you."

"I like being here with you, too."

They sat on the stump.

"Can I tell you something?" Eva Mae asked.

"Sure."

"Sometimes I still think of you as Perfect. I mean, I know you a boy and all. Everybody know it now, but you still Perfect. To me. At first I thought the name was kinda strange, but after we became friends, I started likin' it. And you just as perfect to me now as you always been."

"Thanks."

"Can I call you Perfect sometimes?"

Paul grimaced. "I don't think so. Perfect's a girl's name."

"Not really. I don't know nobody named Perfect, girl or boy. Do you?"

"No."

"So do you mind?"

Paul shrugged. "I don't care. But you can't call me that anywhere but here. If somebody else hear us, we gon' be in trouble."

"Okay. I won't forget." Eva Mae rubbed Paul's hand. Then she stood. "I got a idea!"

"What?"

"Let's look for four-leaf clovers!"

"Why?"

" 'Cause Momma said whoever finds a four-leaf clover is gonna find somebody to love them forever." Eva Mae pulled Paul from the stump.

He thought of Johnny Ray. "Okay."

"You gotta look real close. They're rare and hard to find, but I bet it's one out here somewhere."

She bent to her knees and Paul followed. Together, they split the grass with their hands, tickling each blade until it shivered between their maneuvering forefingers. Abandoning clover after useless clover, they began to uproot them for being despicably ordinary. It became a ritual, this malicious displacement, until dead sprouts lay all about them. "I don't want you!" Eva Mae declared, jerking a fragile seedling from the earth. "Or you!" She jerked another. "Or you, you, or you!"

Paul wasn't as demonstrative—he had learned not to be—but he was certainly as disappointed. "Come on," he growled. "There's gotta be one."

Eva Mae became incensed. "There"—she yanked a plant with each word— "must . . . be . . . love . . . somewhere . . . in . . . this . . . field!" Like a demolition team, the two moved upon their hands and knees, destroying the ordinary in search of the extraordinary. They wanted difference, originality, uniqueness, and they were determined to find it. Each three-leafed reject heightened their disdain for normalcy as the playmates searched for what seemed nonexistent.

Eva Mae's declarations deteriorated into vulgarity. "Where the fuck are you, four-leaf clover!" she bellowed. "You cain't hide forever!"

Paul looked at her and scowled. How would she ever get a man, he thought, talking like that?

"Oh come on! There's gotta be a four-leaf clover somewhere in this whole entire field! Shit!"

"Girls ain't s'pose to say that, Eva Mae. It ain't ladylike."

"Why not? It's just me and you here, and you're my friend."

"I know, but you a girl."

You used to be one, too! Eva Mae almost said, but didn't. "Momma didn't say it'd take a whole day just to find one!"

They paused and huffed in harmony. "I guess love is like that," Paul said. "Sometimes, you look for it a long time before you find it."

"Or you never find it at all."

Paul didn't like that possibility. He wasn't sure he believed in the myth, but he knew he wanted someone to love, so he looked again. Emma Jean had spoken of romance too many times for him to relinquish the hope. He recalled the story she'd told about the girl who, with six brothers, was so beautiful every young boy around sought her attention. He'd loved that story. Emma Jean's theatrical delivery had been priceless. Twirling and dancing across the floor, she had declared Perfect the most beautiful girl in all the land, and Perfect laughed as her self-esteem blossomed. She knew she was the story's protagonist and often closed her eyes and swayed as Emma Jean dramatized the fairy tale. In her mind's eye, she could see the chifforobe of colorful dresses but could only vaguely imagine what a canopy bed looked like. Her mother tried to explain, having seen one in a Sears, Roebuck and Co. catalog, but Perfect couldn't understand why anyone would have a huge piece of cloth suspended in midair above their bed. Was it to block the sun or catch mosquitoes? But that wouldn't make sense, she reasoned, since beds aren't outside.

She'd also imagined quite clearly the tall, handsome suitor in the story. Emma Jean had said, "Just look at your father—then imagine the opposite!" The story led to Emma Jean and Perfect whispering about every young boy they encountered. "Is he one of them?" Perfect would murmur. Usually, Emma Jean rolled her eyes and frowned. "Ugh! Hell naw!" Only occasionally did she affirm, "Now that one's got potential," until Perfect sculpted an image of what the perfect man might look like.

Paul hadn't heard the story in years. He'd never hear it again now. No one had composed any narrative for him as a boy, and he decided that, if he was going to survive, he'd have to create his own story, complete with a fairy-tale ending even he couldn't imagine. So that day in the field of clovers, he began to mentally construct a self-conceived, self-affirming tale that would take him a lifetime to complete.

"I'm gonna find one," he told Eva Mae, resuming the search. "I'm gonna find me a four-leaf clover, and I'm gonna find it today."

His determination was contagious.

"It's probably just some dumb old story grown people tell kids. You know what I mean?" Eva Mae resumed the search.

Paul didn't care. His hope was far greater than his doubt. He wanted a guaranteed love, and he was willing to search the world over for proof that he'd have it.

"Ah, come on," Eva Mae huffed. "I know you're here." Her face was only centimeters from the grass. "Just let me find you. I'll take care of you. I promise. Come on, four-leaf clover. You're in here somewhere. I know you are. You have to be. There's got to be at least one of you. At least one." Moments later, she reclined in the grass and said, "Just forget about it. I don't even care anymore."

Paul wasn't so easily discouraged. "Where are you, Mr. Clover?" he murmured. "I have to find you. I have to. Come on, now. Don't hide from me. I need you." He was now thirty yards from where Eva Mae lay basking in the late afternoon sun. Behind herself, she left a trail of discarded foliage as though knowingly blazing a path others would have to tread. For the next hour or so, Paul ignored the retreating sun, determined to find tangible evidence that, against what Gus believed, he really was perfect, and someone, somewhere, someday would fall in love with him.

"Here's one!" he shouted at dusk. "Oh my God! I found it! Here it is! And it's bigger than the other ones." Paul cupped his hands around it, but didn't pick it. "Come look, Eva Mae!"

Casually, she strolled to where he was kneeling. "Let me see," she mumbled, and knelt.

"Here it is!"

"I see it! You ain't gotta yell," Eva Mae screamed back.

Paul lowered his voice, though only slightly. "Ain't this great? I found a four-leaf clover!" He clapped like a toddler. "This means someone's gonna love me forever, right?"

"That's what they say. I don't know how true it is though."

Eva Mae's skepticism didn't dampen Paul's spirit.

"We'd better be gettin' home. It's late," she said.

Paul looked around and sighed. "Yeah, it is." He plucked the clover from the earth, shoved it in his pocket, and began to run.

"See ya," Eva Mae yelled, sprinting in the opposite direction.

Just as Paul arrived home, the sun vanished. Gus met him on the road.

"Where you been, boy?" he said, shifting his weight to his good hip.

"I'm sorry, Daddy. I just forgot what time it was."

"That ain't what I asked you."

Paul hesitated.

Gus thought to slap him, but instead said, "Get in that barn and get yo' chores done." Then he hobbled away.

Paul thanked a sovereign God. As he carried the cows their portion of hay, then slopped the hogs, he dreamed of the love that was now promised. After returning the slop bucket to its resting place, he waltzed across the barn floor, lost in the arms of an imaginary lover. Twisting and twirling to the silent music, Paul envisioned someone bowing before him, declaring their everlasting love. That's what the clover promised, right? Then, all those mean people in Swamp Creek would have to take back all the ugly things they'd said about him because he'd be lovable and desirable like any other handsome young man.

Suddenly, he conceived an idea. There was no one present, so there would be no harm done. He'd just do it for a moment. Just to remember or, maybe, foresee what his future beheld. Paul glanced around to ensure that he was alone, then extracted old garments of Emma Jean's from the bag in the loft. It was a silly idea, he knew, since he was a boy now, but it couldn't hurt anything. He simply needed a reminder that he was still special. And beautiful.

He slipped the floral-print summer dress over his head and let it fall across his shoulders. It was too big, of course. Emma Jean was a good fourteen on any day, and Paul was barely a four. But it didn't matter. This was all make-believe. It didn't have to be perfect, he thought. It was just a moment. He excavated an old, wrinkled hat from the bag and sat it atop his narrow head. Then he slid his feet into a dusty pair of black heels, which fit better than any of the other items. He laughed at himself. He felt a freedom he had almost forgotten. Returning to the dance floor, he performed a solo waltz, as if a crowd of viewers were watching and applauding. The dress swayed and ballooned with each turn until Paul found himself lost in a mythical world. His steps were constrained and awkward, limited by stilettos he had never worn, but his imagination dwarfed his reality. He was the precious one, at least momentarily, the one whom others admired and desired. He was Perfect Peace again—the child his mother had waited for.

When the barn door flew open, Paul gasped, "Oh!"

Gus stared in bewilderment. "What the hell?" he whispered, closing the barn door behind himself.

Paul tried to make light of the moment. "I was just . . . um . . . Just . . . playing."

Gus shuffled toward him in slow motion.

"It ain't no big deal, Daddy. I was just thinkin' about . . ." He stepped out of the shoes and removed the hat. "It was just a joke—"

Slap!

"A joke? Just a joke? You call this"—he pointed to each item—"a damn joke?"

Paul tried to remove the dress, but his trembling hands couldn't get it over his head. Gus began ripping it from the boy's shivering frame.

"You ain't no punk, boy! I done taught you better! Boys don't wear no woman's clothes!" With each word, Gus ripped the dress until it lay in shreds across the barn floor. Paul covered his naked chest with his arms and prayed Gus wouldn't kill him.

"Is you just determined to be a sissy the rest o' yo' life? Huh!"

"No, sir," Paul mumbled, lying upon mounds of loose hay.

"Then why you keep doin' this stuff?" Gus slapped him again.

"I don't know. I didn't mean—"

"You didn't mean what?" Gus screamed, huffing with rage.

Paul sniffled, but didn't answer.

"Answer me, boy!"

"I wasn't tryin' to be no girl. I was just thinkin' about . . . um . . . different stuff." He almost mentioned the clover and its promise, but he knew it wouldn't make sense to Gus.

"I done told you I ain't gon' have no son like that in my house!"

"Yessir."

Gus grabbed the shoes and slung them against the wall. "Awwwwwww! You gon' be a man, boy! If I have to kill you first, you gon' be a man!"

Paul whimpered, "Yessir."

Gus's nostrils flared and deflated as Paul awaited his fate.

"Get up off that floor. Now!"

Paul rose, quivering. Gus snatched his arm forcefully. "I better not ever catch you doin' nothin' like this again! Do you hear me?"

"Yessir."

"You ain't no faggot, boy! You ain't!"

Paul nodded.

"I done taught you how to be a man, me and your brothers, so ain't no excuse for this shit!"

Paul continued nodding.

"I'll break yo' neck if I ever catch you doin' somethin' like this again. Do you understand me?"

"Yessir."

"I said, do you understand me, boy!"

"Yessir!"

Gus pushed Paul away from him. "Now clean up this crap and get in the house. And I don't wanna hear nothin' more about it." Gus hobbled away heavily.

Paul gathered the shredded dress, shoes, and hat and returned the bag to the loft. He couldn't figure out why Gus hadn't beaten him. That's what he deserved, didn't he? Unaware of the contract Gus had signed with God that night in the yard, Paul gave thanks that he hadn't met his end. He saw the rage in Gus's eyes. Maybe the unmerited grace was God's way of assuring Paul's life, he considered, so the myth of the clover might be fulfilled.

By thirteen, Paul's masculine aura, especially in front of men, was beginning to take shape. His walk had transformed from a sway to a swagger, and his voice had lost its soprano edge. The farm labor was defining his shoulders and arms, and he'd learned not to gawk at Johnny Ray as though desiring to consume him. The tingling sensation still came any time Johnny Ray was around, but he'd learned to conceal it. Even women noted the evolution, remarking that Paul was finally developing into a "handsome ole country boy." The only problem was that he couldn't make himself like girls the way men said he should. At least not yet. But he wasn't through trying.

In the spring of 1954, Paul contracted a fever that threatened to kill him. Covered in sweat from head to toe, he lay semiconscious for nearly a week. Doc Harris came by every evening with a different potion, hoping that something medicinal would break the spell, but nothing helped. Gus watched from a distance until Bartimaeus said, "Help him, Daddy."

"I ain't no doctor, son," Gus slurred.

"I know, but there's gotta be somethin' you can do. It's just gotta be."

Gus recalled the fever of 1912. He'd only been a boy, but he remembered how people were dying faster than the undertaker could bury them. His mother, Momma Lucy, died from the fever and Gus never forget how helpless he felt, watching her sweat and drift away. Chester Sr. tried everything, from boiling roots to prayer, but nothing broke the spell. Gus sat next to her bed the day she expired, and wept far into the night. He never forgave himself for not trying to save her.

"I don't know nothin' to do, son," he said, and collapsed onto the sofa.

Bartimaeus felt his way behind him. "Well, folks say Miss Liza Redfield could heal people. I know she dead now, but maybe some of her folks remember somethin'. It's worth a try, Daddy."

Gus didn't hesitate. "Tell yo' momma I'll be back."

When Gus returned, he told Woody to boil a pot. Then, from the chest pocket of his overalls he retrieved something that looked like dirt and poured it from his palm into the steaming water.

"What's that?" Emma Jean asked. "Smell like you cookin' chicken shit."

"Just be quiet, woman. I'm tryin' to save my son."

He scooped a ladle of the concoction, poured it into a bowl, and went to Paul.

"I need you to sip this, boy," he said as tears streaked his cheeks. "It's hot, but you gotta take it."

Paul shook his head and mumbled, "I ain't hungry, Daddy."

"Don't make no difference. You gotta get some o' this in you. It'll break the fever."

Paul turned away.

"Do what Daddy say, Paul," Bartimaeus encouraged. "You cain't die. You cain't."

Woody supported Paul's head as he struggled to sit up. Gus spoon-fed the broth into Paul's mouth.

"It's too hot," Paul complained.

"I know it's hot, but you gotta drink it like this. It's the only way it's gon' work."

Emma Jean massaged his forehead and promised God she'd serve Him forever if He'd spare her baby. She had some nerve, she knew, asking God for a favor after what she'd done, but she had nowhere else to turn. The fire had left her shamefaced and brutally aware that she had no friends in Swamp Creek. Even Gracie had cursed her and stopped coming around once she learned the truth about Paul. So Emma Jean sneaked into the master bedroom and, in a moment she'd live to regret, ransomed her life in exchange for Paul's. "Do whatever You wanna do with me, Lord," she said. "Just let my baby live. If somebody's gotta die, let it be me." She returned to the living room to see what God decided.

Gus was pouring spoonfuls of the rancid drink into the small opening of Paul's mouth. "Just two more sips, son, and I think it'll be enough."

Paul wanted to vomit, but didn't have the strength. Gus set the cup aside and waited with Emma Jean to see if their efforts would prove fruitful.

At some point during the night, Gus thought about the prospect of burying his baby boy and he couldn't hold his heart any longer. For the first time, he looked beyond what others thought and saw Paul for what he was. Gus also feared that, if the boy died, he'd have to answer to God for having treated him so badly, so Gus took Paul's limp hand and said, "Don't die, boy. Please." He had the same feeling he had the night his mother died. Maybe this was his chance to do something different, he thought. Then his mother's spirit wouldn't trouble him anymore.

Emma Jean stirred in a nearby chair, unable to sleep.

"When you was a baby, I used to sit you on my lap and let you play with my beard. I liked the way you giggled. You was such a pretty baby."

Paul opened his eyes, but didn't move. The room was pitch-black.

"Then yo' momma messed everything up. I never did hate you though. I really didn't. I just couldn't believe you was no boy. You was s'pose to be my baby girl and that's how I saw you, so when I saw yo' thang, I almost lost it." He shook his head. "I ain't neva heard o' nobody experiencin' nothin' like that. I couldn't believe what yo' momma had done done to you."

Emma Jean wanted to explain again, but she didn't.

"My daddy taught me that ain't nothin' worse than a sissified man, and I didn't want you to be one. I still don't. I guess I been too embarrassed to talk to you directly. Folks' whisperin' made me nervous. You know how I am."

Gus scratched the top of his bald head. If Paul died, at least he had said what he needed to.

"I guess this ain't been easy for you, either, huh? I know the kids pro'bly tease you at school and stuff." He paused. "And I'm sorry for beatin' you the way I did that day. When I saw you comin' down the road, you was twistin' like a girl, and I got so mad I couldn't see straight. But I didn't mean to kick you. I even told God I didn't and God told me to tell you, but I never did. I was too 'shamed, I guess. Now you layin' here, and I might not never get a chance to tell you to yo' face. But at least I'm tellin' yo' spirit."

Gus leaned back for a long while, then leaned forward again. "After Momma died, I couldn't seem to stop cryin'. Daddy and Chester poked fun at me and said I was gon' be a sissy when I grew up. I told them I wasn't. They said I was weak and didn't have no backbone 'cause ain't no boy s'pose to cry all the time. But I couldn't help it. I loved my momma and she loved me, and when she died, I felt like I was in the world all by myself. That's a bad feelin', son—to feel like you all by yo'self. I guess you know what that feels like though, huh?"

Do I! Paul wanted to say.

"And I ain't been no help. I knowed this wasn't yo' fault from the start, but I been makin' you pay like it was. I'm sho sorry, boy. I promise to do better if you'll just get well."

When Gus woke at five, Paul was sitting up staring at him. Gus almost burst into tears.

"I didn't die, Daddy. I'm alive. And I'm strong."

Gus patted Paul's head and smiled. "I guess you is, boy. Kinda like yo' old man."

Gus swiveled, grimacing from the pain in his hip, and shouted, "Hallelujah!" as though celebrating Jesus' resurrection from the tomb. Emma Jean raised her hands, as high as she could, and thanked God for answering her prayer.

Then the rains came. Assisted by a homemade walking cane, Gus hobbled toward the Jordan when the first droplets fell, so once again Bartimaeus had to find his own way. The tone of Gus's wailing was lighter than usual, almost falsetto, and people knew that something must have been different. What they didn't know was that, instead of releasing hurt, he was giving praise to a God Who had spared his baby boy. Had they listened closely, they would have discerned phrases like "thank Ya" and "I love Ya" muddled in the midst of dissonant belting, but since no one other than Sugar Baby understood the full purpose of the annual cleansings, most were simply glad when they came and when they ended.

Having found his way for years now, Bartimaeus didn't even need to touch the barbed-wire fence along the way. He could tell, by the sound of the river, how close he was, and when his father's voice sent chills across his body, he knew to turn right with outstretched hands until Gus paused his lamentation and said simply, "Come." Then he waded into the moving water until the pat on his head confirmed that he needn't go any farther. Without preamble, he lent his voice and, together, father and son extracted from the universe the healing—or, rather, now, the thanksgiving—necessary for their souls' redemption. With Gus screeching alto, the river took the tenor part, and, for the sake of balanced harmony, Bartimaeus cried the soprano. Emma Jean stood on the porch and said, "Goddamnit! Sound like a bunch o' women hollerin'!" She knew someone would ask her about the shift in tone, and she didn't know how she'd explain it. Their annual presence at the river never bothered her—everyone had long accepted Gus's and Bartimaeus's irregularity—but at least in years past they had sounded like men crying out in battle. *Men!* Now, folks might be wondering if Emma Jean had joined them.

Oblivious to and uninterested in others' assessment, Gus wept and screamed exultations to God, Who had done exactly as he had requested. Relinquishing his staff, he shuffled waist deep into the Jordan, pounding his chest and arms as though self-flagellation intensified his praise. Bartimaeus moved his small hands across the water's surface, trying hard to sustain the C above middle C while asking God to protect Paul in the future. He had convinced Gus to help Paul, and now he felt better about things. Of course life for all the Peaces might have been different had he told what he knew, but that was in the past now. His hope at the Jordan was that God would build a fortress around his little brother if he'd purge completely, so Bartimaeus took a step forward, filled his diaphragm with air, and hollered, "Yeeeeeeeeeeeeeeeeeeeeeeeeeees!" until he felt certain that God would honor his plea.

The two were home by dark. When they entered, Gus retired his cane to the corner, smiled, and said, "It is finished." Woody retrieved dry clothes and, after father and son changed, they joined the family in the living room and the cleansing of 1954 was history.

Gus decided to love Paul just because he was a Peace. The boy had proven himself strong, like Lucy, and that was all Gus had been worried about. Paul even looked like her, Gus thought, lying on the cot, sweating and fighting for his life, and Gus admitted that if he lost Paul or any of his boys, he'd never be right again. Even the rains couldn't have fixed his heart if that had happened. So, for now, Gus was glad that the broth or Emma Jean's prayer or maybe both had worked the necessary magic. He didn't care what people said anymore.

Paul was his son, and if he was a little effeminate, then, hell, that's simply what he was.

He relaxed his guard in the boy's presence and never hit him again. He'd thought all weak men were sissies, and maybe they were, but Paul had shown him that not all sissies were weak. Now Gus liked him. He didn't know what would become of the boy, but he felt sure that, from now on, Paul could take care of himself.

Chapter 24

King Solomon rose before dawn on August 30, 1954, determined to keep his promise. Tears blurred his vision as he scurried about the living room, packing books he couldn't bear to leave, and bagging the few clothing items he owned. Dressed in a black and green flannel shirt and his good overalls, he stopped suddenly and surveyed the room. What if he failed? What if he was forced to return, days later, to face Emma Jean's doubtful eyes? What if Miss Erma's clandestine tutoring—which would have pissed Emma Jean off had she known—hadn't been enough? No, that couldn't be. It had to be enough. Sol *had* to succeed. If he didn't, he'd die by the roadside, he swore, before he gave Emma Jean the satisfaction of believing he couldn't make it without her.

Paul rolled over and looked into Sol's almond-shaped, weepy eyes. If he hadn't been so dark, he would definitely have been the best looking of all the Peace boys, people said. Standing six foot two, he had a lean, muscular physique that made women lust privately for the comfort of his arms, especially when, in his unusually articulate way, he murmured, "Good afternoon." With teeth white as snow and straight as the spikes in a comb, his smile increased his allure and convinced mothers that some girl would be mighty lucky to get that smart, black Peace boy.

Sol stared at Paul and said, "I gotta go, man. I can't stay here any longer."

"Where you goin'?"

Mister yawned and shook the sleep from his head.

"College."

"College?" Paul said.

Sol paused, momentarily overwhelmed. He would miss everything—his brothers, the array of wildflowers in the front yard, Gus's and Bartimaeus's voices crying in the distance—but he had to go.

"Momma, Daddy," Mister called as though the house were on fire. "Sol's leavin' for college. Right now!"

Bartimaeus jumped and stumbled into Sol's arms. "You'll do fine. If anybody can do it, you can."

"Thanks."

Gus emerged from the bedroom, snapping his worn work overalls. "What's goin' on?"

"I'm going to college, Daddy. Right now." A lone tear tumbled to the edge of Sol's wide, flat nose.

Gus nodded. "All right, son. You a man now."

Paul tried to speak, to ask Sol if he might be willing to wait just one more day, but he couldn't talk past the lump in his throat.

"You got enough money, boy?"

"I got what I saved. I hope it'll be enough."

"Well, hold on a minute." Gus retrieved a five-dollar bill from his pocket. "Take this. Just in case. You don't neva know what might happen."

"Thanks, Daddy."

Emma Jean nodded. What could she say? When she looked at Sol, his eyes suggested that if he never saw her again he'd be the better for it. She wanted to apologize for having hurt him, but how? Nothing she said would've appeased his contempt, and she knew it. The guilt in her heart began to consume her. She wanted at least to wish Sol well, but instead she pursed her lips and remained quiet.

"Take care o' yo'self, boy," Gus said.

Each brother, starting with Woody, said good-bye and good luck, except Paul. He followed King Solomon onto the porch, down the steps, and into the road.

"You'll do real good at college, Sol. I know it. You the smartest person I know."

"Thanks," Sol said, and continued walking.

"I'm sorry Momma didn't let you go to school. She should've. You wanted it more than me, that's for sure."

Sol couldn't restrain his tears.

"I just wanted to thank you for bein' nice to me that day in the barn when Daddy beat me. I ain't never forgot it."

"You welcome," Sol snapped. He hated that he was crying.

"And one more thing. I know you in a hurry, but could you sing something for me before you go? It might be a long time before I get to hear you again."

Sol wanted to deny Paul's request, but he felt he owed him this much. "All of my heeeelp!" he began in the midst of his liberation march.

"Oh yeah! I like that one!"

"Comes from the Looord!"

Paul assumed the response in a different key. "Comes from the Lord."

Sol sang through his tears and continued, "Whenever I need Him, He's right by my side!"

Paul repeated, "Right by my side."

"All of my help . . ."

"My help!" Paul shouted.

"My help . . ."

"My help!"

"My help . . . comes from the Lord. Oh yes it does, oh yes it does." Sol wiped his eyes and embraced Paul. "I love you, boy. I'm not mad at you. I never was. I was just jealous."

"I know." Paul sniffled into Sol's ear. "I know. I'm gonna miss you so much. It's not gonna be the same around here without you."

"I'll miss you, too."

They released and stepped back.

"Just remember to be yourself. That's all you have to do, just be yo'self. Some folks'll like you and some won't, but it doesn't matter. Not really. You're the only one you have to live with. Folks 'round here done talked about you real bad, little brother, and I'm afraid it's not over yet. But I wouldn't trade you for the world. Or change you." Sol cupped Paul's face with his enormous hands. "You're the sweetest person I know, so stay that way, okay?"

Paul nodded.

"I'll be back—one day."

At 8:40 A.M., Sol boarded the train for Little Rock, then transferred to one bound for Washington, D.C. He had never been to a college before, but Aunt Gracie's nostalgic remembrances of Howard convinced him that he'd like it there. The next day, he stood before Howard University's administration building with ten dollars and a heart brimming with hope. Fear almost paralyzed him, but having come this far, he couldn't very well give up and return home, especially since he didn't have enough money to get there.

Like one surveying heaven, Sol gazed at the enormity and grandeur of the buildings. Students buzzed past him, obviously familiar with the place, and Sol desired nothing more than to become one of them. He entered the administration building and rested his two heavy boxes along the wall of the hallway.

"Hi. My name's King Solomon Peace," he said to a friendly looking, well-dressed young man.

The stranger smiled and shook his hand firmly. "Well, with a name like King Solomon, you must be a mighty brother! Hi. I'm Walter Smith Jr. Nice to meet you."

"Nice to meet you, too." Sol liked Howard already. "I was wondering . . . um . . . who I could speak to about going to school here."

Walter frowned. "What do you mean?"

"Well, I want to attend Howard, but I haven't talked to anyone yet."

"Oh, wow. You mean you haven't applied?"

"No, I haven't."

"Well, you have to fill out an application first; then the admissions office decides whether to accept you or not."

"Oh no! What if they don't accept me?" Sol cried. He collapsed against the wall. "I mean, I knew I'd at least have to talk to someone or take a test or something, but then I figured I could just pay my money and start learning."

"Naw, man. It doesn't work quite like that."

"Somethin's gotta work, Walter. I've come too far."

"Well, school starts tomorrow, so it might be too late, but you could go by the admissions office and ask. Maybe they'll let you fill out an application now."

"I hope so."

"Just go to the administration building and ask for the admissions office."

Sol huffed, discouraged.

"Come on. I'll go with you."

Walter carried one of the boxes and together they crossed Georgia Avenue and entered the admissions office.

"Hello, ma'am," Sol said softly to the receptionist.

After sneering at his overalls, she simply continued typing.

"I'd like to go to school here."

"Then you'll have to apply like everyone else," she snarled, shoving an application at him. "Fill this out and return it. You'll hear from us in a month or two."

"Oh no, ma'am! I gotta go to school now. Right now!"

The receptionist paused, reeking with irritation. "Listen, son." She turned to face him. "If you want to go to school here, you'll have to fill out the application, submit it, and wait to hear from us. You obviously want to be admitted for next year's term, is that right?"

"No, ma'am. I want to start tomorrow."

"Well, I'm sorry, son, but you can't do that. You would have had to apply by April thirtieth in order to start now. And of course that deadline is far gone. I'm sorry. You can apply for next year though." She resumed typing.

"But I cain't wait 'til next year, ma'am. I need to start now. I don't have anywhere to go and I've come a long way."

Walter touched Sol's shoulder sympathetically.

"I'm sorry, son, but that's the rules. And, with classes starting tomorrow, we wouldn't have time to process your application anyway. You'll simply have to wait until next term. I'm sorry."

Sol tried desperately to think of something else to say. Walter bit his bottom lip. "I don't mean to be rude, ma'am, but I gotta go to school now. I have to. Is there someone else I can talk to?"

She huffed and rose. "I'll see if the admissions director will see you, but he's gonna tell you the same thing I've already said." She knocked on the director's door behind her desk and entered. Seconds later she reappeared. "Go on in. Good luck."

Walter told Sol he'd wait for him.

"How can I help you, son?" the director barked impatiently.

"I wanna go to school here, sir. Real bad."

"Then get an application from the receptionist out front, and hopefully we'll see you next year."

"But, sir, I wanna go now. I gotta go. I know I can do the work. I'm real smart. My teacher said so."

"I'm sure you are, son, but you can't just walk into a college and begin matriculating."

Sol's hope was fading.

"Where are you from?"

"Arkansas, sir."

"Well, you've certainly come a long way, but I'm sorry, we can't help you. Your high school teachers didn't tell you how to apply for college?"

"I didn't go to high school, sir."

"Beg pardon?" The director's eyes bulged.

"My folks made me stop going to school so my little brother could go. Miss Erma, our teacher, tutored me privately sometimes and said I was real smart. I've read a lot of books though. I brought some of 'em with me, but I left most at home, too. I couldn't carry all of 'em."

The man stared. "You don't have a high school diploma, son?"

"No sir, I don't."

"Then that's the first order of business. You need a high school diploma in order to go to college."

"Oh no," Sol murmured.

"And can you pay tuition?"

Sol didn't respond.

"In other words, do you have enough money to pay for college?"

"I have ten dollars, sir. And I can work."

The man roared. "You must be kidding! Get outta here, country boy! We can't help you. I'm sorry."

The admissions director returned to the paperwork on his desk as though Sol had suddenly vanished. For several seconds, he stood there, unable to envision what he'd do or where he'd go. Upon exiting the office, he closed the door softly as the receptionist sneered, "Told ya."

Sol was too hurt to speak. Walter followed him outside.

"Do you have any relatives here who might take you in and let you work until you save enough money for school?"

They sat on the steps of the administration building.

Sol shook his head and blinked back tears. Walter didn't know how to comfort him.

"I just gotta go to school, man. I gotta."

Walter took his hand and conceived an idea. "Come on."

Sol followed, praying Walter knew something he didn't.

"I don't know if this is going to work, but it's worth a try."

They returned to the administration building and stopped outside the president's office.

"Our president is a legend, but he's pretty down-to-earth, too. He really believes in education. If he says you can get in, you're in. But you'll have to explain your situation. Maybe he'll do something, maybe he won't, but anything's worth a try, right?"

"Right!"

"His name's Dr. Mordecai Johnson. Everybody around here knows him, and, like I said, a word from him would get you in. Let's see if we can talk to him."

Walter led the way and asked Dr. Johnson's secretary if he was available. She inquired about the nature of their visit, and Walter explained as best he could.

"Well, yes, he's in, boys, but I don't know about this."

"Can we try, ma'am?" Sol pleaded. "Please? I don't have any other choice."

Like the first receptionist, she entered an office door behind her desk, then returned almost immediately. "He'll see you now."

Sol and Walter tiptoed into Dr. Johnson's office. Sol thought that maybe this was the university library.

"Have a seat, young men," Dr. Johnson offered. His stern demeanor weakened Sol's resolve. "What can I do for you?"

Sol opened his mouth, but Walter spoke first. "I'm a student here now, Dr. Johnson, and this is my friend King Solomon Peace. He's all the way from Arkansas."

"Mr. Peace," Dr. Johnson said, extending his hand.

Sol shook it firmly. "Good afternoon, sir."

Afraid that Sol's appearance and dialect were strikes against him, Walter took it upon himself to explain King Solomon's dilemma.

"I'm sorry, son, but you must at least have a high school education to come here. This is rigorous intellectual work, and although I'm sure you're smart, you're simply ill-prepared. I'm sorry." He rose and moved toward the door.

"But, sir, I'll work real hard. I know how to work. My daddy taught me that. And I can read real good and I know my times tables backward and forward."

"That's good, son, but it's not enough. Just don't give up hope. Go and get you a high school education, and we'll see you back here in a few years."

"I can't wait that long, sir. I come all the way from Arkansas to go to this school, and all I have left is ten dollars. I don't even have enough money to get home."

President Johnson opened the door. "Good day, gentlemen. You will have to excuse me now."

Walter motioned for Sol to drop the request and follow him.

"I'm sorry," Walter said outside. "I'm really, really sorry."

Sol thanked him.

"I hope we'll meet again someday."

"Hope so."

"I gotta go now. Good luck." They shook hands.

Overcome with grief, Sol tossed the boxes of books into a nearby trash receptacle, then collapsed and wept beneath a small tree. Watching students and parents haul luggage into various buildings only increased his sorrow and made him curse Emma Jean for refusing him education. Paul didn't know how lucky he was, Sol thought, to be on his way to a high school diploma. He'd have everything he needed to succeed in life and, now, Sol had nothing. Paul didn't even want an education! Sol had wanted it worse than anything he could imagine, but still Emma Jean wouldn't relent. "Damn," he mumbled.

"Excuse me, young fella," Sol heard a voice call. He turned and faced President Johnson.

"Yessir?"

"Come with me."

Sol jumped and followed President Johnson into the dining hall.

"Mr. Peace, this is Mr. Pace. He runs our dining facilities." They shook. "Mr. Pace, this young man needs a job. Can you put him to work?"

"I'm sure I can find something for him to do, Dr. Johnson," Mr. Pace teased.

"Well, good. He can start right away. Is that right, Mr. Peace?"

"Oh, yessir!" Sol shouted, military style. He wanted to hug Dr. Johnson, but restrained himself.

"Now. I don't do this very often, but I'ma take a chance on you." He dismissed Mr. Pace and pulled King Solomon aside. "You can work in the dining hall to pay for your room and board. I want you to take these classes." He handed Sol a slip of paper. "You won't get any credit for them because you're not officially enrolled, but if you perform well, and I mean *well*, I'll consider admitting you next semester."

"Yes!" Sol jerked his hand vigorously. "I'll do well, sir! You'll see!"

Dr. Johnson laughed. "You'd better. Chances like this come once in a lifetime."

Sol returned to the Dumpster and scavenged for his books. The stench and filth didn't bother him at all. He then entered the dining hall with more joy than he had ever known.

During supper, Walter gasped to see him mopping the kitchen floor.

"Hey, man! I thought you left. What happened?"

Sol told him, and Walter said, "Aw, wow! That's great, man! I'll help you with your homework if you need it."

Within a week, they were roommates. School was harder than Sol had imagined. Reading was no problem, but algebra kept him up late at night. Walter explained what he could, but much of it Sol simply didn't get. Sometimes Professor Everett tutored him after class until he had to report to the dining hall. He used his lunch break for studying, and Mr. Pace declared, "Son, you 'bout de hardest workin' somebody I ever knowed! You gon' make it." In a letter to his folks, he reported that he was in college and doing all right. He hoped he hadn't lied.

Dr. Johnson summoned Sol to his office at the end of the semester.

"Have a seat, son."

Sol sat uneasily. Dr. Johnson's tone unnerved him.

"I took a chance on you back at the beginning of the school year. Is that right?"

"Yessir."

"What was our agreement?"

Sol shuddered. "Our agreement was that I had to get really good grades from my classes in order to go here officially."

"That's right. How do you think you did?"

"Um . . . I don't know, sir. I studied really hard and I think I did okay. My math class was really hard though."

Dr. Johnson reclined in his seat. "Well, I asked all your teachers to report your final grades directly to me. Here they are." He extended a folded sheet of paper.

Before Sol looked, he repeated, "I worked really hard, Dr. Johnson. I swear I did. Mr. Pace'll tell you—"

Dr. Johnson was unmoved. "Look for yourself."

Sol unfolded the paper and saw three As and one B.

Dr. Johnson smiled and stood. "Congratulations, Mr. King Solomon Peace. You are now officially a student at Howard University."

Sol grabbed his head like James Earl and screamed, "Oh my God! Are you serious? Oh my God! Yes! Yes!" He leapt around Dr. Johnson's office, shouting, "Yes! Yes!" until the secretary peeked through the door, wondering what all the noise was about. "Oh, I'm sorry, ma'am. I'm just so excited!"

Dr. Johnson laughed. "You've done well, son. Your folks would be proud. You're a credit to your people, and I have no doubt you'll go on to do great things."

"Yessir!" Sol was grinning so hard his cheeks hurt.

"Now one more thing. I'm recommending you for the university scholarship. It'll cover your room, board, and tuition until you graduate, provided you keep your grades up."

"What? Are you for real, Dr. Johnson?"

"Of course I'm for real, son. I don't play about education."

Sol shook his head in disbelief. "I'm gon' make you proud, Dr. Johnson. I promise I will."

"You already have, son. You might have grown up poor, but somebody taught you enough about hard work to make sure you'd survive anywhere in the world. That's the greatest gift a parent can give a child."

Sol thought about Gus. "Yessir."

"Then it's settled. You have a merry Christmas and I'll see you next semester."

Sol found Walter and jumped all over him.

"What's wrong with you, man?"

"I'm in! I'm in! Look!"

Walter glanced at the paper. "All right, man!" he cried, and tossed his arms around King Solomon.

The two remained roommates until 1957 when Walter graduated and went on to medical school. Sol finished the following year, summa cum laude, and pursued a graduate degree in psychology. It had been his favorite subject. He loved learning why people do what they do, and he yearned earnestly to comprehend the mind-set of people like Emma Jean Peace.

Gus wanted to attend the graduation but couldn't afford to. Three dollars and forty-eight cents—the total in the coffer—would barely get him to Little Rock, much less Washington, D.C. The rains were recently past anyway, so he knew his crops would soon need his attention.

Emma Jean never considered going—what kind of hypocrite would she have been?—but she wanted to do something, so she emptied the coffer into Authorly's hands, added her own personal money from selling hen eggs, and told him what to do. After traveling all day and night, Authorly pressed his way to the commencement ceremony and screamed, "Yeah, Sol! We love you, man!" when King Solomon received his degree. Sol turned abruptly, searching the massive audience for the familiar voice. When their eyes met, he ran from the stage as Authorly plowed his way through the crowd, crying for the first time in his life. Too overwhelmed to speak, Sol leapt into his big brother's arms and they wept together until Sol's soul was made whole again.

Chapter 25

King Solomon's graduation confirmed to Woody, somehow, that God had called him to preach. He had been reading the Bible for months *just because*, he said, and something about Sol's commencement invitation corroborated that he was supposed to be in the pulpit.

"I have an announcement to make, church," Reverend Lindsey said the Sunday after Sol graduated. "I know everyone remembers Sol Peace, the real smart one o' de Peace bunch, who left here years ago on his way to college."

Some murmured that they didn't know he had left. Others nodded merely as protocol.

"Well, I'm glad to announce that he has just graduated from Howard University at the top of his class."

The congregation cheered.

"I understand that he's pursuing a graduate degree in psychology, is that right?"

Emma Jean stood and nodded.

"Well, bless the Lord!" the Reverend said. "I always knew one of these children 'round here was gon' make us proud." Miss Mamie gave Emma Jean the fakest smile she could muster.

"There's another surprise from the Peace family." He motioned for Woody to join him on the pulpit. "I'm proud to announce that Woody here has been called to the ministry."

Thunderous applause echoed throughout the sanctuary. Gus and Emma Jean beamed. They had suspected as much, wondering why Woody had been reading the Bible all of a sudden.

At his trial sermon a week later, Woody opened with "There was a black man who had lived a righteous life, so God told him he could have anything he desired. Well, he asked God if he could have a highway to heaven. God frowned and told him that that would be kinda difficult, since a highway to heaven would have to float in midair, so He asked the man to think of something a bit more reasonable. The man sat awhile and then said, 'Oh yeah, God! I got somethin'. How 'bout You explain to me why white folks treat Negroes the way they do. I always wondered that.' God nodded to the man and said, 'Two lanes or four?'"

People's laughter reverberated throughout the church. Woody even laughed at himself.

Then, without transition, text, topic, or introduction, he told his neighbors about the power of the blood. "It cleanses the sin-sick soul, ha! It makes the wounded whole, ha! It sets the captives free, ha! It gives slaves liberty, ha! It destroys what the devil, ha, I said the devil, ha, thought he had established!"

Congregants shouted in emotional ecstasy. Woody abandoned the pulpit and walked the aisles.

"Without the blood, there is no remission of sins, ha! Without the blood, ha, we'd all be doomed to the burnin' hellfire, ha! It was the blood of Jesus, ha, streamin' down that old rugged cross, ha, that gives us everlastin' life, ha!"

"Yes, Lord!"

Folks drooled, screamed, shouted, and fainted as Woody discovered the alluring power of the black church pulpit. He had never experienced anything like it. Not even the Laughins in the front yard. Paul and Eva Mae sat mesmerized, smiling at Woody who, just days ago, didn't mean much, but now stood as the messenger of God. He would get married soon, Paul assumed, since he had never met an unmarried preacher, and he hoped that, as a heavenly representative, Woody could answer a few of the zillion questions he had about God and the Bible. Like why God made some people strange and some people regular. Or why He let people have kids who didn't want them. Yes, he'd ask Woody about that later. For now, he was proud that his brother's oratorical skills were being used for something other than mannish clowning.

"Lawd, that boy sho did preach, didn't he!" Miss Mamie said after the benediction. "Who woulda thought that one o' de Peace boys would ever preach de Word? De Lawd shonuff works in mysterious ways, don't He?"

At home that evening, Paul declared, "Wow, Woody! Man! You was real good at church today. Real good."

Woody grinned. "It wunnit me, praise the Lord! It was the God in me."

"Everybody was hollerin' and stuff, and me and Eva Mae was clappin' the whole time. I ain't neva seen church on fire like that!"

"Well, that's what happens when you let de Lawd use you. He'll use you, too, if you let Him. It might not be in the pulpit, but He'll shonuff use you."

Paul didn't want to be used by anyone. "I wanna ask you somethin'."

"Okay. Go 'head."

Paul wasn't sure why he hesitated. "Why does God make some people different from everybody else?"

Woody shook his head. "I don't know. He's a mysterious God. His ways ain't our ways, and His thoughts ain't our thoughts. You just gotta trust Him. And believe on Him. He'll bring you through every time. I'm a livin' witness!"

Paul grimaced. Had Woody answered his question somewhere in the midst of all that useless verbiage? He tried again.

"But why don't God just make everybody the same so nobody can make fun of nobody else?"

"You can't question God, Paul. You just gotta accept Him in yo' heart and let Him change yo' life. Weepin' may endure for a night, but joy comes in the morning. Don't never forget that."

Huh?

"You got any more questions?"

"Yeah." Paul swallowed. "How you get saved?"

"You confess with yo' mouth that Jesus was raised from the dead and believe it in your heart."

"But how would I know if Jesus was raised from the dead?"

" 'Cause the Bible says so."

"I ain't never read the Bible."

"You don't have to. Just believe it. It's in there. I promise."

"What'll happen if I don't get saved? Ain't there some people who don't gotta be saved? And what is you *saved* from?"

"From burnin' in hell! That's what you saved from!"

Reverend Lindsey had preached countless sermons about a place where people burn forever because they don't believe—although Paul never knew precisely what they were supposed to have believed—and now the fire in Woody's eyes frightened Paul even more than Reverend Lindsey's brimstone.

"You just need to pray, boy. God'll answer all yo' questions."

God's voice had proven difficult for Paul to hear. "Cain't you answer 'em?"

"No, I cain't, 'cause you askin' carnal stuff, and I'm a holy man. You sound like a fool, but I know you mean well." Woody stood to leave.

Paul blurted, "I wanna be saved."

"You cain't be saved yet, boy. Not while you still a sissy. You gotta get delivered from that first."

"I been tryin'! What else can I do?"

"Pray and ask the Lawd to deliver you. He'll do it! I know He will!"

"I done asked God a thousand times!"

"Well, obviously you ain't been sincere. If you was, He woulda done it by now."

"I thought all you had to do was believe in Him?"

"You do gotta believe, but you cain't be no sissy. You gotta get rid of that before He can do anything with you. He hates sissies."

"Oh. I didn't think God hated anybody."

Woody smiled. "You don't know Him yet, boy."

"But don't you gotta be baptized or somethin', too?"

"No! You only gotta be baptized if you gon' join the church."

"So can somebody be saved who don't go to church?"

"No!" Woody shouted, irritated. "The Bible say everybody gotta go to church."

"But what if somebody get saved, but then don't wanna go to church?"

"Then they ain't saved!"

"Why not? You said—"

"Listen, Paul! You don't know nothin' 'bout God 'cause you ain't read yo' Bible."

"I know I wanna be saved. I don't wanna burn in no fire forever."

"Then pray and ask God to deliver you from what you is. And really mean it this time."

Paul thought he'd meant it every time.

"Ask God to make you clean. I know you been tryin'. He'll save you one day—soon as you get delivered. Keep fightin'. It won't take long."

Woody walked away.

Paul closed his eyes and said, "God, I hope You can hear me. I don't really understand everything Woody said, but I know I wanna be saved. I don't wanna burn in hellfire forever." He paused, but didn't open his eyes. "Will you take the rest of the sissy out of me? Please?" Paul waited, but didn't feel anything. Maybe he didn't believe, he considered. He'd certainly tried, but believing was hard when there was no proof. How could he be asked to believe what no one could prove?

Paul went to bed troubled and unsatisfied. Would he ever be saved? He loved God in his heart, but obviously that wasn't enough to save his soul. He'd never wanted to be a sissy—had tried desperately to avoid it—but he must not have tried hard enough, he thought. Woody's words left him despondent and less sure than ever that God even liked him. The day would come when he'd need a savior and, on that day, when the savior didn't come, Paul would regret that, years ago, he had never learned how to believe.

With Sol gone and Woody lost in religious rhetoric, Paul became withdrawn and reticent. He and Eva Mae wrote notes to each other in class, but they stopped going to the field of clovers. Most days, he went straight home after school, performing chores with a silent disposition that soon accompanied him everywhere.

By eighteen, his transition into masculinity was as complete as it ever would be. He still switched slightly and never garnered any male friends, but his self-esteem was better than it had ever been since the death of Perfect. Or the birth of Paul. Memories of girlhood days had waned, and, more than anything, he wanted to be left alone. He didn't want to *be* alone; he simply wanted adults to treat him like they treated everyone else. With simple nods of acknowledgment and invitations to "come by and see me sometime." He wanted his peers, especially Johnny Ray, to stop avoiding him and to know that he was just as much a boy as the next. Well, almost. The urge to dress in girls' clothes had disappeared, after that day in the barn when Gus put the fear of God in him, and once he'd recovered from the fever, Paul tried hard to say and do things that would make Gus proud. He didn't want to cook with Emma Jean anymore, and he learned to restrain his normal overflow of tears. The only thing he missed was someone else confirming his worth. No one mentioned how precious he was—like they had said of Perfect—and he was left to believe that, as a boy, he didn't matter. Only Emma Jean reminded him that he was still beautiful, although menfolk taught him to reject such comments. "Boys ain't pretty, Emma Jean!" Gus interjected each time she said it. "They either handsome or nothin' at all." Paul was afraid to ask to which category he belonged, so he began studying his face in the mirror, hoping to discover those features that would qualify him as handsome. Being called "handsome," however, didn't feel the same as having been called "pretty." Paul discovered that when people said "pretty," they meant something or someone innately endowed with traits found pleasing to the eye. Like when a forest dweller happens upon a rare, purple blossom. He marvels at it, then considers its creation as a manifestation of the divine God. Its beauty is simply the fact that it exists. It needs no enhancing or modification. "Handsome," Paul discovered, is a designation used for those people or things that are well put together. A shiny car, for instance, can be handsome. Or a well-built house. Or a man in a suit. Something about the compliment didn't feel as authentic as the former declarations of his beauty. It was as though men *could* be handsome, if they were willing to make the sacrifice, whereas pretty women had been sent from heaven that way.

He knew one thing for sure: he wasn't ugly. Folks in Swamp Creek had expressions, both facial and vocal, for those whom they deemed unattractive. "That Redfield boy? The middle one? Lord have mercy! That child looks like homemade sin!" Miss Mamie said each time she beheld him. Others apparently agreed. They'd shake their heads, observing him from a distance, undoubtedly thanking God their children didn't look like him. What did *homemade sin* look like anyway, Paul wondered. People never said these things about him. As Perfect, she had been affirmed by women and men as a carrier of beauty. Now, as Paul, his caramel, flawless complexion was spoken of only in private by women, and men acted as though they didn't notice. The balanced nature of his facial features rendered most silent with envy. The truth was that he was a bit too beautiful for most people's liking. Authorly kept Paul's hair neat and orderly, and his extra-bushy, perfectly arched eyebrows accented soft, sensual, deep-set, dark brown eyes as though he wore eyeliner. In his teenage years, Paul's face lost its roundness, revealing sharp cheekbones and full, puckered lips that made others look at him longer than they intended. Most agreed, silently, that Paul Peace *was* a pretty colored boy. Yet, because of his history, they didn't dare say it.

Lee Anthony Redfield approached Paul and Eva Mae one day during lunch. The two were sitting on the grass beneath the only tree in the schoolyard.

"Hey, funny boy," Lee Anthony called. His face showed no emotion. He was short for his age, five foot three, and couldn't have weighed more than

120 pounds. Eva Mae had anticipated the day someone would beat the rudeness out of him.

"Shut up!" Eva Mae shouted, and stood. "He ain't botherin' you, so just leave us alone!" She waited for Paul to stand his ground.

"I ain't talkin' to you," Lee Anthony said. "I'm talkin' to *Perfect*."

Paul's head bowed.

"You is funny, ain't you? Everybody says so."

"Kick his ass," Eva Mae murmured.

Paul stood. "Why don't you just leave me alone? I ain't never done nothin' to you!"

"Well, answer my question and maybe I will."

Eva Mae pounced upon him. Having underestimated her strength, Lee Anthony grabbed her lightly, allowing her to toss him aside and punch his nose until blood flowed from it like the Jordan. Paul watched in amazement. Lee Anthony soon realized he was no match for Eva Mae, so he surrendered with his right hand dripping in blood. "I'll get you one day, faggot!" he declared to Paul as he shuffled toward the schoolhouse. "Girls can't take up for you the rest of yo' life."

When Lee Anthony disappeared, Eva Mae turned and slapped Paul's arm angrily. "What the hell's wrong with you?" she shrieked.

"What? What did I do?"

"Nothin'! That's the problem!"

"What was I supposed to do? You definitely didn't need my help."

Eva Mae gasped. "Aw, come on, Paul! *You* was s'pose to fight him, not me! Didn't you hear what he asked you? How come you didn't hit him? You can't walk around bein' no sissy! You gotta be a man—one day!"

"I don't fight, Eva Mae!"

"Well, damnit, you better start. I can't be takin' up for you like you some helpless li'l punk!"

He never thought he'd hear Eva Mae call him those names. "I ain't helpless, Eva Mae, and I ain't no punk!"

"Then stop actin' like one! You big as most of the boys 'round here now. Bigger'n many of 'em. How come you let them treat you like that?"

"I don't *let* them treat me like nothin'! They just do it!"

"And they gon' keep on doin' it 'til you start defendin' yo'self! You ain't no girl no more, so stop actin' like one!"

Paul's mouth fell open. "I ain't actin' like no girl, Eva Mae! I just didn't want to fight!"

"Why not!"

" 'Cause I don't fight. I just don't."

"Well, like I said, you better start 'cause I ain't fightin' for you no more." She brushed her dress.

"Good! I didn't ask you to fight for me anyway!"

Eva Mae walked toward the school. "Just be a man, Paul, okay? If you gon' be one, then *be one*!"

Paul's hurt settled beneath his skin like a lymphoma cancer. How could she, of all people, call him a punk? She knew his story, knew it better than most, and still she had said those ugly things? If he couldn't depend on her, who could he depend upon?

Paul turned his back suddenly to Eva Mae, to the school, to the world, and dashed down the road a bit, crying, "I ain't no punk! I ain't!" His arms flailed wildly as his feet stomped the earth. "And I ain't no sissy! Not now, not ever! You can't make me be that way!" He grabbed a stick from the ground and began beating the trunk of a mighty pine. "I ain't nothin' but a boy, just like any other boy!" Tears flooded his cheeks but he didn't wipe them away. "And I ain't no freak!" Had the stick been an ax, the pine would've been leveled. "I'm a normal"—*wham!*—"Negro boy"—*wham!*—"and nobody's gonna call me a sissy"—*whack!*—"ever again!" When the stick broke, Paul tossed the pieces into oblivion and found another one. "You cain't make me no punk!"—*whack!*—" 'Cause that ain't what I am!"—*wham!*—"I'm a boy!"—*wham!*—"A boy!"—*wham!*—"A BOY!"

A curious squirrel watched Paul purge. Its head jerked right, then left, seemingly unable to discern the source of his madness. Abandoning the attempt, it scampered away, leaving Paul to complete alone what he had begun. "I'll never be no sissy again!"—*wham!*—"Never!"—*whack!*—"I'ma be a man one day! A man!"

The screeches, grunts, yelps, and hollers left Paul exhausted. Within minutes, he collapsed to the earth, panting for dear life and fearing that people's perception of him, like the tree, was immovable. He sighed deeply, unable to think of anything else to do. What difference did it make anyway? Emma Jean always said, *Folks gon' talk about either what you is or what you ain't, so no need wasting good time trying to make them like you. It never works. They ain't God noway!* Paul agreed, but now felt the loneliness of having been rejected by his only friend, his best friend, his one true confidante. That's what hurt most. He knew others didn't care about him, but Eva Mae? Her betrayal stung at the core. He felt weak and tired, like one suddenly drained of the desire to live. Crying had done him no good, and his inability to fight left him as vulnerable as a wounded bird in a forest. What else could he do? Nothing at all, he concluded, so he rose, brushed the seat of his overalls, and, with bowed head, returned to the schoolhouse where, half-listening to Miss Erma drone on about some man named Ralph Waldo Emerson, he sat in misery the remainder of the afternoon.

Chapter 26

After school, Paul went to the Jordan. He couldn't imagine what Gus and Bartimaeus did there, but whatever they did, they returned renewed, and that's what he needed—a renewal, a rebirth, a fresh start—now that Eva Mae had become like the others. He'd never felt so alone in all his life. He'd also never realized how much he needed Eva Mae. Maybe the Jordan would teach him how to survive without a friend in the world.

Once arrived, he stood on the bank with folded arms as the breeze massaged his wounded soul. The rains had long since passed, so he certainly couldn't count on them for assistance, and he was far too shy to wail. He didn't understand why Gus and Bartimaeus did that anyway.

The Jordan had a beauty all its own. It wasn't very wide—fifty yards or so—but its waters rushed as if in a desperate hurry. Fishermen and swimmers alike avoided it until, farther downstream, it spread and calmed into shallower water. Paul bent and submerged his hand in the flow, then jerked it back from the shock of the cold. He was taken by the Jordan's clarity, as though, from the beginning of time, nothing had been allowed to pollute it. It was so clear that Paul noted huge rocks resting on the bottom, far from shore. The water was clearer than any well in Swamp Creek, and he wondered why people didn't come to the Jordan for their drinking water. Wild ferns and other greenery covered both banks as far as Paul could see, and he knew now why the flood of 1915 had claimed so many lives. The turbulent rush outgrew its banks, he imagined, and ran in every direction until its thirst for life was satisfied. Only then did it recede and resume its natural flow. It was a mighty stream, a breathtaking wonder, certainly the most scenic place in all of Swamp

Creek. Maybe all of Arkansas. Yet, beautiful as it was, Paul felt certain that the Jordan was nothing to play with.

Walking a few feet downstream, he attempted to skip a stone across the surface of the water, but the Jordan, like a watery black hole, consumed the pebble in a flash. It was as if the waters were angry at the disturbance. "Sorry," he murmured, then knelt and listened to the song of the current. It was a tumultuous melody, full of chaos and frustration. Had there been words, Paul was sure he could've learned the history of Swamp Creek's people, his people, in the watery uproar. The Jordan would probably have told him everything Gus had ever wept about, and now he would know the inner workings of his father's heart. But there were no words, so Paul closed his eyes and let the Jordan speak for itself, on its own terms, in its own language. He recalled the day's events and began to understand finally, though not fully, why Gus came to the Jordan each spring. There was something medicinal in its chaotic melody, something that reminded him of the big picture, of the minutiae of his troubles. It told him that he was human, and that his emotions were a reflection of the God in him. Paul needed that reminder. His life had been a series of mountains and valleys—mostly valleys—where he found himself depressed and inadequate. The moment he conquered one struggle, another appeared, until he resolved that peace would never be his. As much as he tried, he couldn't seem to please everyone, and, many days, he couldn't please anyone. There was always something unsatifying or unsettling about him. Like when he tried not to switch, someone swore they saw his hips sway, regardless of how constrained he walked. Or when he spoke to boys, simply trying to befriend them, someone inevitably accused him of flirting as if he were bold enough to solicit sexual favors from those who despised him. How could he win, he wondered, if people weren't willing to believe something other than what they already thought about him?

Paul sighed and opened his eyes. What he liked most about the Jordan was that no one could hinder its flow. It had a mind all its own. Others' opinions of its size or depth didn't matter. Only God possessed the power to subvert its course. Whether viewers loved it or not was inconsequential. It was a river, and it was created to flow, and that was exactly what it did. And that's all it did. That was its purpose, and no one could alter that identity, regardless of what they thought. The Jordan enjoyed a life free from external criticism and that's what Paul wanted. Isn't that what everyone wanted?

Recapping his life, Paul chuckled. How had he survived it all? Since age eight, all he'd heard was "faggot" this and "sissy" that. His family had been helpful sometimes and hurtful other times. They'd meant well though, Paul assumed. Maybe others had, too. Yet, when he thought about it, no one had stood with him every step of the way. Not Eva Mae, not Authorly, not even Emma Jean. She'd always loved him and was careful to say so, but after the transition, she surrendered him to the men and turned a blind eye, it seemed to Paul, to his pain and abuse. Paul never saw Emma Jean's tears drip onto her pillow at night or heard the muffled whimpering when her guilt became unbearable. He thought she'd simply made a decision and never looked back. Questioning her about it would've been useless, he determined, since no explanation would've justified what she'd done. Some days he still considered running away, but what good would that do now? It wouldn't change people's opinion of him, and it wouldn't keep him from being—what did others call it?—funny. *Funny?* Paul shook his head slowly. How in the world was *he* funny? What was funny about being mocked and ridiculed and sent to hell? And who actually laughed about it?

Paul's life had changed the night Gus thought he might die from the fever. Even after having beaten and demeaned him, Gus still loved him and that's all Paul needed to know—that his daddy still loved him. He was the only man whose opinion mattered—at least before Johnny Ray came along—and Gus's affirmation freed Paul to consider that he might, in fact, survive as a man. Gus had survived when others thought he wouldn't, so Paul planned to do the same. Dying simply wasn't an option. Paul didn't know how to die anyway.

He stood and he felt better. He didn't know why, but it seemed as if the Jordan had done something to his spirit, or *for* his spirit, and he resolved to make it, if only to prove the world wrong. Emma Jean used to say that he was a perfect child, a God child, and if it had ever been true, then Paul considered that it might still be. Like the Jordan, he had to ignore what others said about him and simply be himself. Sol had said this the day he left. "But who am I?" Paul asked the rushing waters. The Jordan didn't answer. Obviously, he'd have to figure this out for himself.

With his satchel clutched in his left hand, Paul walked away. He was grateful for the Jordan's cleansing power and vowed to return if he needed to. Pressing through the woods, he stumbled upon the pathway home, and that's when his newfound clarity disintegrated into total chaos.

It all happened so fast. In the weeks to come, he couldn't order the sequence of events in a way that made sense. Hard as he tried, he couldn't recall exactly which thing occurred first. Or last. Had he been able to do so, he could've retraced the moment, he convinced himself, and understood. At least maybe. The only thing he remembered clearly was the initial attack.

Like a pack of wild wolves, the bodies descended upon him and wrestled him to the earth. He tried to fight—unlike in the schoolyard—and wielded more strength than he thought he had. "Stop!" he shouted before they stuffed the funky white sock in his mouth and covered his eyes with a heavy strip of cloth. All subsequent screams were muted as Paul struggled in utter darkness. His strength soon faded, however, allowing them to tie his wrists behind his back. They hadn't counted on such a fight. Maybe he had some man in him after all.

"Don't!"

The trees, sky, road swirled about him as the multiple sets of hands restricted his movement. There were at least four assailants. He could tell that much. Some hands were bigger and heavier than others, and one set quivered as though aware it was participating in an evil thing.

"Fuckin' freak!" a voice whispered. The others quickly shushed him. This was a secret, something not to be known. Paul tried frantically to turn his head in hopes of seeing his violators, but, each time, they pressed his face harder into the rough, coarse earth. He was too afraid to cry.

Suddenly, Paul felt the button of his trousers snap. *"No! Please don't!"* he screamed into the sock, but of course it was useless. His head twisted hysterically as someone jerked his pants away from his flesh. Fighting more fiercely than before, he attempted against all odds to toss the weight from his slender frame, but he simply didn't have the strength. Who were these people and why were they doing this to him? He wondered. He knew they were boys. They had to be. Girls never did things like this. Not that he'd ever heard of. And even if they did, the only girl strong enough to hold him down was Eva Mae, and of course this wasn't her doing. She'd save him if she were there, Paul told himself, like she had done earlier. Sure, she'd been upset that he hadn't defended himself, but she wouldn't ever let anyone do this to him, would she? She was his best friend. At least she used to be. No, she still was, Paul decided, and he needed her now more than ever.

One lone tear inched its way down Paul's dirty, marred cheek. His last muffled cry—*"Oh God, no!"*—never reached the ears of his abusers. They were too preoccupied with achieving the goal at hand.

When the elastic waistband of Paul's underwear gave way and slid across his rounded buttocks, he knew he had been defeated. The cool evening breeze, drifting between his bare thighs, brought attention to his nakedness and caused him to shiver with panic. What were they doing?

As abruptly as they had overwhelmed him, they flipped him over. "That ain't no pussy!" the voice from before declared. "That's a goddamn dick!" The others recoiled in horror. Now they knew the truth. Paul *was* a boy. Emma Jean hadn't lied after all.

The truth infuriated the boys more than the rumor had. They recalled how Paul always took refuge in Eva Mae's protection and how his flawless, chestnut-colored skin glimmered in the bright, morning sun, and they began beating him mercilessly. From one side of his face to the other, unexpected blows fell upon him, leaving intersecting streams of blood. Someone's foot, a bit less intense than the fists, kicked his thighs repeatedly until they went numb. Where was Authorly? Sol? Gus? Emma Jean? Somebody?

When the commotion ended, Paul thought the worst was behind him. He tried to stand, with his pants and underwear gathered about his ankles, but the boys leveled him to the earth again. His eyes throbbed, as though attempting to jump from their sockets, and he was sure his lip was busted in several places. Lying upon his stomach once more, he begged God to make those evil boys vanish, but God wouldn't do it. Was it because he wasn't saved? He'd thought he was, but maybe he wasn't. If he had been, none of this would be happening, right? Salvation to Paul meant that one was protected, guarded, exempted—as it were—from Satan's plan, and now he knew he'd never been saved. Had he been, God would've caused him to sprout wings like an angel and fly away. Or He would've killed those beasts on the spot or sent a giant like Goliath to consume them. He would've done something. At the very least He would've told them that Paul was His child and that he was not to be violated. But God didn't say or do anything, precisely because, Paul thought, he'd never truly believed. Or never gotten delivered. Now, in the midst of trouble, Paul trembled and apologized for having fallen far short of God's glory.

In a flash, one of the boys descended upon him from behind, and Paul belted a desperate scream—"NO!"—that sounded like a thousand wounded buffalo. Birds, insects, deer, lizards, and squirrels scampered away in fear. His body quivered as the boy attempted to enter him. *Death? Oh, Mr. Death? Where are you? Come, and come quickly. I ain't scared no more. I need you. Please, please come.*

The boys heard rustling nearby and stopped. Paul felt the load lift from him as suddenly as it had descended, then heard feet rush away into the heavy, sad night.

His saliva tasted like bile. The insertion had only lasted a few seconds, but its memory would linger a lifetime. He couldn't explain it, but he felt dirty and nasty, like someone had pissed and shit all over him. How would he ever feel clean again? All the soap and water in the world couldn't wash that feeling away. Paul never heard the boys say, "He ain't no girl, but he's certainly a bitch!" as they slapped each other's palms excitedly. They'd planned to do other things, but the rustling in the woods had frightened them and altered those plans. *Oh well*, they thought. *He got the point.*

But Paul didn't have the point. Why had they done this? Who were they? What had he done to deserve something like this? He knew what folks believed about him, and he knew that most of it wasn't true. What more could he have done to prove himself worthy of human respect? He never said much to anyone—except Eva Mae—and he tried his best to stay out of people's way. That wasn't enough?

He inhaled and tried, though he failed, to lift himself from the earth. Someone scampered behind him and, with hands warm and strong, bore him up as though he were dead. Paul leaned heavily upon the angel's shoulders as he felt his underwear and pants restored. The angel then untied his hands, removed the blindfold, and lifted him, like a groom hoists a bride, carrying Paul home with swift urgency. Under the moonlight, still semiconscious, Paul couldn't discern who the stranger was although he guessed it was a man. He wanted to say thank you and maybe offer the money in the coffer for his trouble, but Paul hadn't the energy or the will to speak. As they approached home, the man's deep, soothing voice hissed, "Shhhhhhhhhhh" into Paul's left ear. Laying him gently on the porch, he said, "You ain't gotta die. 'Less you want to cain't nobody kill you. Not you." Paul blinked several times and beheld Sugar Baby's soft, scruffy face. His smile was different, as though he knew something Paul didn't. And why didn't he reek of alcohol like he usually did?

Sugar Baby turned suddenly and vanished down the lane while Paul moaned, "Help me!" Mister opened the screen, thinking he had heard the old cat purr, and yelled, "Oh my God, y'all! Come here! Hurry! Somebody done hurt Paul!"

Emma Jean screamed, "My baby!" as the men carried Paul to the sofa.

"What happened, boy!" Gus shouted. "Who done this to you?"

Woody and Mister gathered wet washcloths and began cleaning Paul's face. Sitting at his feet, Bartimaeus removed Paul's shoes and rubbed his numb legs vigorously.

Emma Jean stared in dismay. With her mouth covered and quivering like a dry leaf in the wind, she groaned painfully and blamed herself for everything Paul had endured.

Gus sat on the edge of the sofa, next to Paul's limp, emaciated body, pleading, "Tell me, boy! Who done this to you!"

Paul's light, choppy breathing assured Emma Jean that at least he was alive. She stumbled to a chair at the kitchen table and buried her weepy eyes into her folded arms.

"What happened, Paul?" Mister asked, wiping streaks of blood from his face.

Paul couldn't answer. Everyone's voice sounded far away, as if they were shouting at him across a wide open field. He would've answered had he had the strength. Each time he formulated a response, he couldn't gather the breath with which to say it. The best he could do was nod to assure his family that he wasn't dead—although he felt dead. Pain traversed every pore of his flesh. Even the skin beneath his fingernails ached, as did the soles of his flat feet.

Gus leapt from the sofa and retrieved his shotgun from the wall. "I'll find out myself!" he declared, loading the gun clumsily.

"No!" Emma Jean said, standing slowly. "You too mad. Ain't no tellin' what you might do."

"You right! And you better hope I don't find whoever done this to my boy, 'causen if I do, somebody's goin' to hell tonight! Me or them!"

The door slammed and rattled behind him.

"I'll go with him," Woody said. "Just to make sure he don't do nothin' crazy."

Emma Jean nodded. "Good, good. Hurry up before he get too far gone." At the screen she bellowed, "And fetch Doc Harris!"

Mister lifted Paul's torso and removed his shirt.

"Is he hurt bad?" Bartimaeus asked.

"I don't know. He look bad though. His face is pretty messed up."

"What chu think happened?"

"I don't know!" Mister snapped. "We'll just have to wait 'til he tell us."

Emma Jean took Gus's seat. "Sweetie," she called, reaching forth a trembling hand, "yo' momma's here. Everything's gonna be all right now." She shuddered as she imagined what someone might've done to her youngest son. Her mind conceived possibilities that made her stomach churn. She would never know, now or in the future, that her imagining had been correct, frighteningly correct, down to the smallest detail. What she knew for sure, however, was that this was all her fault. People had never accepted Paul as a legitimate boy, although, biologically, that's all he'd ever been. Even after she cut his hair and Gus changed his name, nobody believed he wasn't a girl. They followed the lie as the truth until the truth of the lie was revealed. Even then they didn't believe it. Emma Jean could tell from the way they looked at her—and at him—that they preferred the lie, had made room for it in their reality, and they hated her for forcing them to relinquish it. Most simply refused. Had they seen his nakedness—like his family and the rapists—there was still no guarantee they'd alter their truth. *A girl with a penis*, many would say, instead of simply calling the child a boy. Evidence doesn't always convince people of the truth, Emma Jean told herself, especially when the lie is what they prefer.

Yet, regardless, Emma Jean knew she had planted the seeds for this harvest. She wished she could go back and do things over. Not just concerning Paul, but everything. Her marriage to Gus, the children . . . everything. Why hadn't she ignored Mae Helen's discouragement and become a dancer? That's the only thing she'd ever really wanted. But of course Mae Helen's dissuasion trumped Emma Jean's self-esteem back then. Now, she was stuck with a life she'd never wanted, unable to fix the things—and the people—she kept destroying.

Woody returned. "I found Doc," he panted, "but Daddy ran off."

"Where is the boy?" Doc Harris asked.

"Over here," Emma Jean called.

"Does anybody know what happened?"

"No, he ain't said a word. He's alive, though, thank the Lord, but I don't know how bad he's hurt."

"Let me look at him."

Emma Jean stepped back and Doc Harris took over. After several minutes, he said, "Somebody beat him pretty good, but he'll survive. That eye'll be black for a few days, but, other than that, he'll be fine." Paul was glad Doc didn't think to examine him all over. "Just keep those bruises clean so infection doesn't set in. Beyond that, there's nothing more any of us can do."

Emma Jean walked Doc Harris to the edge of the porch. He asked, "Do you have any idea who would've done something like this?"

Emma Jean shrugged.

"Well, whoever it was, they sure had it in for him. He'll be okay though. He's tough. Just keep your eyes open, and make sure Gus doesn't do anything he'll regret."

"I'll handle Gus," Emma Jean assured him. "And thank you."

"Oh, no problem. And don't worry about paying me. This one's on me."

Woody walked Doc home and spent the next two hours looking for Gus. Some said they thought they heard a shotgun fire, while others said they hadn't seen or heard a thing. Woody never thought to look for Sugar Baby. If he had, he would've found Gus, too.

Sugar Baby didn't have a home, per se, but only an old shack he inhabited some nights when he didn't feel like wandering. Most had never seen it and, in fact, never would. It was hidden among heavy brush and huge vines, deep in the backwoods of Swamp Creek. No one strolled by leisurely, and, if they had, they wouldn't have noticed it. The forest had overtaken the shack as if to camouflage it from outsiders. It simply looked like a dark green lump, sitting upon the earth, in the midst of massive trees that blocked almost every shred of sunlight.

Whenever he could find them, Sugar Baby lit candles at night, which, from the outside, made the hovel glow like a lime green volcano. Once the short wicks burned out, he sat in total darkness, swatting nagging mosquitoes and drinking cheap liquor. That wasn't hard to come by. He simply gathered discarded bottles during the day and drained them into his own container at night. When he had candlelight. Rum, vodka, scotch, moonshine . . . whatever. He didn't care. He simply needed the escape.

The night of Paul's tragedy he'd been wandering the woods, talking to himself, since he'd run out of liquor. In a sober state, his reality left him restless, so he walked the forest until he'd expended enough energy to return home and, hopefully, fall asleep. That's when he'd found Paul, on his way home. He heard the shuffling of feet and the muted squealing of voices. Sugar Baby approached with the stealth of a lamb, and saw the faces of boys whose fathers he'd known a lifetime. As he stepped on a rotten log for a better view, the log crumbled beneath his weight and caused enough noise to frighten the boys away. But Sugar Baby had seen them. There was no doubt about it. The full moon shone brightly on all four faces, and he recorded their images in his mind. He never wanted to forget.

When Gus came stomping through the woods, Sugar Baby knew who it was. He didn't know what Gus's response would be, but he knew Gus would do something. He met him on the road.

"Somebody hurt my boy tonight," Gus said in the dark. "And I intend to find out who it was. You ain't seen or heard nothin', is you?"

Sugar Baby saw the fire in Gus's eyes and mumbled, "I brung him home. Found him in the road down yonda, close to the river."

Gus nodded his thanks. "Did you see who done it?"

Sugar Baby knew Gus's intention. "Naw."

Gus sighed.

Sugar Baby said, "Come on."

Having no other recourse, Gus followed him to his shack. He'd never been there before, but there was something about Sugar Baby that always made Gus trust him.

Leaning the shotgun against the dilapidated door frame, he ducked beneath overgrown greenery and entered Sugar Baby's cabin. The dark calmed Gus's nerves a bit, and when Sugar Baby lit the small white candle, he noticed that Gus was crying. He gestured for Gus to take a seat and Gus obeyed. Sugar Baby took the other chair, and they sat in silence as though attending a wake. Sugar Baby couldn't tell Gus the truth. Gus was his only friend in the world and he didn't want to lose him. He knew Gus meant to use that gun and, if he did, he'd probably be sent away forever. Then, the Peaces would be destroyed and Sugar Baby would be completely alone.

Having never been a man of many words, Sugar Baby said nothing as Gus sniffled and wiped his tears. The candlelight made them look like ghostly figures in a cave, surrounded by bottles and miscellaneous trash.

"He gon' be all right," Sugar Baby muttered once the candlelight flickered down. "Cain't nobody kill him."

Gus's guilt wouldn't release him.

"Man cain't touch what God send. Not 'til He get through with it."

Gus looked up.

"He'll be all right. Whoever done this gon' get theirs."

Chapter 27

Paul didn't speak for days. He barely ate. When the family gathered at the table, he sat like a zombie, listening to the chomping and smacking of the other Peaces, as the fateful night replayed in his mind. Whose voice was that? It had a familiar cadence, but he couldn't place it. Maybe he'd never heard it before, but that was unlikely in Swamp Creek. Visitors didn't come often, and they certainly didn't stay long. No, it had to be someone he knew. Or at least knew *of*.

Wincing with pain, he moved about the house until he voluntarily returned to his chores. Gus told him he should rest a few more days, but Paul shook his head. He'd had enough of Emma Jean breathing across his face every five minutes, and he didn't intend to let those boys ruin his life. The most difficult part was trying to understand why The Bold One had plowed his way into his private space. Paul didn't see the phallus, but he felt it and he knew what it was. What he didn't know was what the act was supposed to mean. Was the point to demean him? To convince him that he was nothing but worthless, sissified trash? It had hurt like nothing he'd ever felt before, and instinctively he knew he'd never tell it. He couldn't. Not even to Eva Mae.

She tried, day after day, to pry the truth from him.

"What really happened, Paul?"

He blinked, and spoke for the first time. "They beat me."

She followed him to the cows' trough.

"Who?"

He shrugged.

"Why?"

"Why you think?"

Eva Mae didn't answer.

" 'Cause I'm a punk." Paul's voice broke. "And a faggot. That's what people say, ain't it?"

Eva Mae reached to touch him, but Paul wouldn't allow it.

"You ain't no punk."

He turned away.

"Aw, come on! We been best friends our whole lives, Paul. You know what I think about you."

He looked past her.

"You do! I was mad 'cause you didn't fight back. That's all. I didn't have no business callin' you those names. I wish I could take it back."

"Well, you can't."

"You right. I can't. But you know I didn't mean it." Eva Mae wanted to smile but couldn't. "I'll never, ever call you any of those names again. I swear. I guess I was just trying to make you mad enough to fight."

Paul poured the feed until the cows ambled over.

"Now, what happened?"

Shaking his head the way people do when they're overwhelmed, he repeated softly, "They beat me."

"I know that. Anybody can see that. But why? Why would somebody wanna beat you like that?"

Paul rubbed his eyes.

"I know what people think about you, Paul, but that ain't enough to explain this."

"Why ain't it?"

"It just ain't."

"Do you really wanna know what happened? Really?"

She hesitated, then said, "Yes, I do."

Paul closed his eyes.

"Tell me."

Snippets of the attack returned. He felt, all over again, the hands thrust him to the ground and rip his clothes. "I can't. I just can't."

"Yes, you can."

Paul began walking toward the barn.

"I already know somebody beat you up. Everybody know that. So what's the part I don't know?"

Paul wouldn't look at her.

"Oh my God!" Eva Mae screeched. "They did something else to you, didn't they?"

As badly as Paul wanted to confess it, he said, "No."

"You're lying. I can always tell when you're lying."

"Shhhhh."

"You gotta tell me, Paul."

"No."

"You can't let them get away with this!"

"Nothing else happened. They beat me up. That's all."

"You lyin'!"

"No, I ain't."

"Yes you is! I can tell! Those boys . . . touched you, didn't they?"

"Shut up, Eva Mae! Just shut up!"

"You ain't got nothin' to be 'shamed of. The shame ain't on you."

He grabbed her arm forcefully. "Didn't nothin' else happen, all right? Now leave it alone!"

Eva Mae surrendered. "Fine. Didn't nothin' else happen." On her way home, she determined to find out what her best friend couldn't bear to say.

Paul knew Eva Mae wouldn't rest until she knew. That was just her way. She was always sticking her nose in other folks' business. Why couldn't she just leave well enough alone? It was moments like this that made him miss Sol. He would know what to say. Or sing. Yet Sol was nowhere to be found.

Paul returned to school battered and bruised. When he entered, Miss Erma said, "Class, there is no excuse for this kind of behavior. I won't tolerate it! Whoever did this is not welcome in my classroom!"

She studied each face.

"And let me make myself abundantly clear. If I find out that any of you were involved in this I will personally dismiss you from this school forever. Don't make me prove myself."

The vehemence in her voice was undeniable. She was livid not simply because it was Paul, but because she had a feeling who the perpetrators were. She felt sure of it. She'd seen their frowns and heard their snickering far too many times. Her rebuke of them was undermined, however, by the unmitigated sneering of Swamp Creek parents who went so far as to ask Miss Erma

not to seat Paul next to their child. Of course she denied their requests. Whenever she scolded a youngster for making fun of him, she discerned that no one—other than Eva Mae and Caroline—supported her reprimand. That's why this had happened—because children had no fear of reprisal from parents who supported their ignorance. *What is the world coming to?* Miss Erma thought.

Eva Mae and Caroline walked Paul home.

"I just wanna say I'm sorry again, Paul, for calling you those names that day. I really didn't mean it."

Caroline felt tension mounting, but she didn't say anything.

Paul turned and unleashed his fury. "Don't you *ever* call me a punk again as long as you live! I done been called everything, and I mean *everything*, but a child of God by everybody in this town, includin' my own family, so I sho don't need my best friend joinin' in!"

"I'm sorry, Paul. I really am."

Caroline touched his shoulder, but he jerked away.

"I don't need you fightin' for me no more, neither. I'll do my own fightin' from now on."

"Fine with me."

Caroline wanted to ask what happened, but she pieced together the story on her own. "We been friends since we was kids, y'all. Don't mess it up now."

"You need to talk to Eva Mae."

"Okay, Paul, look! I made a mistake. I was wrong. I said that! What more can I do?"

"Nothin'. I don't need you to do nothin'. I need you to be my friend, regardless of what happens."

"I'm gon' always be yo' friend. Always. You know that."

"Me, too," Caroline said.

Paul hesitated. "I know."

At the bend in the road, Caroline went her way. Eva Mae said, "I think I know who it was."

Paul feigned ignorance. "Who what was?"

"The boys who attacked you. I think I know who it was."

"No, you don't. You couldn't."

"You want me to tell you?"

"No! I want you to leave it alone. I already told you that. It's over, so let it go."

Eva Mae chuckled.

"What?"

"Oh, nothin'. It's just funny that I'm madder'n you about this whole thing."

"You ain't madder'n me. It's just that since we cain't do nothin' about it, ain't no need in gettin' all worked up."

"But we *can* do somethin' about it! I'm tellin' you I know who done it, but you act like you don't wanna know."

Paul considered revenge. "Even if you did know, which I doubt, what could we do?"

Eva Mae had several ideas, but decided not to share them. "I don't know, but we could do somethin'."

"What?"

"I don't know! But somebody's gotta make 'em pay. Don't you think so? *Somebody.*"

"Just drop it, Eva Mae. I mean, I 'preciate you wantin' to get back at them on my behalf and all, really I do, but I done had enough trouble for a while. I don't think I could handle anything else. I'll be all right."

"Okay." Eva Mae shrugged. "I'm sure you'll be just fine." She smiled as her retaliation plan crystallized.

"Let's talk about somethin' else."

Eva Mae's expression brightened. "Sure! I been wantin' to ask you something else anyway."

"Like what?"

"Like . . . who you like?"

Paul kicked a stone. "I don't know. I ain't never really thought about it."

"Oh stop it. I don't believe that. You don't think nobody's cute?"

Paul shrugged. He thought Johnny Ray was cute, but didn't everyone? He wanted to ask Johnny Ray if maybe they could go fishin' sometimes or just throw a baseball back and forth, but he didn't. He couldn't. What if Johnny Ray called him one of those ugly names? And what if he cried and Johnny Ray mocked him? How would he ever recover? He didn't care what other boys said. They were stupid and ugly anyway. But Johnny Ray's opinion mattered, and he couldn't bear to know what it was. So he took refuge in indifference and groomed a dream that would never come true. Johnny Ray resembled Sol, Paul thought, with his witty comments and his scholastic aptitude. All the kids vied for his attention and any time Miss Erma left the room, she left him in charge. Who wouldn't have wanted Johnny Ray Youngblood?

Paul didn't admit this. He had tried for years to ignore his feelings, hoping that, with time, they would disappear, but they didn't. Johnny Ray gave him that tingling sensation Emma Jean said would accompany true love. He wished he had known the feeling wasn't always mutual. He would've guarded his heart a little better. Then again, maybe he didn't like Johnny Ray *that way*. Maybe he simply envied the attention Johnny Ray received. Like he used to get back when he was Perfect. But if he did like Johnny Ray *that way*, he could never tell it. He knew that much. Emma Jean would die from embarrassment and Gus would jump into the Jordan. Emma Jean had told him that a man keeps his sexual thoughts to himself, and now he knew why. He'd definitely have to leave Swamp Creek if others found him out and, with nowhere to go, that was out of the question. He'd talk to Sol when he came home—if he ever came home.

He could've named Christina, Mamie's granddaughter, as someone he liked, and it wouldn't have been a lie. Not completely. He recalled how pretty she looked at his eighth birthday party, and marveled that she was even prettier now. No doubt her children would be beautiful and that was definitely a plus for a young man longing for a family. She was the only girl, other than Eva Mae, he'd ever thought about kissing. If he'd had a girlfriend, she'd definitely have been the one—if she liked him, which she probably didn't. Like her grandmother, she could be nosy—Emma Jean called them "uppity"—and the last thing Paul needed was someone trying to figure him out. But if she did like him, he'd be proud to be with her. The only thing was that, in her presence, the tingling sensation never came. Maybe he didn't need it, he told himself. He never saw any indication that Gus tingled at the sight of Emma Jean, and the sensation was obviously a waste of emotional energy with Johnny Ray. But whether he tingled or not, he wanted *somebody,* especially after what those boys did to him. At fifteen, he'd practically take anybody—if they wanted *him.*

He and Eva Mae hugged as a sign that his forgiveness was complete. Paul thanked her for always being there for him, even when she was too much.

"Better too much than too little, don't you think?"

Paul laughed. "Usually I would say yes, but with you—"

"Just be thankful you got me," Eva Mae teased seriously. "You just might need me again."

She waved over her shoulder, switching hips more full and rounded than Paul remembered. At five foot seven, she was taller than most women in Swamp

Creek, and, had it been a different time, she would've made the perfect model. Lean but not skinny, she had perky breasts that bounced excitedly whenever she moved, and her twenty-five-inch waistline made other women smirk with envy. Dresses hung on her slender form as though tailor-made, and Eva Mae enjoyed nothing more than sashaying before others when she knew she looked good. With her long, shapely legs, her walk was more like a strut. Men agreed she had the best pair of legs this side of the Jordan. When women saw her approaching, they frowned, saying, "That black heffa thinks she's cute." Eva Mae had learned to ignore them, to pity them, in fact, for their imperfections, and her "Hey y'all!" greeting only made them roll their eyes. She'd cackle, sling her head back, and walk on. Men usually laughed along.

It was her facial features that kept most men from pouncing upon her. Just like when she was a child playing in Emma Jean's front yard—or beneath her house—her hair was always a mess, at least by others' standards. It was just too hard to comb, so Mrs. Free stopped trying. When Eva Mae grew old enough to groom it herself, she decided she liked it like it was. Ribbons and barrettes looked like they hurt, she'd told Perfect as a little girl, and, as tender-headed as she was, she'd rather have people talk about her than walk around with a headache all day. Had she been cute, she would've had to endure the pain like all the other little girls in Swamp Creek, but since she wasn't, her mother didn't even bother. Her eyes were a bit too far apart, and her lips were so full they appeared swollen. Her daddy's nose sat flat in the middle of her face, and, like him, her nostrils expanded and contracted with each breath she took. He'd told her that they were African people, and that she would've been beautiful—*over there.* So Eva Mae walked around, imagining herself as an African queen, and nothing anyone else said could dampen her pride. Whenever folks called her hair a "wild bush," Eva Mae shook it harder. "Girl, if you pressed that nappy stuff, it'd be so long! And pretty, too!" But Eva Mae refused, having found self-esteem in the self alone.

Lost in his thoughts about Eva Mae, Paul turned and bumped into Sugar Baby as though he'd appeared out of nowhere.

"Oh!"

Swaying like a fragile blade of grass in the wind, Sugar Baby nodded his salutation. Paul didn't know whether to run or to lend the drunkard a hand.

"Thanks for helping me out the other night. Ain't no tellin' what might've happened if you hadn't come along."

Sugar Baby stumbled backward, but didn't fall. He nodded again.

"Did you see who it was?"

Paul didn't see the harm in asking, especially since Sugar Baby had been there and had maybe seen with his own eyes. He didn't want to hear it from Eva Mae, even if she knew. She was a girl, and girls weren't supposed to talk about such things.

"Un-uh," Sugar Baby slurred, shaking his head.

Paul stepped toward the house, then turned abruptly. "What did you mean by I ain't gotta die?"

Sugar Baby stared. "I been watchin' you. From the beginning."

"What?"

The right corner of his mouth turned upward. "You was sent."

The two stared at each other. Sugar Baby didn't answer. "Sent by who? For what?"

"Yeah, okay. You crazy, Mr. Sugar Baby." Paul ascended the steps.

"Sent folk don't die—'til they get through doin' what they was sent to do."

Paul shrugged and entered the house. Sugar Baby staggered away, thinking, *He'll know soon enough.*

Chapter 28

The first Saturday in July 1956, people swarmed the church lawn for the annual picnic. It was the largest crowd ever, Miss Mamie said. She hoped that, maybe this year, instead of simply eating like wild boars, a few unsaved niggas might get saved. Reverend Lindsey opposed her idea of opening the doors of the church as people ate, but he agreed that, at a church picnic, folks should act like they have the Holy Ghost.

Each family was responsible for two dishes of their choice—Mamie was the self-appointed coordinator—and the deacons provided the drinks. Even people who hated church came to the picnic that summer, primarily to hear the latest buzz about the local voter registration drive, which Mister Peace was organizing.

"Them boys better be careful," W. C. told Gus. "White folks ain't gon' like them stirrin' up trouble 'round here."

Mister and Johnny Ray Youngblood were among those who had formed a Swamp Creek branch of the NAACP. Newspaper accounts of the Montgomery Bus Boycott had inspired them to investigate the rights of Swamp Creek Negroes to choose their own government and fight for equal pay for equal work. Mister believed that if they could register locals to vote, then Swamp Creek would become, for all practical purposes, a Negro owned and operated community since Negroes outnumbered whites three to one. He and Johnny Ray had gone from door to door since April, taking names and birth dates of those who they hoped would be persuaded to vote in the fall primary. With over five hundred names already, their hope escalated that Swamp Creek might even get its own township charter. If they could simply get Negroes to the polls, Mister thought, they could change the course of history.

Mister's political motivation was born the previous fall when he witnessed white merchants cheat Gus out of a third of his harvest. The boys accompanied their father to town with wagonloads of peas, corn, tomatoes, squash, green beans, and cured pork sides. Sold by the bushel, the peas alone should have yielded a hefty return, and everyone in Conway County knew that Gus's pork was the best around. Only he was willing to rub salt into his meat for hours each day until every drop of blood had been extracted, and only Gus went to the trouble of finding young hickory saps with which to smoke his meat to perfection. People always paid a little more for his goods, and sometimes his bacon sold for twice the price of others'. That's what angered white merchants in town, Mister concluded, so they felt compelled to remind him that, in their eyes, he was still a nigga.

"Whatcha got there, boy?" Andrew Sullivan asked Gus as he and his sons unloaded the wagon at the outdoor farmer's market in Morrilton.

"Just bringin' in my harvest, sir. That's all."

"Did pretty good this year, did ya?"

"Did fine, sir. Just fine."

"Well, it looks like it."

When Woody and Mister unloaded the meat, Sullivan's admiration disintegrated into jealousy.

"You know we ain't gettin' but ten cents a pound for pork these days, right?"

"What!" Gus hollered. "It was twenty-two cents just last week!"

"I know, I know," Sullivan patronized, "but that's just the way it is, boy. Prices change all the time, you know."

It was the hopelessness in Gus's eyes that enraged Mister. He wanted to beat the white son of a bitch for lying, and had Authorly been there to protect him, he would have. Gus argued lightly, but in the end he took what he could get, coming home with twenty-five dollars instead of the expected forty-five.

That evening, Mister told Johnny Ray what had happened and, together, they solicited a few other bold young souls for the creation of the Swamp Creek NAACP. Most said it was a good idea, but they didn't want any part of it. Including Gus and Emma Jean. Things weren't equal, everyone admitted, but they were equal *enough* to keep food on the table and clothes on children's backs.

"But you have a right to everything you earn!" Mister preached at the church picnic. "We can't keep lettin' white folks steal our crops and our land. We gotta stand up for ourselves!"

People listened to Mister simply out of courtesy. Even the few who genuinely supported him were distracted by the smell of fried chicken and sweet potato pie.

"What cha'll think 'bout them folks down in Montgomery?" W. C. asked a gathering of deacons lounging in fold-up chairs beneath the huge churchyard tree.

"I think it's good," one said. "It's 'bout time colored folks do somethin' 'bout the way we treated."

"Well, I don't know 'bout that," another one said. " 'Cause, now, they walkin' to work instead o' ridin'. That mean they gotta get up earlier and they get home later, and by the time they get to work, they tired already. I mean, I understand fightin' for what's right and all, but seem like to me, the way they fightin' make life harder for theyselves."

"That's what I'm talkin' 'bout," W. C. said. "It's gotta be a better way than that."

"Then what is it?" Mister asked. The deacons hadn't noticed him listening. They fell silent. "If somebody got a better idea than what they doin', I'd sho love to hear it."

"All we sayin'," W. C. defended, "is that if you gon' fight, make sho you winnin' on every level."

"But we cain't win on every level at first. We gotta start somewhere, Mr. W. C."

"That's true, son, that's true."

No one else said anything. They simply waited for Mister to leave. When he did, W. C. said, "Young folks think they know everything. That's why that NAAST or whatever the hell it is ain't gon' 'mount to much, 'cause he and that Youngblood boy think they know everything."

The other deacons agreed.

Mister and Johnny Ray searched the crowd for eligible, unregistered voters. Assuaging their people's fear of white retaliation was far more difficult than either young man had the patience for, and, in a few instances, Mister told folks, "Just forget about it!" and moved on. Johnny Ray was more diplomatic and, therefore, a bit more successful in convincing others to visit the polls during the next election. Whites might try to intimidate, he admitted, but collectively Negroes had the upper hand. People liked his delivery. Yet, in a leader, they preferred Mister's fortitude.

Paul begged Emma Jean to let him join the NAACP, but Emma Jean wouldn't hear of it. "It's too dangerous," she said the night before the picnic. "Ain't no tellin' what might happen to them folks, goin' 'round tryin' to get colored people to fight. I ain't sayin' it ain't right; I'm jes' sayin' you ain't gon' do it."

"Come on, Momma. I ain't a kid no more. I'm sixteen! And what about Mister? He leadin' it! You ain't worried 'bout him?"

"He's grown, boy!"

"But so what! If it's dangerous, it's dangerous for him, too!"

"Well, when you get grown, you can do what you want to. 'Til then, you gon' do what I say, and I say you ain't joinin' that group. Not yet you ain't. You gon' finish school and make somethin' outta yo'self."

At the picnic, Paul told Eva Mae and Caroline that Emma Jean wouldn't let him join the NAACP as they had planned. Caroline couldn't join, either. Eva Mae didn't respond.

"What's wrong, Eva Mae?" Paul asked.

"My momma said I cain't go to school no more."

"Why not? You only got one more year!"

"My brother left home so she said I gotta work now. We need the money. She said don't make no sense wastin' education on somebody don't nobody want anyway, so I might as well go to work."

"I want you," Paul said. The words hadn't sounded strange in his head, but when he spoke them, they sounded sensual. Caroline frowned. Paul opened his mouth to explain, but Eva Mae saved him the trouble.

"Thanks, Paul," she said. Walking away, she whispered intensely, "You still my Perfect Peace!"

Caroline felt invisible. In that moment, Eva Mae and Paul alone populated the world as Caroline looked on, trying to find a category into which she could place this bizarre relationship. Paul didn't know that, as children, once he and Eva Mae began their intimate exchange beneath the house, Eva Mae had told Caroline that Paul—Perfect back then—was *her* best friend, implying, Caroline understood, something exclusive between them that she was not invited to share. She had watched them several times, from a distance, look about nervously and disappear beneath the house, then exit in an aura of pleasure. Afraid to question their interim activity, Caroline often paced the front yard in their younger years, wallowing in jealousy and feelings of abandonment. Fear of Eva Mae kept her from peeking under the house although her curiosity never subsided. The day she asked Paul, "So what you and Eva Mae be doin' down there?" she implored him not to tell Eva Mae she had asked, and Paul promised he wouldn't. In fact, he forgot all about it.

After Eva Mae left, Caroline mumbled from the side of her mouth, "Why Christina keep lookin' over here?"

Paul looked back and smiled. "I don't know."

"She likes you, huh?"

"Who? Me?"

"Yes, you!"

"I doubt it. She's real sweet though. I thought about askin' her to the dance."

"Really? You like Christina?"

"Yup. Well, a little bit."

"How you gon' ask her?"

"I don't know. I ain't neva asked a girl out before. But I know her folks, so it oughta be okay."

"What Miss Emma Jean gon' say? You know she can't stand Miss Mamie."

"I know, but I wanna go to the dance, and I need a date. Everybody's gon' be there."

Caroline nodded.

"What about you? Who you goin' with?"

"I don't know. Nobody's asked me yet. I don't think anybody's going to."

"Wouldn't it be great if you could go with Johnny Ray?" Paul said dreamily.

"Yeah, but he's goin' with Violet. If he go at all. You know how he is, quiet and all."

"Yeah, I know, but he's real handsome, huh?"

"Oh my God. He's the cutest boy I've ever seen."

He sho is! Paul wanted to say. "You never know. Somebody cute might ask you to the dance."

"Maybe."

"Is there somebody else cute you'd *like* to go with? You know . . . somebody *you* like?"

Caroline snickered and covered her mouth. "Yeah, but I can't tell you 'cause you gon' laugh."

"No I won't!"

"Yes you will!"

"I promise I won't."

"Okay. I'll tell you, but you gotta promise not to laugh."

"I promise!" Paul was laughing already.

"Okay. It's yo' brother. Bartimaeus."

"What!"

"Shhh!" Caroline hissed.

"Girl, are you serious?"

"Yes I'm serious. He's so cute to me."

"He's definitely *nice*, but . . ."

"And I don't care that he's blind. I mean, that don't matter to me."

Paul had never considered Bartimaeus's sex appeal. "Wow. Well, you should ask him to the dance."

"What if he says no?"

"He won't say no."

"I don't care about no stupid dance anyway."

"I thought you wanted somebody to take you?"

Caroline shrugged.

"Aw, come on. You gotta go. If you don't go, who I'm gon' talk to?"

"Eva Mae." Caroline smirked.

"She said she might not come."

"Then you can talk to Johnny Ray, I guess."

"Huh?"

"I see how you be lookin' at him."

"Shut up, girl!"

"Oh, don't get mad. It's all right. I won't tell nobody. I know how people are."

Paul sighed. "I can't help it sometimes, Caroline. I'll look up and there he is and I just can't stop starin' at him."

"I know, I know. Jes' be careful."

"I will."

Miss Mamie hollered, "Everybody come eat!"

"If yo' brother don't ask me, I sho ain't goin' wit' none of these knuckle-heads." She surveyed the church grounds. The truth was that, like everyone else, she dreamed of going with Johnny Ray, but weighing 325 pounds, she feared her chances were even worse than Paul's, for although she shared Johnny Ray's butternut complexion, Swamp Creek residents made it clear that no one—man or woman—found her excess flesh attractive. But she couldn't help it, she said. She had tried everything from starvation to no sweets, and she never lost more than a pound or two. Her expansion started during puberty and never stopped. At sixteen, her full cheeks and deep dimples caused people to say, "You sho is a pretty girl—*in the face*!" but they never let her forget the liability of her weight. Eating was all she could think to do after her father pushed himself off of her. It made sense to Caroline to satisfy herself internally since her father desecrated her externally. And since food kept Caroline appeased, her mother cooked as much as the child could hold, which increased each year until, by high school, Caroline ate more than her parents and siblings combined. She wanted to tell Paul and Eva Mae about the abuse, but her father convinced her that no one would believe her since no man in his right mind would ever touch her. So she kept eating and hoping that, somehow, miraculously, someone would kill the bastard.

"Christina's lookin' at you again," Caroline murmured.

"I know. Don't look, girl. I don't want her thinkin' I'm desperate."

"But I thought you said—"

"I do like her, but I don't want her thinkin' I just gotta have her."

"Why not?"

" 'Cause Daddy said when a woman think you gotta have her, she treat you like shit."

"Oh."

Mamie began screaming, "Come and get it, I said!" No one heard her mumble, "You greedy-ass niggas."

"Come on," Paul said. "We'll talk some more after we eat. You can walk me home if you want to." He leaned into Caroline's ear and teased, "So you can see Bartimaeus."

Her sheepish grin made Paul laugh. They sauntered to the long picnic tables covered with more food than the crowd would ever eat. Caroline sat between him and Bartimaeus, dreaming about the day he had spoken to her. He hadn't said anything particularly profound, just "Hello, sweet Caroline." That was all. But the way he said it made her feel special. She froze, and he repeated the greeting. Again, she said nothing and Bartimaeus chuckled.

"Am I *that* ugly?" he had said.

"Oh no, no. Not at all." She almost said he was the most beautiful man in the world.

"Well, let me try it again."

"No," she fumbled. "Um . . . hello." And she ran away.

Bartimaeus smiled. He loved her sweet, lemony scent, like the smell of fresh spring flowers. He sat in the porch rocker and planned how he'd ask her daddy to keep company with her.

Caroline then ate like never before. Food had always been her hiding place, but now it became her personal, private confidant. She gorged as she determined that what she loved about Bartimaeus, or, rather, what she *would* love about him, was his indifference to physical things. She convinced herself that he could love her precisely because he couldn't see her, and that made her feel enormously blessed. She was relieved that someone wouldn't—in fact, couldn't—be repulsed by her enormity, and excited that at least one man in the world might experience her heart. Except for propriety, she would have asked Bartimaeus to marry her, but she didn't want to seem fast.

A week after the picnic, with Mister guiding his steps, Bartimaeus finally conjured the courage to ask Caroline's father if he could take up with her. "Would you please?" the man shouted. Every evening thereafter, Bartimaeus found his way to Caroline's porch and, far into the night, the two giggled like anxious children. Caroline was relieved that he had never tried to touch her and, in fact, wondered if they could live that way forever. It wasn't that she didn't want to be touched; she wanted it desperately. She just feared he might measure her beauty by what his hands felt instead of what his heart knew, then they would be no more. Hand-holding was the most Caroline relented to, but each time Bartimaeus caressed her fingers, her thighs moistened and she imagined him somewhere between them.

When he asked Mr. Burden if he could take Caroline to the dance, she practically fainted. Having decided to go alone, she never imagined she'd actually have a date. Now, she'd have to skip a few meals to fit into her one good dress.

At the Cunninghams', the next day, Paul was even more timid than Bartimaeus had been. He stood at the door for ten minutes, trying to gather the nerve to knock, and when he did, he tapped lightly as though the door might collapse. Christina acted surprised to see him.

"Hi," she whispered through the screen.

Her hair was freshly pressed and pulled back into a ponytail. She might be the prettiest girl in Swamp Creek, Paul thought.

"Hey there."

"I wasn't expecting you."

"No, I guess not." He rubbed his head nervously. "I just thought I'd come by and see if maybe, um, you might like to go to the dance with me." He prepared himself for rejection.

"Okay," she said, smiling, "but you'll have to ask my daddy. You wanna come in?"

"Um, sure."

Paul followed her to the family room. "Good evening, Mr. Frank," he said, and nodded. "Miss Julia."

The couple looked up, but offered no greeting. Dressed as though expecting serious company, they eyed each other, then Frank Cunningham stood. "What can we do for you, boy?" He never extended his monstrous hand. That's how Paul knew something was wrong. He wanted to leave, but there was no turning back now.

"I, um, came by to see if, um, maybe y'all might let Christina go to the school dance with me."

Julia looked away.

"I ain't got nothin' 'gainst you, son, but I cain't lie to ya. I done heard lot o' stuff 'bout you that don't make me very comfortable."

"He's real nice, Daddy."

"I ain't talkin' to you right now, honey. This between me and this boy here."

Paul wished Authorly was there. Or Sol. "Well, sir, um, I don't really know what to tell you."

"Well, tell me this first: is you really a boy?"

"Frank!" Julia snapped.

"I'm gon' ask what I need to ask. If my daughter leave here on a date, I want it to be with a *boy*!"

Paul's eyes watered, but he maintained composure. "I am a boy, Mr. Frank. I always been one, and I'm always gon' be one."

"Well, that's good." Frank resumed his seat. "At least that's a start. Sit down."

Paul and Christina sat in chairs opposite her parents on the sofa. Julia almost smiled at Paul, but thought it better to remain neutral.

"I ain't one to pay much attention to rumors," Frank said, "but all this talk 'bout you bein' a sissy—"

"Frank Cunningham, stop it! You ain't got no right judgin' this boy befo' you talk to him."

"Well, hell, I'm tryin' to talk to him now, but you keep interruptin' me!"

"You ain't *talkin'* to him, babe. You sayin' what you heard about him. Talkin' to him mean he get to talk back."

Paul liked Miss Julia. She was even prettier than Christina.

Frank sighed. "I'm sorry, son. I don't mean to be rude. I just wanna know whoever my daughter leave my house with."

"Yessir. I understand. You can ask me whatever you want." He hoped the man didn't ask to see him naked.

"He's a good boy, Daddy. He's real nice."

"It's okay," Paul said to Christina. "It's really okay."

Julia gave Frank the eye.

"What kinda boy is you?"

"Frank . . ."

"I'm just askin' him what he do!"

"I go to school, sir, and I work in the field with Daddy when I get home. I work real hard and my grades is pretty good. You know my folks."

"I do. I likes ole Gus."

"Well, he'll tell you 'bout me if you ask him."

"I ain't talkin' to him. I'm talkin' to you. A young man's gotta speak for hisself."

"Yessir." Sweat trickled down Paul's back.

"What's yo' intentions wit' my daughter?"

"I don't really have no intentions, sir. I just wanna take her to the dance, if that's all right with you and Miss Julia."

Julia nodded.

"Do you know anything about a lady?"

Paul smirked. *Are you kidding?* "Yessir, I do. My momma taught me real good."

"You know to keep your hands off a young lady, right?"

"Yessir."

"And you know to have her home by a decent hour?"

"Yessir."

"And you know that girls don't kiss on the first date?"

"Frank . . ."

"Would you let me handle this, woman, please?"

"Don't pay him no mind, son."

"He better pay me some mind! Shit. I ain't playin'!"

Christina intervened. "I'd like to go with him, Daddy. If it's okay with you and Momma."

"I know you would, baby, but a man don't give his daughter away easily."

"I ain't takin' her away, sir. We just wanna go to the dance together. That's all. I'll treat her real good, and I'll be real mannerable."

"He's a fine boy, Frank. Let 'em go."

Frank hesitated. "All right. Y'all can go. But you better have my daughter back in this house before eleven o'clock. You hear me?"

"Oh yessir! We'll be back."

Christina beamed. "Thank you, Daddy."

"We'd love if you'd stay for dinner," Julia said after hugging Paul.

"Thank you, ma'am, but Momma's expecting me, and I still got my chores to do."

"Then we'll see you in a few weeks."

Christina walked Paul to the door and onto the porch.

"Thanks for coming."

"Oh sure. I think the dance'll be fun."

"I mean, thanks for asking me."

Was he feeling the tingling sensation? "You welcome. And thank *you* for going with me."

Paul looked up and saw Frank staring from the living room. He turned back to Christina. "I'll see you at school. Bye."

Christina waved sweetly.

At home, Paul relayed the event to Emma Jean, who exploded with fury. "Who does that nigga think he is? He don't have no right questionin' you like that!" The old burn scars itched as though she were on fire again. "Wait 'til I see him Sunday!"

Gus laughed. "You did good, boy."

"It's fine, Momma. He said we can go."

"He better had! I cain't stand them damn Cunninghams. They always thinkin' they better than somebody else. He need to buy his momma a new wig so she can stop wearin' that old matted thang on first Sunday 'cause—"

"Emma Jean, please."

"I ain't mad at him, Momma. Everything's fine."

Emma Jean gasped suddenly.

"What is it?" Gus asked.

This was the moment she'd been waiting for since Paul's transformation. She saw it clearly.

"We gotta find you somethin' to wear."

"I'll just wear one o' Woody's preachin' suits, I guess."

"Oh no you ain't! You ain't wearin' none o' them tired things so Mamie can talk about you and this family the rest of her livin' days!"

"I ain't got nothin' else to wear."

"I know, but we'll find you somethin'. Trust me. You gon' be the handsomest young man at the dance. I"—she tapped her chest—"am gon' guarantee that!"

Chapter 29

Emma Jean spent the next several days thumbing Sears, Roebuck and Co. catalogs for the perfect suit. Her plan was to replicate it on the old sewing machine, since Gus would have died had she mentioned purchasing it outright. She had waited years for the opportunity to redeem herself, and finally it had come.

"That's it!" she shouted one Friday afternoon. "Oh wow. It's gorgeous." What she liked most was that the suit was modeled by a black man. She had never seen a Negro model in a magazine before. He was light enough to pass for white, but he was still black. On top of that, the suit was beautiful. It was a three-piece, navy blue, pin-striped Stanley Becker. She could see her neighbors, in her mind, gawking in awe and envy, and that's precisely what she wanted. For Paul's sake. Whatever they'd said about him, they'd feel bad when they saw him draped in princely attire. At six foot one, he was the ideal height for a suit, and even Mamie would have to admit that Paul had evolved into one of Swamp Creek's gems. Somewhere between fifteen and sixteen, his brows had thickened as his chest broadened, and the field labor had worked the last vestiges of baby fat from his waistline. Whiskers sprouted from his chin like newly planted blades of grass after a rain, and whenever Authorly cut Paul's hair and shaped his burgeoning mustache, Miss Mamie declared, "Ump! That ole sissified boy done turned into a handsome young man after all! Face just as smooth and clear! Cain't even tell that somebody beat him to a pulp last year. Well praise de Lawd!"

Emma Jean studied the image of the suit, trying hard to note every detail. She wasn't a seamstress—in fact, she'd never made anything—but she *be-*

lieved she could. If anyone could do it, she could. Right? She'd certainly need to take her time because, more than ever, she wanted a flawless product. That would let folks know that she was Emma Jean Peace, and she didn't half-do anything.

It took her hours to cut out newspaper pieces that she hoped to use as a pattern for her masterpiece. How she'd afford the cloth was another dilemma. She couldn't very well use the money in the coffer, for then the family would starve the next six months, and without Authorly, Sol, and James Earl, harvest hands had become scarce. But she'd get it somehow. Paul deserved the best, and she intended for him to have it. She had watched him mope around for years, unsure of himself, surrendering to immeasurable ridicule while trying, though failing, to please everybody. Now, he'd be back on top again. Yes, she'd find the money. If she had to pick cotton again, which she swore she'd never do, she'd do it, she told herself.

The suit didn't appear difficult to make, except for the jacket lapels and buttons. She was a little nervous about the shoulders, too, believing correctly that to be off an inch or two in the cutting would mean disaster for the final garment. And how in the world did one get a zipper in the exact middle of those pants? Emma Jean sighed. Maybe this wasn't such a good idea after all, she thought. Then again, she had no other choice. Paul wasn't going to the dance looking like a pauper, and she definitely couldn't afford to purchase the suit. It would work, she told herself. It had to.

A week later, Emma Jean was laundering white folks' clothes. Gus asked her why she needed extra money, and she told him not to worry about it. He'd see. And he'd be proud. She would do it just long enough to purchase the material and other necessary items, since she feared any day now she'd explode and curse out one of those white bitches. "They act like my hands was made for scrubbin' they dirty draws!" she complained to Gus.

"Then why you doin' it?"

Unwilling to expose her scheme, she said, "I'm doin' it for us. For the sake of this family."

The day the material arrived, Emma Jean was as giddy as Perfect on her eighth birthday morning. She ripped the brown butcher paper open and clutched the cloth to her bosom. "Oh yes! It's gonna be so beautiful! I know it is!" The boys marveled at her excitement, wondering what Emma Jean was up to. She immediately cleared the table and unfolded the cloth. Her humming dulled their curiosity, and allowed Emma Jean to work without interruption.

After hours of cutting, she discovered that her patterns simply weren't correct. The pieces weren't even complementary. She proceeded though, trusting that somehow the project would magically come together. More than anything, she was glad not to have to wash white folks' clothes anymore. Thinking about the generations of Negro women who had done it before her—and done it a lifetime—made her honor those who obviously had more enduring power than she had. But that was for another day, she thought. For now, she had to figure out a way to save her dying garment.

Gus rose at 2:30 A.M. after rolling over and feeling nothing but the cold sheet beside him. "You comin' to bed, woman?"

"In a little while. I gotta finish this. Ain't much time left."

"Time for what?'

"Just go on back to bed, man. You'll know soon enough."

By 5:30, Emma Jean sat at the table exhausted and disgusted. There was no way the pieces she had cut out were going to congeal into anything fashionable. She could see that now. But that wasn't the problem. The problem was that she didn't know what to do.

"I don't smell no coffee," Gus said, emerging from the bedroom.

" 'Cause ain't none!" Emma Jean screeched.

"What's wrong with you, woman? Why you hollerin' early in the mornin'?"

Emma Jean huffed. "I'm sorry. I didn't mean to shout."

"But you didn't answer my question. What's wrong?"

The boys began to stir.

"I just gotta figure something out. That's all."

She paced from the kitchen to the living room and back until she knew what she had to do. God was laughing out loud, she told herself. He always gets the last word. She thought He'd forgiven her, but maybe forgiveness doesn't mean you don't pay, she considered. Yes, God was cracking up. He intended to watch every second of the only option available to Emma Jean to salvage Paul's suit. So she bound the pieces and the extra material in a large paper bag, swallowed practically all of her pride, and said, "I'll see y'all later. I gotta handle something."

"We ain't gon' eat?" Gus asked.

"Y'all is if somebody cook," Emma Jean snarled.

She shook her head as she walked down the lane.

* * *

"Knock, knock," Emma Jean called through Henrietta's screen door. The bag of suit pieces rested beneath her left armpit.

"Emma Jean Peace?" Henrietta said, surprised. She neither smiled nor invited her in.

"Well, hey, chile!" Emma Jean said, feigning cordiality. "How you been doin'?"

Henrietta folded her arms and stared at her with repulsion.

"Now I know we ain't best friends or nothin', but, girl, I needs yo' help!" She cackled. "This is my baby's suit for the school dance and it ain't right. It ain't nowhere near right. But I thought—"

"You don't have no shame at all, Emma Jean Peace? None *at all*?"

"Dear heavens, what do you mean?"

"I delivered that . . . that . . . child, and you forced me to go along with some sickness I ain't never forgave myself for, and now you want me to help you fix his suit for a dance?"

"I ain't askin' you to agree wit' nothin', Henrietta. I'm jes' askin' you to give that boy one special evening."

"That's the whole thing!" She clapped in disbelief. "You didn't even raise him as no boy. Not at first!"

"Shhhhhhhh!" Emma Jean hissed. "That ain't none o' yo' business. That's my business. You ain't gon' have to answer to God fu nothin'. I told you that back then. I'll be the one He questions 'bout everything. And don't you worry—I can handle God. I jes' need yo' help right now. I wouldn't o' come if I coulda helped it. Believe me, I wouldn't've."

Henrietta cracked the screen door, and Emma Jean rushed in.

"You know I quit midwifin' after that day, don't you?"

Emma Jean ignored her, removed the pieces from the bag, and laid them across Henrietta's kitchen table. "It don't need much. Some of the pieces don't fit together too good though. I probably didn't cut 'em out right."

Henrietta glanced at the material. "Then you askin' me to make a whole suit from stratch!"

"Well, whatever it takes. You the only seamstress 'round here I know of. That's any good anyway." Emma Jean couldn't look at her.

"Don't act like you didn't hear me," Henrietta said, pushing Emma Jean away from the pieces as she examined them closer. "That don't matter to you, do it?"

Emma Jean didn't respond.

"Well, it matter to me. I'll never forget that evening long as I live." Henrietta looked at Emma Jean, who turned away. Henrietta had the pieces in her arms now. "I sat in that chair like a zombie all evening and into the night. I couldn't believe a mother could do what you had done, but I couldn't say nothin', neither. That was the worst part about it. I had to keep yo' secret."

"Can we fix the suit?"

"*We* cain't do nothin'!"

"Well, can *you*?"

"Maybe," Henrietta shrugged, "but you gon' hear me out first or I ain't fixin' nothin'. And cain't nobody this side o' heaven do nothin' with these rags but me."

Emma Jean sighed.

"I been wonderin' how de Lawd was gon' make you come back to me, and now I see." She snickered. "And you need my help this time. Ha! Ain't life somethin'?"

Just fix the suit, heffa! she wanted to say but couldn't.

"So let's get this straight. I'll fix the suit—on one condition."

Emma Jean knew an ultimatum was coming. "What is it?"

Henrietta returned the pieces to the table. "I want the rest of your life."

"What?" Emma Jean scowled.

"That's right. You ruined my sleep, my health, and my midwife practice," Henrietta explained with her back to Emma Jean. "Now, I want the life I never had."

"My life ain't worth a damn!"

"Oh no! I don't want your *existence*—I want your work, your energy."

"What is you talkin' 'bout, Henrietta?"

"See, I wanna open up my own little boutique. Right in downtown Morrilton. Trish moved away last year, and with my husband gone, I ain't got nothin' else. I been wantin' to do this for years, but I ain't had no money."

"Well, shit, I ain't got none, either!"

"But you can work enough to make some. That's what I want."

"You want some money? I'll pay you some money. You didn't think I'd ask you to do this free, did you?"

Henrietta laughed. "You don't get it, do you? I don't want no one-time payment. I want you to work for me. For free. For the rest of yo' life."

Emma Jean howled. "Sheeeeeeeit! You must be crazy, woman! I ain't no fool. I ain't workin' for you or nobody else for free, and I sho ain't 'bout to do it for de rest o' my life! You must think I'm stupid or somethin'!"

"You ain't gotta do nothin', Emma Jean Peace. Unless you want this suit fixed."

"I'll fix it myself before I let you swindle me into something that crazy! I cain't sit for no long time noway!" Emma Jean snatched the garment pieces from the table.

"Suit yourself. That child is gon' look a mess at the dance in some ole botched-up suit. But if you okay with it, it sho don't bother me."

Henrietta held the screen door open as Emma Jean stomped through it. "I ain't neva been that desperate, Ms. Henrietta Worthy. Never!" She pranced away, mumbling her indignation.

"That hussy must be crazy!" she panted, trudging through the screen door.

"What is it?" Gus asked.

Emma Jean was too embarrassed to say. "I just cain't believe she said that. I just cain't believe it."

"Who said what?"

"I can't tell you. Not yet."

"All right," Gus said. He and the boys went to the field.

"She wanna charge me a arm and a leg just to fix a suit? It'll be a cold day in hell befo' I work for that heffa for free! She must think I ain't got no sense!" Emma Jean marched around the kitchen table, speaking as if someone were sitting before her. "Shit. I ain't crazy. Let me try this one more time. Maybe I just got too frustrated too soon."

She poured the pieces from the bag onto the table and immediately became discouraged all over again.

"Let's see. . . ."

She tried to align the parts of the suit, but they simply didn't fit together. "Goddamnit!" she shouted, and pounded the tabletop. There was nothing else she could do.

Throughout the day, Emma Jean tried to think of someone or something else to ameliorate her situation, but she kept drawing blanks. Surely someone other than Henrietta Worthy could sew who could help her out. Emma Jean thought of several women—including Mamie Cunningham—but their garments always looked homemade. And she wasn't about to ask Mamie Cunningham for anything. No, Henrietta was the only one who could make an outfit and folks thought it came straight from the store. And that's what she wanted.

By midnight, Emma Jean knew she had no other choice. She had moved the pieces around all day, but they never merged into the suit she had imagined.

"Where you goin' at this hour, Momma?" Woody asked as Emma Jean opened the front door.

"I got somethin' I gotta do, son. Don't worry about me. I'll be all right." She took Gus's flashlight and walked into the night.

Henrietta thought she heard a woodpecker, then, when the knock came stronger, she concluded that somebody must be dead. She rushed to the door.

Emma Jean glanced everywhere except into Henrietta's eyes.

"What's de matter?"

"This suit. That's what's de matter."

"What chu doin' here at this hour?"

Emma Jean pushed past Henrietta and into her living room. "Fix the damn thing," she mumbled, and tossed the bag onto the sofa.

"Why didn't you bring it tomorrow? I can't do nothin' wit' it tonight."

"Yes you can," Emma Jean returned, and nodded. "And you will. If I'm gon' give you the rest o' my life, you gon' give me tonight. And I don't want none o' my folks knowin' nothin' 'bout this suit or our little . . . arrangement."

Henrietta yelped. "You can't come in my house and—"

"Oh just fix the goddamn suit, will ya!" Emma Jean paused. "Please."

Henrietta cleared the table and laid out the pieces. She mocked Emma Jean's mess, then put on a pot of coffee. "I thought our dealings were over years ago."

Emma Jean sat silently on the sofa.

"God gon' always bring it full circle, ain't He?"

She wanted Henrietta to shut up and fix the suit as quickly as possible.

"When that child was born and you did what you did, I promised myself I wouldn't bring another baby into this world. I came home that evening and threw my medicine bag into the fire and cried. You made me carry somethin' that was too heavy for me. But I didn't have no choice, did I?"

Fix the damn suit, woman, and close yo' mouth!

"I was so scared you wuz gon' tell my business. Ha! If I knew then what I know now, I woulda let you tell whatever the hell you wanted to 'cause wunnit nothin' worth that."

"It didn't cost you nothin'. It was my doin'."

Henrietta shook her head. "You wrong. It cost me everything. I didn't sleep for days."

"Why didn't you? It didn't have nothin' to do with you."

Henrietta looked at Emma Jean as though she had transformed into a cyclops. "You made it have somethin' to do with me! You made me agree to destroy somebody's life."

Emma Jean rolled her eyes.

"Yeah, okay. But you gon' pay. You gon' wish to God you had let that boy be a boy."

Emma Jean whispered, "He *is* a boy."

"He is *now*! But he gon' always have some girl in him. Always. Thanks to you."

"He's still gon' be my sweet baby, don't care how much girl he got in him. I'ma love him just like he is."

"Yeah, but the world ain't. That's why somebody beat him up. You and Gus can't protect him a lifetime, Emma Jean. He ain't gon' live with you but a little while longer, then what?"

"I don't know, but he'll be all right."

Silence wanted to settle between them, but Henrietta ran it away. "The next time I saw that child, she was 'bout two. I couldn't believe my eyes. She really looked like a little girl. I couldn't figure out how you had done it. But I told myself to be patient. Time would reveal the truth. But it never did. So, one day, I just decided not to carry it any longer. I gave it over to God and told Him to do whatever He wanted to do with you. I was mad for years 'cause seem like God wunnit gon' do nothin', then, all o' sudden, you show up on my doorstep." Henrietta laughed hard. "He may not come when you want Him, but He's always right on time. Ain't that what they say?"

Emma Jean cleaned her fingernails with a toothpick.

"Now, you need me again. Well, ain't that some shit?"

Emma Jean wanted to slap Henrietta, but, under the circumstances, she held her peace.

"How did you do it, Emma Jean? I mean, even now, folks ain't figured out how you pulled it off. How did you keep it from Gus and them boys?"

Silence.

"Huh? How'd you do it?"

Emma Jean ignored Henrietta and watched her work. Her sewing skills made Emma Jean envious. Piece by piece, the suit began to take shape the way Emma Jean had envisioned. Things that would have taken her days Henrietta did in minutes and did it much more meticulously.

"None o' them boys never asked you nothin'?" She poured herself a cup of steaming hot black coffee.

"There wunnit nothin' to ask."

"I guess you right. They didn't know to ask."

She connected the shoulders and reinforced the stitch. "You cut these shoulders like that child is a li'l boy. He near 'bout tall as Gus now, ain't he?"

"Yes, he is."

"And what if that boy get married one day and then start thinkin' 'bout boys? Ain't you gon' blame yo'self?"

Emma Jean's patience was fading. Sighing and huffing weren't deterring Henrietta, and Emma Jean knew her abrasive tongue wouldn't remain silent much longer.

"Ump, ump, ump. Yeah, you done created more than you can handle, Miss Emma Jean. I hope that chile gon' be all right."

"He'll be just fine, thank you. If he get married, I expect him to honor his vows like everybody else s'pose to."

Henrietta's head jerked around. "How do you do it? Huh? How do you just ignore truth and create the reality you want?"

"Oh come on, Henrietta! Finish the suit!"

Henrietta shrugged and continued sewing. "I don't get it. I couldn't do it. I wouldn't get a wink o' sleep if I did some o' de stuff you did." She stared at Emma Jean. "At least I could sew. That saved my life. When I burned my medicine bag, that's the only thing I had to fall back on. And thank God folks need clothes, 'cause otherwise me and Trish woulda starved to death."

The mention of Trish was the break Emma Jean needed. "How is the preacher's daughter?"

Henrietta's flappable tongue calmed. "Trish is doin' just fine."

It was Emma Jean's turn to cackle. "So! Did you ever tell her the truth?"

"Don't start that again, Emma Jean. You know good and damn well it ain't the same thing."

"Well, like I said years ago, every woman gotta fight for whatever piece of life she gon' have. You fought for what you wanted, and so did I, so let's just leave things be."

"You better pray somebody don't hurt that boy for real. He got a long, hard road in front o' him and you know people ain't sympathetic to boys like that."

"Somebody done already hurt him for real and he survived, so don't worry 'bout my child. And the next person lay a hand on him gon' have to deal with me!"

Within the next several hours, Emma Jean watched Henrietta work magic on the mess she had created. Just before six, Henrietta said, "I'll give you until after the dance. But from then on, I intend to see you at the crack of dawn every day." Henrietta displayed the suit for Emma Jean's inspection.

"It's beautiful. Thank you."

"Yes it is, if I must say so myself. No need for thanks. You'll earn every penny of it. I promise you that."

Chapter 30

Gus and the boys were lounging at the kitchen table when Emma Jean returned.

"Where you been at, woman?"

"Don't you worry about that, Mr. Gustavus Peace!" Emma Jean said. "I got a surprise for everybody."

The boys stared in anticipation.

"I been workin' on somethin' the past couple o' days, and now it's complete. Paul, this is for you." She pulled the suit from the bag.

"Oh wow," he murmured, walking slowly toward Emma Jean. "It's real nice, Momma. Real nice!"

"Yes it is," she sang with a smile.

Paul touched it as though it were fragile. "Where'd you get it from?"

"I didn't get it from nowhere. I *made* it."

Woody and Mister gasped.

Gus said, "You made it?"

"That's right! I had a little help, but, for the most part, I did it all by myself."

"When did you start sewin'?"

"I *been* sewin', man. You don't know everything about me."

"It looks really good, Momma," Mister said, struggling not to be jealous.

"Thank you, son. Now, Paul, go try it on."

Emma Jean placed the cast-iron skillet on the stove and extracted eggs from the icebox. When Paul emerged, the men moaned with admiration.

"You looks mighty fine, boy," Gus said, nodding. "Mighty fine!"

Woody and Mister gawked in silence. Bartimaeus asked, "What does he look like, y'all?"

"He look like a handsome, black prince," Gus said.

"Ah, Daddy. I don't look *that* good."

"Oh yes you do! I ain't never seen a Peace man in a suit who didn't look good."

Emma Jean turned and beheld her dream. "Oh my Lord! Look at my baby." She clasped her mouth. "It's perfect. It's just perfect! You look incredible, son."

The boys surrounded Paul and whispered their praise. Gus told Emma Jean, "You outdid yo'self this time, woman."

"Didn't I!" Emma Jean sassed. "But, really, it wunnit nothin'. He had to have somethin' to wear to the dance."

Mister smiled beyond his hurt. "I hope Christina got a real pretty dress, 'cause if she don't, you gon' make her look bad!"

The family laughed as Mister exited to feed the chickens.

"I appreciate this, Momma," Paul said, peering into Emma Jean's eyes. "You didn't have to do it."

"Well, of course I did. You deserve it. And, anyway, it ain't nothin'. I just want you to be happy." She kissed Paul's cheek and became giddy, temporarily forgetting the price she'd soon have to pay. For now, his joy was the point and that alone was her pleasure.

"Don't get it dirty, son. We sho ain't got no money to clean it. Take it off and go hang it back up. You'll get to wear it soon enough."

After obeying his mother, Paul joined the others at the kitchen table and said, "You musta sat up all night sewing."

"Don't you worry 'bout that. You jes' focus on yo' part and I'll always make sure I take care o' mine."

"I didn't even know you could sew."

"Well, like I said, don't you worry 'bout that. What you don't know could make another world, chile." She placed the scrambled eggs on the table and extracted biscuits from the oven.

Paul imagined the look on his peers' faces when he appeared at the dance. He hadn't been this anxious since seeing the chocolate-covered lemon cake on his eighth birthday. He couldn't wait for Johnny Ray to see him. Maybe then he'd speak.

"Well, y'all come on and eat," Emma Jean called, placing chipped plates and mismatched cutlery on the table. "Where did Mister go?"

"He went to feed the chickens," Woody said.

Gus frowned. "It don't take nobody this long to feed no chickens. Paul, go get yo' brother and tell him to come on and let's eat."

Glancing around outside, Paul called for Mister but didn't see him. Before reentering the house, he saw Mister's shirttail disappear into the nearby forest. "Mister!" he screamed, but Mister never turned. What was he going into the woods for? Paul stood on the porch momentarily, staring at the space where Mister had vanished. He felt awkward, as though having witnessed something he shouldn't have. He decided not to mention anything to the others and to ask Mister about it later.

"I didn't see him," Paul said, and took his seat at the table.

"Well, he'll just have to eat later," Emma Jean said. "Gus, bless the food before it gets cold."

Mister hoped the family would ignore his absence long enough for him to do what he needed to do. At twenty-one, against everyone's prediction, he had blossomed into the most virile, physically desirable of the Peace boys—even beyond Paul—and most agreed that his only rival was Johnny Ray Young-blood. His chiseled chest, arms, abs, and thighs caused Authorly to say, upon viewing Mister's naked torso, "Boy, you done got fine as hell!" His entire childhood was filled with visions of leaving home and moving to a place where he had his own bed and maybe even his own room. But what would Gus and Emma Jean do without him? Woody would leave soon, he thought, and Bartimaeus was useless, for the most part. Paul would probably go to college since he had gone to high school, so Mister feared his escape would mean the starvation of his parents. Gus would always work, Mister knew, but, with a stubborn hip, he certainly couldn't work the farm alone, and, since the fire, Emma Jean's productivity had never quite rebounded. Yet the real reason Mister stayed, the reason churning in his soul, went far beyond the welfare of his parents, or his brothers' future. In fact, a year or so later when Bartimaeus married and moved out, shortly after Woody, Mister cried. Not because of some fraternal longing, but because along with Bartimaeus went the cover for the truth of Mister's stagnation. No one understood why such a handsome young man didn't take a wife and raise countless children the way other southern black men did. But he couldn't tell it—not if he wanted to live in Swamp Creek—for had he followed his heart, he would have announced to the world his love for Johnny Ray Youngblood. Women—including Emma Jean—had worshiped Johnny Ray so much that, as a child, Mister wanted to be like him and, as an adult, he wanted to be with him. Maybe Emma Jean would have approved, Mister considered, happy that Johnny Ray found at least one of her children desirable, but Mister wouldn't have dared to mention such a thing. In various sermons, Woody made the community's position on sexuality quite clear, calling same-sex attraction a disease, an abomination, a reproach to humanity as the congregation shouted, "Amen!" The last thing Mister wanted was to be the source of familial shame. He was certain Gus knew nothing of homosexuality—he knew about sissies, but that was different—and mentioning as much would surely have incited unbridled confusion in an already mentally fragile man. So Mister hid in his parents' house, trying frantically, on bended knees, to pray away desires that seemed only to intensify. Out of sheer desperation, he confessed his struggle to Paul the evening of the day Emma Jean unveiled the suit, believing that, if anyone would love him unconditionally, Paul would.

"Where'd you go this morning? I saw you run off in the woods."

Mister closed his eyes. "I had to meet somebody."

"In the woods?"

"Yeah."

"Why?"

Mister sighed. "I need to tell you something."

"Okay. Go 'head. What is it?"

"Well . . ."

"Just say it. You can tell me anything."

Mister huffed and said, "I have . . . um . . . feelings for boys."

"What!"

"Shhhhhh. Be quiet, man. I ain't tryin' to tell the whole world."

Paul was lost somewhere between surprise and curiosity.

"I jes' can't help it. God knows I tried. I don't know where the feelings come from and I sho don't know how to get rid of 'em. I wish I could. I done asked God to take 'em away, but He won't do it."

Paul bit his fingernails.

"Say something, please. Anything."

"I don't know what to say, Mister."

"Ain't you never had no feelings for a boy? I thought that maybe you had, considerin' everything you been through."

"Naw, I ain't never had no feelings for a boy. Not like *that*." Paul hated himself for lying.

"No? Really?" Mister glanced at Paul in disbelief, then shrugged. "Well, I don't know what to do."

"And I don't know what to tell you." Why, he wondered, hadn't he trusted Mister as much as Mister had trusted him?

"Sometimes when we sittin' in the NAACP meetins or goin' 'round talkin' to folks, I can't hardly concentrate for lookin' at Johnny Ray."

"Johnny Ray!" Paul shouted.

"Yeah. Johnny Ray Youngblood. You know Johnny Ray, right?"

"I know him." Paul feared he couldn't hide his disappointment.

"I try to get him outta my mind, but most times I can't."

"Johnny Ray?"

"Yeah. What's wrong with him?"

"Nothin'."

"You actin' like it's somethin'."

"Oh no. It ain't nothin'. Really. I'm just a little surprised, I guess. He seems so . . . I don't know . . . quiet." Paul became dazed.

"Well, he's the one."

Oh no, Paul thought. *This can't be.*

He'd never tell anyone about his feelings for Johnny Ray now, and he assumed it wouldn't matter anyway. Johnny Ray wanted Mister, and Paul didn't know how to abort the contempt growing in his heart. *What does Mister have that I don't?* he wondered. *And what is it about me that Johnny Ray doesn't like?* His brows furrowed as he realized that the man he'd always wanted, the only one his mother might've approved of, loved his brother instead. He couldn't imagine what they did out there in the woods, but he knew they must have been driven by love, for had anyone caught them, their own fathers would have hanged them.

"We can't live this way," Mister whispered into Johnny Ray's mouth. They sat on the edge of a tree stump.

"I know. I know," Johnny Ray said, caressing Mister's thick brows with his thumbs.

"And we can't keep meeting like this. What if somebody sees us?"

Johnny Ray sighed. "I'd just tell 'em how much I love you. And why."

Mister stood. "This ain't funny!"

"I ain't makin' no joke."

"We can't live like this!" Mister repeated.

"Then leave me," Johnny Ray said matter-of-factly.

"What?"

"If you so tortured, just leave me and let's be done with it."

Mister resumed his seat. "I never said I was tortured."

"Well, you act like it."

"I'm sorry, man. I just don't want this . . . this thing between us to get out."

"It can't long as we keep quiet. Anyway, if it did, we'd just have to confess our love for each other. To hell with what the rest of the world thinks. I'd even give up the organization if I had to in order to be with you."

"It ain't that easy, and you know it. What would your father say?"

Johnny Ray hesitated. "You right. He wouldn't be happy."

"Happy? He'd kill both of us. And my father would help him."

"Well, let's just take it one day at a time."

"That's what we been doin'."

"You got a better plan?"

They held hands and dreamed of different, though equally liberating scenarios in which people celebrated their union. Neither thought of quaint cottages surrounded by blooming violas or a wedding akin to anything Emma Jean had once dreamed for Perfect. They weren't even sure if two men *could* marry. Certainly they had never heard of such a thing. And certainly not in Arkansas. To think of it occurring in the church was even more challenging— until they remembered that drunkards, liars, whores, divorcées, and non-virgins married in churches all the time. So, even though preachers denounced men lying with men, Mister and Johnny Ray guessed that if they simply claimed to love God, like everybody else did, they, too, might be joined in holy matrimony in the Lord's house.

But that hope was for another day. For now, they simply fought to envision a life, a forever and ever, free from degradation. Mister wished he were Paul, with a mother who would give anything to secure his happiness. Even as a child, Mister knew that Paul—Perfect back then—was the parental favorite, and maybe that's when he began to long for Paul's life. As a girl, she had gotten all the pretty things, including her own room, while Mister and the others were treated as ordinary, disposable vagabonds. For every dress, she had matching accessories, although one pair of pants and an old hand-me-down shirt was apparently sufficient for the boys. He wanted to be special like Perfect, but boys weren't supposed to be special. Authorly told him constantly that to be jealous of Perfect was tantamount to sissihood, so Mister learned to ignore his feelings. Even the suit, which Emma Jean handcrafted for Paul, was more than anything Mister had ever gotten from her. He was always made to feel insignificant and unworthy, and as long as he stayed in that house, he knew he'd always feel that way.

Some days, Mister wished he was Authorly. He was the one Emma Jean adored. Once, when Authorly cursed her about having opened his mail, Mister overheard Emma Jean say, "Now that's a man who don't take no stuff!" Mister's desire to please her, which manifested in an impeccable reputation and a sweet, kind disposition, only repulsed her, causing her to ask on ocassion, "Why don't you be a man sometimes?"

His only option, he thought, was to leave and take Johnny Ray with him. Where they'd go he didn't know, but he'd find someplace out in the world where he could live unashamed. He had worked hard all his life for people's approval, and had gotten it—everyone's except his mother's. Now he had to figure out how not to need it.

Chapter 31

"Gus! Boys!" W. C. shouted frantically from the road the following Sunday morning. "Come give us a hand! The Redfield house is on fire! Hurry up!" It was dawn.

The Peace men leapt from the table and stumbled out the door, buckling overalls and zipping pants all the while. Even Bartimaeus scurried along, unsure of what he could do, yet determined to do something.

"Get the buckets from the barn!" Gus yelled to Woody. "Run!"

Mister and Paul were amazed that their speed and stamina were no match for their father's. On an ordinary day, they would've bet him top dollar that they could outsprint him, and now they knew they would've lost badly. When they arrived, Gus was already amid the other men, slinging streams of water onto a virtual inferno.

"Grab a bucket and come on!" Gus screamed.

Within minutes, the house was totally engulfed in flames. Paul drew water from the well as the others dashed it onto the burning structure. His arms ached from the constant lowering and pulling of the chain, but as long as they were trying, he knew he couldn't quit. There were at least twenty men present, and all of them moved as if the house were their own. They knew their efforts were useless; anyone could see that. The blaze was simply too hot to battle. Those at the end of the line were tossing more water on the ground than on the fire, but they had to try.

Once exhaustion took its toll, W. C. stepped back and said, "Let it go, boys. Ain't no use."

The men dropped their buckets and moved away with bowed heads. Frank Cunningham told Gus, "It's a shame, man. That whole family's gone."

Paul stumbled and fell. "What do you mean 'gone'?" he cried. "Nobody was in there, was it?"

Gus motioned for Mister to assist Paul.

"All of 'em were in there, son," Frank said. "By the time we got here, wasn't nothin' nobody could do."

Paul leaned on Mister and trembled. "Oh my God." He tried not to look weak in the company of men. "All of 'em?"

"That's right. It's a sad day, but you can't question the ways of God. He knows best."

Paul thought of Lee Anthony and his brothers, sitting in school, making fun of him, and he shivered at the thought of them consumed in a ball of fire. He imagined how they must've screamed and fought to get out, running to doors and windows, which apparently barred their way. He could see Lee Anthony, with his bulged eyes and protruding forehead, searching desperately for a way of escape, but finding none. Paul wondered if their screams had been heard, if maybe Sugar Baby had been awakened by strange screeching he couldn't understand. But Sugar Baby was nowhere to be found, and since the surrounding trees couldn't talk, Paul resolved that he'd never know.

Yet someone knew. She was standing just in the shadow of the forest, watching the men grieve in their silent, stoic manner. She wanted to comfort Paul, to tell him that, now, his abusers would never touch him again, but fearing exposure, she remained nestled among the trees. It hadn't been as bad as the men imagined, she thought. In fact, it had all happened rather quickly. The fire wasn't supposed to claim the entire family. It was only meant for the boys. Yet it took on a mind of its own, consuming everything and everyone in its path. *Fires do that sometimes*, she thought. But those boys had to pay. It was only right. They had violated her best friend—Caroline had overheard them boasting about it and she'd told Eva Mae—and it was her job to make them pay since Paul couldn't do it. He was too embarrassed, and she understood why. But someone had to. *You can't treat people like that and get away with it*, she justified in her heart. Especially someone like Paul who had never bothered anybody. He deserved love and friendship and kindness, so for those boys who did what they did, they deserved what they got. The whole family did. None of them were innocent. If they had raised those boys right, she thought, they would've known to respect other people and they wouldn't have called Paul those mean, hurtful names. They definitely wouldn't have beaten and touched him that day. The oldest boy, whom none of them even knew, had participated without ever having encountered Paul. Ain't that the devil? So she sent them all to hell forever and ever, amen.

Sugar Baby had awakened to the smell of smoke. He dashed outside and followed the scent until he saw flames billowing from the Redfield house. His first instinct was to run inside and save whomever he could, but the blaze blocked his way. He then ran to the back of the house and saw, through a window, the faces of the same boys he had beheld beating Gus's youngest boy that night. Still, he would've helped them if he could've, but the window was too high to reach. He thought to search the barn for a ladder, but suddenly his mind returned him to the dusky evening on the road leading to the Jordan River. And he relaxed and watched them writhe in agony. God was collecting His debt, Sugar Baby told himself, and although it was painful, it had to be paid. *That boy hadn't done anything to them*, he thought. *Still they beat him like a dog.* They would've done worse, Sugar Baby knew, if he hadn't come along. Now, God was punishing their wrong.

He saw Eva Mae dash, like a frightened fawn, into the nearby woods. He assumed she was going for help, then he wondered why she was there at all. It didn't make sense that a young lady would be found, before dawn, loitering around the Redfield place, unless she was having a fling with one of the boys, and even then, shouldn't he have been the one to make his way to her? Sugar Baby didn't put the pieces together until he noticed that Eva Mae had stopped just beyond the edge of the forest and turned to watch the flames engulf the house. He didn't know if she'd started it—maybe it had begun inside—but she definitely wasn't committed to putting it out. The look on her face was one of retribution, not horror, and Sugar Baby squinted harder as he tried to discern exactly what she was thinking. Unable to do so, he stood still among the trees, as though he were one of them, and watched her smirk until she went away. Again, he would've helped if he could've, but there was nothing he could do. Whether it had been inspired by God or Eva Mae, he resolved that the Redfield boys had it coming. In terms of the others, he decided that not only do the sins of the father visit the sons, but sometimes the sins of the sons visit their fathers.

The community was somber until the funeral. Of course there were no bodies, but the church was packed with moaners who remembered the Red-fields as hardworking, giving people. No one said so, but they were really referring to Martha Mae, since Sipio was known as the laziest man the Good Lord ever made, and everyone knew the boys were good for nothing. People asked for her peach cobbler as though it were medicinal, and Martha Mae worked hard to meet every request. Reverend Lindsey said, "His ways are not our ways, and His thoughts are not our thoughts." Paul wondered if there'd ever be a time when he'd know the ways of God. Or the thoughts of God. And how could a man know?

Eva Mae sat next to him, contented. It had to be this way, she thought. Someone had to submit themselves as a vessel in the hands of the Almighty God. For Paul's sake. He'd thank her one day, she determined—if he ever became bold enough to know the truth.

Chapter 32

The evening of the dance, Paul called on Christina at six and brought her to see Gus and Emma Jean before going to the party.

"Good evening, Miss Emma Jean, Mr. Gus," Christina said, tiptoeing into the living room. She looked radiant in the powder blue evening gown, but Emma Jean refused to say so. Instead, she murmured a casual "Hello."

Gus extended the warmth. "Come on in, baby," he said, standing quickly. "Have a seat. You looks mighty purty. Mighty purty!"

"Hey, Christina," Mister said. "You really do look nice."

"Thanks."

Emma Jean gave a fake smirk. "How yo' folks?"

"They fine, ma'am, thanks for askin'."

"How'd they like Paul's suit?"

"Emma Jean!" Gus huffed.

"What! I just asked a simple question."

Mister shaded his brow with his right hand.

"They said he looked real handsome, ma'am. My mother loved the suit. She said Paul would probably be the best-lookin' boy at the dance."

"Well, that was nice of her to say. And she's right!"

Christina smiled awkwardly, like an actor who'd forgotten her lines in the middle of a play.

"It's just a suit, Emma Jean. Don't make such a fuss over it."

"Just a suit? I beg your pardon? Do you know how hard I worked to get that suit together? Huh, man? Do you?"

"It's great, Momma, and I thank you for it."

"I think it's nice, too," Christina said. "Real nice."

"We better be gettin' on," Paul said before Emma Jean's drama embarrassed him further. "We don't wanna be late."

"Well, you kids have a nice time," Gus said. "And make sure you have that young lady home at a decent hour. Don't let Frank Cunningham get after you."

Christina chuckled. "It was nice to see all of you."

"You be sure to come back, hear?" Gus said.

Emma Jean rose, but didn't speak.

Once they left, Gus said, "What's the matter with you, woman? You act like you ain't got no manners at all. That girl was just as sweet as she could be, and all you did was show yo' ass."

"I don't like her. Not for Paul."

"Why not? She's pretty and comes from a good family. What's wrong with her?"

Emma Jean shrugged. "I didn't say nothin' was wrong with her. I just don't like her for Paul. That's all. Didn't you see how she strutted in here like she was some big movie star or somethin'?"

"Aw, stop it, Emma Jean! That girl was just as nice and down-to-earth as she could be!"

"I think so, too," Woody said.

Mister agreed.

"That's 'cause y'all men and don't pay attention to stuff like that. A woman can pick up on another woman's nastiness a mile away."

"She wasn't nasty!" Mister hollered.

"I say she was! And, like I said, you woulda seen it if you was a woman. But y'all men, so I don't expect y'all to recognize that kind of stuff."

"Woman, you crazy."

"Call me what you want, but I know a stuck-up heffa when I see one."

"Stuck up? Christina?" Woody asked.

"I ain't gon' argue with you. I'm a woman and I know 'bout women. Menfolks don't even notice what a woman been lookin' at for years." Emma Jean switched to the kitchen and washed the evening dishes.

Eva Mae watched Christina waltz like Cinderella through the gym door. Having come alone, Eva Mae envied her and all the other girls who clung to boys their mothers hoped they'd marry. Eva Mae had wanted to come with Paul, since he was her best friend, but they were far past the age when others thought of their union as adorable. "Get you a real man!" her mother advised, but none of the local boys called on her. They said she had the body but not the face. Eva Mae dismissed them in jest, then realized, at the dance, that she was falling in love with her childhood playmate.

"Hey!" Paul called, and waved enthusiastically.

Eva Mae tried to smile.

He and Christina approached. "How do I look?" Paul raised his arms and swiveled slowly.

"Really good. And Christina, you look nice, too."

"Thanks, Eva Mae. I like your earrings."

"Thanks."

Eva Mae almost asked Paul if they could escape to the field of clovers, just for a little while, but instead she told Christina, "Blue's my favorite color," and proceeded to stroke her puffed sleeves. Christina wanted to tell Eva Mae that she looked nice, too, but since Paul hadn't said it, she feared the lie wouldn't be believable. Eva Mae's brown, obviously cheap dress clashed with her navy blue skin tone, and, as always, her hair sprouted from her head like a field of wild dandelions.

"Where's Caroline and your brother?" Eva Mae asked.

"I don't know. He went to get her before I went to Christina's."

Eva Mae smirked and asked Christina, "So . . . how much do you like Paul?"

"Pardon me?" she whispered.

Eva Mae practically shouted. "I said, how much do you like Paul!"

"Eva Mae! What's wrong with you?"

"I just wanted to know how much she likes you, that's all. Did I ask too much?" Her feigned innocence frustrated Paul.

"Just drop it, okay?"

"Okay, fine. I didn't mean any harm. I'm sorry, Christina, if I embarrassed you."

"It's okay."

Eva Mae's jealousy swelled. Paul narrowed his eyes at her and she knew they'd fall out later. For now, she tried to ease the tension with "Paul, you look better than any of these other guys. Don't you think so, Christina?"

Christina nodded and excused herself to greet other friends.

"What's wrong with you, Eva Mae?"

"Nothin's wrong with me. I can tell she likes you, and I just wanted to know how much."

"But don't ask her in front of all these people!"

"Ain't none o' these folks listening to us. Plus, who cares?"

"I care!"

"Why? 'Cause you like her, too?"

"Maybe. And I don't want her to feel shame. Just back off, okay."

"Whatever. You can have Christina Cunningham if you want her. Far be it from me to be in the way."

"Oh! You're jealous."

"No I ain't jealous. Why I gotta be jealous of her?"

" 'Cause you think I like her more than I like you."

Eva Mae looked away.

"Girl, listen. You my best friend. Ain't nothin' gon' change that. You was there when my own family wasn't. I'll never love anybody the way I love you."

"Never?"

"Never."

"Okay." Eva Mae brightened. "Now I won't have to whip Christina's ass for messin' with my man."

"Get outta here, girl!" Paul said playfully, but Eva Mae wasn't playing.

Suddenly, everyone gasped. Caroline entered with Bartimaeus, draped in Gus's good suit. He looked rather handsome, many said. Yet it was Caroline who took people's breath away. Cloaked in a flowing yellow chiffon dress, she wore an air of confidence no one had ever seen on her. Her size, which had once been a liability, was clearly an asset now as she pranced across the dance floor, flaunting rotund hips with pride and delight.

"Go 'head, girl!" Eva Mae hollered, shattering the silence. Youngsters roared and applauded.

Bartimaeus beamed with pride. Earlier in the evening, he had hugged Caroline and told her, "Hold your head up, honey. I feel yo' beauty all over you." He lifted her chin. "Can't you see it?"

She said no.

"Well, I can. It's a shame what folks wit' eyes can't see."

"I'm too fat to be pretty," she whined.

Bartimaeus felt for her hands. "You de most beautiful girl I know. I know how big you is, and I likes every bit of it."

Caroline snickered.

"I ain't jokin'. I'm serious. I likes you 'cause you a lotta human. Big don't mean ugly, baby, and thin sho don't mean pretty. If a person wanna be pretty, they gotta walk pretty and act pretty and talk pretty. Can't nobody take pretty from you. Every time I hold yo' hand all I feel is pretty all 'cross yo' finger-tips."

He tickled her fingers with his own, and Caroline squealed. Bartimaeus's words had unleashed an instantaneous transformation in her. That was all she had ever wanted—someone to search for and find beauty in her. Having been on the verge of suicide countless times, she gladly considered that the world had been wrong about her. Maybe she *was* pretty and she *was* desirable and she *was* worthy. And, anyway, if she wasn't, Bartimaeus believed she was, and that was all that mattered.

She sashayed across the dance floor and posed in front of Eva Mae and Paul.

"Oh my God, girl! Look at you!" Eva Mae screamed. Paul covered his mouth.

Caroline fingered her mother's dangling silver earrings. "How I look?"

"Amazing," Paul said.

"Girl, you look fabulous!"

"Well, if a blind man call you pretty," she said, winking at Paul, "you shonuff oughta believe it!"

They giggled and studied the room for fashion faux pas they'd gossip about later. Christina returned.

"Will you dance with me?" Paul asked her.

"Um . . . sure . . . but I'm not really good." She feared others would immediately notice her self-conscious movements.

"Well I am," Paul boasted. "So follow me."

In the center of the room, he slid his left arm around her waist until it rested at the base of her spine. With his right hand he clutched her left, and her right hand rested naturally on his left shoulder. They stood closer than they ever had.

"Just flow with me," Paul whispered in her ear.

Christina followed, and found herself floating across the dance floor. Paul's ease, comfort, and authority impressed her, yet the enmity in Eva Mae's eyes stifled Christina's pleasure. Each time Paul swung her in the other girl's direction, Eva Mae's expression asked her, *How could you?* and Christina stiffened with guilt. Paul noticed the nonverbal exchange and maneuvered

Christina until her movements escaped Eva Mae's purview. Then he pulled Christina closer, wanting to feel the warmth of her body, and she surrendered. The outer edge of her bra brushed his muscular chest, and Paul backed a bit to conceal his budding erection.

"You wanna dance?" Caroline asked Bartimaeus.

"Okay, but I ain't never danced before."

He stepped on her feet repeatedly but Caroline didn't care. She was enjoying her newfound confidence. With each compliment, her ego had grown throughout the evening, until now, twisting and twirling in the center of the dance floor, she felt gorgeous for the first time in her life. Bartimaeus giggled, enjoying her graceful flow and giving thanks that God had used him to initiate it.

Eva Mae watched her and waved. If Caroline could get a man, she thought, what was her problem?

Bartimaeus pulled Caroline close and whispered, "Will you marry me?"

She froze. "What did you say?"

"I said, will you marry me, Miss Caroline." He was smiling.

"Me? You askin' me?"

"Yeah, I'm askin' you."

She dropped his hands and clutched her chest. "You wanna marry *me*?"

Bartimaeus laughed. "Of course I wanna marry you, silly. You the prettiest girl I know and you sweeter'n sugar."

"Oh my God."

"Does that mean yes or no?"

"I don't know."

"What's the problem? You don't like me?"

"Oh no! It's not that. It's not that at all."

"Then what is it?"

Caroline exhaled. "Is you really sure you wanna marry me? I ain't nothin' special. And I'm real fat."

Bartimaeus reached for her face. "Listen to me, Caroline, and I ain't gon' say this again. You're everything I need. I know what size you is, and I like it. I told you that already. Don't you never say you ain't special no more. You exactly the way you s'pose to be, and I wouldn't change nothin' 'bout you."

He felt Caroline's tears crawl over his fingers.

"Ain't nobody never said nothin' to me like that before."

"Well, I'm gon' keep sayin' it 'til you believe it."

Caroline embraced him so tightly he teased, "Okay, woman. Don't squeeze me to death."

She kissed his cheeks. "Marryin' you would make me the happiest girl in the world."

"Is that a yes?"

"No," she said. "It's a Lawd-have-mercy, thank-you-Jesus yes!"

Bartimaeus hollered, and the couple danced the night away.

When Johnny Ray entered, cloaked in a tan worsted wool tweed jacket, dark brown pants, and a white shirt, Paul feared Christina would notice him staring. He tried to hang his head and turn away, but somehow, seconds later, he was looking again. Violet hung on Johnny Ray's arm as though she were already his wife, and Paul thought, *If she only knew.* He liked Violet. She wasn't particularly pretty, but she had an hourglass shape everyone admired, and that alone made her beautiful to most. Her hair was pulled into a bun, making her already huge eyes look even bigger. The mustard yellow, straight-cut dress hung nicely on her, Paul thought, and reminded him of the yellow dress he wore to his eighth birthday party. Their eyes met, Paul's and Johnny Ray's, and, for an instant, Paul swore he felt a connection. Johnny Ray nodded a greeting—which was more than he usually did—and Paul responded with a smile wide enough to show every tooth in his mouth. Did Mister know that Johnny Ray liked Violet? *Did* Johnny Ray like Violet? They had probably talked about it out in the woods, Paul assumed. He probably accompanied Violet to the party just to be nice. He was sweet like that, and that's why Paul couldn't stop glancing at him.

"She must be pretty," Christina said.

"Huh?"

"The girl you keep lookin' at. She must be pretty."

"Oh no! I ain't lookin' at nobody. I'm just lookin' around in general. You know. Just to see who came with who."

"Sure."

"No, really," Paul lied. "I'm just nosy, you know?"

"Un-huh."

Damn! He closed his eyes and finished the dance. "Would you like some punch?"

"Yes, please."

They followed the crowd to the refreshment table where Eva Mae had been left standing the entire evening.

"He's cute, ain't he?" she whispered to Paul.

"Stop that!" he mouthed. "You can't say that out loud!"

Eva Mae's uproarious laughter made others gaze in wonder. The more she thought of it—what she knew that Christina and Violet didn't—the louder she bellowed.

"Stop it, Eva Mae!" Paul screeched. "Just stop it!"

She was out of control. Had she followed her heart, she would have taken Paul to the field of clovers and performed their childhood ritual, thereby reminding him that she, not Christina, had always been his lover. She would have told Violet that Joshua Henson loved her more than Johnny Ray Youngblood ever would, and that, in fact, Johnny Ray didn't love her at all. She would have informed Christina that dating Paul was a monumental waste of time, although he was a wonderful person, and she would have bet a week's wages that Paul would never marry her. Yet since she couldn't say any of this, she found it all the more hilarious.

"Eva Mae!" Paul grabbed her arm. "Will you stop this, please?"

Each time she glanced at one of the girls, she screamed louder. Everyone was looking now, wondering why Eva Mae had suddenly become obnoxious.

"What's wrong with you, Eva Mae!" Paul muttered into her ear.

"Me? What's wrong with *me*? Are you kidding?"

The question unleashed a cackling that made others nervous. In their curiosity, the youths subconsciously formed a circle around Eva Mae and whispered about her erratic behavior.

"What's going on?" Caroline asked Paul. "Why is Eva Mae laughing like that?"

"I don't know," Paul murmured, embarrassed.

Eva Mae shook her head and panted, "Wooo weee!" as she clutched her sides. "Ump, ump, ump. Lord have mercy!"

Violet drew nearer to Johnny Ray, and Eva Mae's laughter intensified. Tears streamed from her eyes as she stumbled toward the exit like a woman possessed. Paul followed.

"I'll be back in a minute," he told Christina. "I'ma see if I can figure out what's going on."

Christina nodded, and the others returned to dancing.

Outside, Eva Mae collapsed to her knees.

"What the hell is wrong with you, Eva Mae?"

She stood slowly, still overwhelmed with it all. "Wow. How do men do it?"

"What are you talking about?"

"Y'all get everything you want. And then some."

"What?"

"It's true. You get to have girlfriends and flirt with each other, too."

"Shut up, Eva Mae! You don't know what you're talking about."

"Oh really? I watched you dance with Christina and make eyes at Johnny Ray—all at the same time. She didn't even notice!"

Paul couldn't deny it.

"And is somebody gonna tell Violet about Johnny Ray?"

"Tell her what?" *Eva Mae couldn't know, could she?*

She began to chuckle again. "Everybody ain't dumb, Paul. Most people 'round here is, but everybody ain't."

If she didn't mention anything specific, he certainly wasn't going to.

"Oh, don't worry. I ain't gon' say nothin' to nobody. I just think it's funny."

"Just leave it alone, Eva Mae. It's none of your business."

"Oh! I see! You're my best friend, supposedly, but who you love is none of my business?"

"I didn't mean it like that."

"It don't matter." She patted his shoulder. "I'm a woman, so I ain't supposed to know anyway. That's how it works, right?"

Paul huffed. "Why are you doing this now?"

" 'Cause it's just so crazy! Everybody wants a man—men and women—but women think they're the pretty ones. Ain't that crazy!" Her chuckling evolved into uncontrolled laughter again.

"I'm going back inside."

"Yes, you should. I'm sure Christina's waiting for *her man*!"

Eva Mae howled. Paul walked away more frustrated that he couldn't counter her claim than irritated by what she'd said. Before he reached the entrance, he bumped into Johnny Ray.

"Oh . . . hey," Paul stammered.

"Hey," Johnny Ray said.

"I like your jacket. It's really nice."

"My jacket? Man, everybody's talkin' 'bout your suit! Where'd you get it from?"

"Momma made it."

"Wow. That's cool. I didn't know Miss Emma Jean could sew like that."

"We didn't, either."

They endured ten seconds of awkward silence, unaware of Eva Mae's lurking eyes. Then, without thinking, Paul reached out and lightly touched the lapel of Johnny Ray's jacket, like one attempting to smooth out a stubborn wrinkle. And Johnny Ray didn't stop him. In fact, Johnny Ray sighed and closed his eyes at the touch, unaware of the return of Paul's budding erection.

Eva Mae's laughter broke the trance.

"Oh . . . um . . . I'm sorry," Paul said, shaking his head. "I didn't mean to—"

"It's okay. It's nothing." Johnny Ray smiled warmly. "I'ma just go to the outhouse for a minute, and I'll see you back inside."

"Okay."

Paul studied Johnny Ray's strut, noting his thick buttocks and extra-wide shoulders. Why couldn't Johnny Ray love him? Mister could have anybody he wanted. Everybody said so. Paul would have done anything—*anything*—for Johnny Ray's heart. Like Eva Mae had done for his. *But I guess you can't make nobody love you*, Paul told himself. The more he imagined Johnny Ray in his arms, the more clearly he saw the hurt on Mister's face.

"Your girlfriend's waiting," Eva Mae snarled. "I'll see you later." She began walking home in the dusk.

"Why you leavin'?"

" 'Cause I don't wanna walk home in the dark." Over her shoulder, she shouted, "*By myself*."

Chapter 33

Gus and Bartimaeus missed Woody's wedding announcement in the spring of '57 because of the rains. It had never poured like that, people said. One moment the sun was shining brilliantly, then, suddenly, dark clouds gathered and unleashed as they must have in Noah's day. Gus rushed to the Jordan when the rains commenced, and Bartimaeus followed, losing his way among the monsoonlike winds. The rain fell all day, as if from a waterfall, then, as abruptly as it began, it stopped, and the setting sun was instantly unveiled. Gus and Bartimaeus heard exultant rejoicing as they approached home that Saturday evening, and Authorly intercepted them down the road with dry clothes and news of Woody's engagement.

"He said God came to him the other day and told him he needed a help-mate," Authorly explained.

"Well, good for him," Gus said. "Good for him."

Bartimaeus asked, "Who's the girl?"

"Puddin' Jenkins," Authorly chuckled.

Gus screeched, "Puddin' Jenkins? That ugly girl from Damascus? One o' David Jenkins's girls?"

"Yep! That's the one!"

"He couldn't do no better'n that?"

Authorly hollered. "He said God showed her to him in a dream and told him to go get her. I told him he was havin' a nightmare!"

The men laughed heartily.

"She can't be *that* bad," Bartimaeus said.

"If you only knew! You better be glad you can't see!"

"All right, boy. Ugly folk need love, too." Gus tried not to laugh.

"He said they gettin' married pretty soon."

Gus and Bartimaeus congratulated Woody when they arrived home, and Gus confirmed that a preacher should have a wife. He wasn't too sure about it being Puddin' Jenkins, but, hell, why not? She needed a husband as much as any other girl.

At the wedding a week later, which lasted all of fifteen minutes, folks scowled when Puddin' appeared before the opened double doors of the church. Her dress was pretty enough, but all the makeup in the world couldn't alter what Emma Jean called "bone ugliness." Her forehead protruded like a cliff, and her crazy left eye swiveled while the right one never moved. People didn't know if she was looking at them or around them, so they smiled and waited until after the ceremony to voice their comments.

W. C. said, "If God had sunt me a girl lookin' like that, I'd o' told God, 'No thank Ya!'"

Deacons hollered.

Miss Mamie said, "Woody Peace is shonuff a man o' God 'cause nobody *but* God could o' made him marry Puddin' Jenkins. Seem like to me that girl just *wants* to be ugly! She could do better if she just would."

The crowd marched to Emma Jean's front yard to consume barbecued coon, squirrel, chicken, and rabbit that Authorly had slow-roasted throughout the night. People congratulated Gus on getting another son married off, and patted his back sympathetically for having endured the recent rains. Everyone had heard his and Bartimaeus's strong baritones announce the arrival of yet another spring, but by the end of the day their voices had disintegrated into hoarse, scratchy cries of fatigue. They persisted, nonetheless, sure that if they didn't, the residue of pain in their hearts would overwhelm them before the rains came again. Gus especially would've been honored to know that countless Swamp Creek residents sat on their porches and listened to the melodious lamenting until their hearts, too, were made clean and pure. When the wailing ceased, people returned their chairs to their kitchen tables and began revisiting those obstinate neighbors whose offenses they now forgave.

At the wedding reception, Paul told Eva Mae, "I think Christina wants to marry me."

"Really?"

"Yeah. At least I think so. Every time we together, she talks about wantin' a husband and kids. She asked me what I thought about the possibility of bein' her husband."

"What'd you say?"

"I told her I hadn't never thought about it. Not really." Paul turned to see Eva Mae's reaction.

"Paul . . . um . . ."

"What?" he said, smacking on a rabbit leg.

"I don't want you to get hurt. Just take yo' time. Okay? You ain't like most men."

"What's that suppose to mean?"

"Just what I said. Don't rush into nothin'. Most folks ain't got nothin' to lose. You got everything to lose."

Paul grimaced.

"Aw, boy, please! Can we just tell the truth for a change?"

"What truth?"

"The truth that you don't know what you like. Not yet. You look at Johnny Ray harder than you look at Christina. Tell me I'm lyin'!"

Paul didn't challenge her.

"That means you don't know who you are."

"I know who I am!"

"I don't mean your name. I mean your spirit. Who you really are deep down inside, regardless of what other folks say. That's what you got to figure out." Eva Mae could tell Paul didn't want to hear it, but she continued anyway. "Yo' life has been crazy, Paul, to say the least, and figurin' out who you is sometimes takes years. You gotta know what you think and what makes you happy and what you can live with, and some of that I don't think you know yet."

Her nurturing tone softened his guard. "You're probably right."

"Me, on the other hand, I didn't have no other choice. Ain't nobody never thought much about me, so I started thinkin' about myself really early. Remember how I used to come to y'all's house all the time?"

"Yeah."

"Well, it was only because my folks didn't care where I went, so I had to pretend somebody liked me. That somebody was you."

"Why me? I didn't even know you."

"Yeah, but Miss Emma Jean adored you and that's what I wanted. I used to walk by y'all's house all the time, hoping she'd ask me to come over and play with you, and maybe then I might be important. At least to somebody. I thought it might work since you didn't have no sisters."

"Oh! So that day Momma saw you and Caroline in the road and asked y'all to play with me wasn't the first day you walked by?"

"It wasn't the second or third, either. Like I said, I just wanted to be your friend 'cause yo' momma thought you was God."

Paul laughed. "Yeah, right!"

"She sure acted like it. Wherever y'all went, you always looked like a doll. You had the prettiest dresses, and the part down the middle of yo' head was always straight as a arrow. Me and Caroline used to talk all the time about how jealous we was of you."

Paul sighed as his memory ran amuck. "I miss those days sometimes."

"I'm sure you do. That's why I'm sayin' go slow with Christina. Or whoever. You gotta figure out what part of Perfect you want and what part you don't. Then you gotta put that part with who you is now. It'll all come together when you get clear about who you wanna be."

"I don't know where to start."

"Well, just start by talkin' to yo'self and admittin' the truth. You ain't gotta tell nobody else, but you gotta tell yo'self. Then you'll be able to answer some of the other questions."

"How do you know all o' this stuff?"

"My grandmother. She used to say that a person gotta *make* theyselves, and I never understood what she meant." Eva Mae paused long enough to speak to Emma Jean, then continued: "But now I see. Just don't let what other people think and feel make you think and feel like them. If you different, be different. People'll get used to it. They ain't got no other choice."

Paul smiled. "You right about that."

"Don't give people God's power. Yeah, they have opinions and stuff, but they ain't got no power to change your world unless you give it to 'em. Keep all the power you got. You'll need it. I promise."

Bartimaeus and Caroline didn't want a wedding. They simply asked Reverend Lindsey to marry them and he did so—right in Gus and Emma Jean's living room. The newlyweds then moved into Caroline's grandmother's abandoned house. It had been vacant for more than a year, and Mr. Burden said they could have it if they wanted it. It was just south of Highway 64, walking distance from the church, so Bartimaeus asked his brothers to examine the house and tell him what it needed. "Everything!" Emma Jean said upon seeing it. "That thang's 'bout to fall down!" Gus rolled his eyes and said, "It's not that bad, son. We'll get it together for you. Don't worry. I ain't gon' have you livin' in no shack." Emma Jean said, "Then you 'bout to build a whole new house!" Gus and the boys took a week and repaired what they could, and Bartimaeus and Caroline moved in.

Lying in bed with another person felt strange to Bartimaeus, who only now fully appreciated the security, silence, and confinement of the coffin. He wondered if there were double-occupancy models, or maybe triple, since Caroline consumed the space of two. But not knowing whom to ask, he dropped the notion and tried to adjust to a normal bed, complete with Caroline's incessant shifting and monstrous snoring. Most nights, he lay awake long after her bestial growling began, or, upon the rare occasion of falling asleep first, found himself awakened in the middle of the night by the same. Sleepless nights came often. Lying there, staring into darkness, he couldn't tell if it was two o'clock or five thirty. His mind wandered, from one topic to the next, until, one night, he found himself thinking about Paul. What kind of life would he lead? Caroline had told him about Paul's feelings for Johnny Ray, making him swear never to divulge the secret. Bartimaeus promised he wouldn't, but admitted he wasn't surprised. He said it made sense for Paul to be that way since he had been a girl all those years. "But what about Christina?" Caroline asked. "Paul likes her, too." Bartimaeus had no explanation. He said that maybe Paul liked both of them, although he'd never heard of such a thing. "He's confused, honey. Anybody who's been through all of that oughta be." Caroline agreed.

Bartimaeus rolled to his left side, trying in vain to sleep. Sometimes he buried his head beneath the pillow, and other times he simply endured. He loved Caroline—all of her—but the sleepless nights made his love less dreamy and more actual. He wanted his coffin back, yet, afraid Caroline might feel rejected, he kept the fading wish to himself. Only in these moments did he desire a slimmer wife, and that was only because he believed Emma Jean's theory that "fat folks snore the loudest." Authorly had proven it. At any given hour, when they were kids, he would begin hollering—as Mister called it—and none of the others would sleep again until Authorly rolled onto his stomach. Bartimaeus soon discovered that, by lowering the coffin lid, he could shut out most of Authorly's noise and sleep dead to the world. Now, after months of marriage, he knew the days of sound, uninterrupted sleep were gone. *Oh well*, he thought. If this were the price he'd have to pay for living with a woman who cooked like Caroline, he counted himself blessed. He never knew a chicken could be prepared so many different ways. Their union also introduced him to foods he'd never heard of like broccoli, asparagus, and eggplant. Gus had told him that "any man who finds a cookin' woman gon' love her forever," and now he knew his father wasn't totally crazy. What Bartimaeus liked most about Caroline's food was that she didn't overseason and overcook the way his mother did. She could baste a coon so tender others thought they were eating roast turkey.

Food was also Caroline's nemesis. She ate nonstop and, at every meal, cooked enough for ten although there were only two. Conscious of waste, she felt compelled to eat what Bartimaeus couldn't, and fussed at him for making her eat all that extra food. Her escalating weight didn't trouble him as much as her deteriorating health, but Bartimaeus decided not to complain. The last thing she needed was another man unsatisfied with her.

Chapter 34

How hard could sewing be? Anybody could thread a needle and cut out shapes of cloth from patterns, then sew them together. There was nothing difficult about that. The sitting would be the hard part, Emma Jean reasoned, and she'd simply have to stand whenever she needed to. Henrietta had offered the ultimatum as though believing Emma Jean would be tortured by the work. It just couldn't be *that* hard, Emma Jean told herself as she walked. She had always worked, even as a child, so it would take more than physical labor to break her down. That's what Henrietta wanted, wasn't it? To break her spirit and make her regret what she had done? Emma Jean cackled. "Henrietta Worthy don't know me! Shit, I'm a survivor. If I can live with Mae Helen Hurt and come out alive, I can stand anything!" There was simply nothing she could foresee about sewing that would torture her into believing she had not done the right thing for Perfect. Well, Paul. She hadn't meant to twist up the child's mind, as Authorly had put it, until he didn't know right from left. She had simply wanted a daughter, and she didn't understand why she couldn't have one. Since her days with Mae Helen, she had heard nothing but "no" and "you're not good enough" and "you ain't nothin'" and "you don't deserve this or that," so she promised herself that, when she got grown, she would have something she wanted and something she loved. And nobody would keep her from it. "Henrietta's got another thing coming if she thinks I'm gon' apologize for what I done!" Emma Jean declared, stomping her frustration into the dirt road. "She ain't gon' make me hate myself for lovin' my child!"

The first day wasn't so bad. It was actually pretty boring. Emma Jean's hands ached from cutting out countless garments with scissors that Henrietta knew were too dull for the job. But it didn't kill her, and because of that, Emma Jean left for home at 5:16 with her head held high. She was tired, of course. She couldn't lie about that. Ironing cloth in preparation for cutting, then pinning patterns atop it, then bending and stretching around those patterns as she attempted to cut the cloth with precision had been far more exhausting than she had anticipated. A few times, Henrietta had glanced at her and burst into unbridled laughter, but Emma Jean didn't let the ridicule bother her. She simply pressed on as though Henrietta wasn't there. By day's end, Emma Jean couldn't hide her fatigue, and Henrietta said, "See ya in de mornin'!" as though knowing Emma Jean's destruction was nigh.

Shortly after six that evening, the menfolk entered and saw Emma Jean asleep at the kitchen table. A light fire brewed in the woodstove, but Gus smelled no food.

"What's the matter with you, woman? You sick or somethin'?"

Emma Jean lifted her head slowly, wiping saliva from the corners of her mouth, and blinked her way back to reality. "Lawd have mercy. I musta dozed off for a minute. Y'all 'cuse me." She rose quickly and began cooking.

"You mean to tell me you ain't cooked yet?"

Emma Jean huffed. Her nerves were already frayed, and, tired as she was, she had absolutely no patience for Gus's mouth. "I had a lotta things to do today, man, so don't start with me!"

"What'd you do?"

"Don't worry about that, okay? I don't need you givin' me the third degree!"

Gus let it go. He washed up and waited.

"Somethin' wrong with Momma," Paul whispered to Mister, sitting next to him on the sofa.

"Yeah, I know, but I don't know what it is. Where'd she go this morning? She left before we did."

"I don't know, but wherever she went she must've stayed all day 'cause this house is a mess."

Emma Jean noticed the exchange, but chose to ignore it. It was already 6:30—an hour past dinnertime—and dinner was nowhere to be found. She sliced potatoes and fried them with onions in the cast-iron skillet and rolled out dough for biscuits. The leftover cabbage and yams from Sunday's meal she simply warmed and placed on the table. At 7:15, she said, "Y'all come on."

Gus blessed the food, then, before serving himself, asked, "Where de meat?"

"You ain't gotta have meat *every* time you eat, man. Just go 'head and be satisfied with what you got."

"But we got plenty o' meat in de smokehouse. Why can't we eat it?"

" 'Cause I ain't had time to fix it today, okay! Damn! You ain't never satisfied with nothin'!"

The boys looked at each other.

"Y'all go 'head on and eat! Y'all acted like y'all was starvin' to death!"

The boys filled their plates and ate in silence. The cabbage was lukewarm, and the potatoes were burned on the bottom, but they feared what Emma Jean might say if they complained, so, like Gus, they ate with bowed heads.

Afterward, Emma Jean was so tired she could hardly tidy the kitchen. She heard Henrietta in her head, roaring with laughter, and she hated her. Having underestimated how the agreement would affect her family, Emma Jean now understood that Henrietta had tricked her into more than she had bargained for. It wasn't that the work of sewing was so exhausting; it was that, by the time she arrived home, she wasn't fit for anything else. *Damn bitch*, Emma Jean thought. Of course she couldn't quit. That would mean she wasn't a woman of her word, and, if nothing else, Emma Jean Peace kept her word. And Henrietta knew it. That's why she had taken advantage of her during a desperate moment. "Black hussy," Emma Jean murmured. And all the while Emma Jean thought she'd had the upper hand.

By 8:30, Emma Jean collapsed across the bed as if she'd been shot.

"You actin' mighty funny, woman," Gus said, unlacing his work boots.

Emma Jean found enough strength to roll to her side of the bed. "I'm all right. I just got somethin' I gotta do for a while."

"What chu mean, 'a while'?"

"I mean . . . a while. I can't really explain it to you, so don't ask me, but supper gon' be late every day."

"Every day?"

"I'll try to put somethin' on in the mornings before I go, but—"

"What de hell you doin', Emma Jean?" Gus turned and stared at her.

"It ain't nothin' for you to worry about. It's just somethin' I gotta do 'cause I said I would."

"Well," Gus said, shrugging, "I sho hope it don't last long, 'cause eatin' at damn near eight o'clock ain't gon' work."

Emma Jean drifted off before confessing that the change would probably last a lifetime.

Henrietta and Emma Jean never talked. Henrietta simply told her what to do and Emma Jean did it. By the end of the first month, Emma Jean discovered that the biggest torture of the job was the silent contemplation it forced. Endless hours passed with Henrietta either quiet or absent, and, in that time, Emma Jean's mind, without her heart's permission, wandered back to moments and decisions she never thought she'd reconsider. That was the agony of the job—sitting in silent discourse with herself, then, because of the burn scars, standing, subject to the same mental contemplation. Emma Jean had never known the power of silence. Her life had been filled with sound, noise, speech, and she liked it that way. She could control what she said and to whom she said it. Even when someone's words pissed her off—like that damn Sugar Baby—she liked that her sharp tongue came to her rescue and put folks in their places. And of course with seven children, someone was always asking or telling her something, and by the time she tired of talking, she was ready for bed. Not now. Now, Silence ruled her and made her think about things. It was so inconsiderate. It didn't care that some memories were too painful to revisit. It didn't care that Emma Jean wept aloud each time it forced her back to places and experiences she had forgotten for the sake of sanity. It wasn't the least bit moved that it sometimes made Emma Jean wonder if she were losing her mind. Silence seemed to enjoy the game. Could Henrietta have known Silence? Could she have known this would happen?

Emma Jean saw Claude Lovejoy's face one day, buried within the threads of a yellow garment. He was weeping and looking at her as though asking, *Why did you reject me?* Emma Jean turned away, shaking her head violently, but the image remained. "I was a child," she mumbled. "What was I suppose to do?" The face continued staring, unmoved. Angrily, she bunched the cloth and threw it across the room. After retrieving it and still beholding her father's face, she ripped it to shreds. Henrietta found her sobbing at the table.

"Something wrong, honey?"

Emma Jean hadn't heard her enter. "I'm fine." She wiped her eyes and said, "We'll need another bolt of yellow fabric. This one fell apart."

Henrietta smiled. "I see. Well, don't worry about it. If it happens again, we'll just have to get Gus to pay for it."

"This ain't got nothin' to do with Gus. You leave him out of this."

"Fine. But if you get so mad you destroy any more of my cloth, you gon' have to pay for it—in cash."

Henrietta walked around the house for the next hour, envisioning Emma Jean engulfed in a rage of fury, ripping yellow strips of cloth and probably cursing all the while, and taunted, "Are you having fun yet?" There was nothing Emma Jean could say or do. Belligerence was useless since, for better or worse, she couldn't go anywhere, and Henrietta would undoubtedly have welcomed a physical brawl. Ignoring her was the best Emma Jean could hope for, and Henrietta's mocking laughter made that practically impossible.

By Christmas of 1958, Emma Jean's balancing of home and work had fallen apart. She was simply too tired to clean and cook after twelve hours of tedious sewing. Still, Gus didn't know about the arrangement, but he stopped questioning her once she started crying her nights away. In the mornings, she'd soak her hands in hot water, hoping to ease the tension from her joints, but it never helped much, and squeezing the small rubber ball repeatedly only intensified the pain. Henrietta recommended that she sit upon her hands and rock like her mother used to. It relieved her arthritis, Henrietta said, and maybe Emma Jean would find a similar relief. "Of course Momma's mind wasn't too good, either, so rocking helped her steady herself."

"I ain't no old, crazy woman!" Emma Jean said. Yet, after dropping and breaking half of her good dishes, she knew she needed to do something. She tried Henrietta's suggestion, and, much to her chagrin, it worked. Gus frowned, wondering why in the world she was rocking like that, but her quivering mouth kept him from asking.

Henrietta opened her boutique in March of 1959 with grand success. Women marveled at the variety of dresses, skirts, and blouses it offered, and wondered how one woman could produce such volume. Henrietta smiled and said, "The Lawd always makes a way!" Within a week, she had sold half her merchandise—mostly to white women—and she told Emma Jean, "Guess we gon' have to double our production." Henrietta gave Emma Jean a brand-new pair of scissors, and Emma Jean received it like a Hebrew slave might have received straw for bricks. Although the cutting was easier, the sheer volume of cloth being cut had doubled, so the pain in Emma Jean's hands never subsided. With Henrietta tending the boutique, Silence came more often. It asked Emma Jean, one day, why she had abandoned King Solomon.

"I didn't abandon him."

Sure you did.

"No, I didn't."

Then why didn't you let him go to school? He's the one who wanted it.

" 'Cause we couldn't send but one."

Oh yeah. And you wanted Perfect to go.

"His name's Paul."

Paul. Perfect. Same difference.

"No it ain't!"

Sure it is. And you loved her most. That's why you abandoned the others.

"You don't know what you're talking about. It didn't happen like that!" Emma Jean looked around quickly. Was she losing her mind? Who was she screaming at?

All he wanted was to learn, and you denied him. What kind of mother are you?

"Kiss my ass!" she shouted.

"Emma Jean?" Henrietta said slowly, coming through the screen door. "Who are you talking to?"

Snapping back to reality, she said, "Oh . . . um . . . nobody. We're out of black thread though."

Henrietta had noticed that the confident, self-assured Emma Jean had been replaced by a sullen, discomposed one. She had stopped grooming her hair—something the old Emma Jean would never have done—and some days her clothes looked as though she had slept in them. Mamie Cunningham noticed the change weeks earlier.

"What's wrong with Emma Jean?" she asked another deaconess.

"I don't know, but she don't seem like herself, do she?"

"Naw, she don't," Mamie said, staring at her archenemy from a distance. "I spoke to her 'fo church this mornin' and she smiled like somebody tryin' to keep from cryin'."

"You don't guess she sick, do you?"

"I don't think so. It's somethin' else. Somethin' deep down."

"Maybe she thinkin' 'bout what she done to dat boy."

"Maybe so."

If Emma Jean had had her way, she would've stopped attending church altogether, but Gus wouldn't hear of it. He said a family ain't a family if they don't go to church on Sunday mornings. Emma Jean hadn't the strength to argue. She knew she wasn't her old self. Her spunk and drive had dwindled to barely enough motivation to speak to others, and many days she considered quitting Henrietta's and simply letting her integrity crumble. But she couldn't. It was all she had of her former glory, and if she gave that up there'd be no reason to live. She didn't care about much else now. She didn't have the energy. Every morning when she looked in the mirror, she saw Mae Helen's face taking shape over her own and she cursed the day she agreed to be Henrietta's slave.

Was it really worth this? Really?

"Please leave me alone," Emma Jean muttered. She would've stabbed Silence if she could've.

You shouldn't have done that to that boy.

"Don't you talk about my baby. Ever!" To this point, Silence had avoided the issue, and Emma Jean had been grateful. "You don't know nothin' 'bout that."

But you do.

Emma Jean didn't respond.

You should be ashamed. You have no idea what you've done. And all because you wanted something you didn't have.

"That's right! I wanted something I didn't have. Why don't people understand that?"

'Cause you destroyed somebody else to get it.

"My momma did it!" Emma Jean declared before realizing what she'd said.

Yes. She did. And you hated her for it.

Emma Jean leaned her head back to stop the tears. "She was such a pretty baby."

He.

"You know what I mean."

But why did you do it? He was an innocent child.

"I was a innocent child, too!"

Yeah, but didn't you grow up?

Emma Jean paused.

Now look at him. He don't know who he is.

"He's still my baby. And I love him."

Sure you do. But does he love himself?

Emma Jean went to the window and studied the rain. Sometimes Silence went away when she sang, so she began, "All of my heeeelp."

That's Sol's song.

"You don't bother me when I'm singing! You know that!"

Yeah, but that's Sol's song and you don't have no right to sing it. Not the way you treated him.

"What are you talkin' 'bout? I loved him just like I loved the others!"

Really? He never knew it. You didn't even go to his graduation.

"Yeah, but I sent Authorly! Ain't that enough? I can't do everything." She returned to her work. "I've done the best I could by all my children."

Yeah right!

"Nobody's perfect."

Somebody was.

"Don't start that again!"

I'm just wondering how you justified it. That's all. It really didn't bother you?

"No, it didn't bother me 'cause I didn't do nothin' wrong."

Oh, sure you did. You just didn't care. You didn't think about anyone but yourself.

"Well, who else was thinkin' about me? Huh?"

No one.

"That's right! So I had to think about myself." She stuck her thumb with a pin and shouted, "Shit!"

You're still selfish. Even if others didn't think about you, you didn't have the right to mess up that boy's life. Especially as a baby.

"Leave me alone, goddamnit! You don't know nothin' 'bout me, so you can't judge me!"

You've already been judged. Now you're being sentenced.

"To what?"

Silence paused. *To the truth.*

Henrietta's business flourished. A month after opening, she purchased a storefront on Main Street in Morrilton. No colored person had ever done that. Above the door hung a huge sign that read TRISH'S THINGS. Swamp Creek residents boasted with pride. They said God had worked a miracle for Henrietta, and maybe now Morrilton whites would welcome other black businesses into the downtown area. In the midst of it all, Henrietta never mentioned Emma Jean.

Weeks passed. Emma Jean's screaming increased as Silence tormented her.

Emma Jean? she heard one still, quiet, gray morning.

"Please leave me alone."

I can't do that. Not yet.

"Why not?"

'Cause you ain't told the truth.

"About what?"

You know about what.

"You can't make me say I'm sorry for what I done!"

You already sorry for what you done. You just ain't told the truth about it.

"The truth is," Emma Jean sassed, "that I didn't have no other choice."

Sure you did.

"No, I didn't! You don't know what was in my heart then."

Yes I do. I live there. Remember?

"Then you oughta know why I did what I did."

I do know. But that don't make it right.

"What's right changes from day to day." Emma Jean was becoming exasperated.

Not this time. You was just wrong.

"And if I was, what can I do about it now?"

Admit it.

"But I wasn't wrong. I didn't have nothing else."

You had everything. A husband, six boys, your—

"That ain't what I wanted! You know that! I had been dreamin' 'bout a daughter since I was a little girl. I just wanted to love her right."

Unlike Mae Helen had done you?

Chills raced across Emma Jean's arms as she touched the crescent-shaped scar. "This ain't about her."

There you go lying again.

"Why don't you just leave me alone!" Emma Jean's hands trembled.

Mae Helen's gone now. She can't hurt you anymore. You can let it go.

"Let it go? If it was that easy, I woulda let it go years ago!"

Oh! So you admit Mae Helen hurt you?

"That ain't nothin' to admit! She almost named me Nobody! Of course she hurt me. Anybody wit' eyes can see that."

But they can't see the scars. Not the real ones.

"I don't wanna talk about her."

I'm sure you don't, but you gotta. You can't get to the truth 'til you settle the past.

"I'm through with all of that!" she shouted. "And I don't wanna hear nothin' else about it."

Remember the baby doll Mae Helen bought?

"Shut up!" Emma Jean screamed, covering her ears as if the inner voice were too loud. Her body quivered like a condemned convict sitting in the electric chair.

And remember washing dishes as Pearlie and Gracie combed each other's hair?

"Shut up!"

And remember how Mae Helen burned your forehead with the hot comb?

"No!"

And remember how you fainted in the chicken coop after—

"No! No! No!"

No one heard Emma Jean's protestation. She wilted to the floor, surrounded by strips of cotton, polyester, and silk, and begged Silence to spare her. It did, but only for a while. Once she recovered and returned to work, Silence returned.

I'm never going away, you know.

Emma Jean closed her eyes as tears formed. "I wish you would."

Well, I won't. Not until you admit the truth.

"Fine! What is it you want me to say?"

It's not what I want you to say. It's what you need to say.

"Whatever! Just tell me and I'll say it—if it'll shut you up."

And you gotta mean it, too. It don't mean nothin' if you don't mean it.

Emma Jean repeated, slowly, "Just tell me what to say."

Silence hesitated. *No. You gotta look in your heart and see the truth for yourself. Then say whatever you see.*

"Well, I don't see nothin' in my heart 'cept love for my boys. And respect for my husband."

Anything else?

Emma Jean sighed and sat at the kitchen table. "Nope."

Then I gotta stay 'til you see it. That's what I'm for.

As the days passed, Henrietta could tell something was wrong. Emma Jean's outbursts frightened her at times and reminded Henrietta of her mother's descent into dementia. Henrietta almost told Emma Jean to go home, but then she remembered why Emma Jean was there at all, and if Henrietta never did another living thing, she intended to make Emma Jean suffer. So she watched and listened as Emma Jean's mind ran away.

Are you ready now?

"Ready for what?" Emma Jean said in the middle of her lunch break. She no longer cared that Henrietta witnessed the exchange, gawking in stark dismay.

Ready to tell the truth.

"You know what? Fine!" Emma Jean slapped her palms onto the kitchen table. "Let's get this over with."

Good. I'm ready whenever you are.

Henrietta froze. Was Emma Jean going completely off the deep end? "Emma Jean? Are you okay?"

Emma Jean stood and paced Henrietta's kitchen floor. "I was a terrible mother. Okay? Is that what you want me to say?"

No, it isn't. That's not the truth. I want you to say the truth.

Emma Jean burst into tears. "Okay! I was wrong. I shouldn't've done it."

You shouldn't've done what?

"I shouldn't've turned that boy into a girrrrrrrrrrrrl!" Emma Jean wailed like Gus at the Jordan. She hadn't meant to mean it, but her spoken words ruined a lifetime of peace. So right there, with Henrietta watching, she whirled in circles, screaming, "I didn't mean to do it! I didn't mean to do it! I didn't mean to do it!"

"Emma Jean!" Henrietta cried. "Don't do this to yourself!" The sight of Emma Jean's deterioration was far worse than the thought of it, and all Henrietta wanted now was for Emma Jean to go home. "Emma Jean! Pull yourself together!"

Emma Jean tumbled cups, plates, pans, and saucers onto the floor as she continued twirling like a hypnotized ballerina. "I didn't mean to hurt you!"

You didn't mean to hurt who?

Henrietta couldn't restrain her.

"I loved you! I really did! I didn't mean to hurt you!"

Emma Jean looked like a crazy woman possessed. Henrietta ran from the house, but Emma Jean never noticed.

Very good, Emma Jean. Very good.

Sweat streamed across her forehead and down the circular scar. She collapsed onto the floor, panting heavily. "I've been a bad girl, Mommy, haven't I?"

Yes, you have.

"I'm sorry. I won't do it no more. I promise."

Okay, Emma Jean.

"Am I in trouble?" She coiled into a fetal position beneath Henrietta's table.

Yes, Emma Jean. You're in trouble.

"But I said I won't do it no more!"

You're in trouble 'cause you already done it.

"I said I'm sorry, Mommy!"

Sorry won't fix this.

"I'll do anything! I just don't want no whippin'!"

You ain't gettin' no whippin', Emma Jean.

"I ain't?"

No, you ain't. You're too old for that.

"Then what's my punishment?"

Something worse than a whippin'.

"What's worse than a whippin'?"

A painful memory. Silence laughed.

"I thought you said if I told the truth I'd be set free?"

I never said that. I said if you told the truth, I'd leave you alone. And, now, that's what I'm going to do.

"Oh no! Not yet! You can't leave me. I need you now. I know I said all those bad things before, but I need you now. No one else understands me the way you do. You wouldn't really leave me, would you?"

There was no response.

"NO!"

Henrietta and Gus burst through the front door. They found Emma Jean crawling upon her knees, begging someone not to leave her. Henrietta told Gus about the arrangement and Gus asked, "Why didn't you come tell me the truth? Way back then?"

" 'Cause Emma Jean blackmailed me, and I was scared." Henrietta frowned at the absurdity of it all. "She promised to tell my business if I didn't keep hers, so I kept my mouth shut. I know it was wrong, but I felt like I didn't have no other choice. At least not then. You know how Emma Jean is."

Gus nodded. "Yeah, I know. Guess ain't no need in blamin' you. It's over with now anyway."

Gus lifted Emma Jean from the floor.

"You can take her home now. I'm through foolin' with her. God'll do the rest."

Chapter 35

Emma Jean never recovered. At Paul's high school graduation on May 4, 1959, she stumbled through the church doors, like Sugar Baby, and sat on the back pew as though she'd never been there. Dressed in a wrinkled black dress and snow-white shoes, she rocked atop her hands, hoping desperately that Silence might come along and comfort her. It never did. Her neighbors' voices wouldn't allow it.

"Is that Emma Jean back there?" Mamie asked another woman.

"Chile, yes. Don't she look a mess?"

"Oh my Lord! What happened to her?"

"I don't know. Some folks say she just went crazy all o' sudden. Gus found her at Henrietta's, naked and screamin' under the table."

"What? You don't say. My, my, my. The Lawd shonuff works in mysterious ways, don't He?"

"Yes He do!"

Miss Mamie studied Emma Jean's shrunken form. "Ump. I never thought I'd see that woman like that. But you know what? She had it comin'."

Sugar Baby proclaimed, "The King is comin'! The King is comin'!"

Emma Jean ignored him. She ignored everyone. Throughout the ceremony, she never lifted her head. When Paul's name was called, her tears fell like raindrops and she apologized all over again. "I didn't mean to do it," she mumbled. "I didn't mean to do it."

Too embarrassed to celebrate, Paul escaped immediately following the commencement exercises. He encountered Johnny Ray on the road. They smiled as they approached each other.

316 *Daniel Black*

"Congratulations, Mr. High School Graduate."

"Thanks." Paul said.

"You the first in the family, huh?"

"Well, I'm the first to graduate from high school, but of course Sol done already graduated from college."

"Oh yeah, that's right. Well, congrats anyway."

Paul thanked Johnny Ray again.

"I'm sorry to hear about Miss Emma Jean."

"Yeah," Paul said, shaking his head.

"What happened?"

"We don't know. She just started actin' real strange one day, and it kept gettin' worse. It's like she's talkin' to somebody, but ain't nobody there."

Johnny Ray sighed. "If there's anything I can do, just let me know."

"Okay. Sure. Thanks."

The awkward silence came again. Paul wanted to touch Johnny Ray's face, just to see if it felt as smooth as it looked, but his hand wouldn't move. He wondered, if he leaned forward, would their lips meet halfway.

"You're really handsome, you know," Paul said.

Johnny Ray smiled bashfully. "I think I better go."

"Oh, I didn't mean nothin' by that. I was jes' sayin' that—"

"It's fine. Don't worry about it. Thanks for the compliment."

With that, Johnny Ray strolled away. Paul watched his swagger disappear in the distance as the tingling sensation overwhelmed him. He'd made a fool of himself and he couldn't imagine how he'd ever fix it.

Later that evening, someone banged loudly on the flimsy screen door.

"Who in the world . . . ?" Gus said. Emma Jean looked toward the door, but never moved from the sofa. Mister dashed to answer it and beheld a nervous, panting Johnny Ray. "I gotta talk to you."

"Who is it?" Gus called.

"It's just . . . Johnny Ray, Daddy. It's for me."

Paul strained for a glimpse. What did Johnny Ray want? Were his eyes still shimmering like they were earlier? What if he asked for Paul instead of Mister? Paul's curiosity calmed when he turned and beheld Emma Jean's narrow, piercing eyes.

"I thought we said we wunnit gon' meet at each other's houses?" Mister whispered, stepping onto the porch and closing the door behind himself. "This don't look right."

"I know what we said, but I gotta talk to you right now. It's important."

"Cain't it wait 'til later? My whole family's here. We're gonna have supper soon. You know it's Paul's graduation day."

"Yes, I know that, but, no, it cain't wait. I gotta talk to you right now."

Mister told the family that he and Johnny Ray needed to handle some NAACP business and that he'd be back shortly. No one—other than Paul and Emma Jean—thought to question him further. Through the window, Paul watched Mister lead Johnny Ray across the lawn and into the woods.

"What's so important?" Mister asked with a tone of frustration.

Johnny Ray took his hand. "Well, remember I was tellin' you 'bout my brother in Atlanta who does civil rights organizing?"

Mister nodded. "Yeah."

"Well, I got a letter from him this morning." Johnny Ray extended it, but Mister didn't take it.

"What he say? Is he all right?"

"Yeah, he's fine, but . . . um . . ."

"But what?"

Johnny Ray put the letter in his pocket and took Mister's other hand. "He got me a job. And I gotta take it. It pays three dollars an hour."

Mister studied Johnny Ray's face to make sure he wasn't joking.

Johnny Ray's eyes moistened. "My brother works in a steel mill and he said he asked his boss about a position for me. At first the man didn't say nothin' but then he told my brother yesterday that he'd hire me if I could get there by Monday morning."

"Monday?" Mister blinked. He couldn't believe what he was hearing.

"Ain't nothin' here for me, Mister. Except you and the organization."

"We ain't enough?"

"I ain't worried 'bout the organization. More people comin' all the time. It's you I want. You know that. That's why I'm here right now, 'cause I want you to come with me."

"Come with you?"

"Yeah! Come with me. What you got to lose?"

"De same thang you got to lose. My folks. Memories. Not to mention all the organizing we done done."

"But we can make some new memories. Together. Just you and me and Big Ole Atlanta. Somebody else can lead the NAACP here. Plus, we can make some money. So get yo' stuff and let's get outta here. That's what we always wanted, right?"

As often as he'd dreamed of escaping, Mister now hesitated. "I don't know, Johnny Ray. I ain't thought about movin' that far away, especially with Momma sick and all." He paused. "I guess it could be okay though."

"It could be great! Mr. Gus and your brothers'll take care of Miss Emma Jean. We could stay with my brother until we got our own place. Course we couldn't let on 'bout our feelin's, but that would come soon enough. He wouldn't mind. I'm sure of it. I just gotta leave this place." He thought of what Paul had said earlier. "Somethin' bad's gonna happen if I don't. I can feel it." His breathing intensified. "Whatcha say?"

Mister released Johnny Ray's hands. "I don't know, man. This is all happening so quick."

"Yeah, I know, but I just got the letter."

"When would we leave?"

"Well, that's the thing. We'd have to catch the noon train on Friday in order to get there by Monday. The next train don't come 'til Monday afternoon."

"Aw, man!"

"What is it?"

"Momma's birthday is Saturday, and we givin' her a big party. Daddy said she always wanted one, so maybe it'll help her feel better."

"Oh no."

"I cain't miss that, Johnny Ray. I just cain't. Ain't no way. Daddy would kill me!"

Johnny Ray's pursed lips increased Mister's anxiety.

"But it's our only chance. If we ain't on that train, I can kiss that job good-bye."

Mister paced between two cypress trees. "Can't I come later?"

"Naw," Johnny Ray murmured, " 'cause I done already bought de tickets." He extracted them from the breast pocket of his overalls.

"Oh my God."

"Just take a chance and come on. Miss Emma Jean's gon' be all right."

Mister's impulse was to run back to the house, grab his good overalls, shake Gus's hand, kiss Emma Jean, hug his brothers, and follow his heart to Atlanta. But he couldn't do it. "I wanna go. You know I do."

"Then let's go!"

"I can't miss the party. I just can't."

Both heads bowed.

"Can I use the ticket Monday?"

"Naw. The man said they're only good for Friday."

Mister touched Johnny Ray's face and whimpered, "Then I can't go. I just can't go."

Johnny Ray fought on. "Miss Emma Jean would understand! I know she would. Ain't nothin' you can do to make her no better. Don't make me go without you."

"I'll always love you, Johnny Ray Youngblood. Don't neva forgit that. Neva."

"Aw, Mister, please! You gotta come. We've talked about it a million times. And, anyway, I don't know when I'd get back or when you'd save enough to come on your own. Or even if you'd come on your own at all."

"I don't know, either, but I'd never forgive myself if I missed Momma's party. Not in the condition she's in."

"But you could forgive yourself if you let me go? Is that it?"

"Don't make this harder than it already is."

Johnny Ray kissed Mister lightly. "I'm sorry. I understand. I'm not mad at you. I'm just disappointed. Tell Miss Emma Jean happy birthday for me, okay?"

"You know I will."

They embraced tightly and held on for several seconds. Locals would have frowned at the scene, two striking young men crying in the woods about a love they weren't supposed to have. Someone might have told them to get some help or to ask God for deliverance and, in the moment, deliverance was precisely what they wanted—from caring about what other folks thought and from believing that God didn't sanction their union. They might have turned, that very second, and told Swamp Creek residents to go to hell or at least to consider that, since they had already wrestled with God, a human battle would be easy.

Their lips met and melted in an exchange of love and sorrow. For the first time, they didn't care who was watching.

"If you don't come with me now, I'll never love again. It hurts too bad."

Mister wiped Johnny Ray's tears, then forced a smile. "You'll find someone in Atlanta. That's a big place, I hear."

"I don't want nobody—not if I can't have you."

Their foreheads touched.

"Here's the other ticket if you change your mind. I'll be at the station at eleven—with my fingers crossed."

Johnny Ray kissed Mister again and walked away. Mister retrieved his pocketknife and did what, the day before, he wouldn't have dared. With vehement rage and meticulous precision, he carved the letters into the trunk of the cypress tree, then stepped back to look at his work.

MP
LOVES
JRY

His heart felt lighter. He and Johnny Ray had discovered—or created—something beautiful that the world deemed diabolical. The proof of their love would forever be etched into the universe now, and Mister decided that whoever figured out the initials would simply have to know.

Paul sensed Mister's distress when he returned, but offered no sympathy. He hoped that, maybe, the two had parted ways and Johnny Ray was now free to love *him*.

Chapter 36

Emma Jean's birthday began with a brilliant sun and a light, cool breeze. "Yes!" Gus declared as sunshine poured through the kitchen window. The day was becoming everything he'd hoped for—clear and warm, but not too hot. "Come on, y'all! Rise and shine!" he called to Mister and Paul shortly after five.

Mister emerged from the bedroom, rubbing his eyes. "What time is it?"

"Time for lazy Negroes like you to get up off they asses and get ready for this hyeah party!"

"What's the rush, Daddy? I thought you said it wunnit 'til this evening," Mister grunted.

"And leave it to Negroes like you to wait 'til the last minute to get ready! Well, not today! Yo' momma's sick. You know that. And I want everything just right. Now come on and get to movin' so we can make sure everything's in place." Gus snatched the quilt from Paul, who wanted to curse him, although he knew better.

Throughout the day, the boys straightened up around the house while Eula Faye, Caroline, and Puddin' prepared food. Paul decorated the living room with yellow ribbons, just as he'd done years ago, while Emma Jean observed silently. Her mind wasn't completely gone; she simply entered and exited reality like one might move from one room to the next and back again. As Paul moved about, she saw him—in her mind's eye—at eight, dancing around the living room in the frilly yellow dress, and, now, after having been beaten with the truth, the memory saddened her.

"I didn't have no right to do what I did, son," she murmured in a whisper.

Paul stopped abruptly. He thought his mother's days of lucidity were gone. "It's all right, Momma. I'm fine. You just worry about gettin' yo'self better."

Emma Jean smiled as the painful memories resurfaced.

See! Didn't I tell you? This is worse than a beatin', huh?

"You can't come here!" Emma Jean yelled. "It's my birthday and you ain't welcome!"

I go wherever you go.

"I said, leave me alone!"

Paul watched Emma Jean slip further away. Then, kneeling before her on the sofa, he said, "Momma? It's all right. I'm here."

"I know you here, baby, but I'm tryin' to get this"—she didn't know what to call it—"*thing* to leave me alone."

"What is it? What do you see?"

Emma Jean didn't try to explain.

It's sorta funny, ain't it? Now he's worried about you.

"I'm fine, baby," she said, patting Paul's spongy Afro. "It's just that sometimes I hear . . ."

"It's okay, Momma." Paul resumed sweeping.

"Honey?"

"Yes, ma'am?"

"Would you do me a favor?"

"Sure. What is it?"

"Would you put on yo' suit for me?"

"My suit? Today? It's Saturday, Momma."

"I know, but would you put it on anyway? I need to see you in it."

"Okay. Anything you want. It's your birthday."

He finished sweeping, then went into the bedroom and emerged more handsome than Emma Jean recalled. She covered her mouth and longed for bygone days. "I'm so sorry," she managed to say. "I never meant to hurt you."

"I know, Momma. I know."

"No, you don't know. When you was born, you was the most beautiful baby I had ever seen. You just happened to be a boy." She smiled and gazed into his eyes. "I hadn't never seen no baby that pretty, and you was all mine. All I wanted was to love you and give you pretty things and make sure you knew how beautiful you was. I didn't mean to confuse you."

Well, you did.

"Shut up!" she shouted to the ceiling.

"I'm fine, Momma. It didn't kill me."

Gus almost did.

"I shouldn't've done it, baby. You was a boy and you didn't have no business bein' no girl."

That's right.

"All I'm askin' is that you forgive me for what I done."

Very good, Emma Jean.

"I done already forgave you, Momma. I know you didn't mean no harm. Stop worrying about me."

Emma Jean smiled. "All right, honey." She looked him over. "You sho do look nice."

Paul glided and swayed before Emma Jean like a model on a runway. They laughed together.

"You all grown up now, son. I ain't gon' be 'round forever. You gotta fight for yourself."

"I know, Momma. I ain't weak."

No thanks to you.

"Leave me alone, I said!"

Paul's look of pity embarrassed her.

"It's that voice again, honey," she said, trying to laugh away the shame.

"I understand." Studying the yellow ribbons plastered throughout the room, Paul added, "You know what, Momma? I miss bein' Perfect sometimes."

Emma Jean frowned. "Forget about that. That was all in the past."

"I don't wanna forget it. Not all of it. I know I can't live that way, but I can remember. I had so much fun, playin' with Eva Mae and Caroline, and dressin' up on Sunday mornings. I felt special then, Momma, like I was really somebody."

"You still special, baby. I shouldn'ta done what I done though. I messed up yo' mind."

You sure did!

"You didn't mess up my mind, Momma. I had fun back then. I don't neva talk about it no more, but it was the funnest days of my life. I was thinkin' about it the other day."

"Just leave it alone! Go forward, son. Let the past die. You'll never be Perfect again."

The past don't never die.

"You know what I hate most, Momma? The way we stopped talkin' and doin' stuff together."

"It had to be that way, son."

You're gettin' good with this truth tellin', Emma Jean.

"I know, but I still miss it. We had our own little world, just you and me. We used to laugh and cook and—"

"Look, boy! I said, forget about all that!"

Paul was startled. "Why! Why cain't I have my own memories? It don't hurt nothin' to remember."

"Yes it do! Memories hurt the most, especially if they bad memories."

"My memories of bein' a girl ain't bad. The bad memories came when Authorly and Daddy started beatin' me, tryin' to turn me into a boy. Then everybody else started talkin' about me."

"It was for yo' own good, son."

"My own good? Beatin' me was for my own good?"

"That's right. There was no other way." Emma Jean nodded confidently. "You couldn't live out yo' life like that."

"All right, Momma. Let's just stop talkin' about it."

"Okay, baby. I didn't mean to upset you."

You can't do nothin' right, Emma Jean, can you?

Emma Jean rose slowly and exited to the backyard, where she wept bitterly. Paul's effeminate nature assured her that he'd always have some residue of his former life, and now she knew that all the beatings in the world wouldn't change him. She'd hoped the men's influence could diminish the girl in him, and it had, but it hadn't erased it. Not completely. That would never happen, and Emma Jean would be tortured with that truth for the rest of her life. She had loved him more than she had meant to, and far too much for him to forget. He still spent most of his time with girls when Emma Jean would rather him marry one. She'd even take Christina. He obviously hadn't forgotten his days as Perfect, and from the looks of things, he didn't intend to. At nineteen, he was precisely what he'd always been, and Emma Jean would never forgive herself for having made him that way.

You're on your own now.

"Don't leave me, Momma."

I have to go. I'm glad you told the truth.

"Yeah. It just hurts so bad."

It usually does.

Emma Jean hugged herself. "It got out of hand." She marveled at the magnitude of it all. "And ain't nothin' I can do about it now. The boy's grown. He gon' have to figure thangs out on his own. Yeah, I shoulda told him sooner, but I didn't know how. I mean, how do you tell yo' own daughter that she ain't really no girl? And I needed a girl. You know I needed a girl, right?"

I know you wanted *one.*

Emma Jean's eyes followed the erratic movements of a bird outside the window. If only she could fly away . . . "All I'm gon' ask is that somebody love him. I don't care who, but don't let him be lonely the rest o' his life. It's gon' be hard as it is. I know that. But there's gotta be somebody who can make him happy. He's a good boy. Don't let him suffer because of me."

No one can guarantee love, Emma Jean.

"I know that! But can't you?"

No. Not even you.

Chapter 37

The party started shortly after five. Gus had hoped for a cheerful, jubilant atmosphere but, under the circumstances, the somber, gloomy air made sense. Authorly tried to talk, but no one really paid him any mind, and Woody's jokes just weren't funny. It was as if Emma Jean had died and people were now gathered for the wake. Gracie was there, as was Eva Mae, who came with a cake her mother had sent. Miss Mamie brought a pretty yellow and green quilt she'd made for herself, but decided to give away once she messed it up. Much to Emma Jean's horror, Henrietta came and spent the afternoon shaking her head sadly, mumbling "ump, ump, ump" each time she glanced at Emma Jean.

The only consolation was the food. The daughters-in-law were superb cooks, much better than Emma Jean, so everyone ate far past their appetite instead of looking at Emma Jean drool at the mouth and rock on her hands. It was a humbling sight, Eva Mae thought. One minute you're up and thriving, and the next you're shriveled and dying. Her grandmother used to say, "You know neither the day nor the hour," and, watching Emma Jean from the corner of her eye, Eva Mae knew her grandmother had been right. But who could feel sorry for Emma Jean after what she'd done?

When the feasting ended, Gus beckoned everyone to the living room. The boys brought chairs from the kitchen table and sat them in a semicircle before the sofa where Emma Jean sat. Mister and Paul joined her, sitting on either side, and the married boys stood behind their seated wives. Gus stood like one about to convene an important meeting.

"I jes' wanna say how much I 'preciate all o' y'all for comin'. 'Course Emma Jean ain't well, but I'm sure she feels better, havin' all o' y'all here."

Emma Jean tried to smile, but didn't want to speak, fearing that the voice would return and contradict her words. She peered at everyone, especially her sons, imagining how she'd raise them differently if given the opportunity, and only now did she realize how she had privileged Paul over the others. A tear ran down her right cheek as a nonverbal apology which, apparently, the others understood and accepted. They smiled sympathetically.

Suddenly, Paul's head twitched. Was he hearing things, too? He closed his eyes to listen more intently, and that's when he identified the voice. It was unmistakable.

"All of my heeeelp!" he heard faintly in the distant breeze.

Paul lifted his hands and sang off-key, "All of my help," as water gathered in his eyes.

"Oh my God!" Mister jumped and shouted. "It's Sol!"

Everyone but Paul and Emma Jean ran through the screen door and into the yard to welcome King Solomon Peace home. Gus waited at the edge of the porch.

"Comes from the Looooord!" Sol continued to sing.

The family smiled at King Solomon, approaching from the weeded lane.

"Comes from the Lord!" Paul sang inside.

"All of my heeeelp," Sol belted louder.

"All of my help," Paul muttered, shaking his head in joyful disbelief.

Sol hugged his brothers first, crooning and crying all the while. "Comes from the Looooord!"

"Comes from the Lord."

"Whenever I neeeeeed Him! He's right by my siiiiide! Oh, thank Ya, Lord! All of my help!"

"My help!" Paul declared.

"Myyyy help!"

"My help."

"My help, comes from the Lord, oh yes it does, shonuff it does!"

"Go 'head and sang yo' song, boy!" Gus whispered from the porch, squeezing his staff to keep from crying.

"Hey, man! You made it! I hoped you would!" Authorly scooped Sol from the earth in an enormous embrace. "You got the letter, huh?"

"Yep, I got it. Wow. Y'all look so good!"

The girls chuckled.

"Eva Mae, you look good, too, girl! Where's your husband?"

"Where's yo' wife?" she sassed playfully.

The crowd roared. Sol never relinquished Bartimaeus's hand.

"Come on, man," Authorly said, retrieving Sol's bag. "Let's put yo' stuff in the house so you can say hey to Momma and Paul."

"Man, you still tellin' folks what to do?"

"Yes, Lord!" Woody hollered.

"You know he is," Bartimaeus said. "He don't know how to do nothin' else!"

Mister shouted, "Put him in his place, Sol, for God's sake!"

The boys laughed as they ushered Sol onto the porch. Gus grabbed him and slapped his shoulders as though Sol had been gone a lifetime.

"How you doin', Daddy!"

"Doin' good, boy! Doin' good! You looks mighty fine."

"Yes I do, don't I?"

Woody and Authorly chuckled.

"You just got here?"

"Yessir. Just got off the evenin' train."

"Well, that's good. It sho is good to see you, boy!"

"It's good to be home, Daddy." Sol restrained his emotions. "I was hopin' I hadn't missed the party."

"Oh no! It's just gettin' started! You right on time!" He wanted to hug Sol again, but he didn't. "What you doin' wit' choself now? You teachin' school somewhere?"

"Not yet. I'm in graduate school, studying to be a psychologist."

Gus frowned.

"It's the study of human behavior. You know, why people do the things they do."

"Un-huh, I see." Gus nodded several times. "Well, that's all *right*!"

James Earl finally said, "Hey, King Solomon," as though only now recognizing him. Sol hugged him again, then stepped through the front door.

Paul stared and trembled, like the disciples beholding their resurrected Savior. Sol smiled, freeing Paul to leap into his brother's arms as if the two had been separated during slavery. Weeping freely, Paul didn't care what Gus or Authorly or anybody else thought. He held on to Sol the way he used to hug Olivia and wouldn't let go. Sol needed the embrace, too. He had been away from the family long enough to convince himself he no longer had a place or a people in Swamp Creek. Paul's quivering arms reminded him of who and what he was.

"Come on, boy," Sol soon whispered. "You gon' make all of us cry."

Paul relaxed his hold and sniffled, "My brother's home."

"Yes, I am."

"King Solomon . . . you just don't know."

"I don't know what?"

Paul sighed. "You just don't know. You just don't know." Tears came again as years of pain vanished. Sol rubbed Paul's back.

"All right, all right," Gus said. "Say hey to yo' momma."

When Emma Jean first heard Sol's voice, she tried to decide what she'd say. He hadn't been home once in all the years he'd been in college, and so much had changed. Or so little. Silence had reprimanded her for how she hadn't loved him, and now she didn't know how to fix it. "Let me handle this," she murmured.

Authorly had informed Sol of Emma Jean's condition—he dictated the letter to Eula Faye, who sent it on behalf of the family—and he'd sympathized with her. Now, staring at Emma Jean's sullen, shrunken figure, Sol looked past the last vestiges of hurt in his heart and said simply, "Hey, Momma. How you doin'?" He knelt before her.

Emma Jean looked up, prepared to behold vengeance in Sol's eyes. When she saw compassion, she said, "Hi, baby," reaching for his hand. Sol surrendered it. "I didn't know you was comin'."

"I know. Authorly asked me not to tell anyone. Happy birthday." His voice cracked. He never thought he'd see Emma Jean this way.

"Well, it sho is good to see you. It's been a long time."

"Yes ma'am, it has."

He looks good, no thanks to you.

"I said, let me handle this!" Emma Jean shouted to the air. "He's my son!"

Sol looked at his brothers, confused. They dropped their heads.

"I'm sorry I didn't let you go to school. Back when you shoulda gone."

That's right!

"Shut up!"

"It's okay, Momma. I went and I'm all right now."

"I know, baby, but please don't hate me. I just thought that since Paul—"

"You don't have to explain."

"Yes I do! I *need* to explain."

You sure do.

"Leave me alone!"

Emma Jean's wild eyes and unpredictable outbursts made Sol uneasy. "Why don't you get some rest, Momma."

"I don't need no rest, son! I need for you to understand how sorry I am for what I done."

Very good.

"And how wrong I was. If I could do it all over again—"

But you can't.

"I know I can't!"

"Momma, I'm all right now. Don't worry yourself about me. God took care of me."

"I know, honey, but *I* didn't! And I should've."

Right!

"And I don't want you to hate me"—Emma Jean sobbed—"the rest o' yo' life."

"I don't hate you, Momma." Sol closed his eyes as Emma Jean's tears dripped onto his right hand. "You did what you thought was right."

"But it wasn't right! It was wrong! It was so wrong!"

"I understand. I know." For a brief moment, Sol's hurt resurfaced. He remembered his childhood longing and he felt, once again, the pain of Emma Jean's rejection, yet he refused to pick back up what it had taken him years to let go of. "I've survived, Momma. I'm okay. You can let it go now."

"No! I cain't let it go! I hurt you and I didn't mean to! I need to fix it now!"

It's too late for that.

"It's all right, Momma." Sol gently pulled his hand away. Seeing her like this was more than he could bear.

"Don't worry about it, Emma Jean," Miss Mamie said, rubbing Sol's long, slender arm. "He's gon' be just fine."

"This is my business, Mamie Cunningham, and I don't need you in it!"

"Emma Jean!" Gus admonished. "She's our guest."

"Oh, it's okay," Mamie said, smiling. "She don't mean it. She ain't in her right mind noway."

"I *am* in my right mind, and I meant exactly what I said!"

People began to retreat.

You're messing up again!

"Leave me alone!"

"Why don't we all go outside," Gus suggested, "and give Emma Jean time to calm down."

"I don't need to calm down!"

Yes you do. You're starting to scare everyone. You're even starting to scare me.

"Why?"

Because you're screaming and no one knows why.

Emma Jean watched everyone scramble away. Gus touched her arm lovingly as he passed.

Did you ask Sol for forgiveness?

"No. Not yet. I was getting to that."

You cain't do nothin' right, Emma Jean.

"Kiss my ass! I'm tired of you anyway!"

Fine! Then I'll just go away. For now.

"No! Don't go! I need you. I ain't got nobody else."

Silence went away.

"Hello? Are you there?"

Outside, folks bombarded Sol with questions about the outside world. Gus asked about a wife, and Sol said he was looking. Authorly wondered where Sol got his snazzy clothes from, and Mister asked if he had a bedroom all by himself. The distant laughter and cheering, without Emma Jean, made her believe she wasn't needed anymore, and that's what initiated her final descent. Mae Helen had been right after all, she thought. Everybody deemed her crazy now and maybe she was, but after a lifetime of giving to Pearlie and Gracie, Gus and the boys, then that damn Henrietta, the sad thing was that she was back where she'd started from.

There was only one answer, one way to be made whole again. Why hadn't she thought of it before?

Emma Jean wiped her tears, put on her best Sunday dress, and slipped into her good black shoes. She even took a pocketbook, although she didn't know why.

"Where're you goin', woman?" Gus called as she stepped into the yard.

"Don't worry 'bout me. I just need to do somethin'. I'll be back in a little while."

"You ain't got no business walkin' 'round by yo'self! You know you ain't well. I'll come with you."

"No! No." Emma Jean's trembling finger, pointed at Gus's nose, got everyone's attention.

"I'll be fine."

Miss Mamie and Henrietta shook their heads. Eva Mae and Paul tried to guess where Emma Jean was going and why.

"Let her go, Daddy," Sol said. "She can't get lost around here."

Her guests left the house shortly after she did. Most saw no reason to loiter if the birthday girl was gone, so they told Gus to take care and keep on praying. Sol walked Miss Mamie home. Mister accompanied Henrietta. Eva Mae never warranted an escort.

Passing the bend in the road, Emma Jean headed toward the Jordan. If it had cleansed Gus and Bartimaeus all those years, then it could cleanse her, too. Sugar Baby saw her, zigzagging along the same path where Paul had been assaulted, looking more drunk than he ever had, but he paid her no mind. *She probably just needs a little air,* he told himself.

The Jordan welcomed her. A comforting breeze blew as Emma Jean folded her arms and breathed deeply. She looked around, like one who'd never been there before. She'd been a child, hunting berries with Gracie and Pearlie, the last time she was there, and now it looked different. Was it always so broad? Why did it flow like it was angry?

Emma Jean stood on the banks and reviewed her life. What a mess she'd made! Everyone she'd tried to love, she ended up hurting. Maybe she'd been cursed from the beginning, she thought. Maybe the point of her life had been to show people what *not* to do, and, with such a mission, she'd been doomed from the start. Gazing across the water, she shook her head and sang, "I need thee! Oh, I need thee! Every hour, I need thee!" Her arms stretched toward the heavens as she continued: "Oh, bless me now, my Savior! I come to thee!" Waiting for the magical moment, she swayed and hummed as the roar of the Jordan promised an imminent transformation.

It's up to you now.

"I did the best I could."

It wasn't good enough.

"I'm not a bad person."

Oh really?

"Really! My momma hurt me!"

Don't start that again.

"It's true!"

Then come and be with me forever. I'll love you. There's nothing more you can do here. No one else needs you now.

"What about Paul? He's so young."

You'll never fix what you did. Never.

Emma Jean believed it.

I'm your only friend now. Come, and be with me.

"How?" Emma Jean whimpered. "How can I be with you?"

Meet me in the water. I'll carry you away.

"Will you love me?"

Yes I will.

"Forever?"

Forever.

"Do you promise?"

Yes, Emma Jean. I promise.

Emma Jean didn't hesitate. Unable to foresee herself in the future, she marched boldly to the edge of a jutting rock and, with the help of God's heavy hands, plunged headfirst into the chilly Jordan. It swallowed her whole and rocked her in its tumultuous bosom. It loved her and accepted her for who she was. And who she wasn't. It embraced her with loving arms and never let her go. The Jordan was no respecter of persons, so it stripped Emma Jean of everything she had—clothes, memories, guilt, shame—as it prepared her for the land of everlasting love. She couldn't swim and, even if she could, she wouldn't have tried. She'd gotten precisely what she'd come for. She was cleansed now, and no one—including Mae Helen—could tarnish her again. The hope for perfect peace had finally been realized, and now she'd have it forever.

She'd get a new body and a new spirit, too. That's what Reverend Lindsey had said. And maybe, if she got the chance to live again, she'd come back as a pretty little black girl, she thought, one others would smile at and want to give sweets to. She'd ask God not to make her so dark this time that her mother would beat her for it, but to give her hair like her sisters' and soft, caramel skin like Paul's. But if she couldn't live again, she wouldn't be angry. She'd lived once, and once had certainly been enough.

* * *

When Sol returned, Paul met him on the front steps. The sun was beginning its descent.

"You ain't seen Momma, have you?" Paul asked.

"No. She's not back yet?"

"Un-uh. But she shoulda been by now."

"I'm sure she's fine."

Several seconds passed before Paul gathered the nerve to ask, "Is you still mad at her, Sol?"

He stared across the horizon. "Naw, I don't think so. Some days are harder than others, but for the most part I've let it go."

Paul nodded. "I know it was hard."

"You have no idea."

"Well, Momma was definitely glad to see you today. I could tell."

Sol chuckled. "Yeah. I guess she was."

"It must be painful for her, lookin' at how you done done so good, even after what she did to you."

"Ha! I'ma tell you a secret, little brother: God has a way of making sure you reach your destiny, regardless of what others do to you."

"You think so?"

"Trust me. It's true. Sometimes, when people think they're putting obstacles in your path, they're actually laying your stepping-stones. You just gotta recognize them as one and the same."

Paul chewed his left thumbnail as he listened to Sol's wisdom.

"It's funny, you know. When I saw Momma today, I wasn't sure what I felt at first. The only thing I knew for sure was that I wasn't going to start hating her all over again. It took me too long to drop that burden. I've never forgotten what she did. I just decided that she couldn't have my *whole* life. I wanted to move forward, so I had to stop looking back."

"I wish I knew how to do that." Paul thought of the assault.

"There's no trick to it. You just put your energy into what you want to be, and you try to let the past go. You don't ever forget though."

"Well, if you don't forget, how you stop lookin' back?"

"By figuring out how the experience can help you move forward. That's the point of why it happened to you in the first place. There's something you're suppose to get from the moment that'll get you closer to your mission if you can see it. Most people can't."

"But what if the experience wasn't for you?"

"It was. It always is. Sometimes it's hard to see, and sometimes we don't want to believe it, but every experience you have is for you. You just gotta figure out how."

"Ump. That's hard to believe."

"I know."

"You're even smarter now than you used to be!"

Sol placed his arm around Paul's shoulder. "I don't know about that!"

"I do! That's why you're my hero."

"You're mine, too, sir."

Paul blushed.

"So what's next for you?"

"I don't know."

"What about farming?"

"No way!"

They giggled.

"Can't say I blame you for that."

"Daddy and Authorly love it, but I don't."

"You ever thought about college?"

"Yeah, that's what Momma wants me to do, but I don't like school. Not that much. Is college hard?"

"Hell, yes! It's a lot of reading and writing."

"Then it's not for me."

"You'd probably better leave it alone. If you don't love knowledge, and I mean *love* it, going to college is a waste of time."

"Then I don't know what to do."

"Anybody you thinking about marrying?"

"Nope."

"No? There must be someone around here you've been looking at."

Of course there was *someone*, but Paul couldn't name *him*.

Sol leaned onto Paul's shoulder and whispered, "What's his name?"

"Oh my God!" Paul covered his face. "How'd you know?"

"It wasn't hard to figure out."

"You think Daddy knows?"

"I don't know, but I wouldn't worry about it."

"Why not!"

"Because you're grown now. And, anyway, people ain't God. Whatever they think they know, God already knows, and if He hasn't troubled you about it, you can pretty much ignore other folks."

Paul thought a moment. "I guess you right."

"Don't ever give others the power to destroy you, little brother, because they'll take it. Your fear is their invitation."

"Wow. Then I've given a lot of power away over the years."

"Haven't we all? Now it's time to take it back. Folks'll kill you and enjoy doing it if you let them."

"That's true. I could name a few people standing in line right now!"

Sol laughed.

"I got the fever a few years ago, and everybody thought I was gon' die, but I didn't. I lived."

"Well, good for you. Now you have to live *well*."

Paul studied a squirrel, scampering from one tree to another.

"If you do find someone you like, just be careful. The heart'll trick you, man, if you let it. It'll make you think you'll give up everything and everyone you know for someone you don't."

"Ain't that the truth!"

"Everyone gets the chance to love, but we don't all get to love who we want. Take your time. Your day'll come."

Paul thought of the dried, brittle four-leaf clover nestled between the pages of his Bible.

"You have to get clear about the kind of life you can live *here*. Life can be lived anywhere, but not every life can be lived everywhere."

"I ain't never thought about it like that."

"Keep on livin', and you'll start thinking about a lot of things."

"I guess I gotta figure out somethin', huh?"

"Yeah, you do. Maybe you're too scared to know."

"Maybe I am, 'cause there is somethin' I like that I ain't never told nobody."

"What is it?"

Paul laughed at himself. "Clothes. I know it sounds crazy, but when Momma made me that suit and I put it on, I felt somethin' I ain't never felt before."

"Really?"

"Yeah. I wondered what it would be like to make one myself."

"Okay."

"I'm real creative. Eva Mae says so all the time. But I don't know nothin' 'bout makin' no clothes."

"Well, what about Miss Henrietta? Does she still sew?"

"Does she! Man, she got a shop in town that's sellin' out fast as she can make the stuff."

"Then I'm sure she could use some help. She'd probably be glad to teach you what she knows. You can make a lotta money doing it, too. It might be what you was sent to do."

"Hmmm." *Sent?* He thought of Sugar Baby. "It just might be."

"Of course folks 'round here don't think much about a man making clothes, but that doesn't matter. Not if you want it bad enough."

"You right."

"Just make sure you can handle the pressure. People'll talk about you, but who cares? When you're a famous designer, they'll praise you as a son of Swamp Creek."

"I hate when people do that."

"Yeah, but we all do it. We talk about people we don't like until they become famous. Then we love 'em."

Paul sighed.

"You'd make an incredible designer, man. You've had enough experiences to bring a whole new perspective to fashion. Plus, you're strong. You gotta be. Who could've endured what you have? Now, take those experiences and create something the world has never seen."

Paul's excitement shone in his eyes.

"But remember this: you're strong *because of* your people—not *in spite of* them. You come from resilient folks, man. Don't ever forget that. I know what Momma did to you, and I know it wasn't right, but that's a price she'll have to pay—not you. *She* was crazy, but that doesn't mean you have to be. Peace men are strong, Paul, and you're one of us. Take the best from us and add to it. But whatsoever you do, don't ever forget that you're a Peace."

"I won't."

"And remember this, too: sometimes you have to grow up before you appreciate how you grew up. I'm still learning that one."

Paul promised he wouldn't forget.

* * *

At dusk, Gus and the boys went searching for Emma Jean. Sol said he'd wait at the house, just in case she returned, but of course she didn't. By dawn, half of Swamp Creek was combing the woods and knocking on doors, inquiring about Emma Jean's strange disappearance. Most knew something bad had happened, but they went along with the search for Gus's sake.

Sugar Baby found her downstream a few days later, faceup and bloated. Holes punctured her face as if piranhas had tried to consume her, and her eyes were bulged like one in mid-fright. The only thing familiar to Sugar Baby was the moon-shaped scar, which seemed more pronounced now. He didn't remember it being quite so rounded, but maybe the swelling had stretched it, he thought. He never dreamed he'd see Emma Jean Peace like this. He would've carried the body to the house, but the stench was unbearable, so he ran and told Gus what he'd found.

On a cloudy Friday morning in late May of 1959, they buried Emma Jean in Bartimaeus's sealed casket. The funeral was beautiful, people said. Folks everywhere and food galore. Miss Mamie sat behind the family, marveling at how handsome the Peace boys had turned out—all except Woody—and Gus thanked God that Emma Jean had lived long enough to see Paul survive. His sobbing was the saddest part of the service. All he could think about was the pretty lemon cake Emma Jean had made for his birthday and the fun he and other kids had had eating it with homemade ice cream. That's why he wept—because no one other than Emma Jean understood how precious and beautiful those days had been. She'd tried to love him— Paul knew that in his heart—but she just hadn't done it right. Now she was gone forever, and no one else in the family cared to remember who or what he'd once been. Burying Emma Jean was tantamount to burying Perfect, and Paul simply wasn't prepared to let either of them go. Yet he had no choice. Sitting on the front pew in the suit that had cost Emma Jean everything, he sighed as they buried the woman who insisted on having what God wouldn't allow.

Woody gave the eulogy, talking about things that had absolutely nothing to do with Emma Jean, and, at the end, Authorly rose and asked Sol to render a selection. He almost sang "All of My Help," for Paul's sake, but then, for his own, he belted, "When peace, like a river, attendeth my way! When sorrows like sea billows roll!" Tears poured as Sol gave thanks that his hurt hadn't consumed him. "Whatever my lot, thou hast taught me to say, it is well, it is well, with my soul!"

* * *

Paul escaped the repast and found himself at the Jordan. He hadn't meant to go there. His aim had been to gather wildflowers for Emma Jean's grave, then return to the church, but the rumble of the river drew him until, unwittingly, he stood upon the rock where his mother had recently stood.

"I'm all right, Momma. The world didn't kill me."

He thought he heard Emma Jean's laughter amid the rushing waves.

"I'm a man now. Can you belive that? A man."

He didn't need anyone's confirmation. He'd discovered that, like the Jordan, he simply had to be who he was. That was the secret of life, right? That's what Sol had been trying to tell him, wasn't it? To be himself regardless of what others thought? Wow. *Death has a way of breeding clarity,* he thought. As sad as he was about Emma Jean, he gave thanks for finally understanding.

"You did the best you could. I know that. And I thank you for my life—all of it."

Sugar Baby watched from the woods, unable to hear Paul's words, but discerning his actions clearly.

"Take care, Momma. I'll be fine now."

And with that, Paul knelt and splashed his face with the healing powers of the Jordan. The water was cold and sharp, but it was also refreshing and satisfying. He couldn't imagine how fish dwelt in the frigid flow, much less how his father and brother waded in it. But there was something magical there. He felt it now and he needed it, so he splashed his face repeatedly until he felt renewed.

Just as he stood, the Jordan began to sing him a lullaby. He closed his eyes and swayed. The rough, coarse melody, bubbling up from the deep, soothed his aching soul. He listened, for what felt like an eternity, to the cry of the currents until the notes reverberated in the abyss of his memory. He would recall the tune years later and hum it whenever his past threatened to overwhelm him. For now, he listened until his heart was clean. Until he was free. Until, with his scars and wounds, he was sure he'd been made whole.

The rains came at nightfall. They hadn't been this late, Gus recalled, since the day of Paul's birth. But, unlike then, there was no rush this time, so father and son walked hand in hand to the place of cleansing. As the moon rose, so did their voices. Gus couldn't figure out why Emma Jean had jumped into the river. She knew she couldn't swim. Was she *trying* to die? Had the voices in her head led her astray? It didn't make sense, but there was nothing he could do about it now, so he thanked God for all his boys and wept with joy that Sol was home again. Gus had missed him deep in his heart. He regretted that he'd stood with Emma Jean on the decision to halt Sol's education, but he couldn't do anything about that, either. Sol had succeeded against the odds anyway, and that's what mattered, so Gus thanked a faithful God for making Sol strong enough to withstand it all. Neighbors had expected wailing and mourning, but when they heard exultation and praise, they knew that ole Gustavus Peace would be all right. He wouldn't live to see Paul prosper, but the brothers would. They'd meet in New York in 1965, all seven of them, and watch models display, in radiant splendor, Paul's breathtaking creativity. They'd clap as they remembered little Paul Peace, the one few—other than Sugar Baby—thought would survive, and they'd know that God's hand had always been upon him. For now, Bartimaeus said, "So long!" to Emma Jean as he and Gus waded into the Jordan. By morning, their burdens had been lifted, and it was finished.

"Any o' y'all seen Mister?" Gus called, emerging from the bedroom at dawn.

They would learn, days later, that he had hitchhiked to Memphis on his way to Atlanta. They'd never know how surprised and elated Johnny Ray was to see him. In his letter, a week later, Mister reported that he was working in Atlanta and doing fine. He asked Paul to check in on the NAACP meetings—now that Emma Jean couldn't stop him—and to let him know what happened in the fall election. He also told Paul that there was something waiting for him in the barn loft. Sol wrote back that everybody missed him and that Authorly said he was going to whip his ass for running off without saying goodbye. Sol explained that the enclosed dried-up clover was from Paul, who said to tell him that he loved him. Mister sniffled as he placed the clover in the middle of his own Bible.

Paul had abandoned the loft the day Gus found him in Emma Jean's clothes. Yet curious to see what Mister was talking about, he climbed the ladder and looked around. Eva Mae was with him.

"What is it?"

"I don't know. I don't see anything." He shifted a small pile of hay and gasped, "Oh my God. I don't believe it. All this time."

"What?"

Paul descended the ladder with Olivia swinging from his right hand.

"He had her all these years?"

"I guess so." Paul brushed the dirt from the doll's face and clothes. He smiled. What was he supposed to do with her now? He didn't need her anymore. She didn't even seem real, like she once did. He remembered how much he'd loved her and how much she'd meant to him—back in another lifetime.

"What chu gon' do with her?"

Recalling what Emma Jean had done with the rest of Perfect's things, Paul laid Olivia on the pile of rubbish Gus was burning behind the barn. Then, hand in hand, he and Eva Mae went to find Henrietta.